Legends from China
THREE KINGDOMS

Vol.
06

Three Kingdoms

Many centuries ago, China was made up of several provinces that frequently waged war with one another for regional supremacy. In 221 BC, the Qin Dynasty succeeded in uniting the warring provinces under a single banner, but the unity was short-lived, only lasting fifteen years. After the collapse of the Qin Dynasty, the Han Dynasty was established in 206 BC, and unity was restored. The Han Dynasty would last for hundreds of years, until the Post-Han Era, when the unified nation once again began to unravel. As rebellion and chaos gripped the land, three men came forward to take control of the nation: Bei Liu, Cao Cao, and Ce Sun. The three men each established separate kingdoms, Shu, Wei, and Wu, and for a century they contended for supremacy. This was known as the Age of the Three Kingdoms.

Written more than six hundred years ago, *Three Kingdoms* is one of the oldest and most seminal works in all of Eastern literature. An epic story spanning decades and featuring hundreds of characters, it remains a definitive tale of desperate heroism, political treachery, and the bonds of brotherhood.

Wei Dong Chen and Xiao Long Liang have chosen to draw this adaptation of *Three Kingdoms* in a manner reminiscent of the ancient Chinese printing technique. It is our hope that the historical look of *Three Kingdoms* will amplify the timelessness of its themes, which are just as relevant today as they were thousands of years ago.

THREE KINGDOMS
Vol. 06

Blood and Honor

Created by WEI DONG CHEN

Wei Dong Chen, a highly acclaimed and beloved artist, and an influential leader in the "New Chinese Cartoon" trend, is the founder of Creator World in Tianjin, the largest comics studio in China. Recently the Chinese government entrusted him with the role of general manager of the Beijing Book Fair, and his reputation as a pillar of Chinese comics has brought him many students. He has published more than three hundred cartoons, which have been recognized for their strong literary value not only in Korea, but in Europe and Japan as well. Free spirited and energetic, Wei Dong Chen's positivist philosophy is reflected in the wisdom of his work. He is published serially in numerous publications while continuing to conceive projects that explore new dimensions of the form.

Illustrated by XIAO LONG LIANG

Xiao Long Liang is considered one of Wei Dong Chen's greatest students. One of the most highly regarded cartoonists in China today, Xiao Long's fantastic technique and expression of Chinese culture have won him the acclaim of cartoon lovers throughout China. His other works include "Outlaws of the Marsh" and "A Story on the Motorbike".

Original Story
"The Romance of the Three Kingdoms" *by Luo, GuanZhong*

Editing & Designing
Design Hongs, Jonathan Evans, KH Lee, YK Kim,
HJ Lee, JS Kim, Lampin, Qing Shao, Xiao Nan Li, Ke Hu

Original Chinese edition published by Anhui Fine Arts Publishing House.

BEI LIU AND HIS SWORN BROTHERS

Bei Liu's plan to challenge Cao Cao's supremacy relied on the temperamental Shao Yuan, who initially pledged his support but suddenly withdrew it. Unable to defeat the enemy on his own, Bei Liu must flee before he is overrun by Cao Cao's army. Cao Cao's army led by Liao Zhang advances to XiaPi, defended by Yu Guan. After much persuasion, Liao Zhang convinces Yu Guan to end his defense of the fortress and fight for Cao Cao's by telling him that Bei Liu's family is in danger. Not knowing what has happened to Bei Liu, and not wanting to endanger his family, Yu Guan accepts the offer on the condition that he be allowed to leave when he learns of Bei Liu's whereabouts. Cao Cao tries to win more than Yu Guan's sword, and showers him with riches in order to win his loyalty. But Yu Guan's unwavering loyalty is part of his greatness, and he will not break the oath he swore to Bei Liu and Fei Zhang.

Meanwhile, Bei Liu has taken refuge in Shao Yuan's camp. When Shao Yuan finally sends an army to attack Cao Cao, his forces are repelled by Yu Guan, who beheads a succession of field commanders. Shao Yuan blames Bei Liu for the deaths, but Bei Liu knows that Cao Cao is behind it all. They try to reach Yu Guan, but he is too heavily guarded. When a spy is finally able to speak with Yu Guan and tell him about Bei Liu, Yu Guan keeps his word and leaves to rejoin his brother.

CAO CAO

Cao Cao has for some time been the most powerful man in China, a cunning and ruthless strategist who has allied himself with the emperor to maximize his leverage over the people of China. His ambition is boundless, and he is always looking to further strengthen himself. With Bei Liu and Fei Zhang driven away after the battle of XuZhou, Cao Cao turns his attention toward winning the loyalty of Yu Guan, who defends the fortress of XiaPi alone. Yu Guan is both feared in battle and revered for his commitment to living an honorable life, and Cao Cao knows that having an ally like him would consolidate his power even more. But even Cao Cao underestimates the depths of Yu Guan's loyalty, and he is unable to win Yu Guan's allegiance. As a result, Cao Cao pledges to become so powerful that losing the allegiance of someone like Yu Guan will seem trivial.

LIAO ZHANG

Liao Zhang is a young soldier who formerly served under Bu Lu. When Bu Lu was captured by Cao Cao, Liao Zhang was only spared from death by the intervention of Yu Guan. Since then, Liao Zhang has treated Yu Guan with the respect of a savior. Thus, it is Liao Zhang who attempts to convince Yu Guan to fight under Cao Cao's banner.

Characters

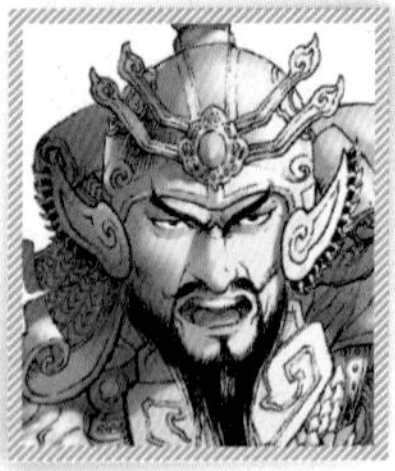

SHAO YUAN

Shao Yuan is a fickle lord whose words do not always match his deeds. Having pledged to send an army to help Bei Liu defeat Cao Cao, Shao Yuan decides at the last minute not to join the fight. Bei Liu is forced to flee Cao Cao's army and ends up a guest of Shao Yuan's camp. Some time later, Shao Yuan finally decides to send his army into battle against Cao Cao's forces. Unfortunately for Shao Yuan, Yu Guan is now fighting for Cao Cao and winning battles almost single-handedly.

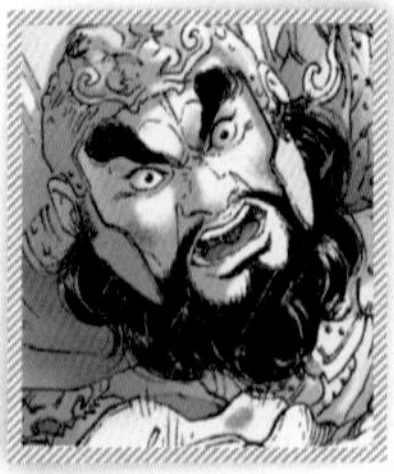

LIANG YAN

Liang Yan is one of Shao Yuan's most senior commanders. He is a ferocious warrior who is feared in battle and kills two of Cao Cao's commanders before driving away a third. But Cao Cao has a new soldier among his ranks, and Liang Yan's winning streak is about to end.

CHOU WEN

Chou Wen volunteers to lead an army of 100,000 soldiers to face Cao Cao's forces when he hears of Liang Yan's failure in battle. Chou Wen neutralizes the enemy by ordering his archers to fire waves of arrows, but ultimately one thing stands between him and victory: Yu Guan.

SHOU JU

Shou Ju is an advisor to Shao Yuan who is often at odds with his master. It is Shou Ju who advises Shao Yuan to turn down Bei Liu's advice regarding the mobilization of his army; Shao Yuan replies that Shou Ju is destroying the morale of his army.

Chapter 1

Yu Guan's Choice 199 AD

Summary

After thwarting an attempted coup and killing hundreds of people, Cao Cao leads an army of 200,000 soldiers to attack Bei Liu, who was one of the principal figures of the coup. In response Bei Liu asks Shao Yuan for help, but Shao Yuan changes his mind and refuses to deploy his army after initially pledging his support. Following Bei Liu's humiliating defeat, Fei Zhang flees to Mount MangDang in the west, while Bei Liu retreats to Shao Yuan's territory.

Meanwhile, Yu Guan is making a last stand to defend the palace at XiaPi, as he swore to Bei Liu he would defend it to the death. At Cao Cao's request, Liao Zhang, who is leading the attacking force, asks Yu Guan to abandon the defeated Bei Liu and pledge his loyalty to Cao Cao. Yu Guan refuses and flees to a nearby mountain, after which Liao Zhang's forces destroy the palace. Liao Zhang follows Yu Guan to the mountain and again tries to persuade him to join Cao Cao. When Yu Guan again refuses, Liao Zhang tells him that XiaPi has been destroyed and suggests that not relenting might result in harm coming to Bei Liu's family. Fearing for his brother's family and without a city to defend, Yu Guan relents, pledges his full loyalty, and swears to fight for him, winning numerous concessions in the process, including a promise that Bei Liu's family won't be harmed.

ChangShan
BeiHai
B
PuYang
XiaoPei
HuLuo
XiaPi
GuanDu
C
LuoYang
XuZhou
ChangAn
XuChang
A
NanYang
ShouChun
River Huai
HeFei
XiangYang

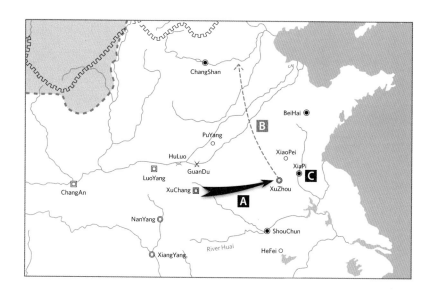

A Cao Cao leads a large army to attack Bei Liu at XuZhuo.

B Bei Liu retreats to Shao Yuan's camp, and Fei Zhang flees to the west.

C Yu Guan surrenders to Cao Cao and reluctantly agrees to fight for him.

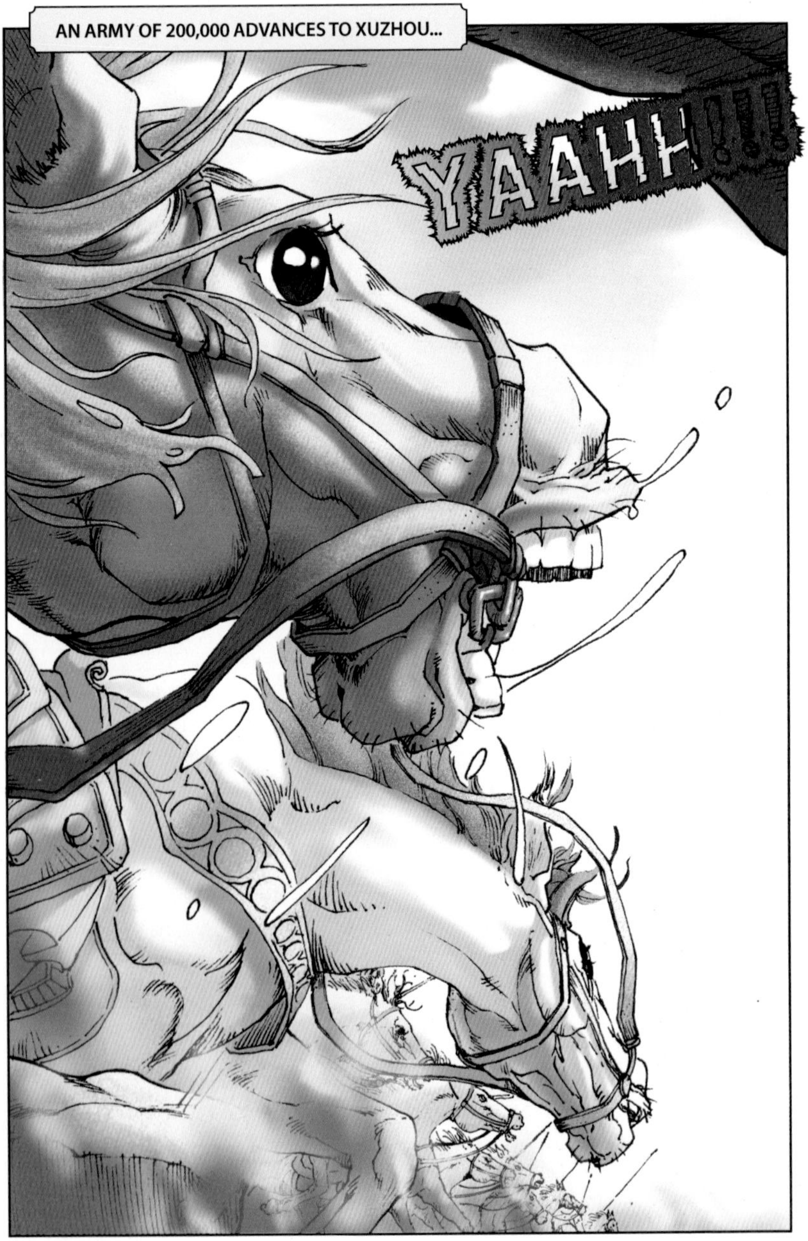
AN ARMY OF 200,000 ADVANCES TO XUZHOU...
YAAHH!!!

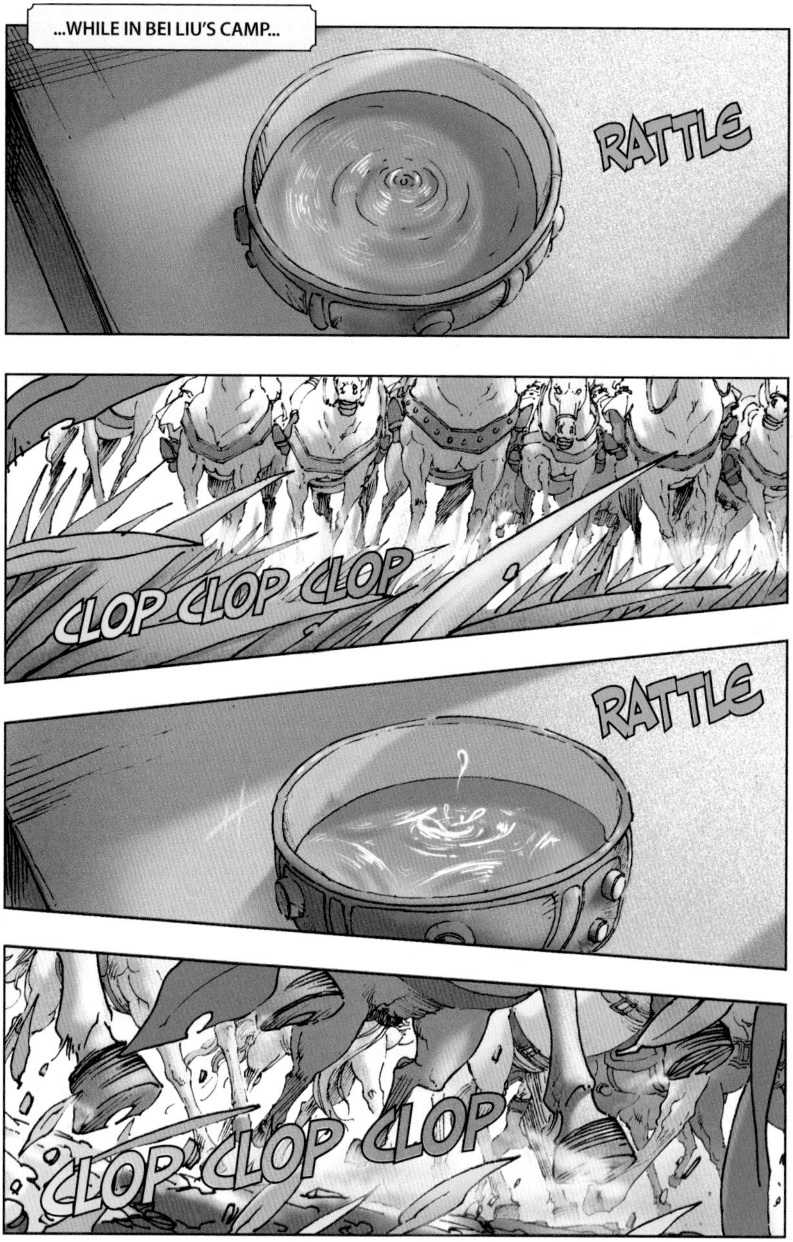
...WHILE IN BEI LIU'S CAMP...
RATTLE
CLOP CLOP CLOP
RATTLE
CLOP CLOP CLOP

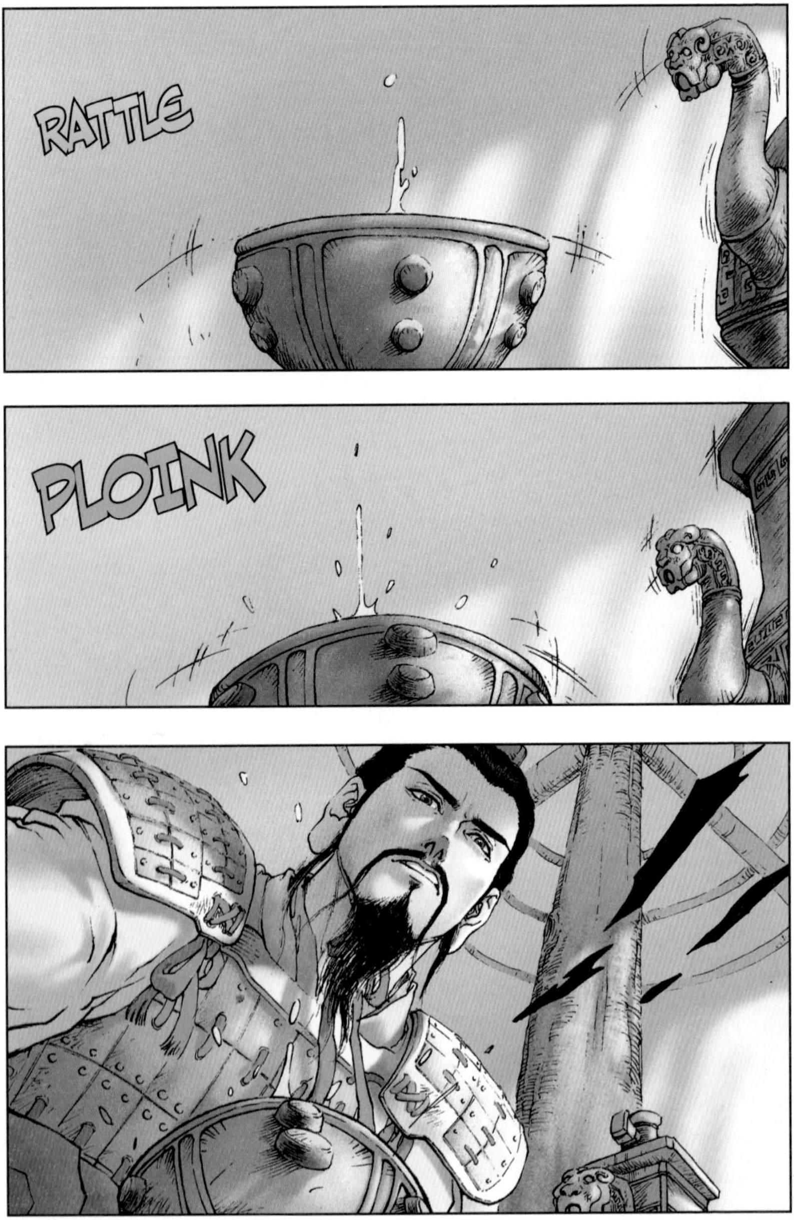
RATTLE
PLOINK

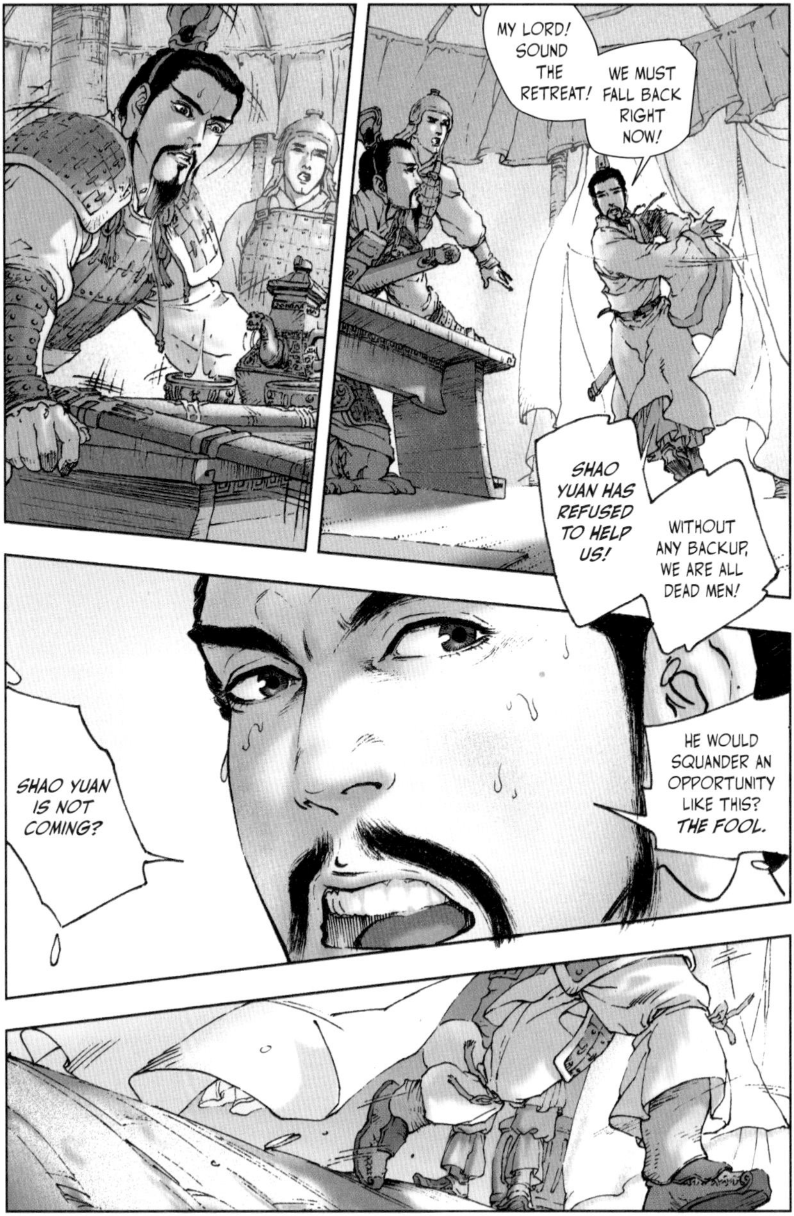
MY LORD! SOUND THE RETREAT!
WE MUST FALL BACK RIGHT NOW!
SHAO YUAN HAS REFUSED TO HELP US!
WITHOUT ANY BACKUP, WE ARE ALL DEAD MEN!
SHAO YUAN IS NOT COMING?
HE WOULD SQUANDER AN OPPORTUNITY LIKE THIS? THE FOOL.

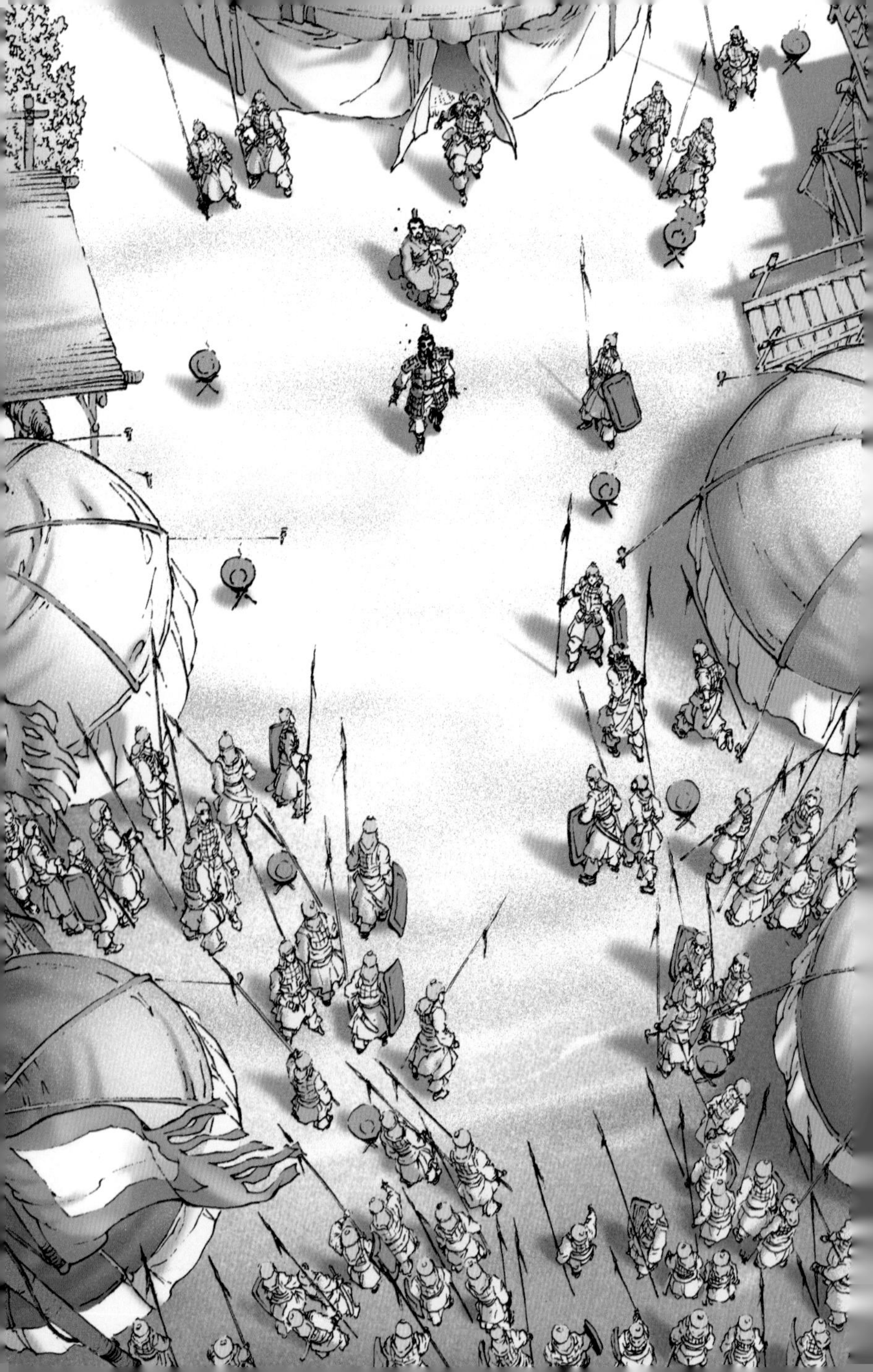

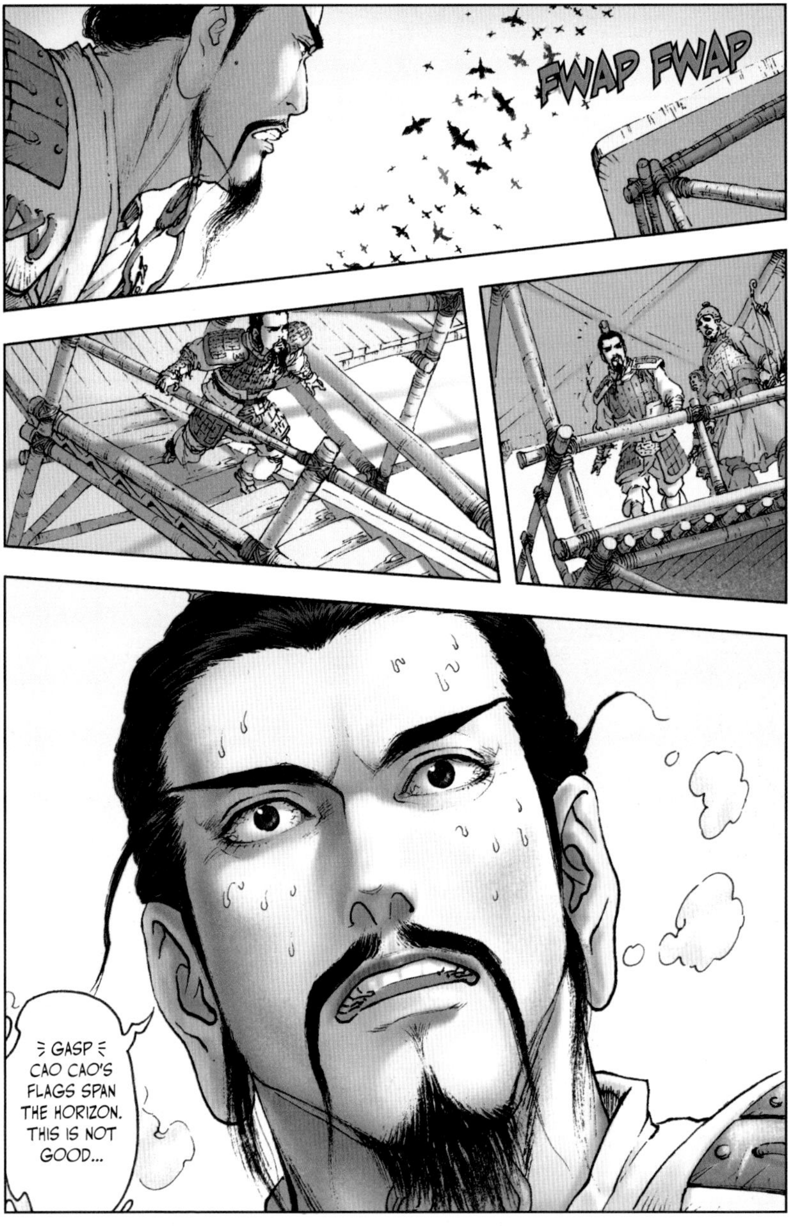
FWAP FWAP
≶ GASP ≶
CAO CAO'S
FLAGS SPAN
THE HORIZON.
THIS IS NOT
GOOD...

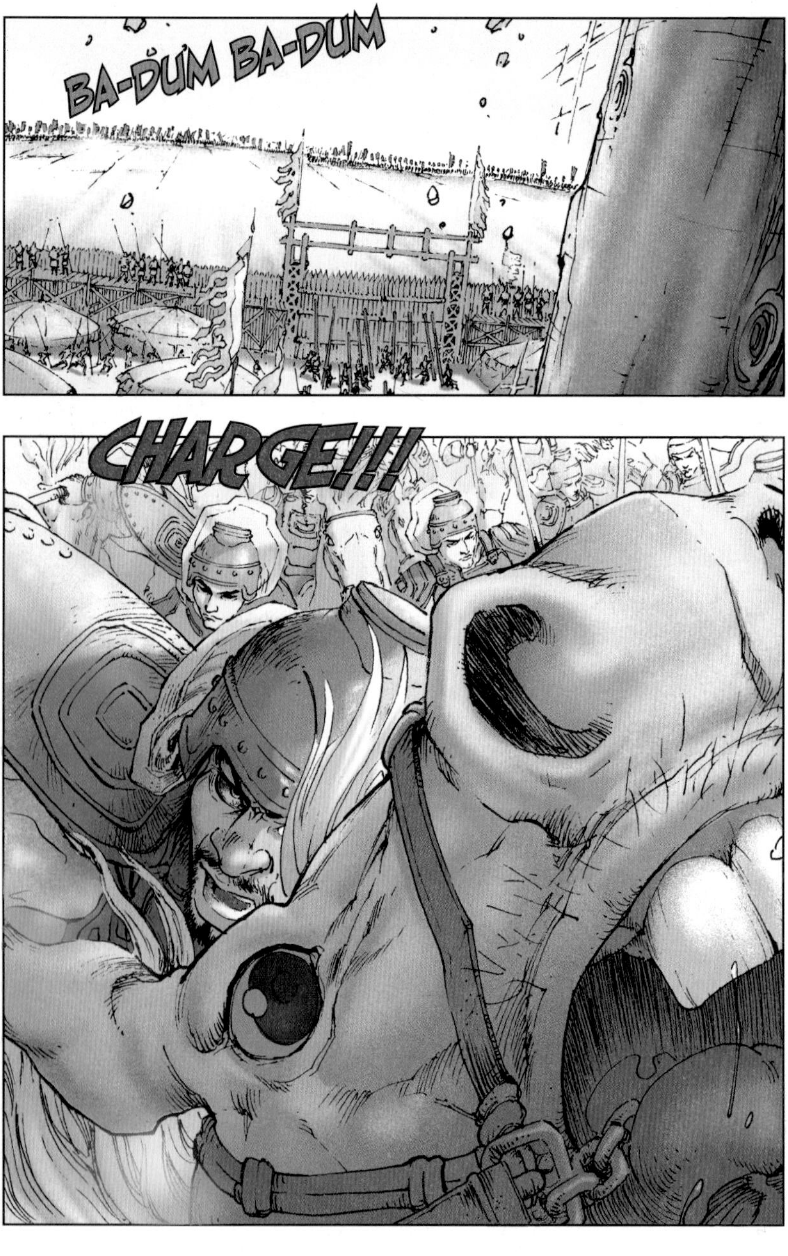
BA-DUM BA-DUM
CHARGE!!!

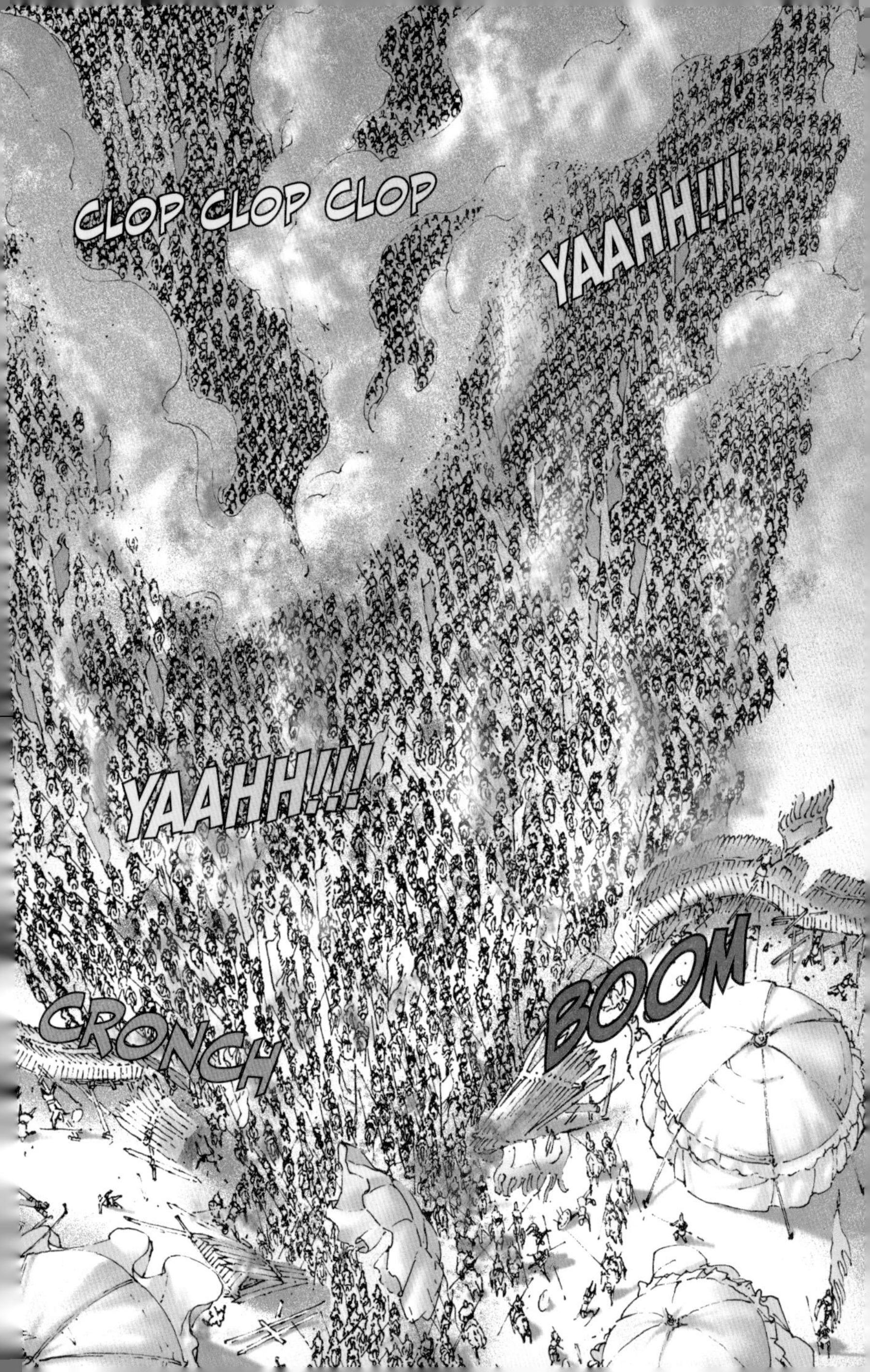
CLOP CLOP CLOP
YAAHH!!!
YAAHH!!!
CRONCH
BOOM

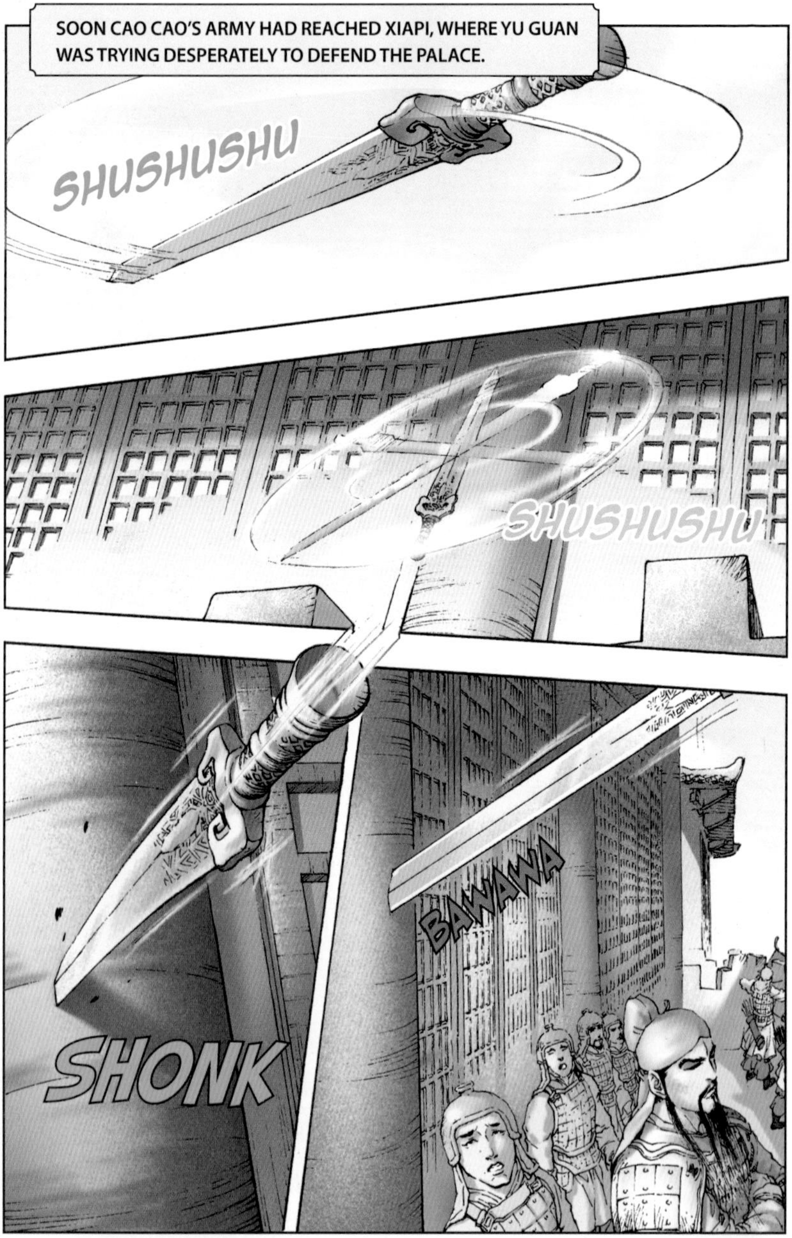
SOON CAO CAO'S ARMY HAD REACHED XIAPI, WHERE YU GUAN WAS TRYING DESPERATELY TO DEFEND THE PALACE.
SHUSHUSHU
SHUSHUSHU
BAWAWA
SHONK

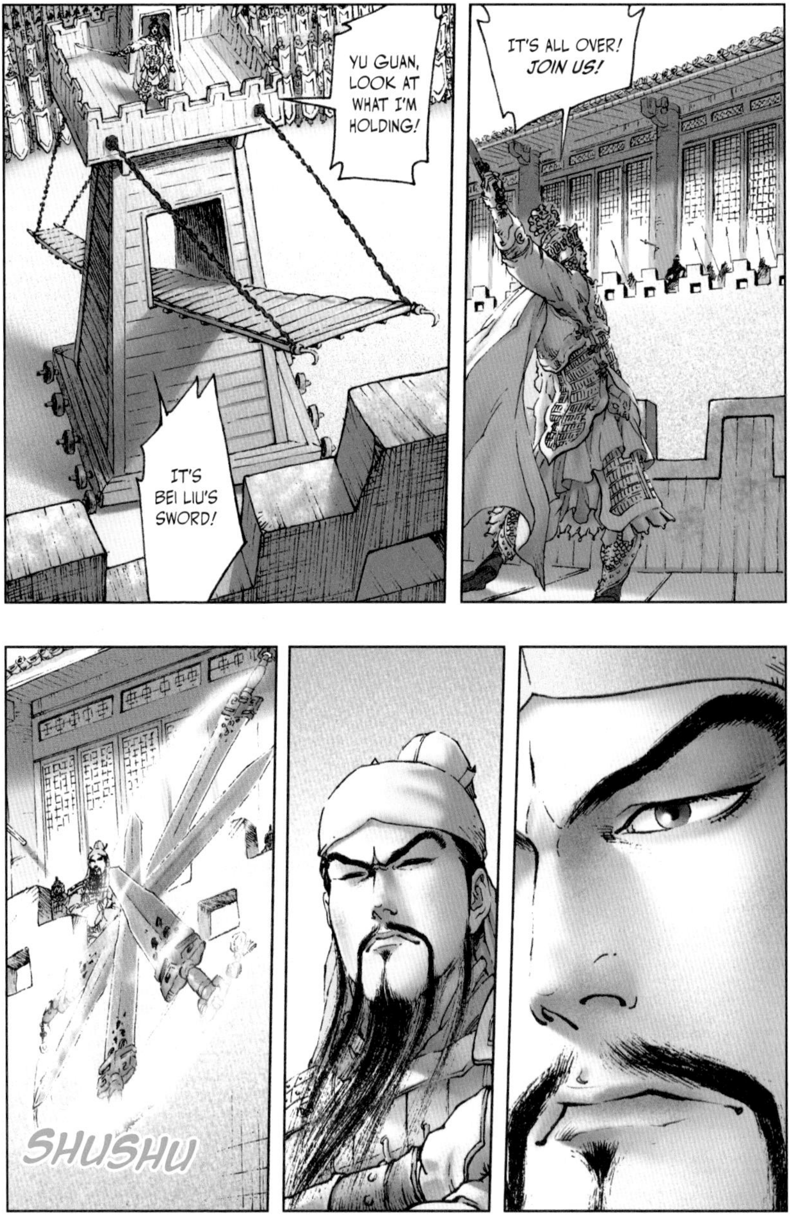
YU GUAN, LOOK AT WHAT I'M HOLDING!
IT'S BEI LIU'S SWORD!
IT'S ALL OVER! JOIN US!
SHUSHU

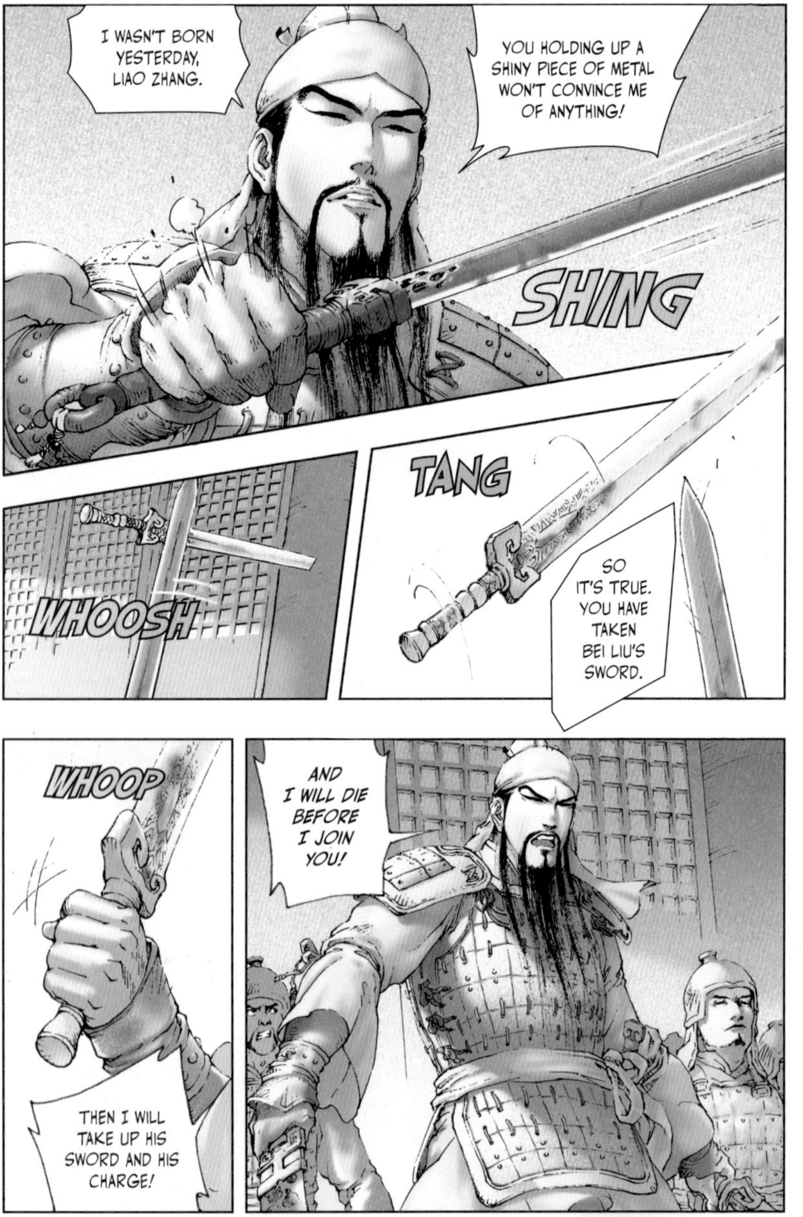
I WASN'T BORN YESTERDAY, LIAO ZHANG.
YOU HOLDING UP A SHINY PIECE OF METAL WON'T CONVINCE ME OF ANYTHING!
SHING
WHOOSH
TANG
SO IT'S TRUE. YOU HAVE TAKEN BEI LIU'S SWORD.
WHOOP
THEN I WILL TAKE UP HIS SWORD AND HIS CHARGE!
AND I WILL DIE BEFORE I JOIN YOU!

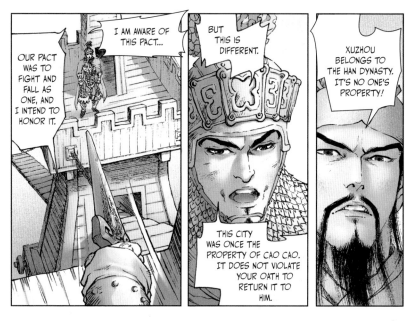

OUR PACT WAS TO FIGHT AND FALL AS ONE, AND I INTEND TO HONOR IT.

I AM AWARE OF THIS PACT...

BUT THIS IS DIFFERENT.

THIS CITY WAS ONCE THE PROPERTY OF CAO CAO. IT DOES NOT VIOLATE YOUR OATH TO RETURN IT TO HIM.

XUZHOU BELONGS TO THE HAN DYNASTY. IT'S NO ONE'S PROPERTY!

IF WE CANNOT AGREE, THEN WE MUST SETTLE THIS HONORABLY. I AM SENDING FORTH FOUR OF MY COMMANDERS.

IF YOU LOSE, WE TAKE OVER XUZHOU. IF YOU WIN, I WITHDRAW OUR FORCES.

THINK, YU GUAN. NO MORE INNOCENTS NEED TO DIE. THIS IS THE ONLY WAY.

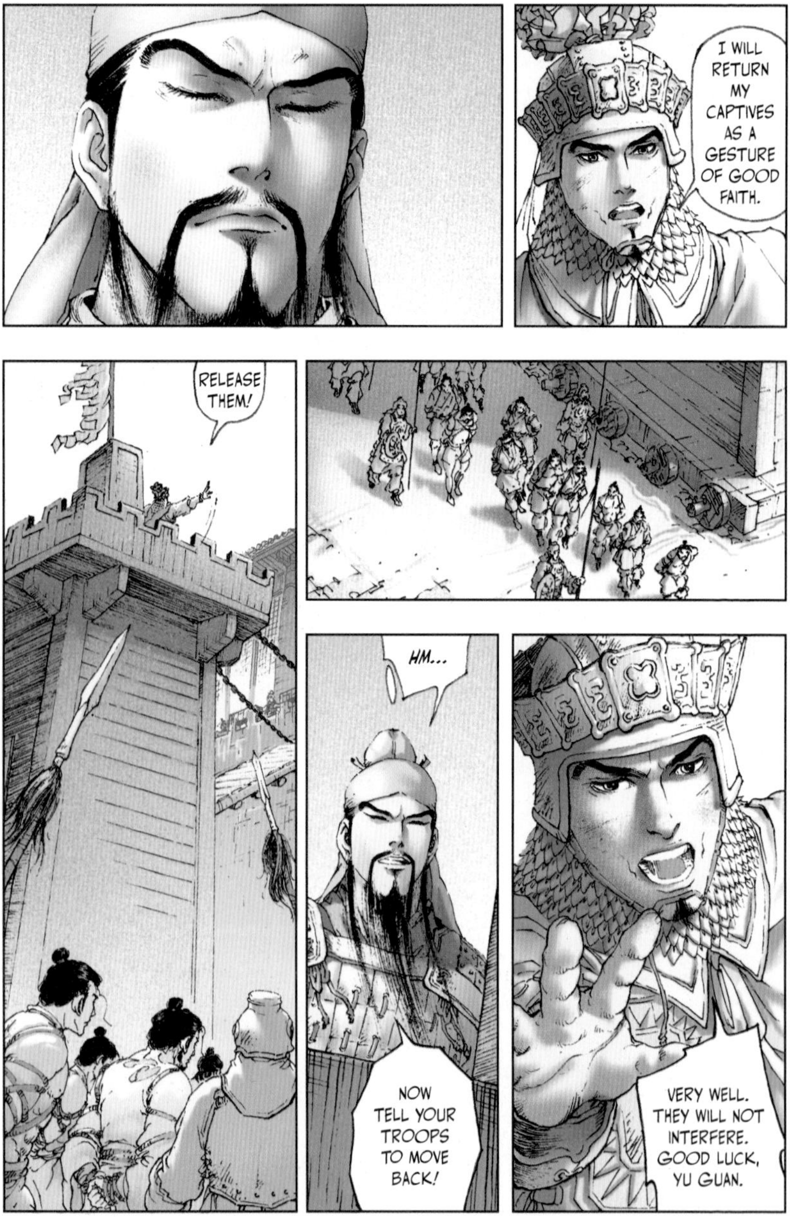
I WILL RETURN MY CAPTIVES AS A GESTURE OF GOOD FAITH.
RELEASE THEM!
HM...
NOW TELL YOUR TROOPS TO MOVE BACK!
VERY WELL. THEY WILL NOT INTERFERE. GOOD LUCK, YU GUAN.

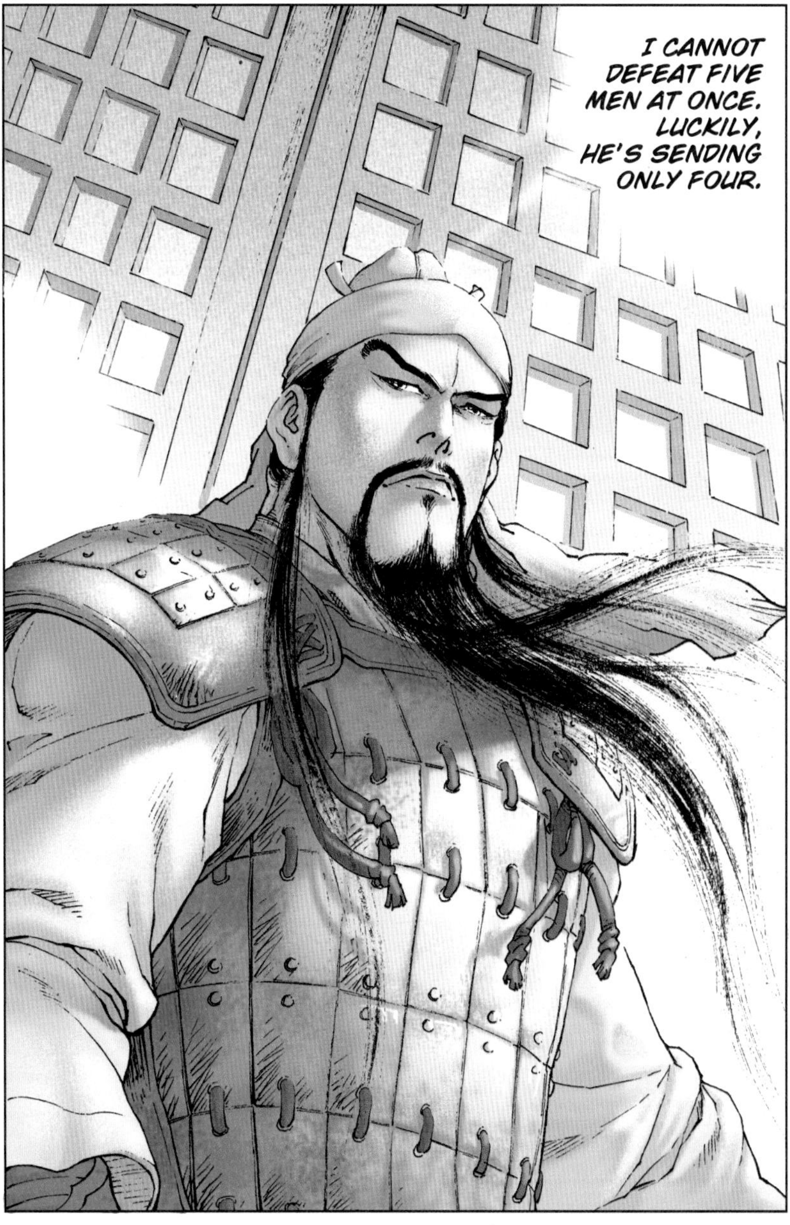
I CANNOT DEFEAT FIVE MEN AT ONCE. LUCKILY, HE'S SENDING ONLY FOUR.

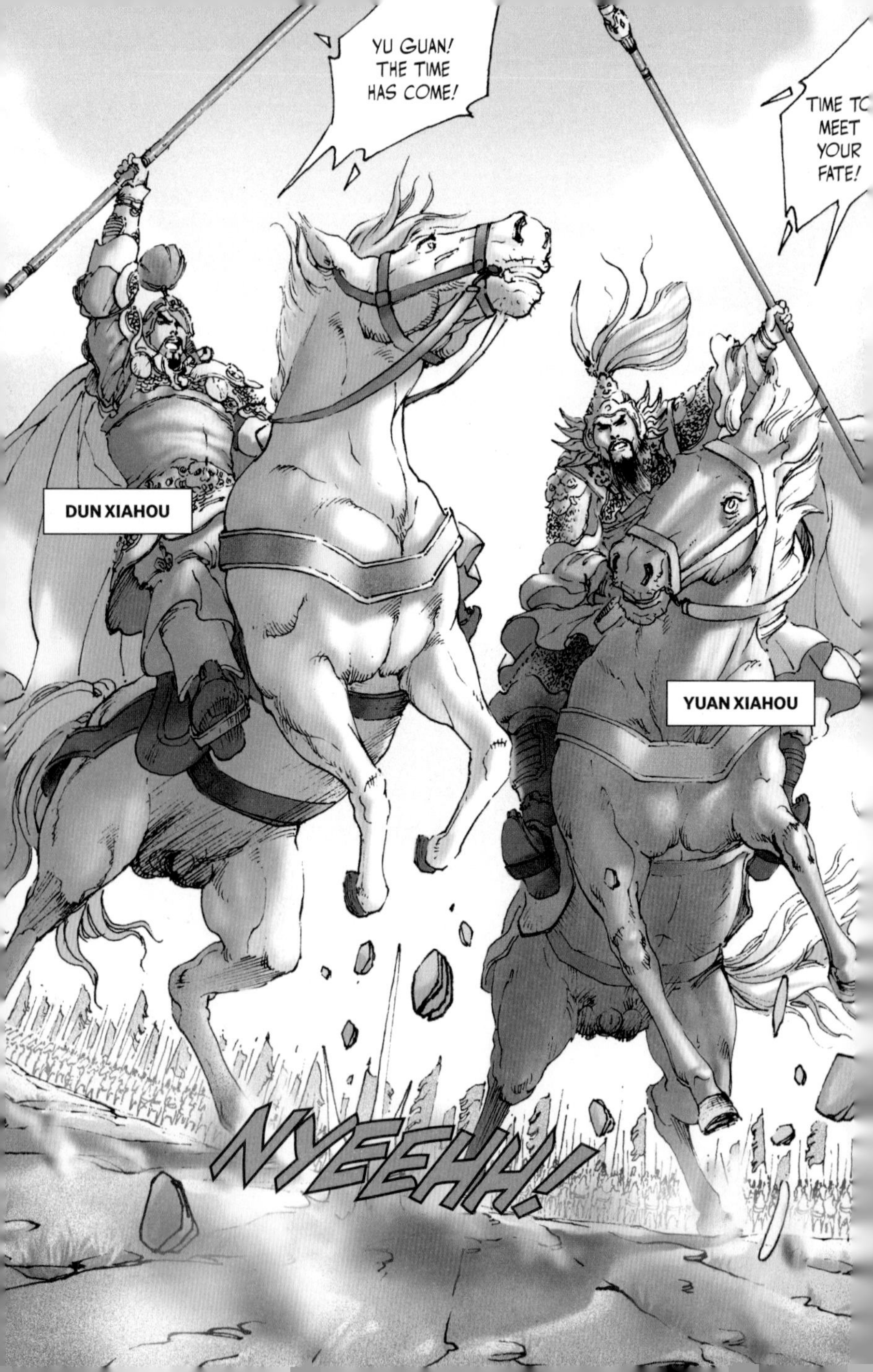
YU GUAN! THE TIME HAS COME!
TIME TO MEET YOUR FATE!
DUN XIAHOU
YUAN XIAHOU
NYEEHH!

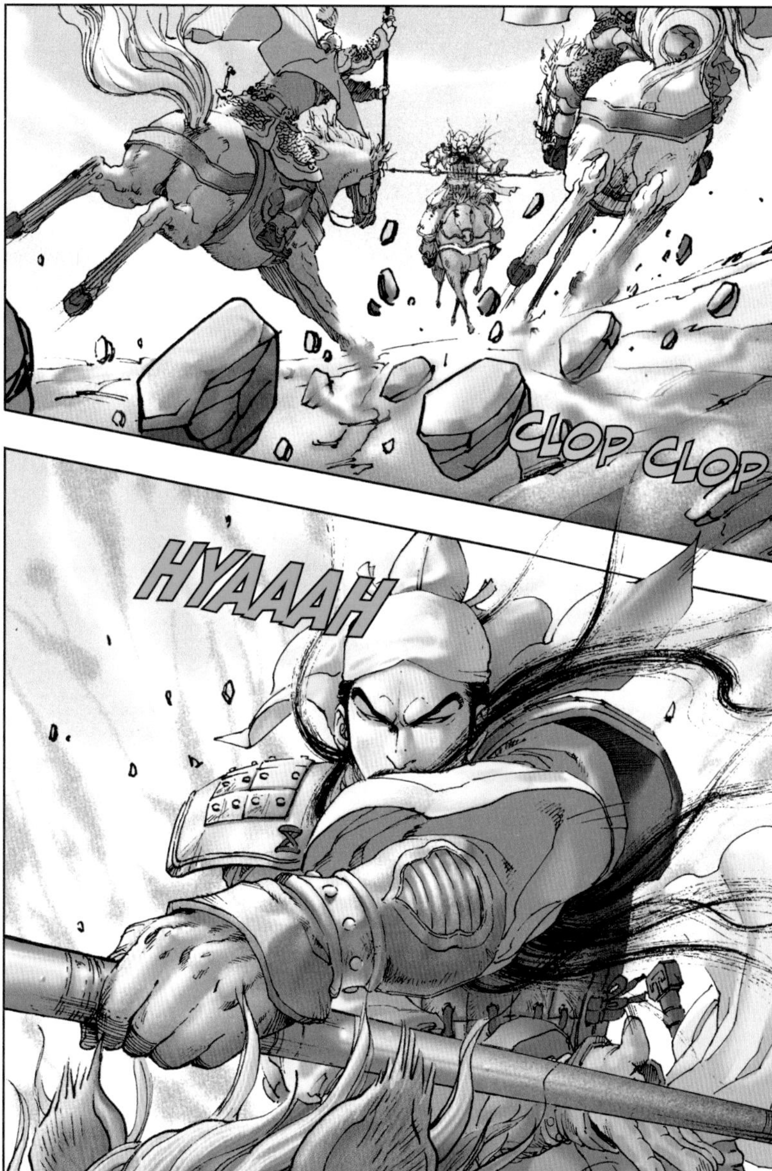
CLOP CLOP
CLOP
HYAAAH

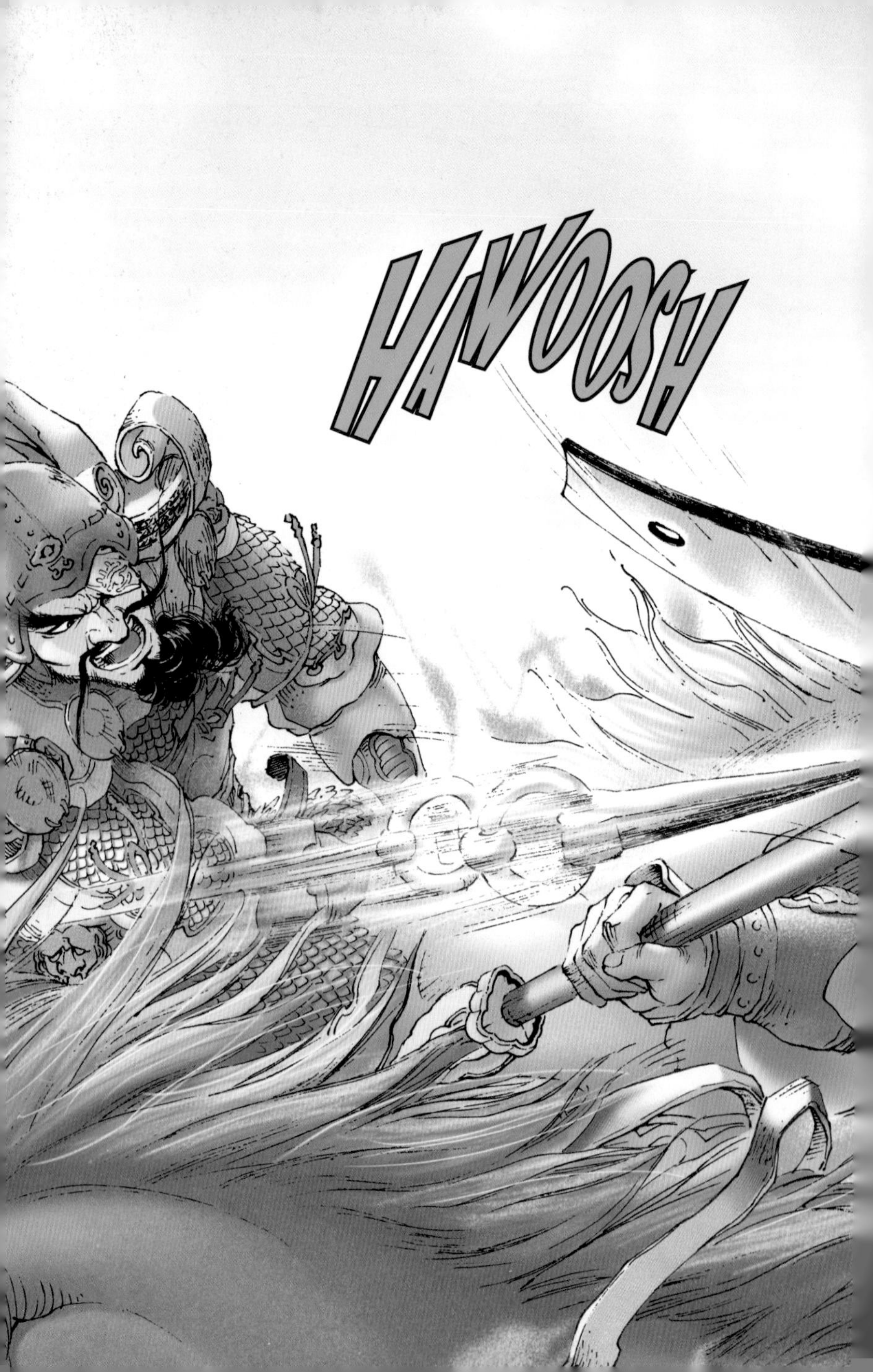
HWOOSH

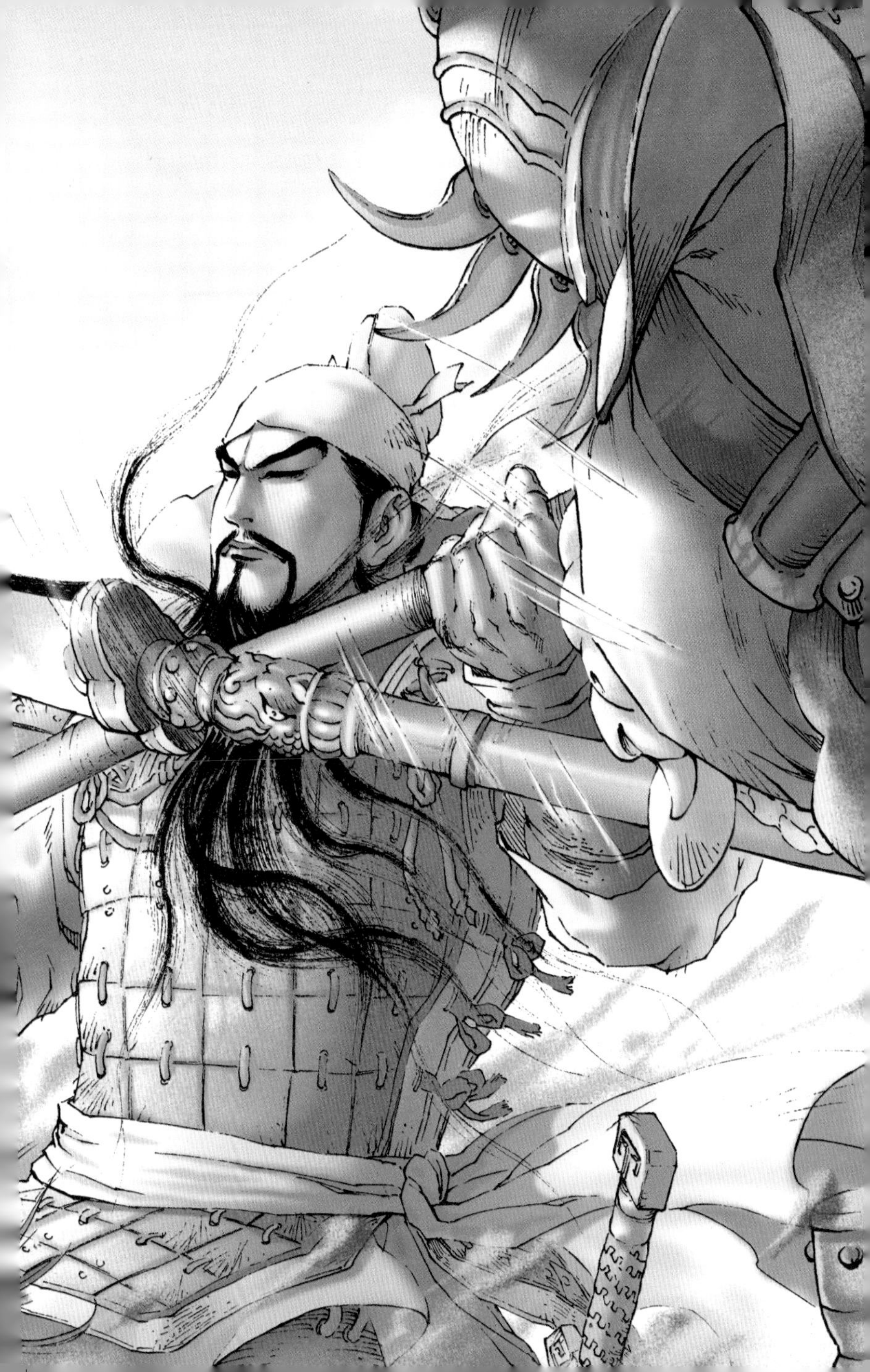

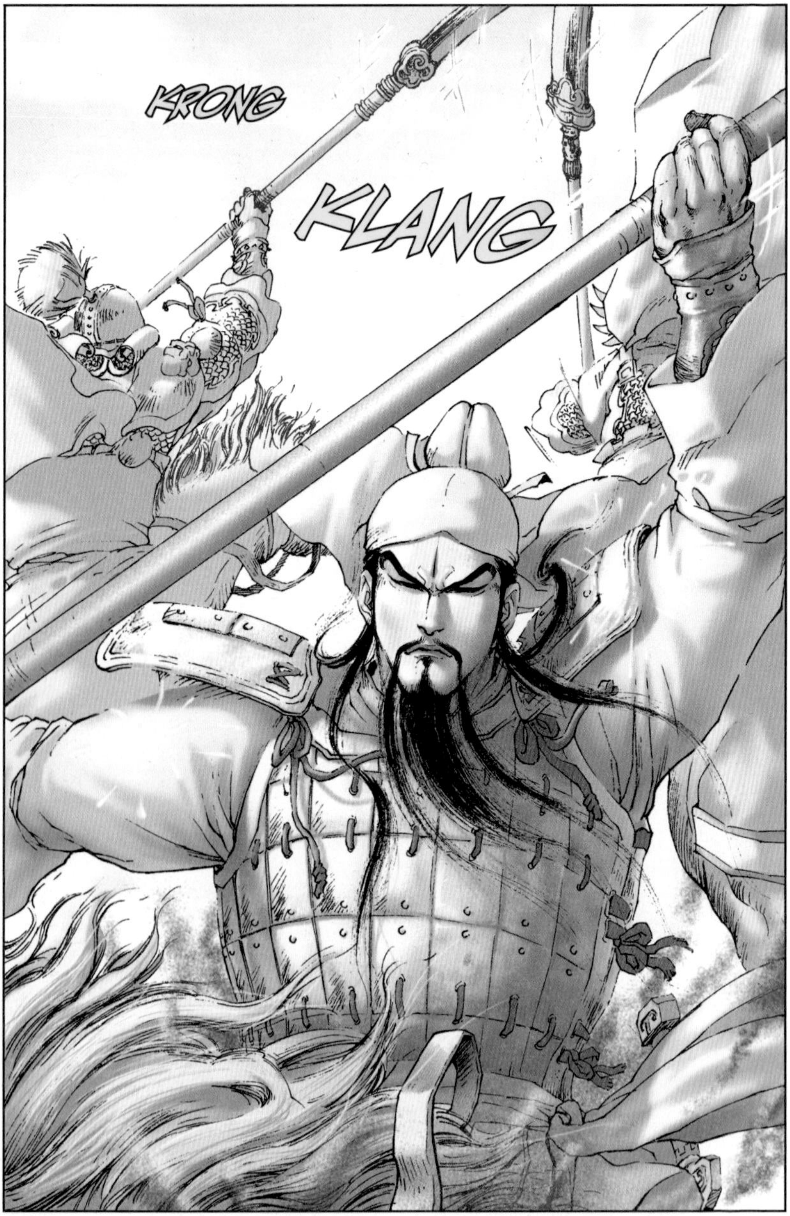
KRONG
KLANG

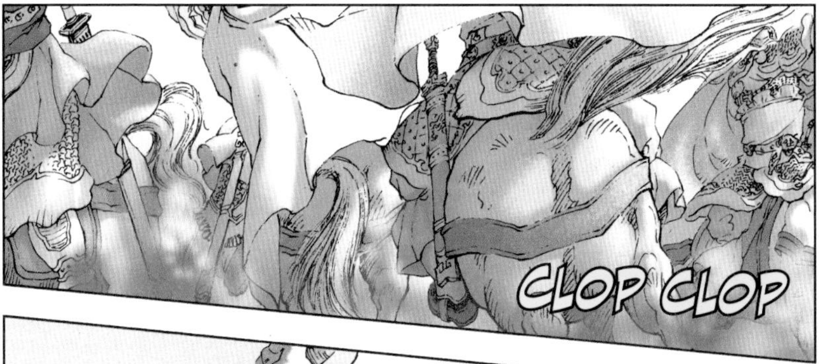
CLOP CLOP

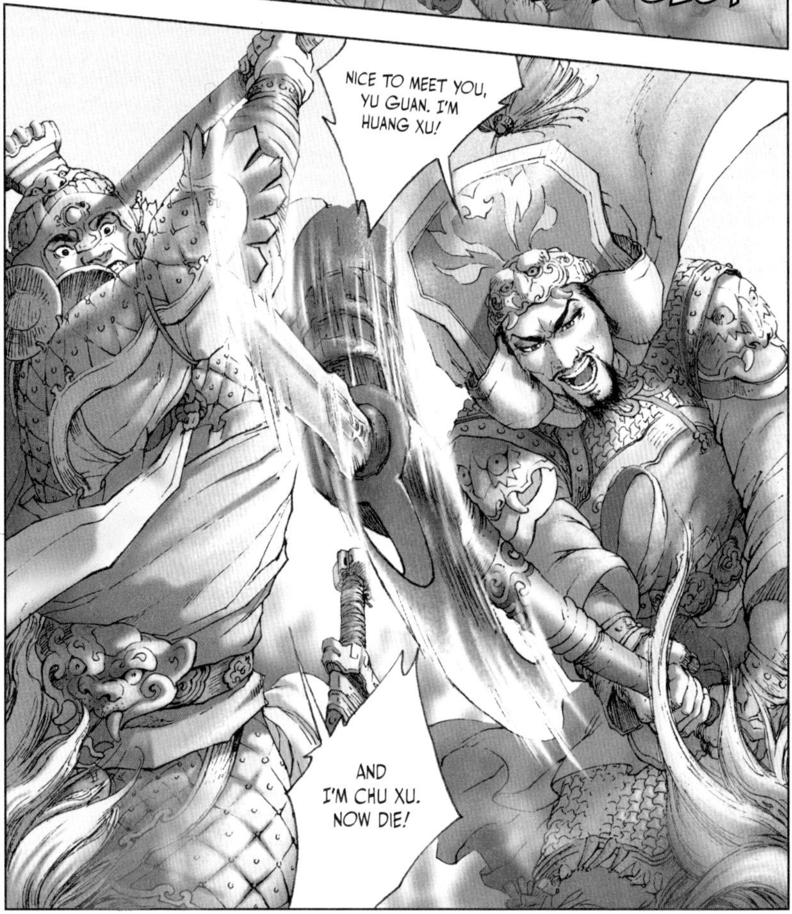
NICE TO MEET YOU, YU GUAN. I'M HUANG XU!
AND I'M CHU XU. NOW DIE!

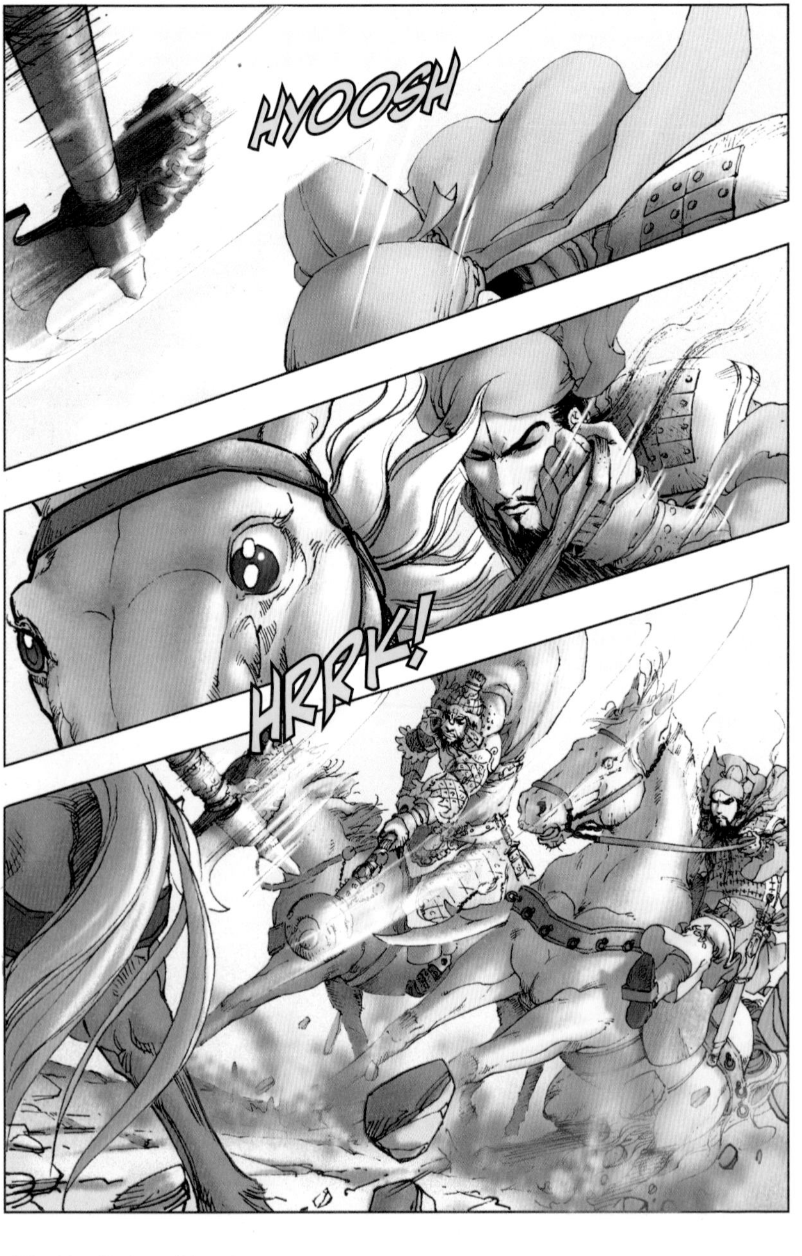
HYOOSH
HRRK!

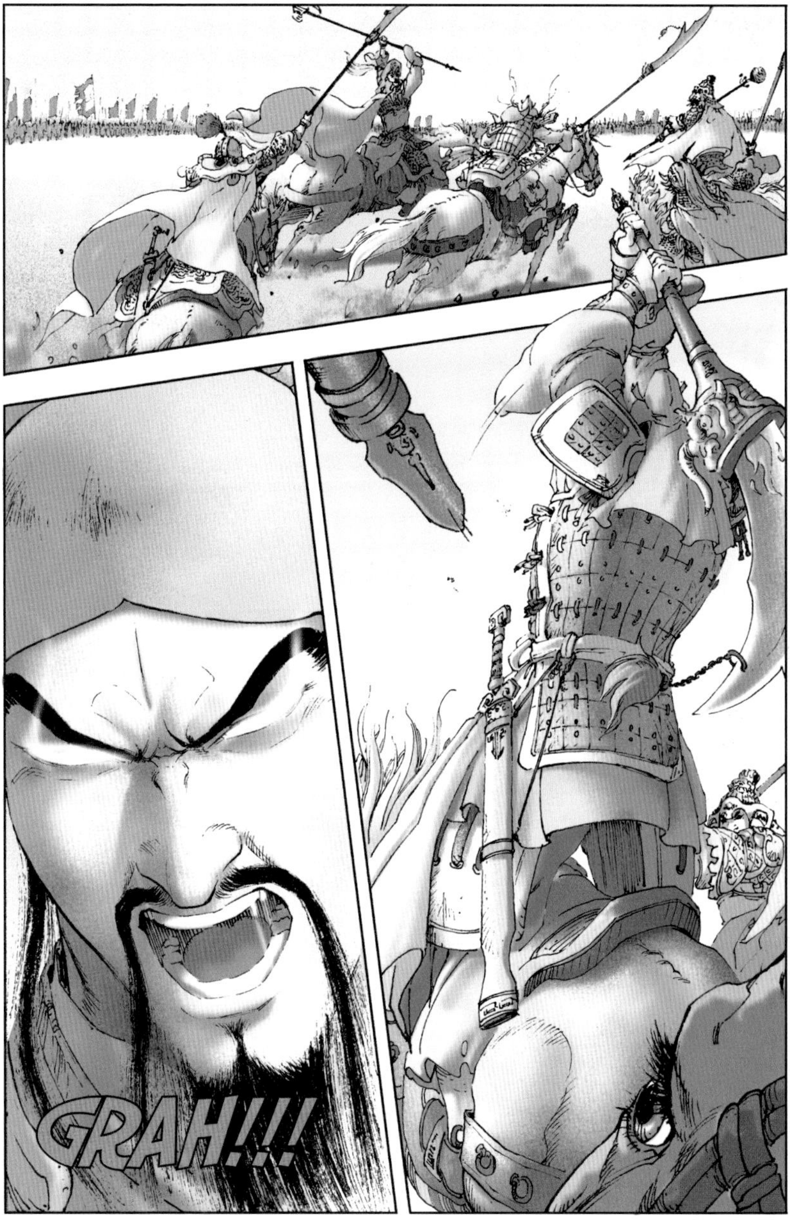
GRAH!!!

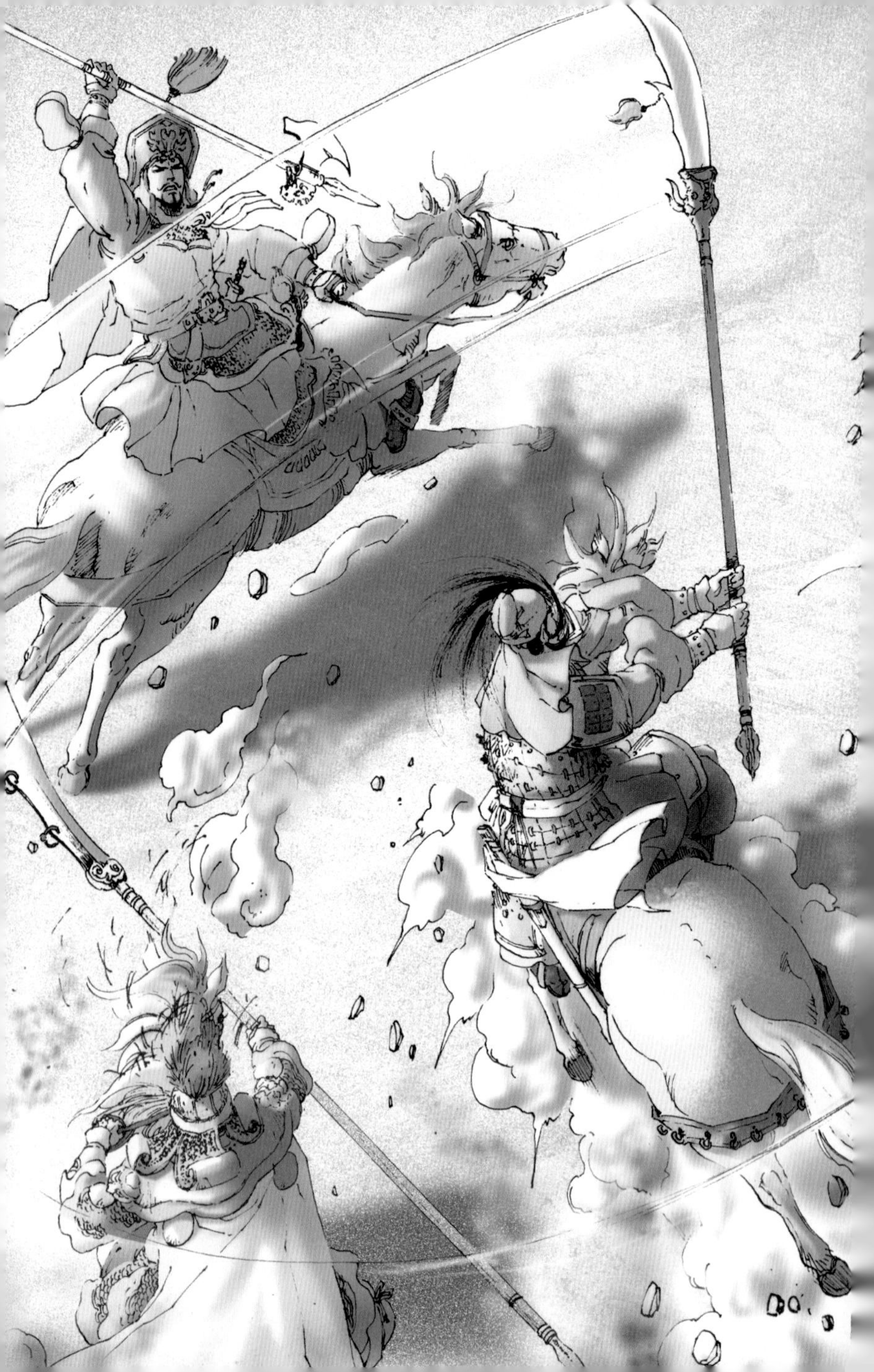

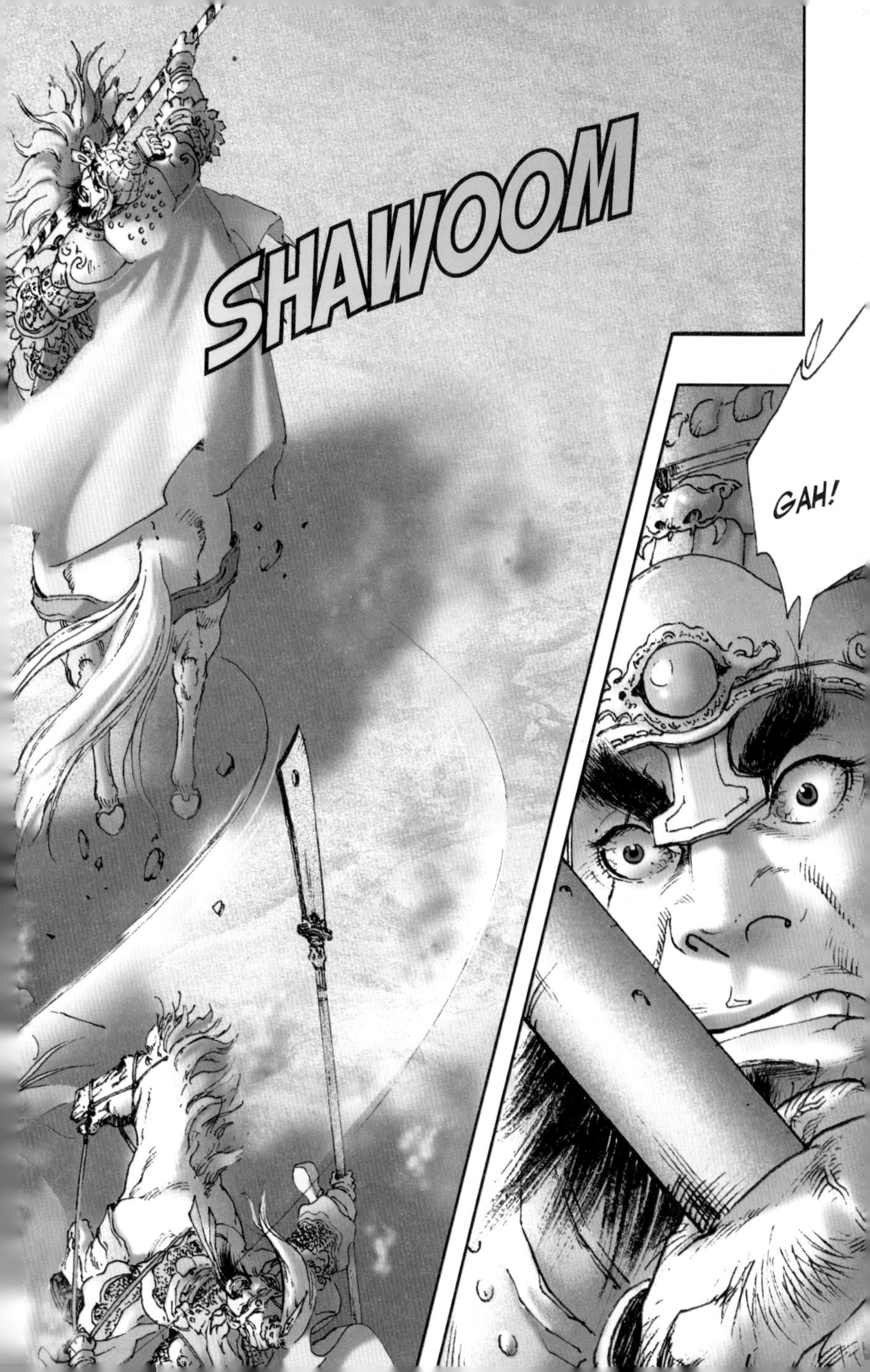
SHAWOOM
GAH!

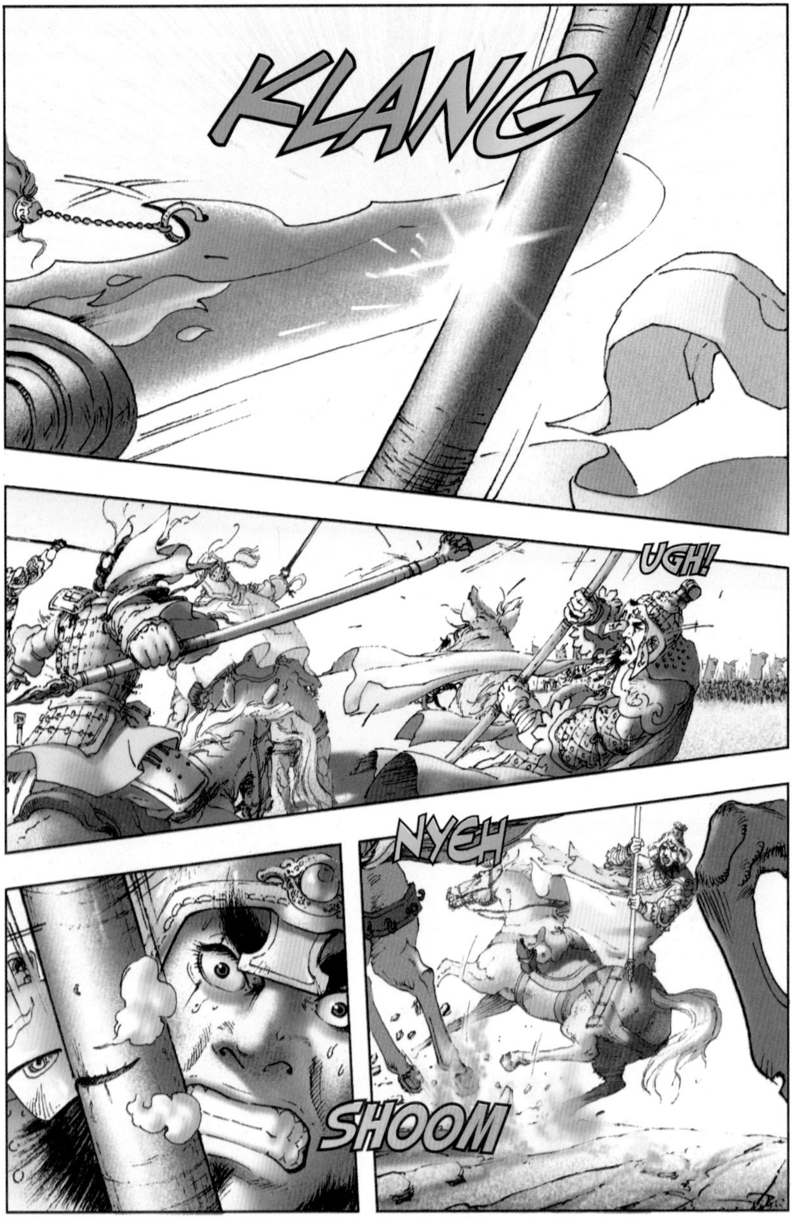
KLANG
UGH!
NYEH
SHOOM

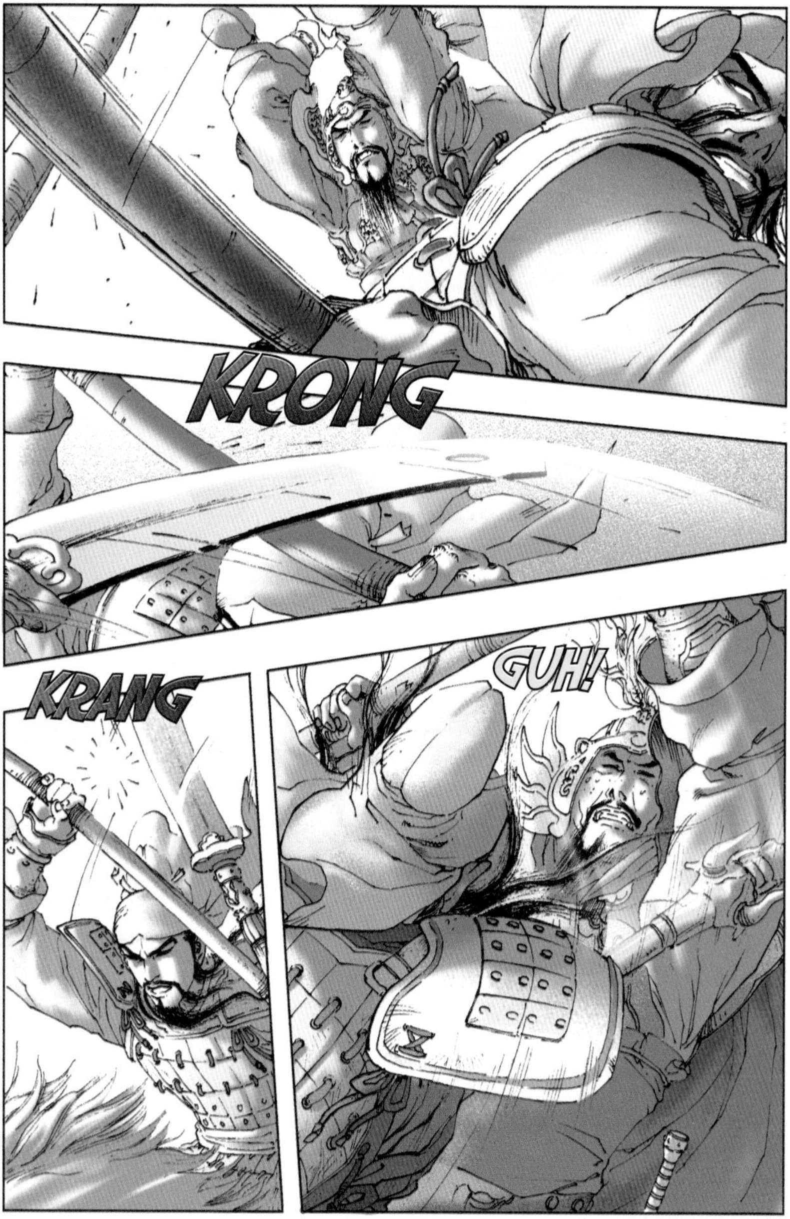
KRONG
KRANG
GUH!

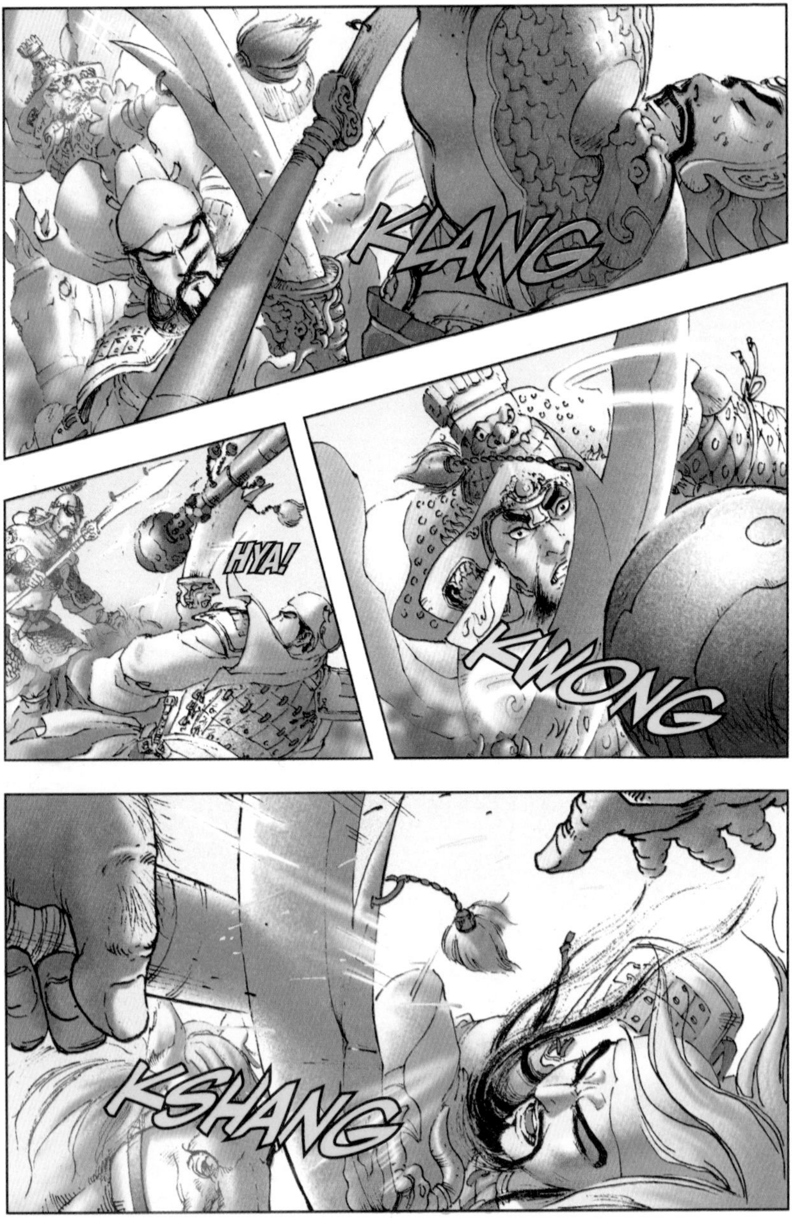
KLANG
HYA!
KWONG
KSHANG

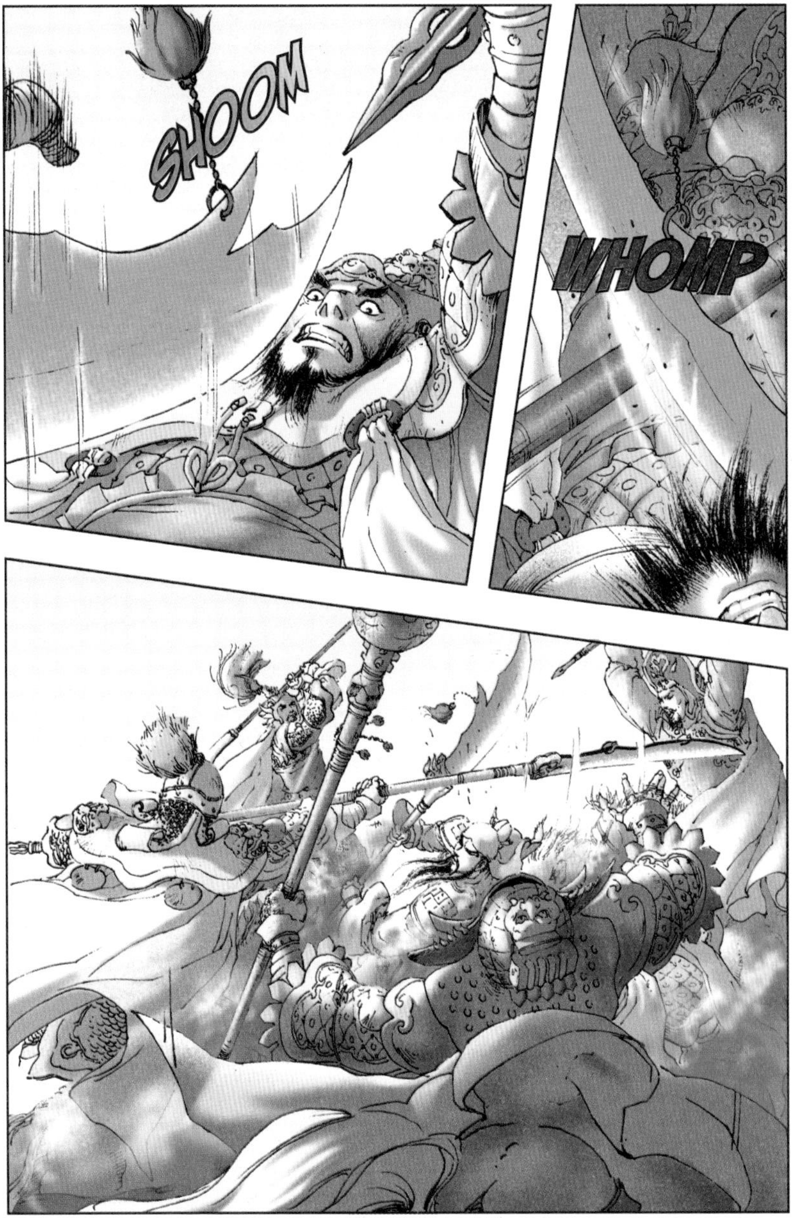
SHOOM
WHOMP

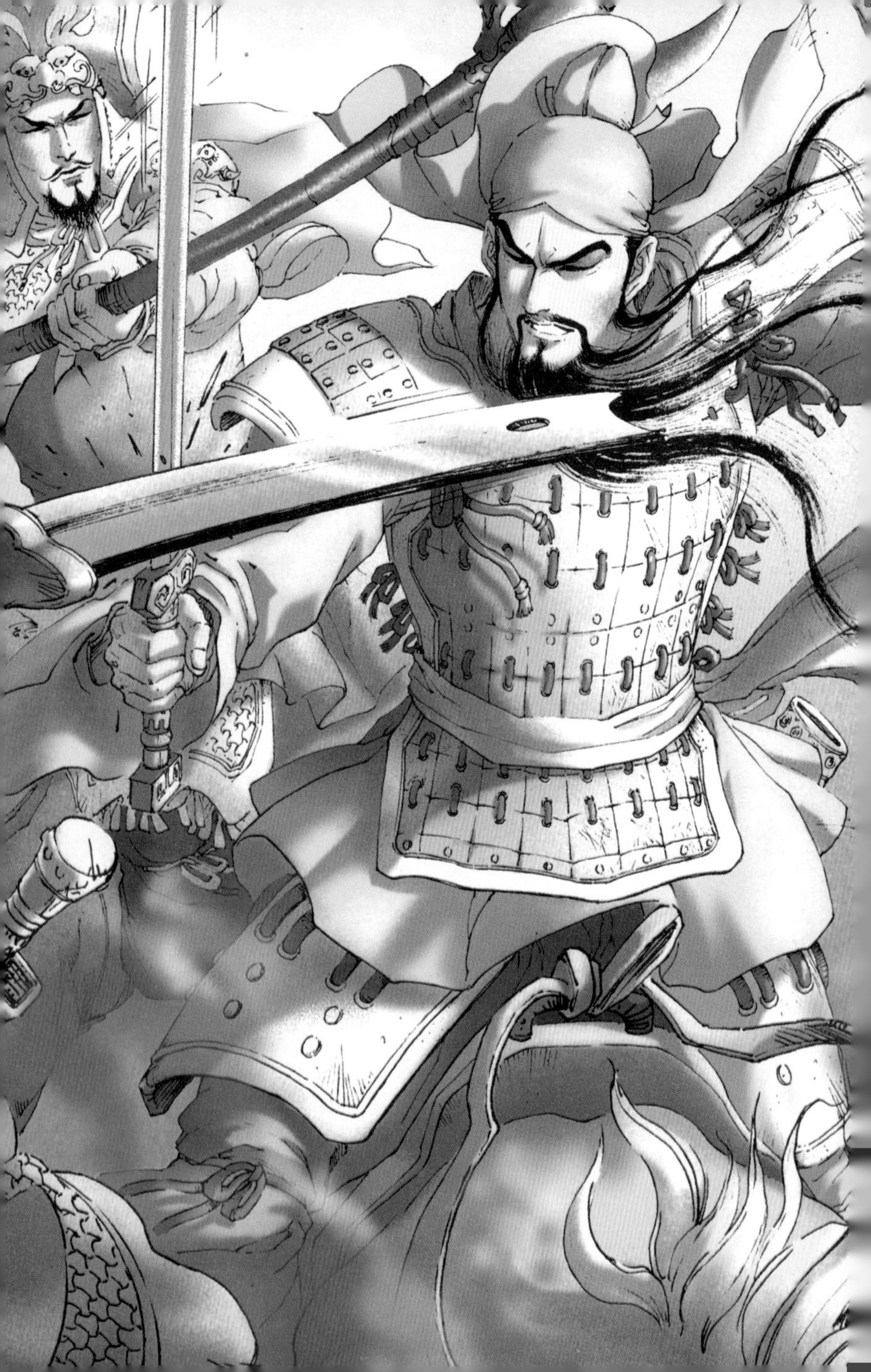

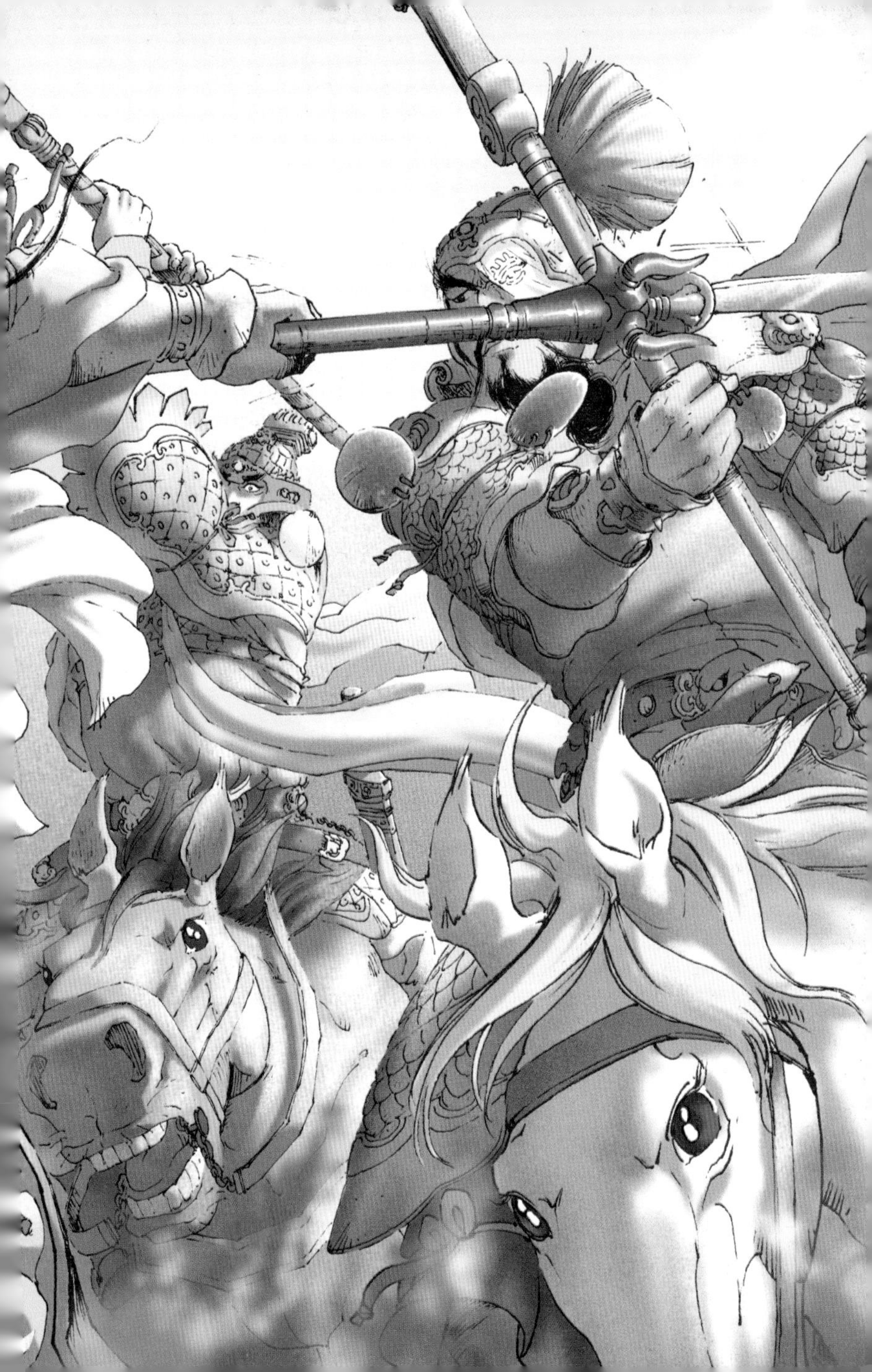

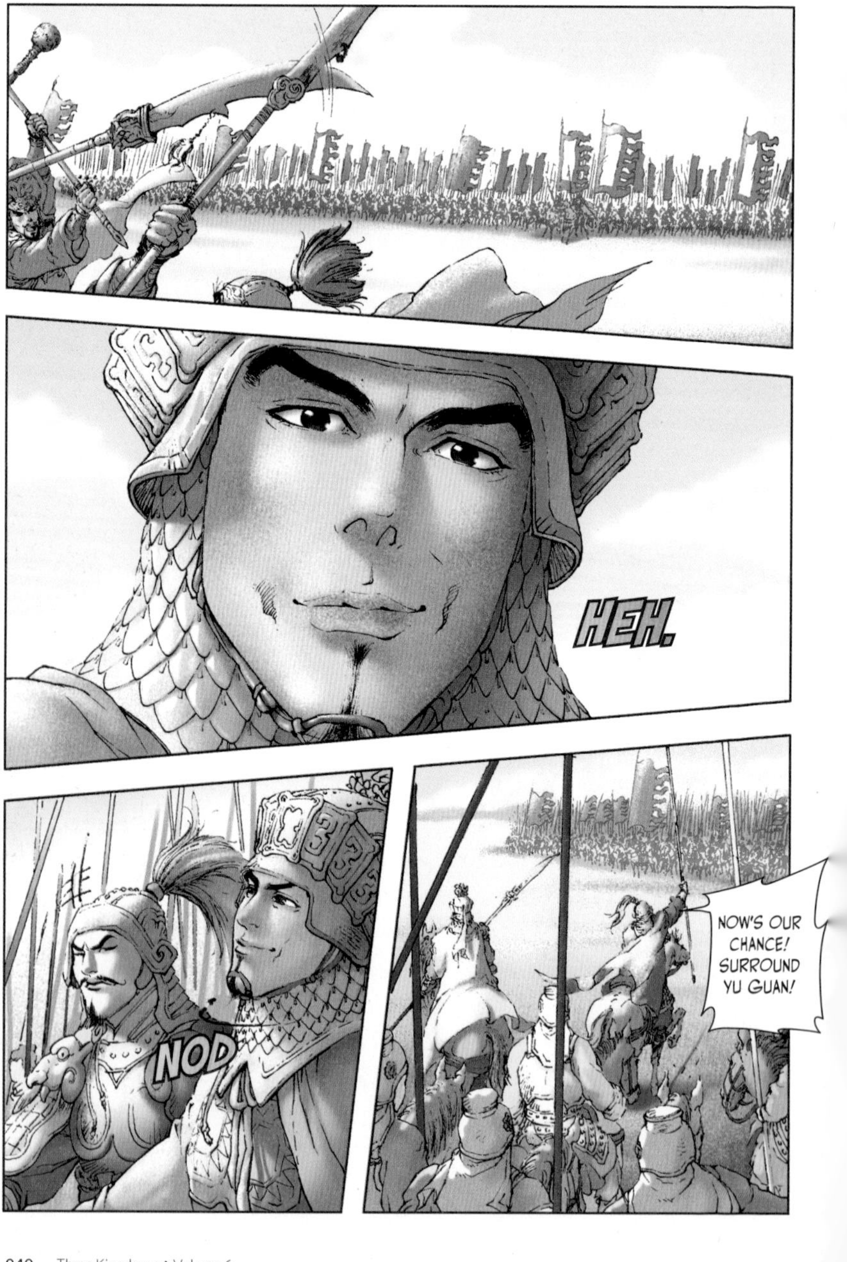
HEH.
NOD
NOW'S OUR CHANCE! SURROUND YU GUAN!

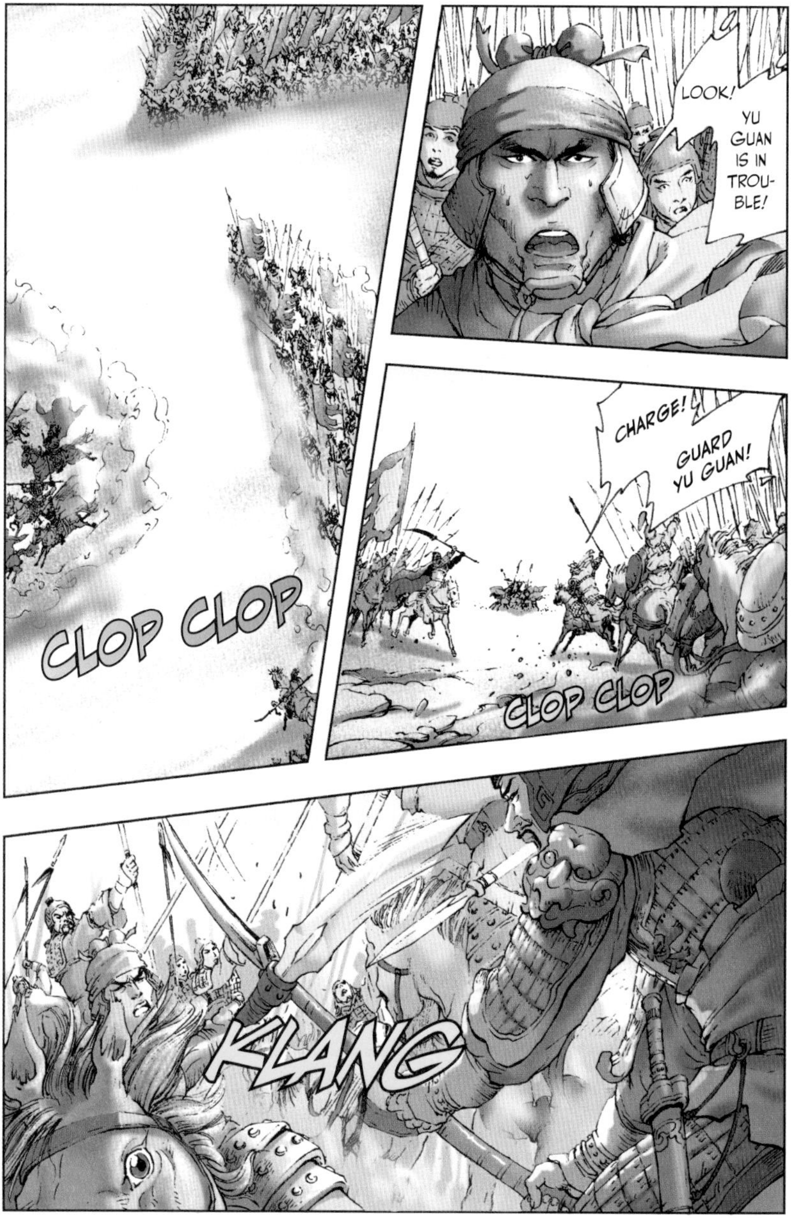
LOOK!
YU GUAN IS IN TROU-BLE!
CLOP CLOP
CHARGE!
GUARD YU GUAN!
CLOP CLOP
KLANG

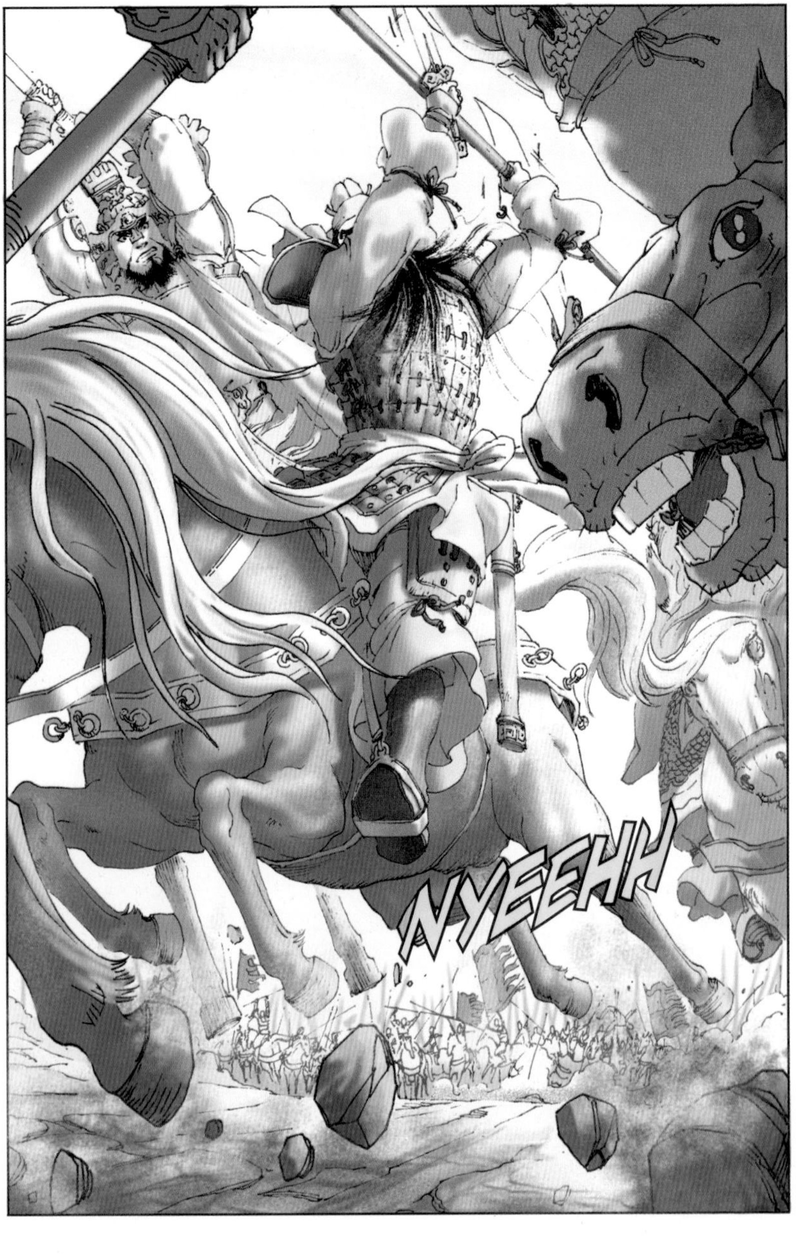
NYEEHH

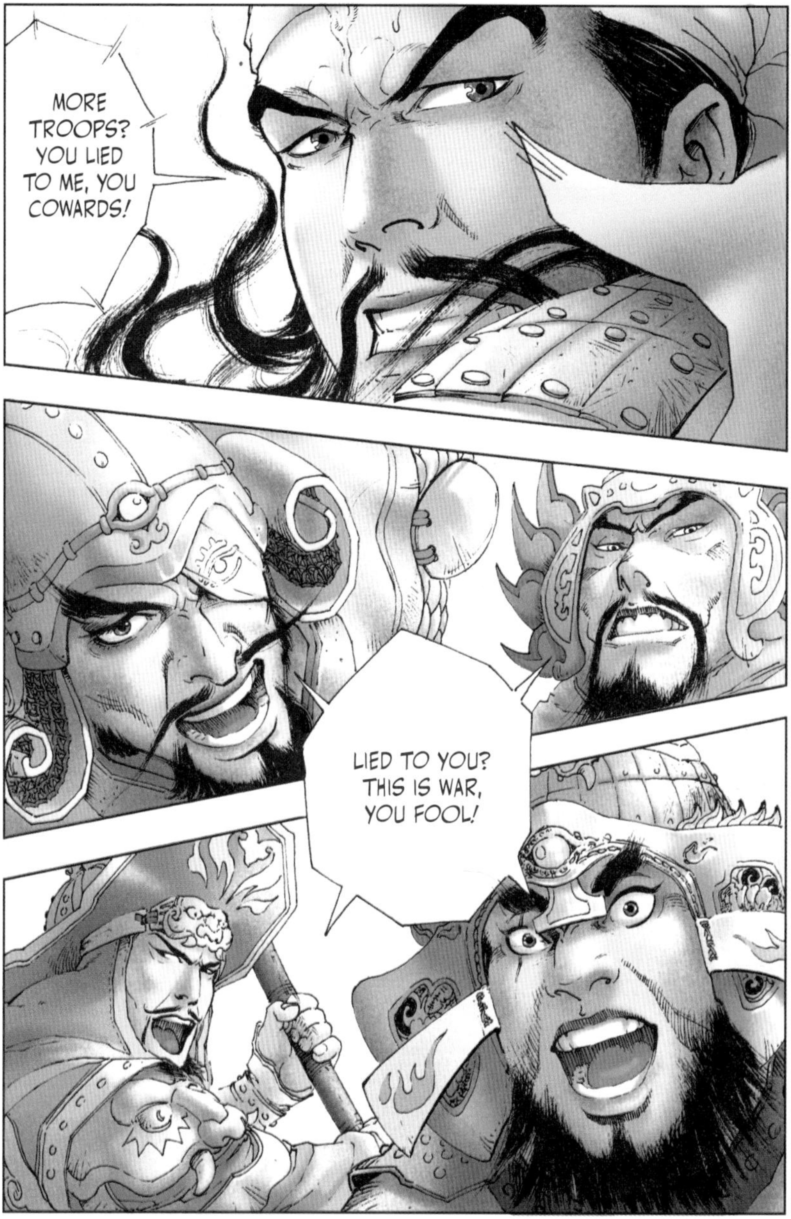
MORE TROOPS? YOU LIED TO ME, YOU COWARDS!
LIED TO YOU? THIS IS WAR, YOU FOOL!

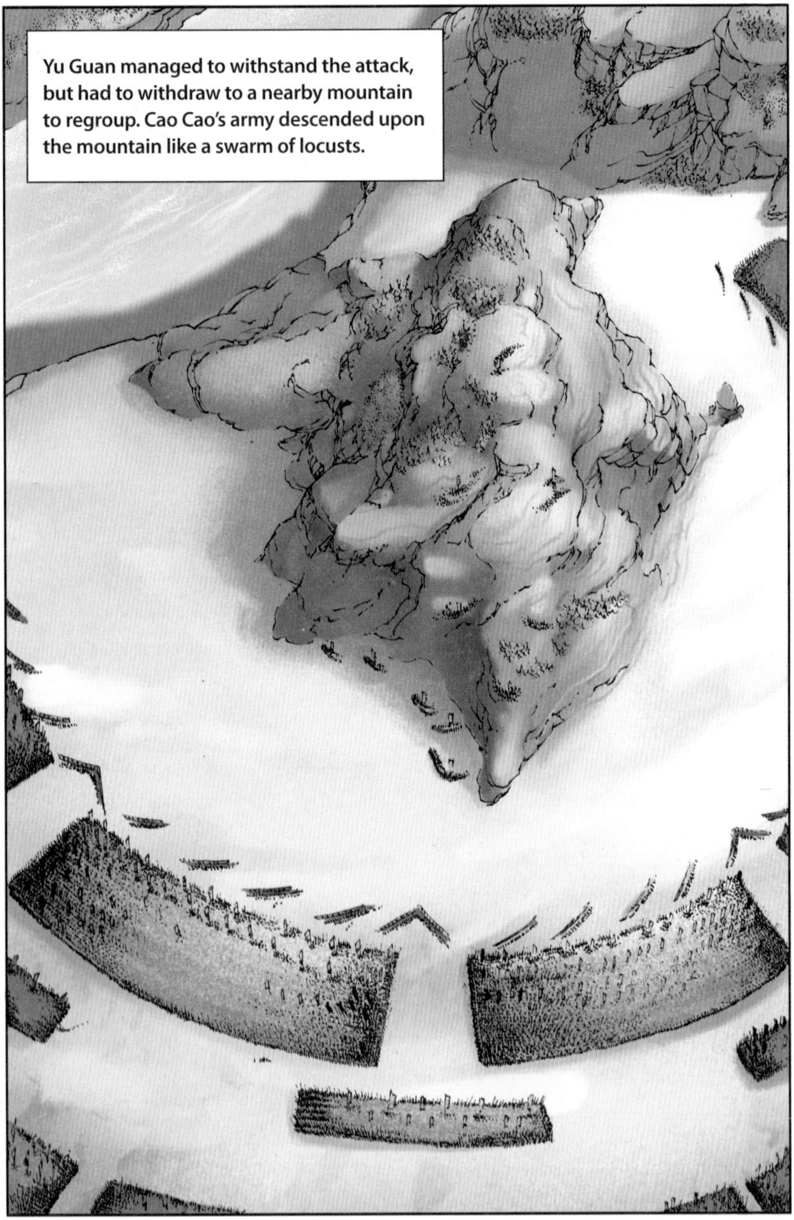
Yu Guan managed to withstand the attack, but had to withdraw to a nearby mountain to regroup. Cao Cao's army descended upon the mountain like a swarm of locusts.

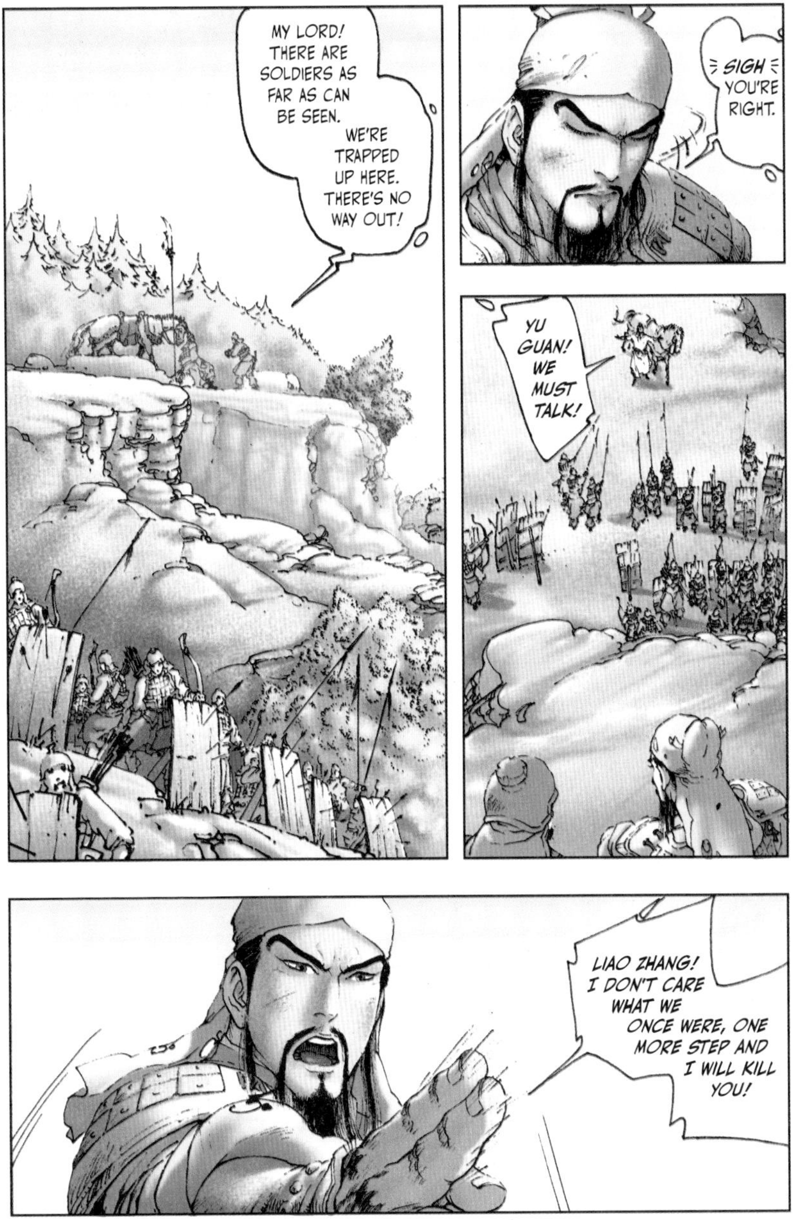
MY LORD! THERE ARE SOLDIERS AS FAR AS CAN BE SEEN.
WE'RE TRAPPED UP HERE. THERE'S NO WAY OUT!
SIGH YOU'RE RIGHT.
YU GUAN! WE MUST TALK!
LIAO ZHANG! I DON'T CARE WHAT WE ONCE WERE, ONE MORE STEP AND I WILL KILL YOU!

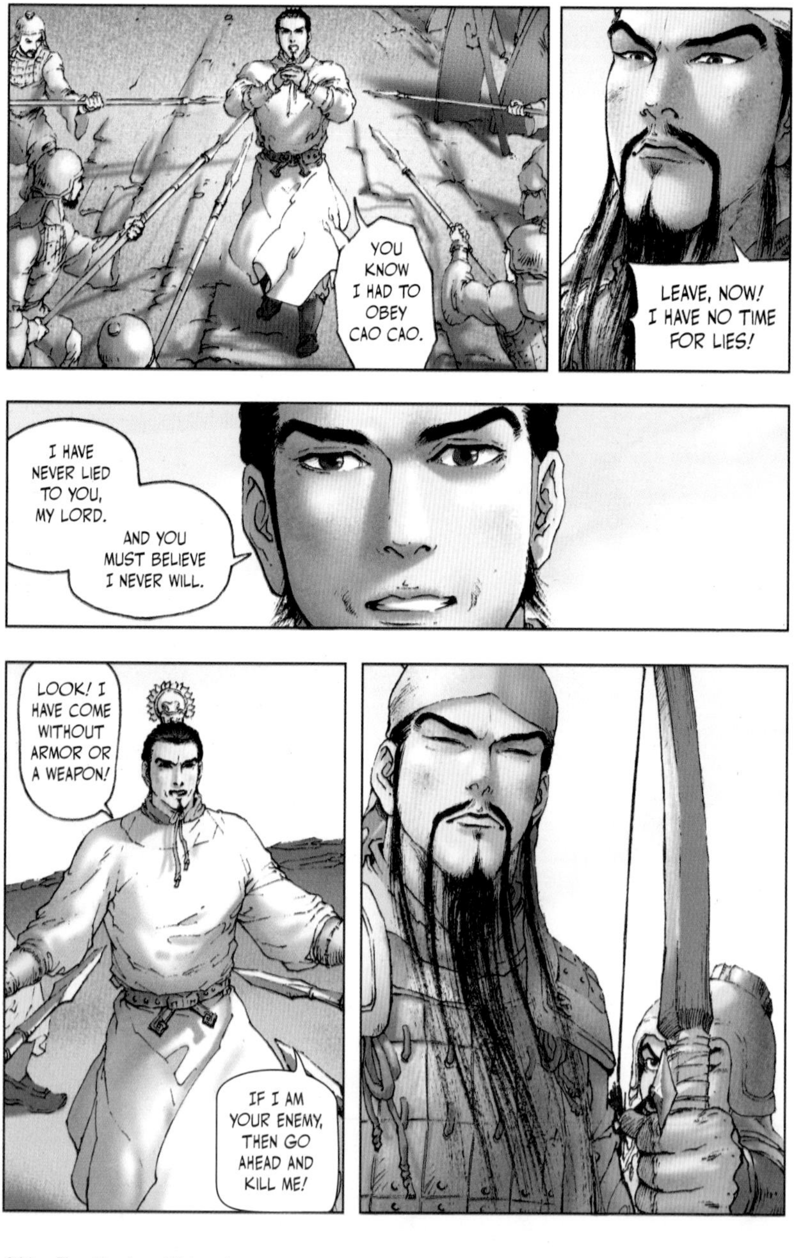
YOU KNOW I HAD TO OBEY CAO CAO.
LEAVE, NOW! I HAVE NO TIME FOR LIES!
I HAVE NEVER LIED TO YOU, MY LORD.
AND YOU MUST BELIEVE I NEVER WILL.
LOOK! I HAVE COME WITHOUT ARMOR OR A WEAPON!
IF I AM YOUR ENEMY, THEN GO AHEAD AND KILL ME!

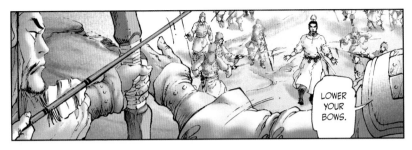

LOWER YOUR BOWS.

YOU MAY BREAK MY NECK, BUT NOT MY WILL.

I HAVE NO INTENTION OF BREAKING EITHER ONE.

THERE ARE TIMES WHEN A MAN NEEDS TO CHANGE HIS MIND. IT'S WHY I'M STILL ALIVE.

AND FOR ALL WE KNOW, BEI LIU AND FEI ZHANG COULD STILL BE ALIVE. IF SO, YOU WOULD DO THEM NO HONOR BY DYING.

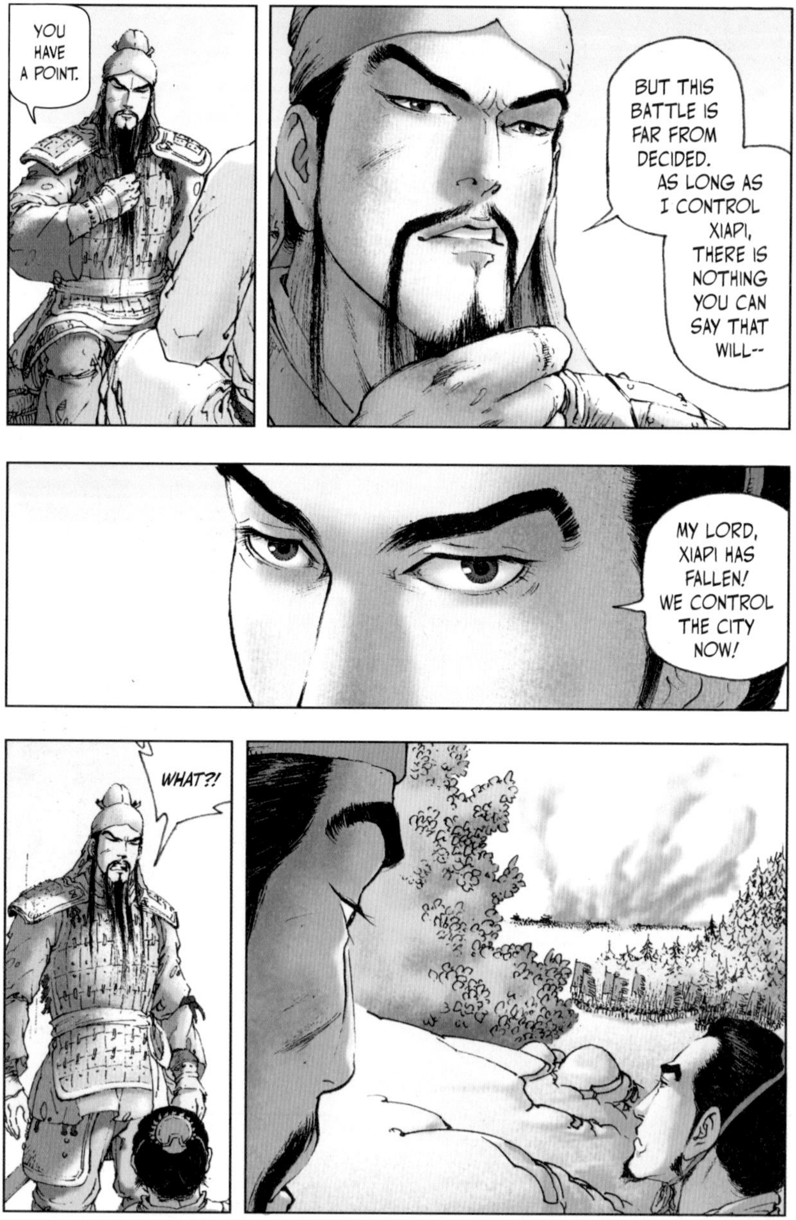
YOU HAVE A POINT.
BUT THIS BATTLE IS FAR FROM DECIDED. AS LONG AS I CONTROL XIAPI, THERE IS NOTHING YOU CAN SAY THAT WILL--
MY LORD, XIAPI HAS FALLEN! WE CONTROL THE CITY NOW!
WHAT?!

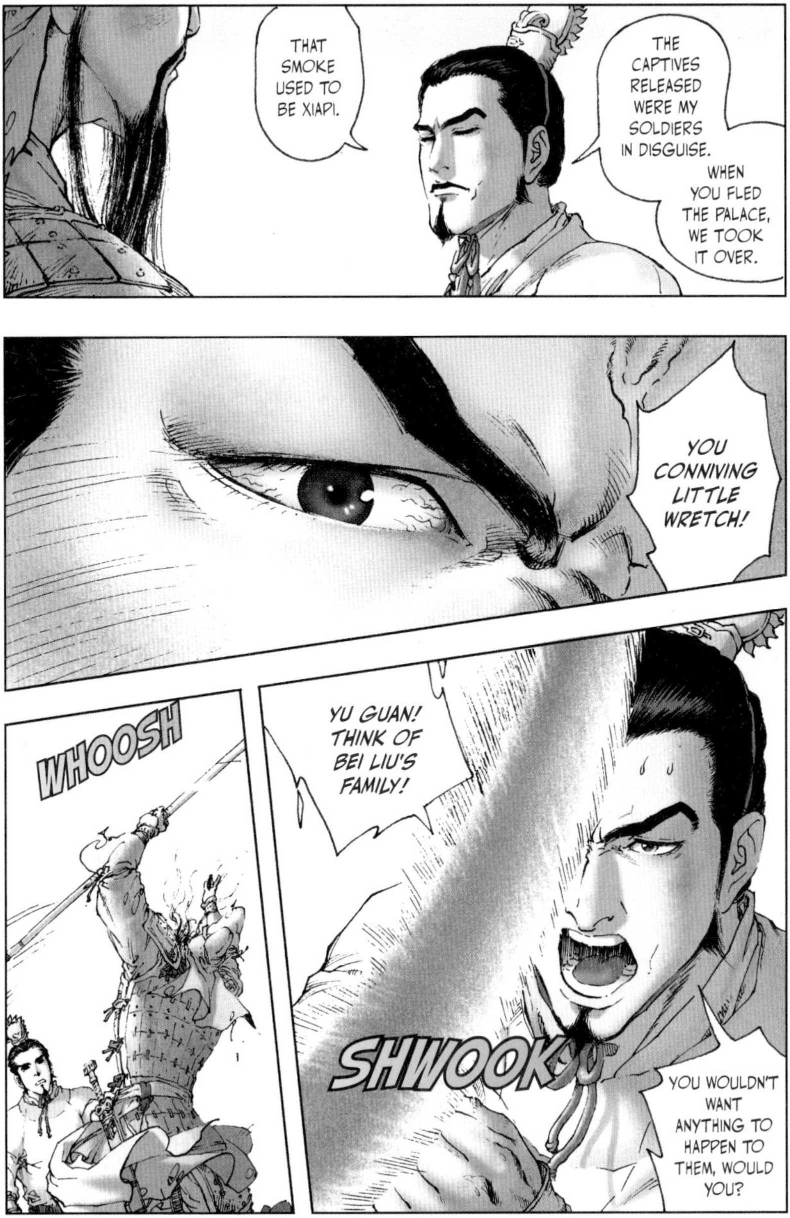
THAT SMOKE USED TO BE XIAPI.
THE CAPTIVES RELEASED WERE MY SOLDIERS IN DISGUISE.
WHEN YOU FLED THE PALACE, WE TOOK IT OVER.
YOU CONNIVING LITTLE WRETCH!
YU GUAN! THINK OF BEI LIU'S FAMILY!
WHOOSH
SHWOOK
YOU WOULDN'T WANT ANYTHING TO HAPPEN TO THEM, WOULD YOU?

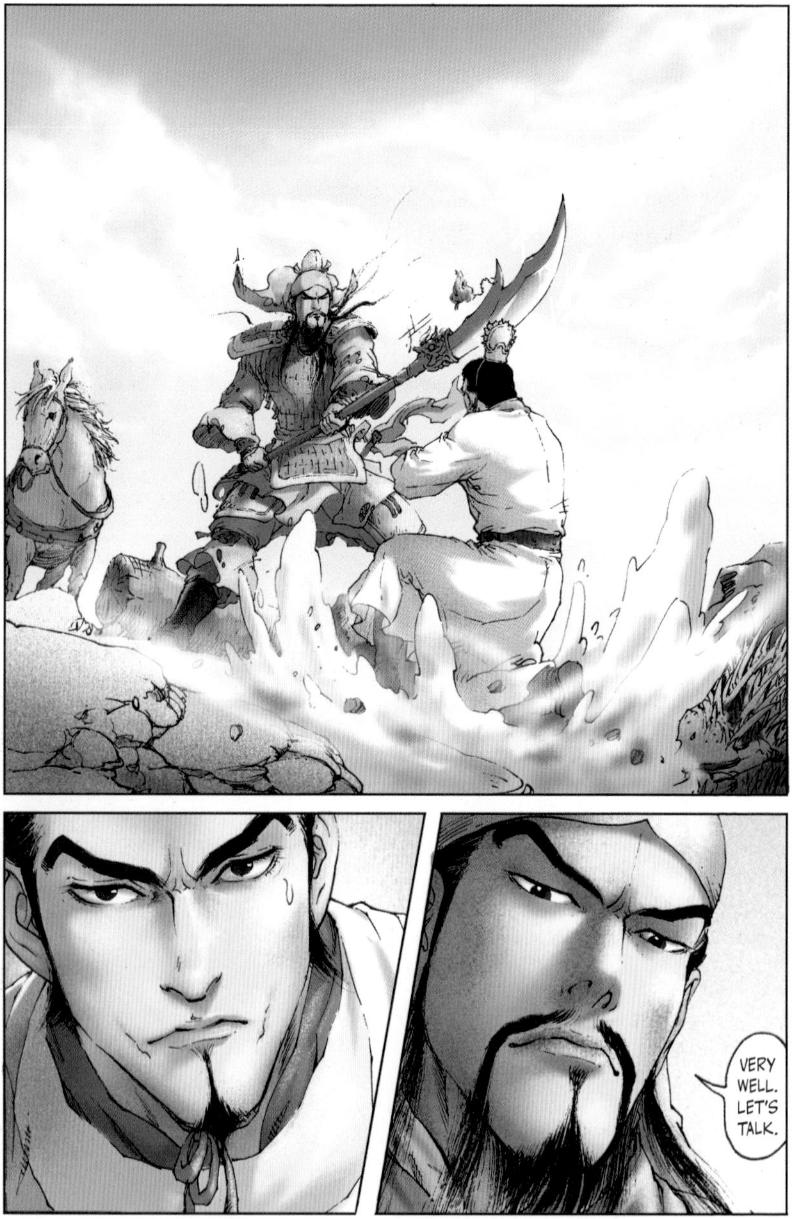
VERY WELL. LET'S TALK.

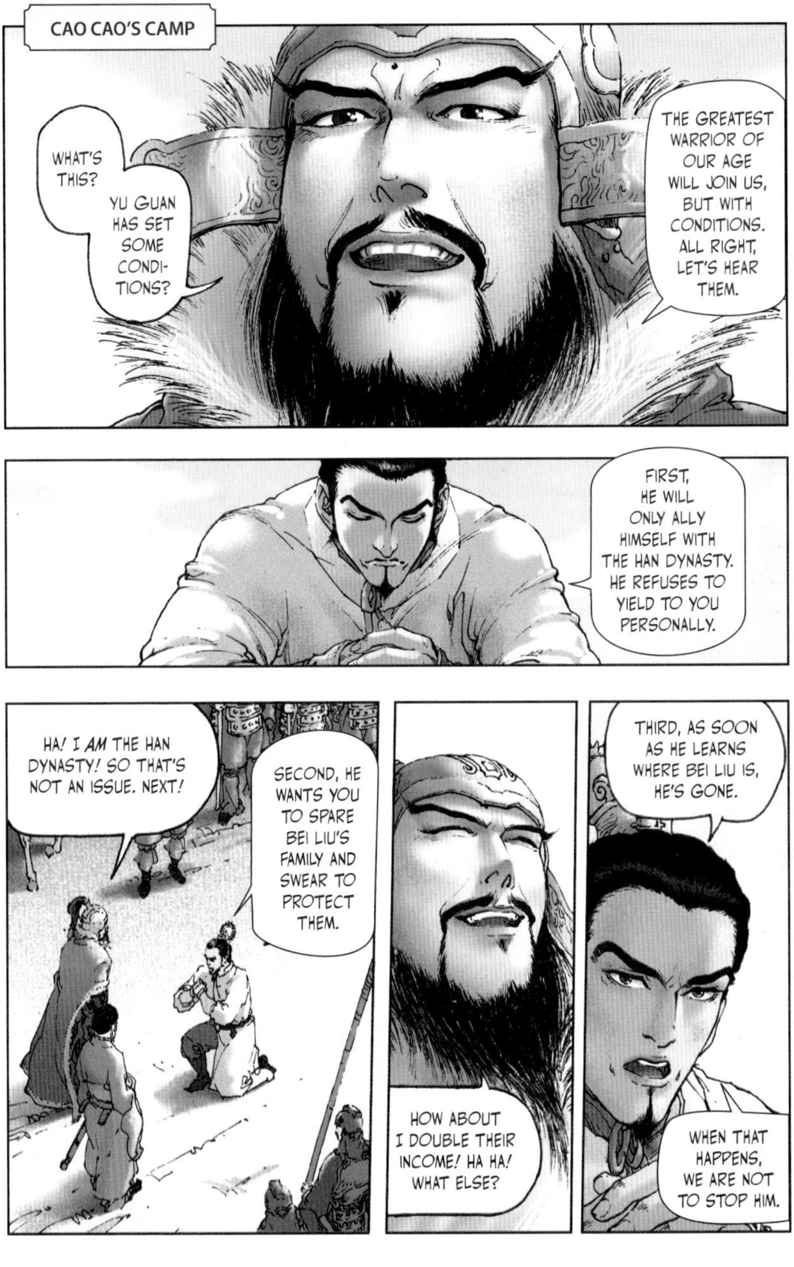
CAO CAO'S CAMP
WHAT'S THIS?
YU GUAN HAS SET SOME CONDITIONS?
THE GREATEST WARRIOR OF OUR AGE WILL JOIN US, BUT WITH CONDITIONS. ALL RIGHT, LET'S HEAR THEM.
FIRST, HE WILL ONLY ALLY HIMSELF WITH THE HAN DYNASTY. HE REFUSES TO YIELD TO YOU PERSONALLY.
HA! I *AM* THE HAN DYNASTY! SO THAT'S NOT AN ISSUE. NEXT!
SECOND, HE WANTS YOU TO SPARE BEI LIU'S FAMILY AND SWEAR TO PROTECT THEM.
HOW ABOUT I DOUBLE THEIR INCOME! HA HA! WHAT ELSE?
THIRD, AS SOON AS HE LEARNS WHERE BEI LIU IS, HE'S GONE.
WHEN THAT HAPPENS, WE ARE NOT TO STOP HIM.

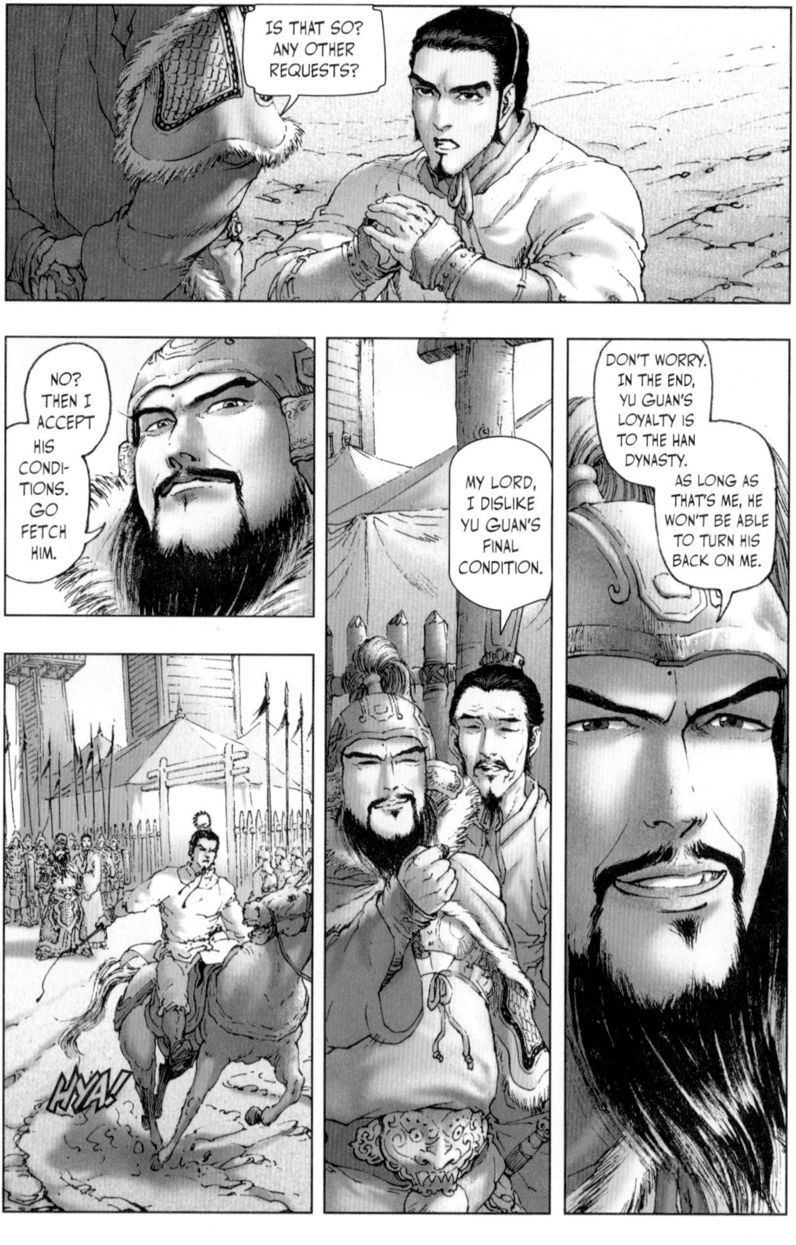
IS THAT SO? ANY OTHER REQUESTS?
NO? THEN I ACCEPT HIS CONDITIONS. GO FETCH HIM.
MY LORD, I DISLIKE YU GUAN'S FINAL CONDITION.
DON'T WORRY. IN THE END, YU GUAN'S LOYALTY IS TO THE HAN DYNASTY.
AS LONG AS THAT'S ME, HE WON'T BE ABLE TO TURN HIS BACK ON ME.
HYA!

DUN XIAHOU

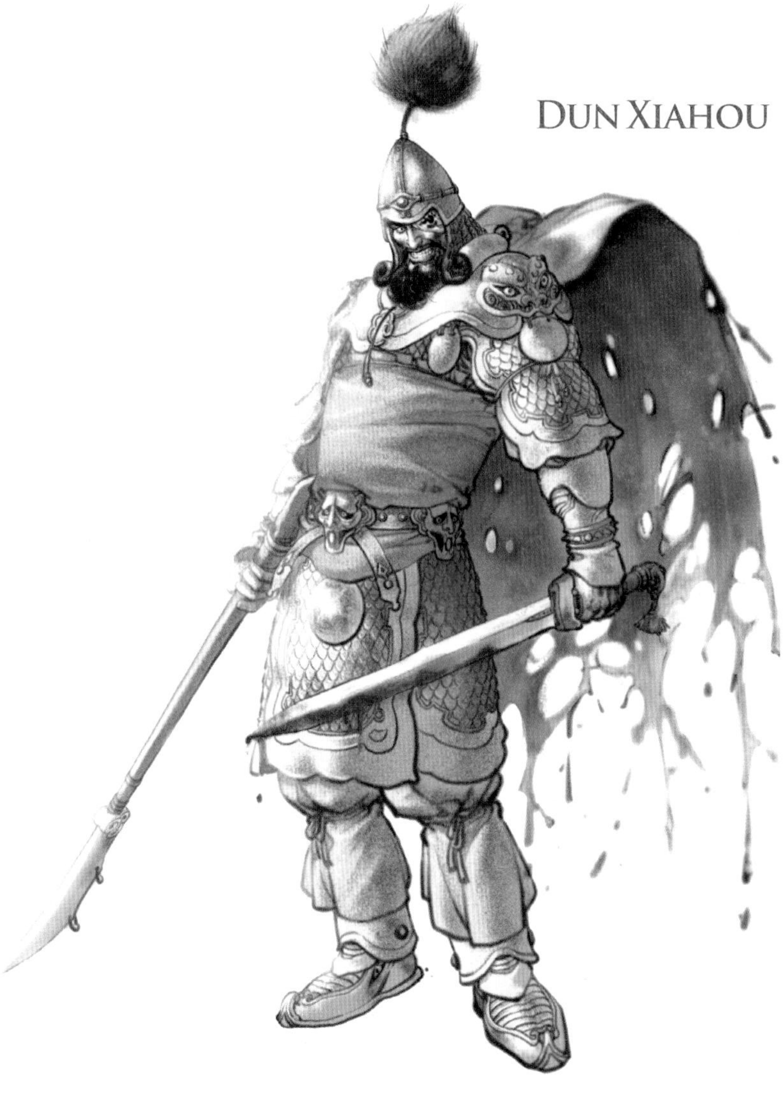

Chapter 2

The Battle of BaiMa ^{200 AD}

Summary

Cao Cao is relieved to have won at least the tentative allegiance of Yu Guan and celebrates the alliance. But Yu Guan is impervious to Cao Cao's vigorous attempts to win his full allegiance and insists he will remain only until he learns of Bei Liu's whereabouts. Cao Cao is distressed by this and asks Liao Zhang to speak with Yu Guan yet again. But yet again Yu Guan will not be persuaded.

Meanwhile, Shao Yuan finally decides to send his army into battle against Cao Cao's forces and dispatches 100,000 soldiers to BaiMa. When Cao Cao learns of this, he decides to personally lead an army of 50,000. Cao Cao's advisors are reluctant to go along with Cao Cao's plan, because it relies to heavily on Yu Guan, whose allegiance is not entirely certain. But Cao Cao is adamant and departs for battle.

On the battlefield, Shao Yuan's forces, led by Liang Yan, have the advantage and are driving Cao Cao's forces into full retreat when Yu Guan is sent onto the field. Distracting the opposing army with a herd of charging horses, Yu Guan leaps into the fray almost undetected, and Liang Yan has barely enough time to realize that something has gone wrong before his head has been lopped from his body.

Zhuo
ChangShan
B
BeiHai
PuYang
BaiMa
XiaoPei
HuLuo
C
XiaPi
LuoYang
XuZhou
A
XuChang
ChangAn
NanYang
River Huai
ShouChun

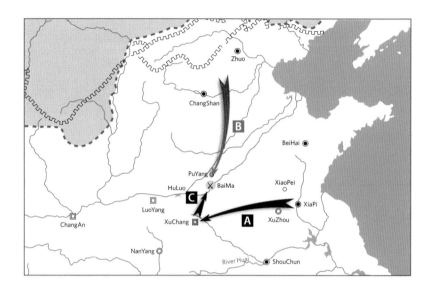

A Yu Guan agrees to temporarily join Cao Cao and comes to XuChang. But he is adamant that he will leave and rejoin Bei Liu as soon as he learns of his sworn brother's whereabouts.

B After much delay, Shao Yuan sends his forces into battle against Cao Cao.

C Cao Cao's forces are nearly defeated, but the situation changes as Yu Guan is sent into battle and almost single-handedly defeats the enemy army.

Once Yu Guan had agreed to join Cao Cao, a party was thrown to honor the alliance.

MY GLASS IS EMPTY.

SURELY, THIS CANNOT STAND!

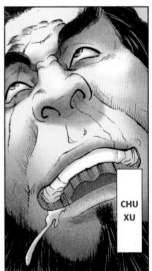

CHU XU

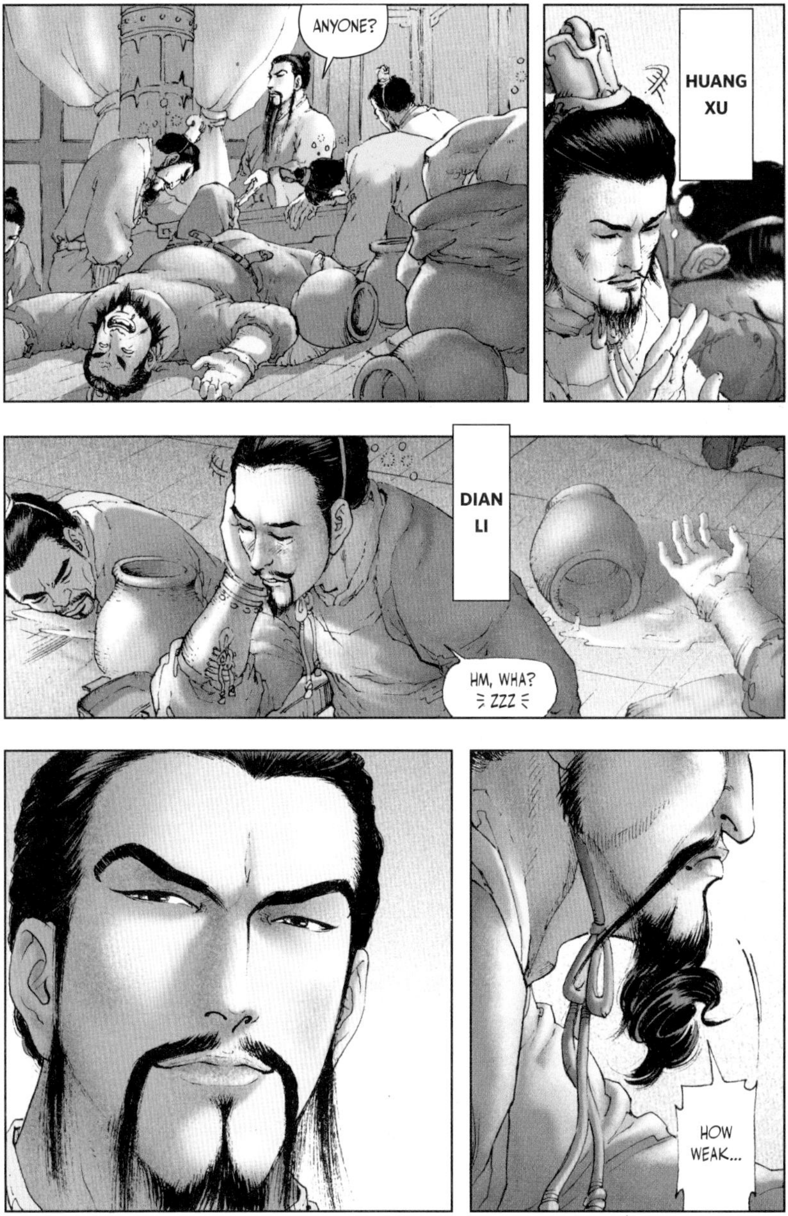
ANYONE?
HUANG XU
DIAN LI
HM, WHA? ZZZ
HOW WEAK...

GLUG GLUG

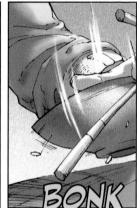

BONK

GRUH! I'M AWAKE!

YES, POUR ME ANOTHER!

ξ ZZZ ξ HUH? YES...YES. NO ONE CAN DRINK DUN XIAHOU UNDER THE TABLE.

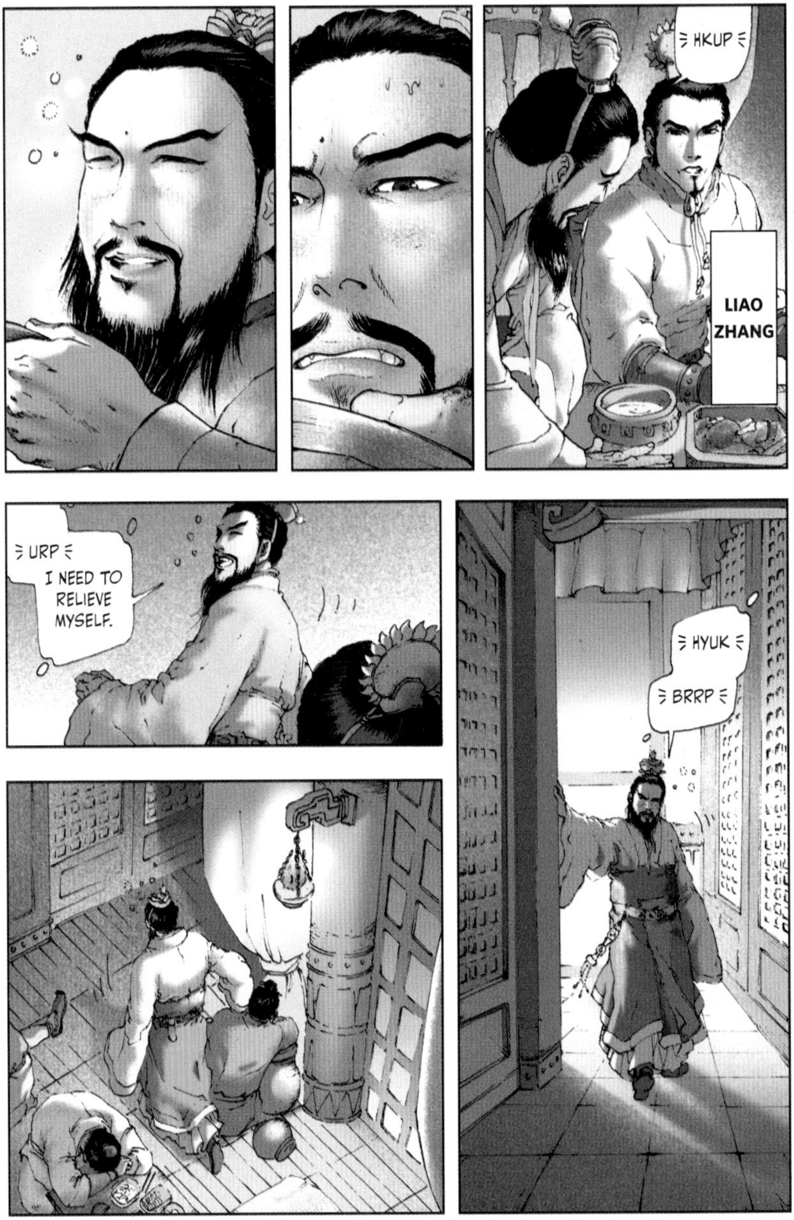
≋ HKUP ≋
LIAO ZHANG
≋ URP ≋ I NEED TO RELIEVE MYSELF.
≋ HYUK ≋
≋ BRRP ≋

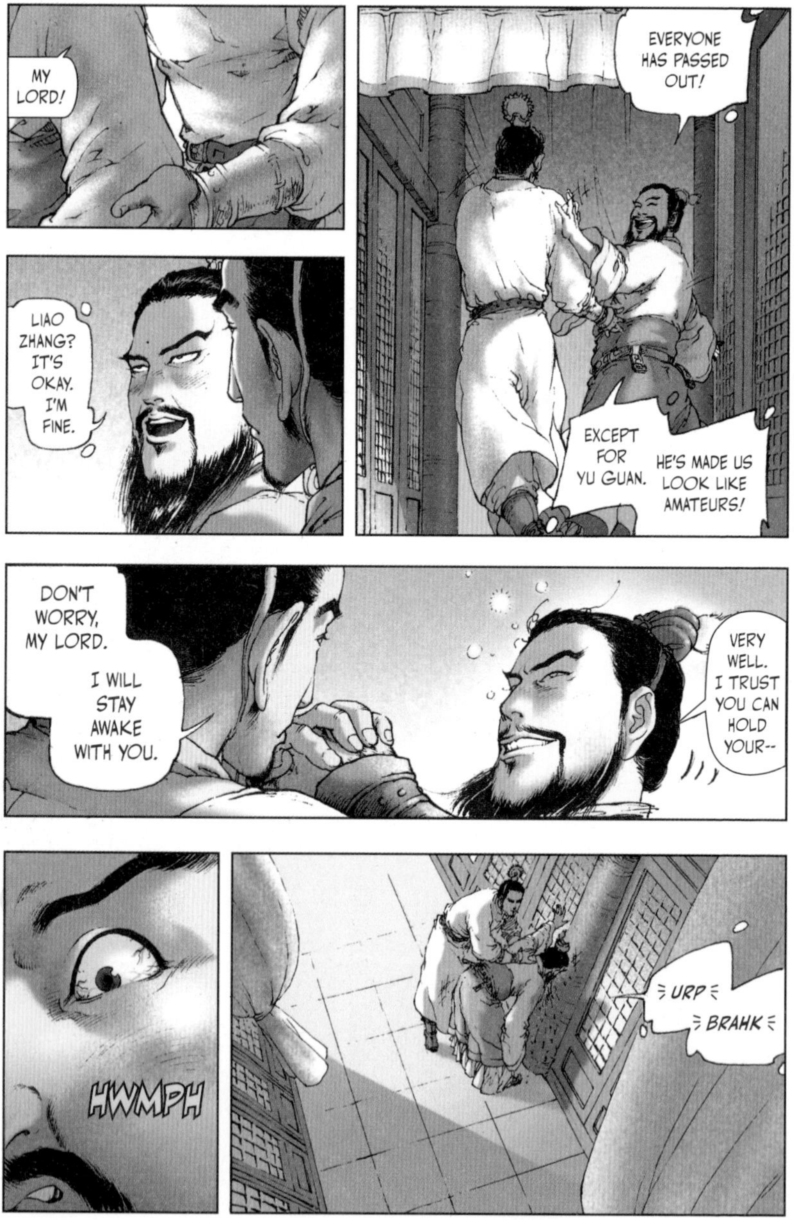
MY LORD!
EVERYONE HAS PASSED OUT!
LIAO ZHANG? IT'S OKAY. I'M FINE.
EXCEPT FOR YU GUAN.
HE'S MADE US LOOK LIKE AMATEURS!
DON'T WORRY, MY LORD.
I WILL STAY AWAKE WITH YOU.
VERY WELL. I TRUST YOU CAN HOLD YOUR--
HWMPH
URP
BRAHK

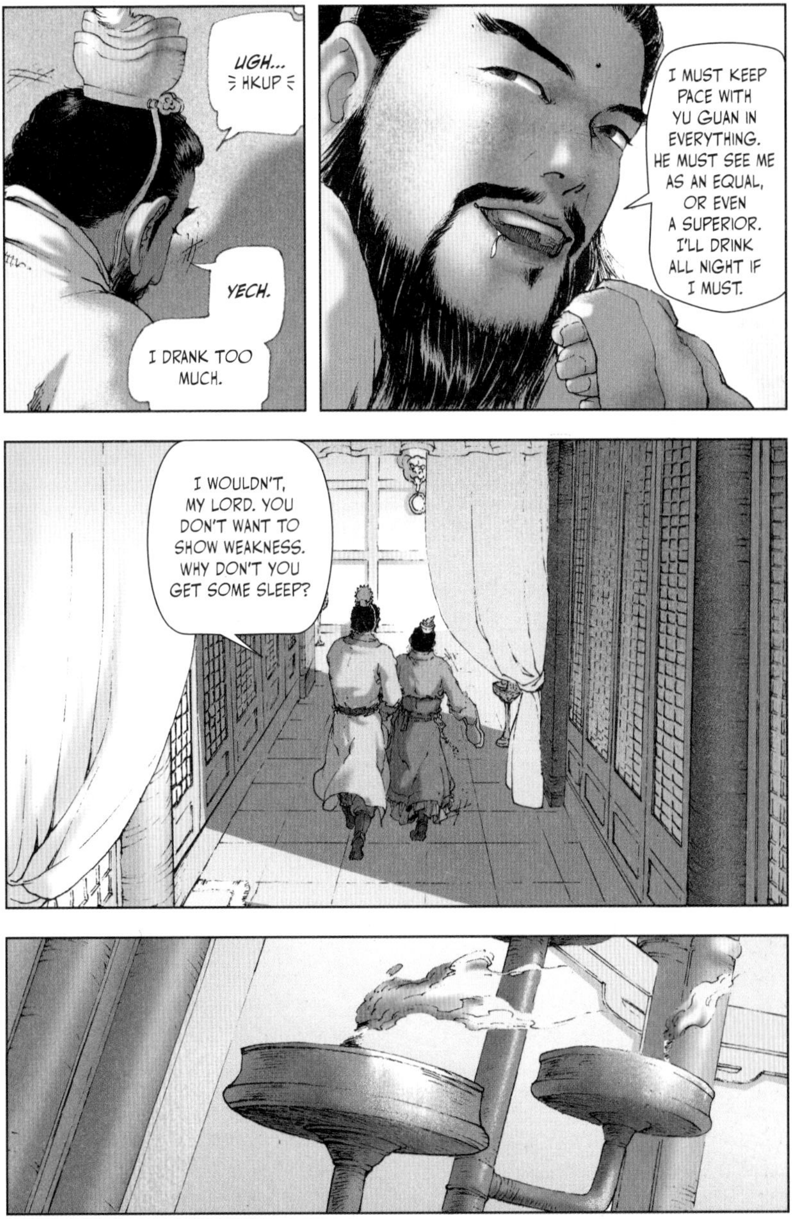
UGH...
HKUP
YECH.
I DRANK TOO MUCH.
I MUST KEEP PACE WITH YU GUAN IN EVERYTHING. HE MUST SEE ME AS AN EQUAL, OR EVEN A SUPERIOR. I'LL DRINK ALL NIGHT IF I MUST.
I WOULDN'T, MY LORD. YOU DON'T WANT TO SHOW WEAKNESS. WHY DON'T YOU GET SOME SLEEP?

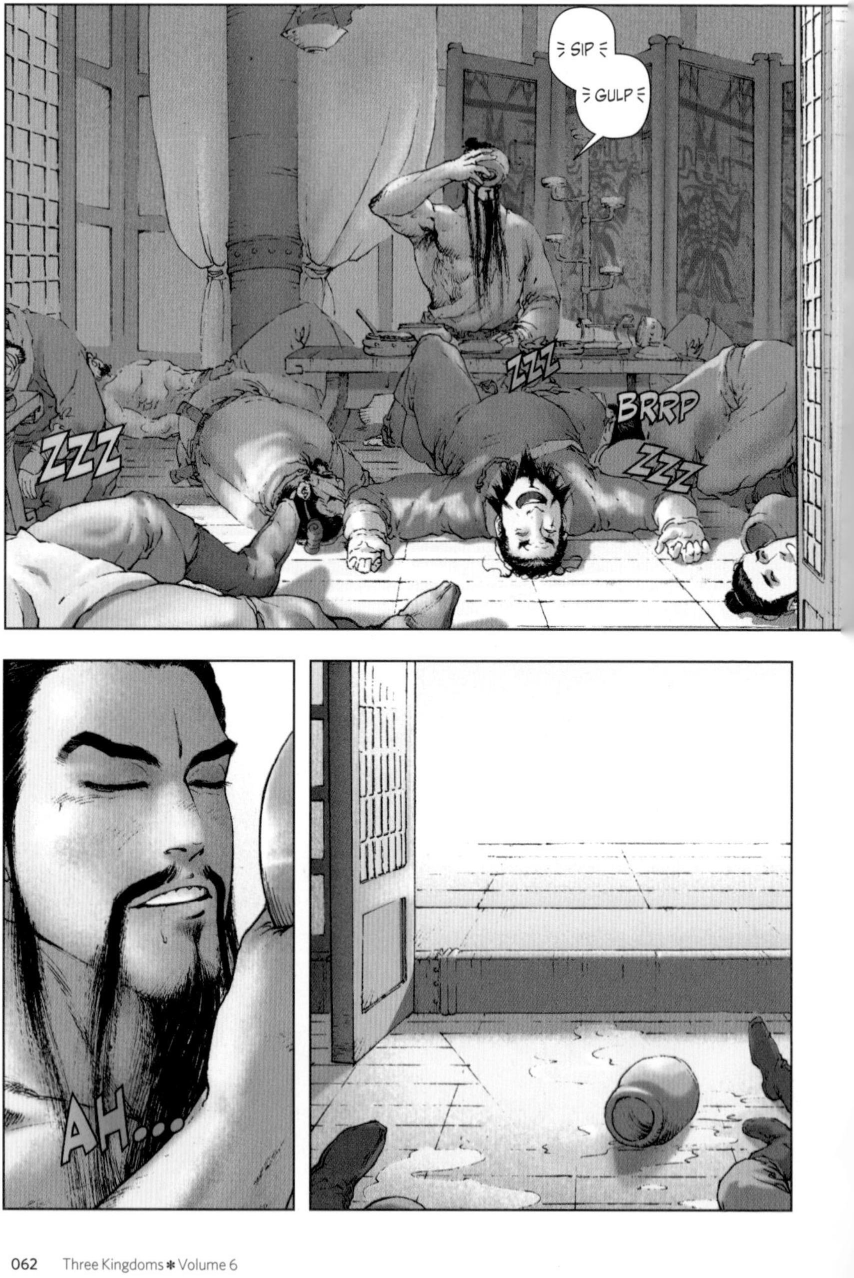
SIP
GULP
ZZZ
BRRP
ZZZ
ZZZ
AH...

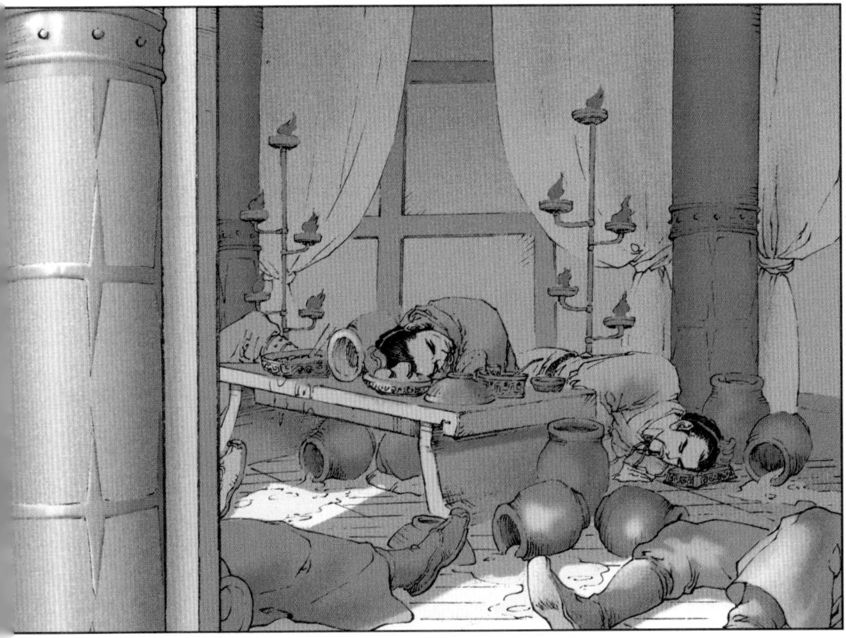

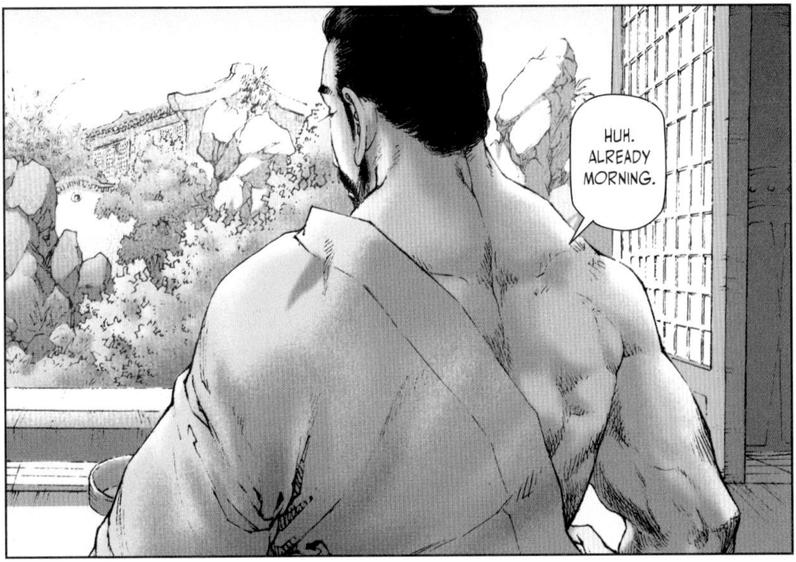
HUH. ALREADY MORNING.

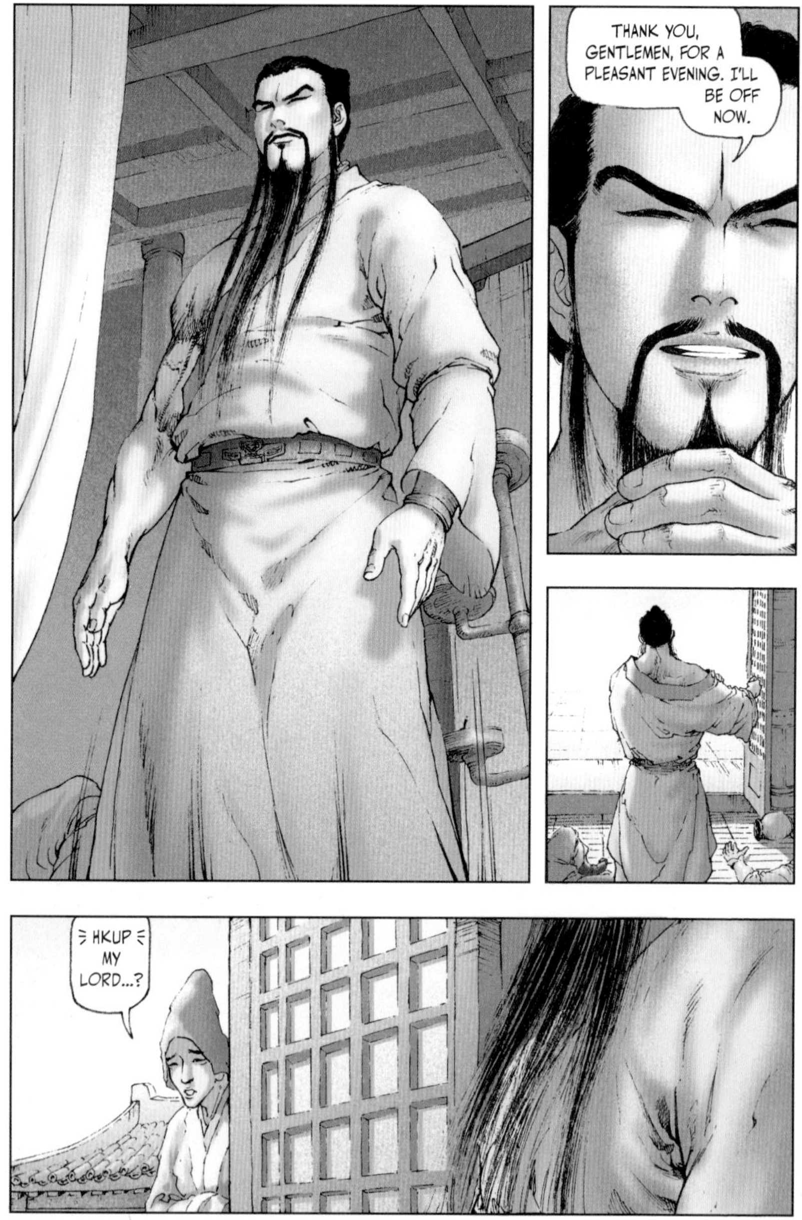
THANK YOU, GENTLEMEN, FOR A PLEASANT EVENING. I'LL BE OFF NOW.
HKUP
MY LORD...?

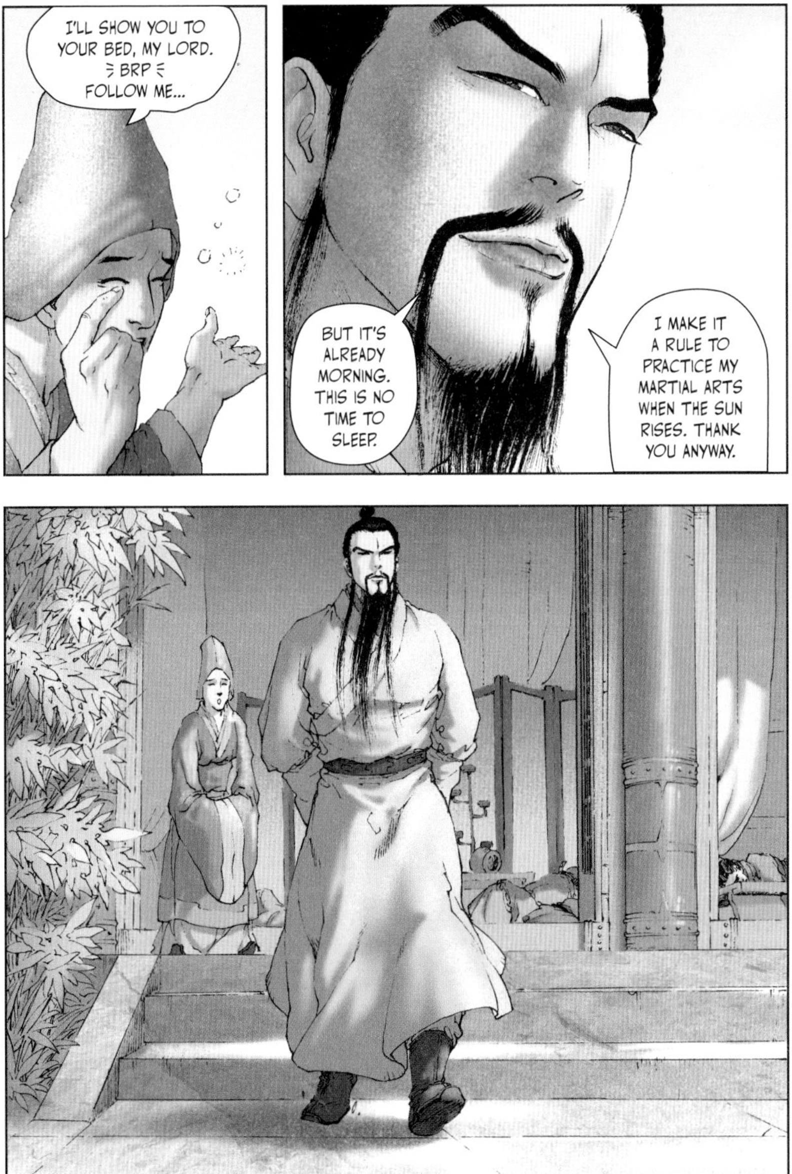
I'LL SHOW YOU TO YOUR BED, MY LORD. ⋛ BRP ⋚ FOLLOW ME...
BUT IT'S ALREADY MORNING. THIS IS NO TIME TO SLEEP.
I MAKE IT A RULE TO PRACTICE MY MARTIAL ARTS WHEN THE SUN RISES. THANK YOU ANYWAY.

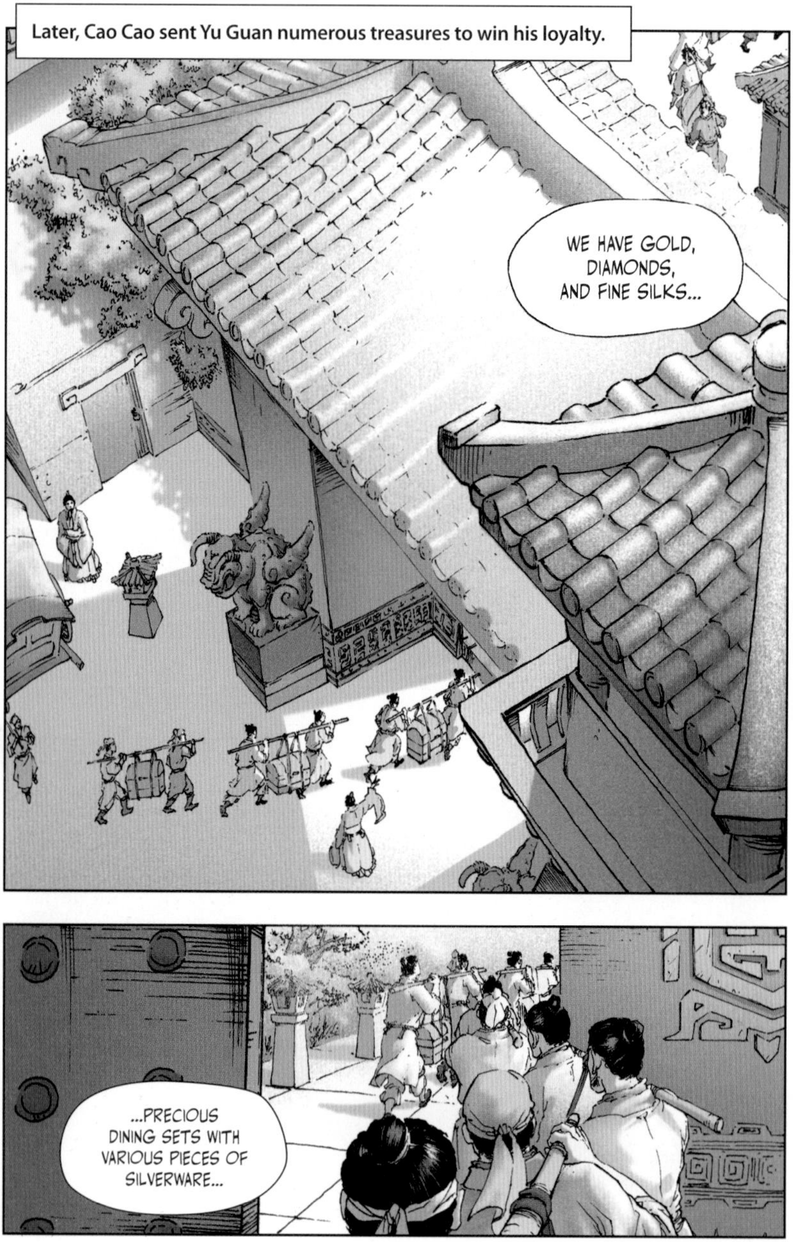
Later, Cao Cao sent Yu Guan numerous treasures to win his loyalty.
WE HAVE GOLD, DIAMONDS, AND FINE SILKS...
...PRECIOUS DINING SETS WITH VARIOUS PIECES OF SILVERWARE...

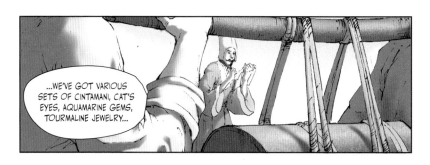

...WE'VE GOT VARIOUS SETS OF CINTAMANI, CAT'S EYES, AQUAMARINE GEMS, TOURMALINE JEWELRY...

WHAT ELSE? UH... STRANDS OF PEARLS, BOWS FROM GAO LI, AND EVEN BU LU'S HORSE...

WHOOSH

OH, ALSO 30 SLAVES AND 10 MISTRESSES. ALL OF THESE ARE COMPLIMENTS OF THE PRIME MINISTER.

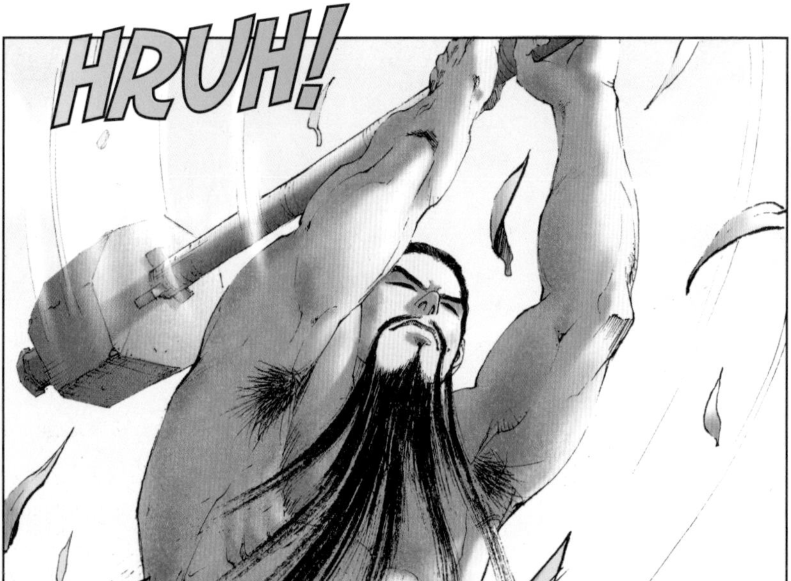
HRUH!

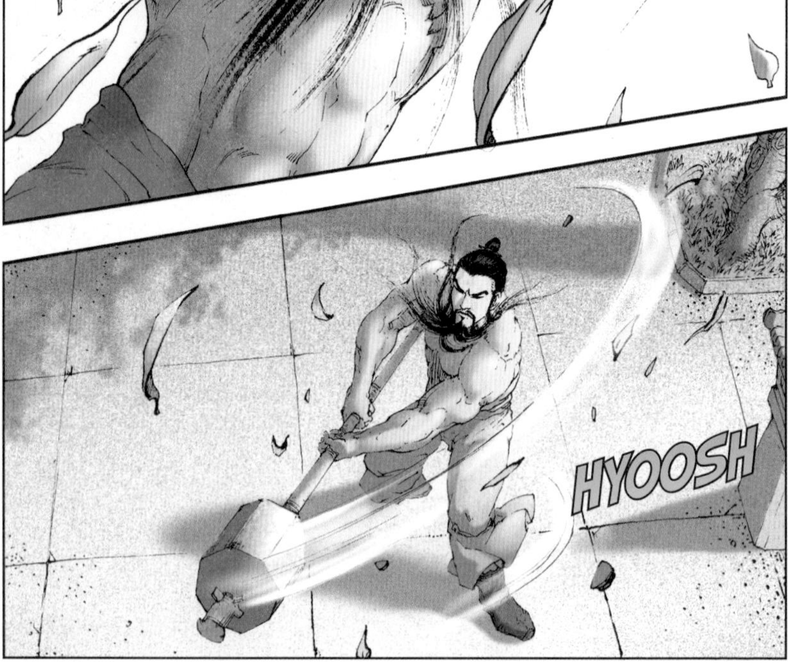
HYOOSH

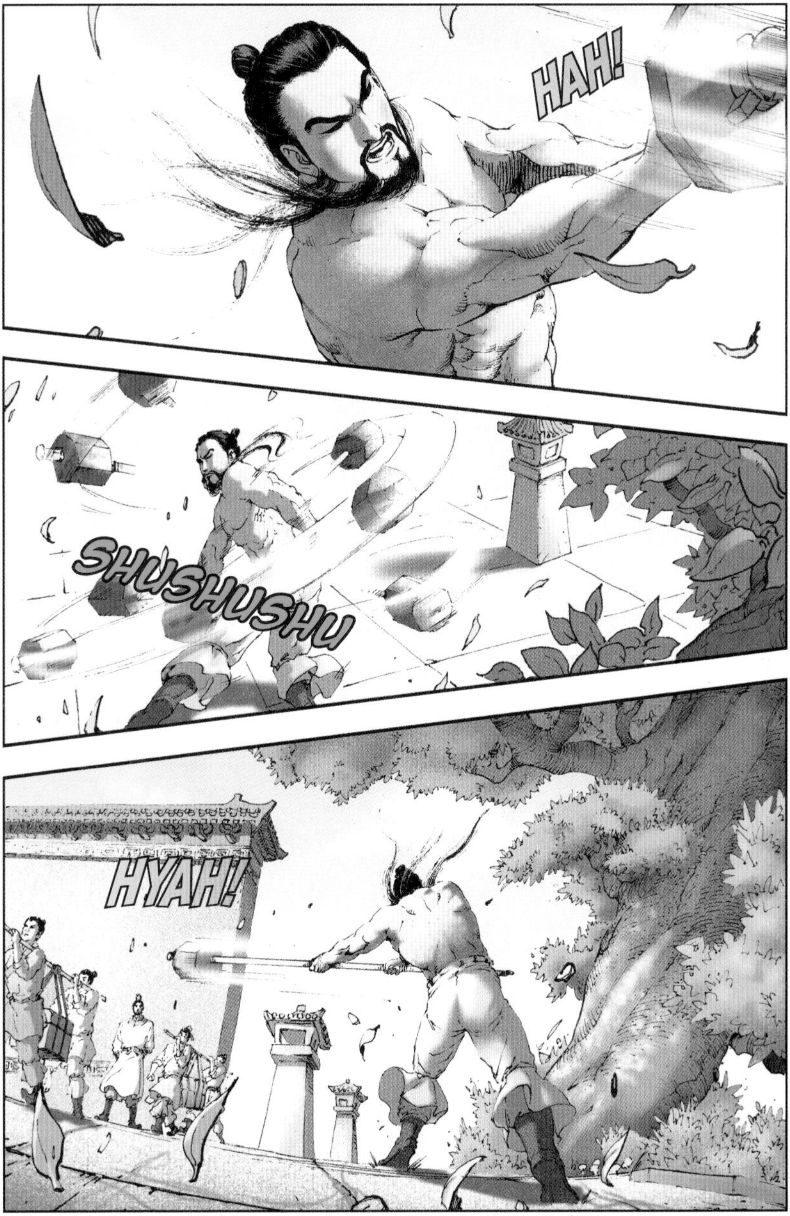
HAH!
SHUSHUSHU
HYAH!

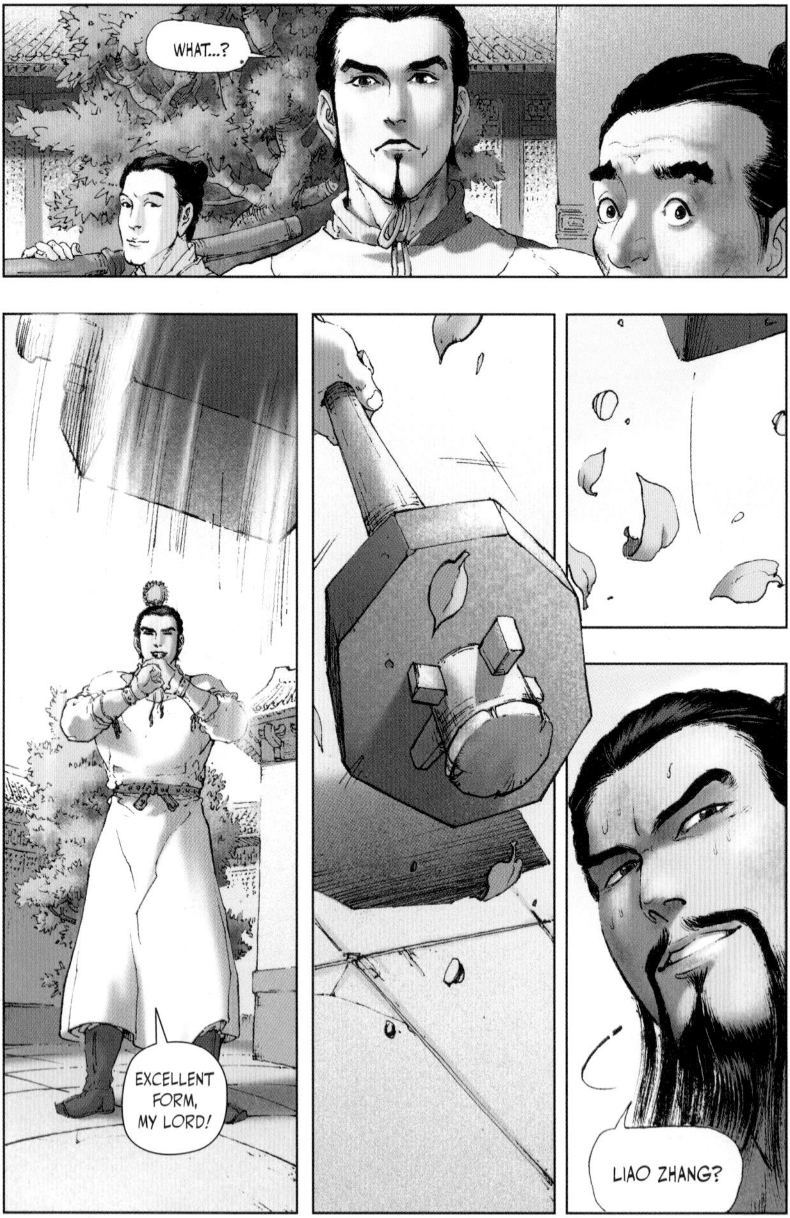
WHAT...?
EXCELLENT FORM, MY LORD!
LIAO ZHANG?

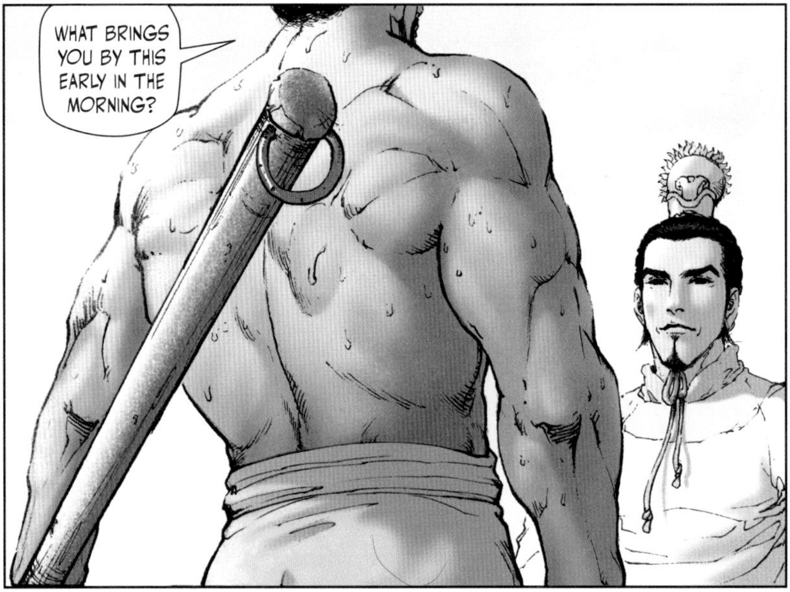
WHAT BRINGS YOU BY THIS EARLY IN THE MORNING?

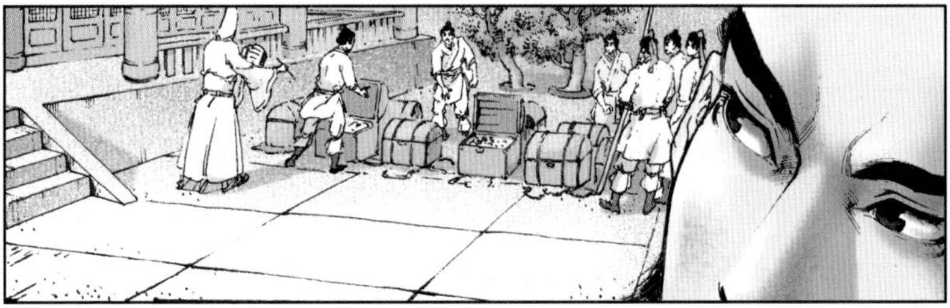

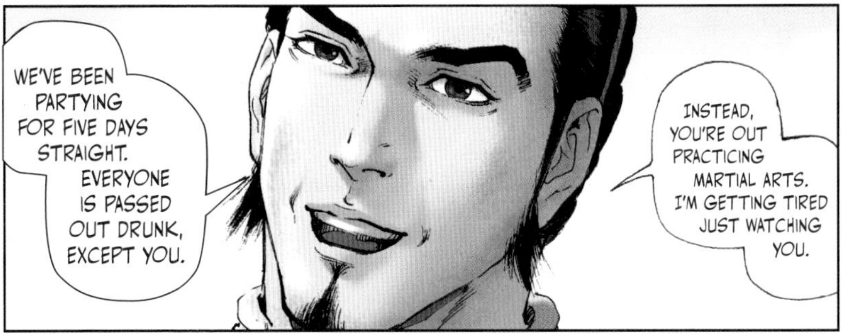
WE'VE BEEN PARTYING FOR FIVE DAYS STRAIGHT. EVERYONE IS PASSED OUT DRUNK, EXCEPT YOU.
INSTEAD, YOU'RE OUT PRACTICING MARTIAL ARTS. I'M GETTING TIRED JUST WATCHING YOU.

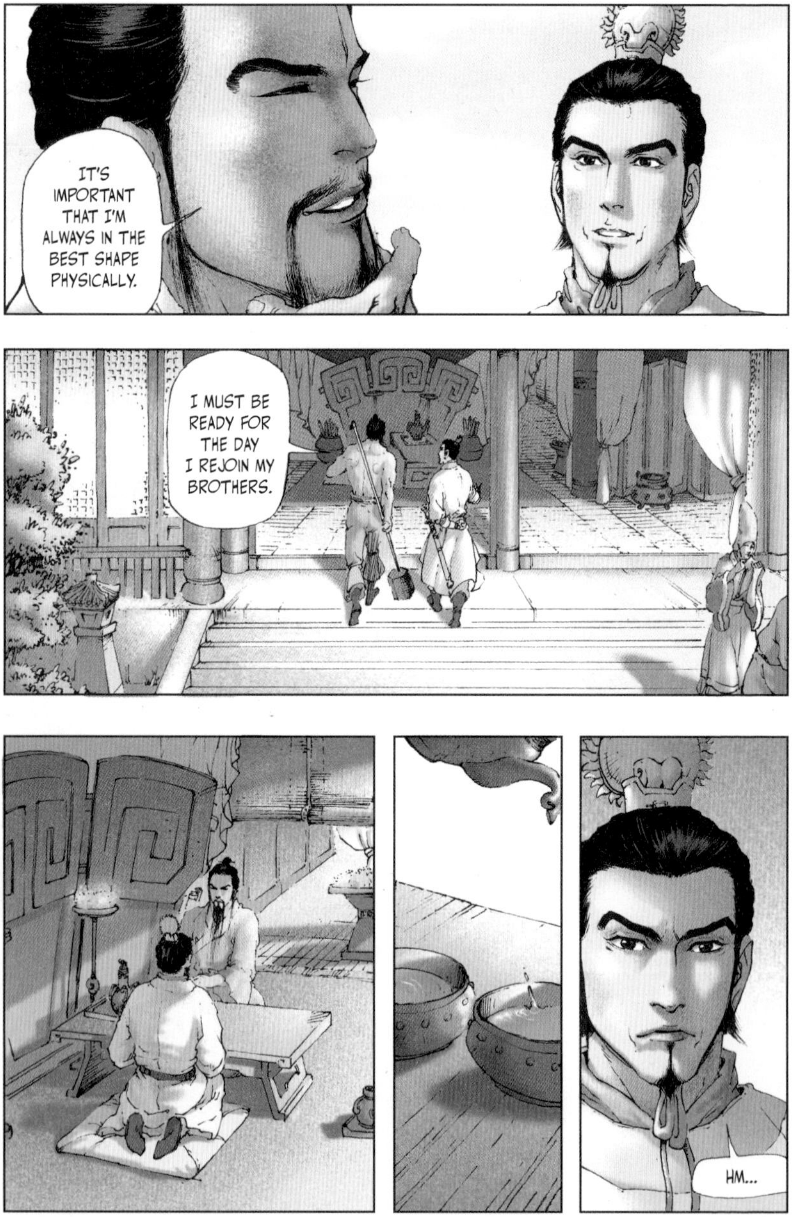
IT'S IMPORTANT THAT I'M ALWAYS IN THE BEST SHAPE PHYSICALLY.
I MUST BE READY FOR THE DAY I REJOIN MY BROTHERS.
HM...

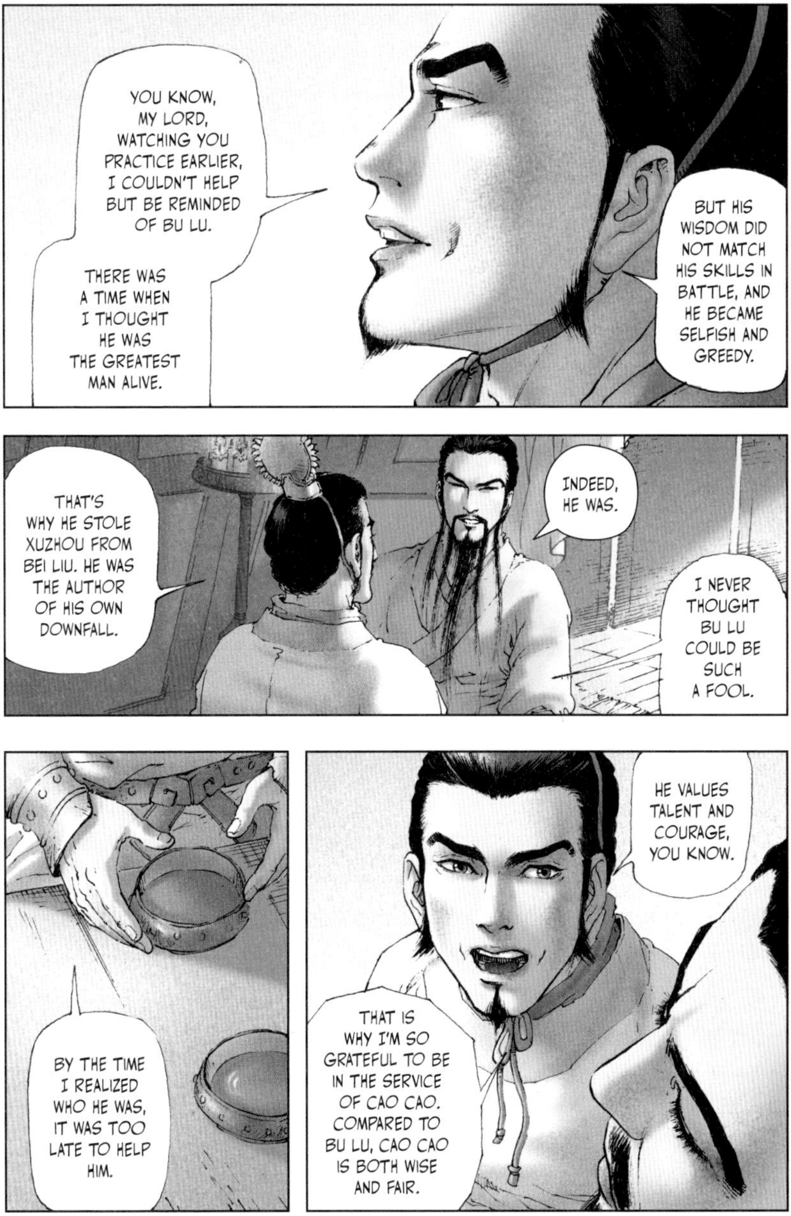
YOU KNOW, MY LORD, WATCHING YOU PRACTICE EARLIER, I COULDN'T HELP BUT BE REMINDED OF BU LU.
THERE WAS A TIME WHEN I THOUGHT HE WAS THE GREATEST MAN ALIVE.
BUT HIS WISDOM DID NOT MATCH HIS SKILLS IN BATTLE, AND HE BECAME SELFISH AND GREEDY.
THAT'S WHY HE STOLE XUZHOU FROM BEI LIU. HE WAS THE AUTHOR OF HIS OWN DOWNFALL.
INDEED, HE WAS.
I NEVER THOUGHT BU LU COULD BE SUCH A FOOL.
BY THE TIME I REALIZED WHO HE WAS, IT WAS TOO LATE TO HELP HIM.
HE VALUES TALENT AND COURAGE, YOU KNOW.
THAT IS WHY I'M SO GRATEFUL TO BE IN THE SERVICE OF CAO CAO. COMPARED TO BU LU, CAO CAO IS BOTH WISE AND FAIR.

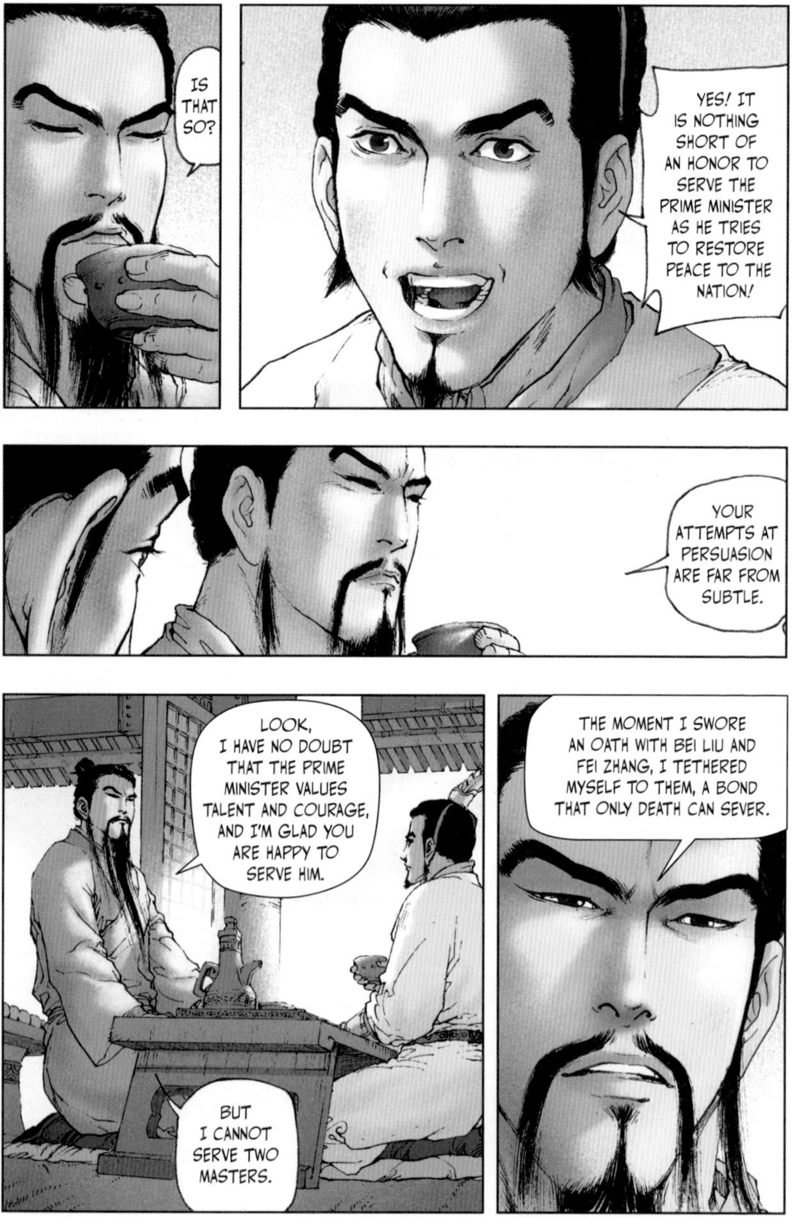
IS THAT SO?
YES! IT IS NOTHING SHORT OF AN HONOR TO SERVE THE PRIME MINISTER AS HE TRIES TO RESTORE PEACE TO THE NATION!
YOUR ATTEMPTS AT PERSUASION ARE FAR FROM SUBTLE.
LOOK, I HAVE NO DOUBT THAT THE PRIME MINISTER VALUES TALENT AND COURAGE, AND I'M GLAD YOU ARE HAPPY TO SERVE HIM.
BUT I CANNOT SERVE TWO MASTERS.
THE MOMENT I SWORE AN OATH WITH BEI LIU AND FEI ZHANG, I TETHERED MYSELF TO THEM, A BOND THAT ONLY DEATH CAN SEVER.

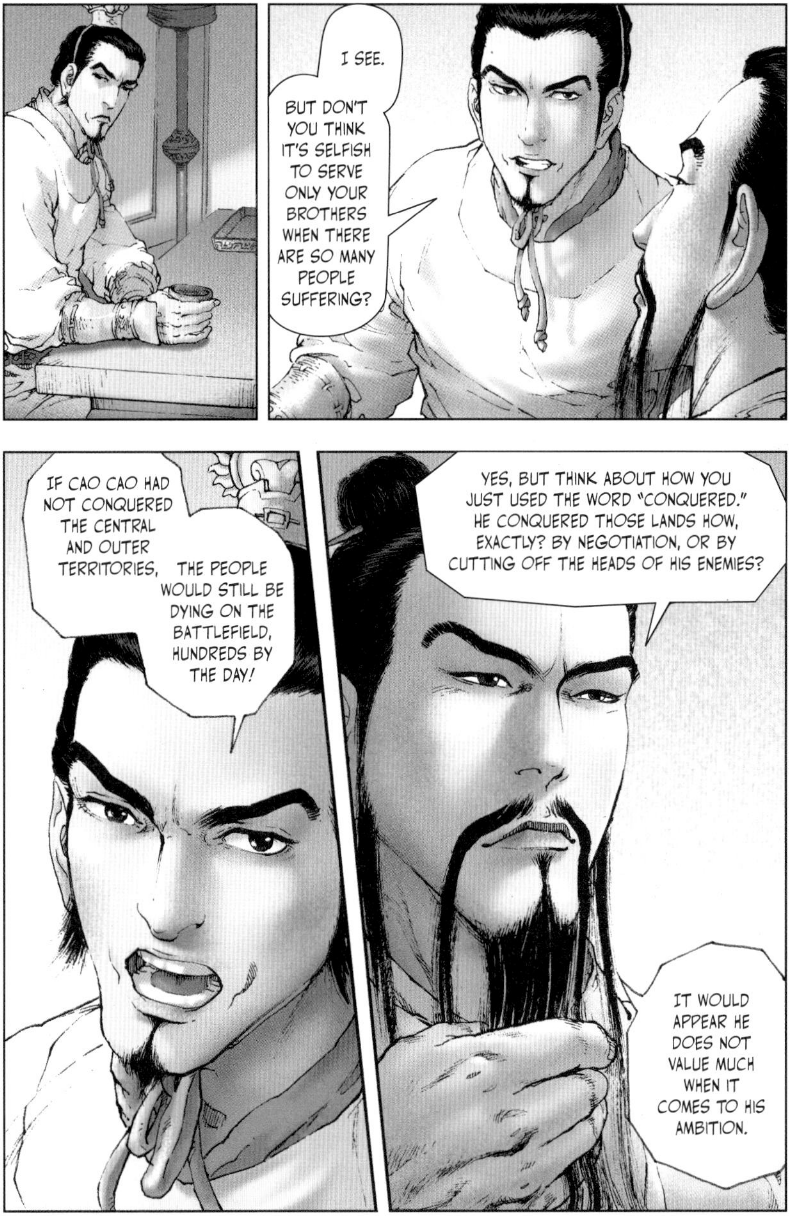
I SEE.
BUT DON'T YOU THINK IT'S SELFISH TO SERVE ONLY YOUR BROTHERS WHEN THERE ARE SO MANY PEOPLE SUFFERING?
IF CAO CAO HAD NOT CONQUERED THE CENTRAL AND OUTER TERRITORIES,
THE PEOPLE WOULD STILL BE DYING ON THE BATTLEFIELD, HUNDREDS BY THE DAY!
YES, BUT THINK ABOUT HOW YOU JUST USED THE WORD "CONQUERED." HE CONQUERED THOSE LANDS HOW, EXACTLY? BY NEGOTIATION, OR BY CUTTING OFF THE HEADS OF HIS ENEMIES?
IT WOULD APPEAR HE DOES NOT VALUE MUCH WHEN IT COMES TO HIS AMBITION.

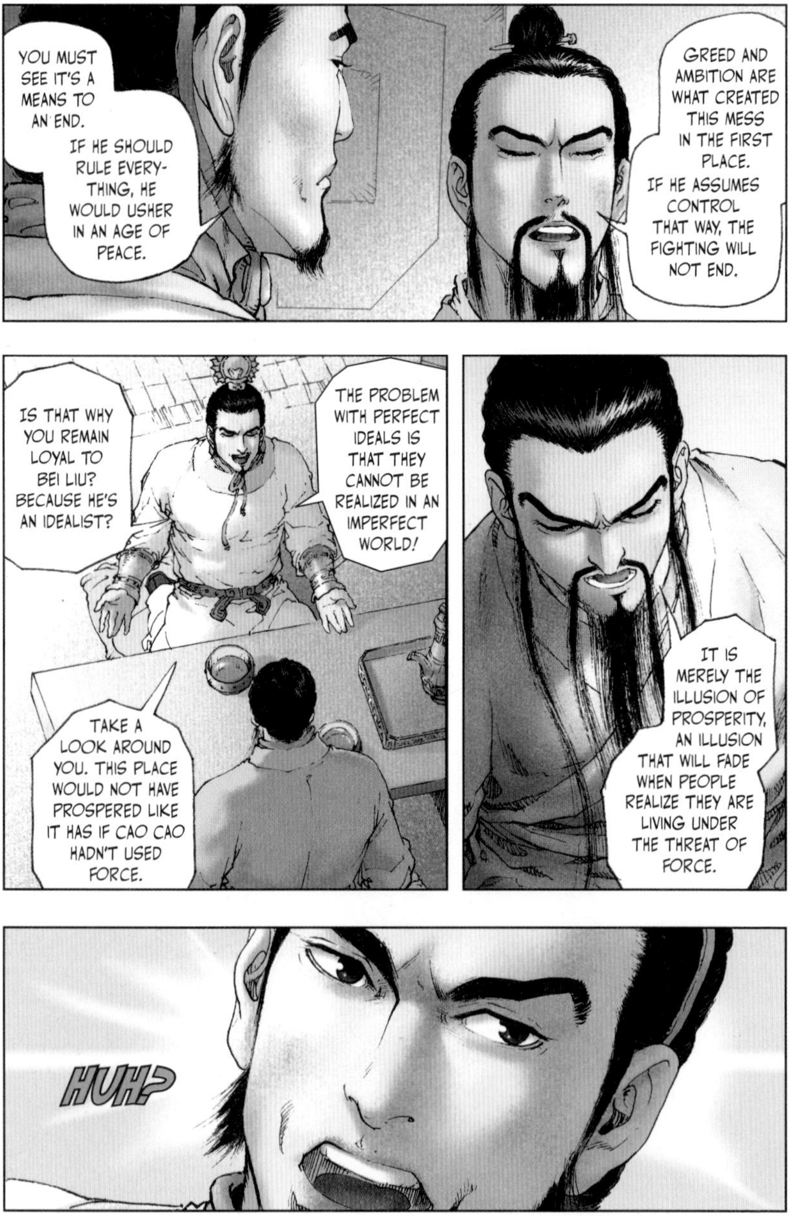
YOU MUST SEE IT'S A MEANS TO AN END.
IF HE SHOULD RULE EVERY-THING, HE WOULD USHER IN AN AGE OF PEACE.
GREED AND AMBITION ARE WHAT CREATED THIS MESS IN THE FIRST PLACE.
IF HE ASSUMES CONTROL THAT WAY, THE FIGHTING WILL NOT END.
IS THAT WHY YOU REMAIN LOYAL TO BEI LIU? BECAUSE HE'S AN IDEALIST?
THE PROBLEM WITH PERFECT IDEALS IS THAT THEY CANNOT BE REALIZED IN AN IMPERFECT WORLD!
TAKE A LOOK AROUND YOU. THIS PLACE WOULD NOT HAVE PROSPERED LIKE IT HAS IF CAO CAO HADN'T USED FORCE.
IT IS MERELY THE ILLUSION OF PROSPERITY, AN ILLUSION THAT WILL FADE WHEN PEOPLE REALIZE THEY ARE LIVING UNDER THE THREAT OF FORCE.
HUH?

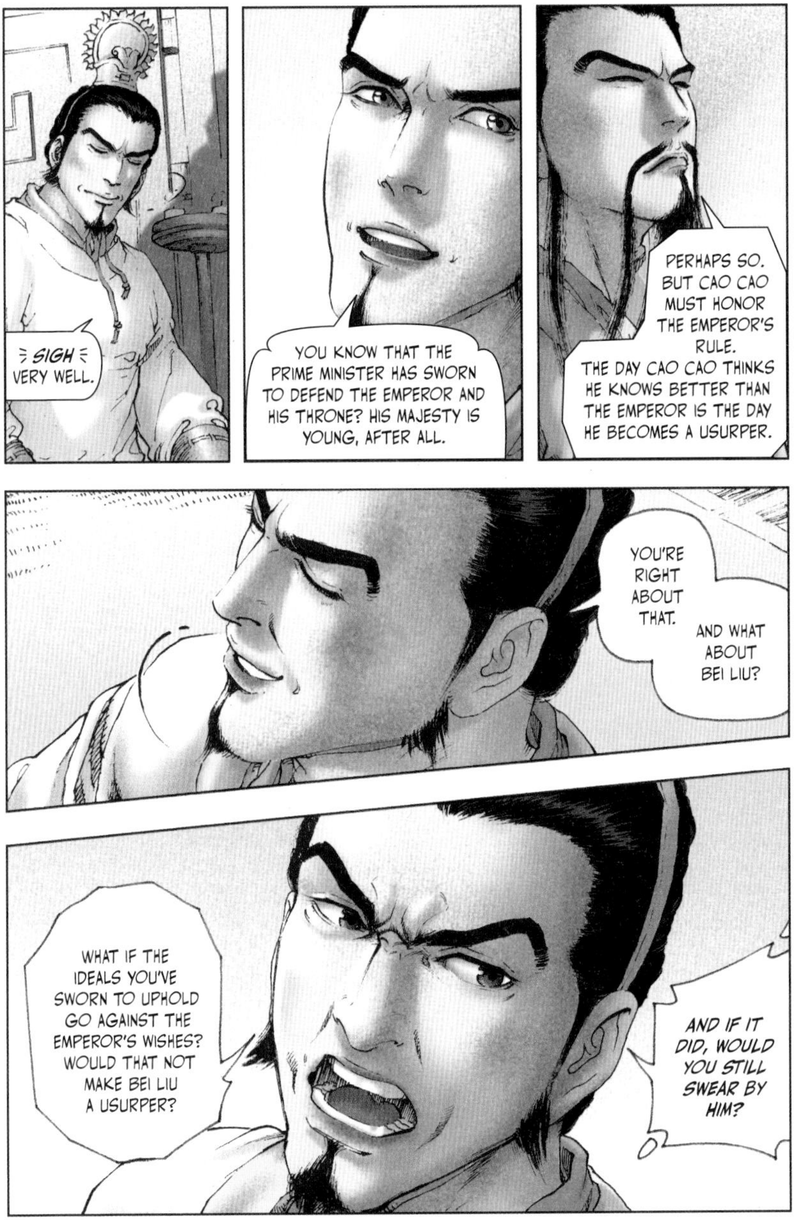

≡ SIGH ≡ VERY WELL.
YOU KNOW THAT THE PRIME MINISTER HAS SWORN TO DEFEND THE EMPEROR AND HIS THRONE? HIS MAJESTY IS YOUNG, AFTER ALL.
PERHAPS SO. BUT CAO CAO MUST HONOR THE EMPEROR'S RULE.
THE DAY CAO CAO THINKS HE KNOWS BETTER THAN THE EMPEROR IS THE DAY HE BECOMES A USURPER.
YOU'RE RIGHT ABOUT THAT.
AND WHAT ABOUT BEI LIU?
WHAT IF THE IDEALS YOU'VE SWORN TO UPHOLD GO AGAINST THE EMPEROR'S WISHES? WOULD THAT NOT MAKE BEI LIU A USURPER?
AND IF IT DID, WOULD YOU STILL SWEAR BY HIM?

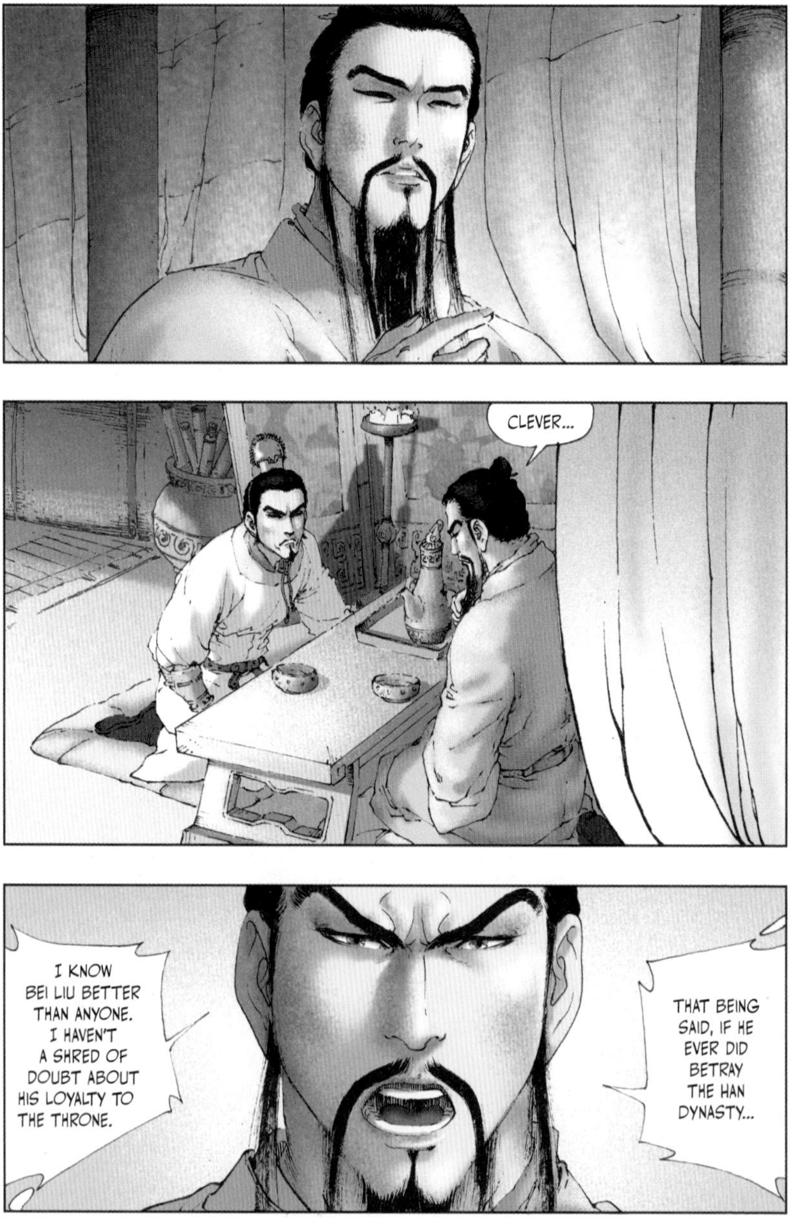
CLEVER...
I KNOW BEI LIU BETTER THAN ANYONE. I HAVEN'T A SHRED OF DOUBT ABOUT HIS LOYALTY TO THE THRONE.
THAT BEING SAID, IF HE EVER DID BETRAY THE HAN DYNASTY...

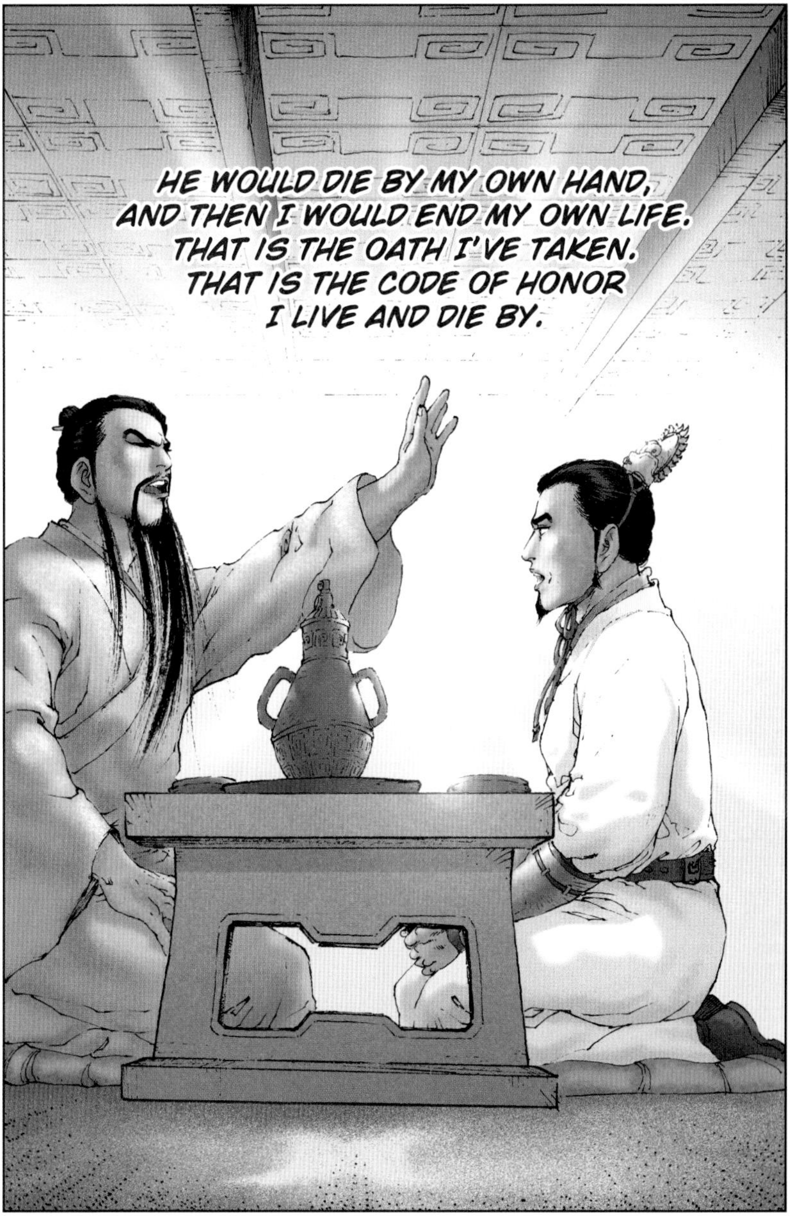
HE WOULD DIE BY MY OWN HAND,
AND THEN I WOULD END MY OWN LIFE.
THAT IS THE OATH I'VE TAKEN.
THAT IS THE CODE OF HONOR
I LIVE AND DIE BY.

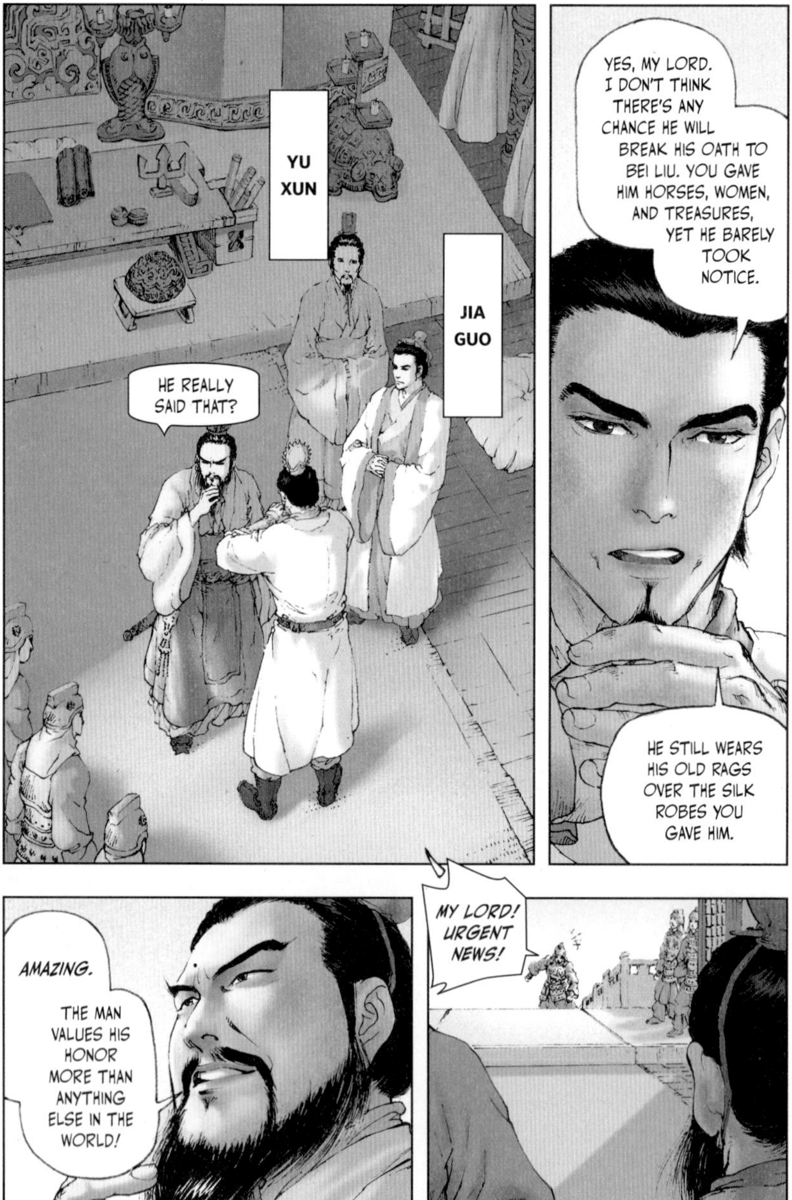
YU XUN
JIA GUO
HE REALLY SAID THAT?
YES, MY LORD. I DON'T THINK THERE'S ANY CHANCE HE WILL BREAK HIS OATH TO BEI LIU. YOU GAVE HIM HORSES, WOMEN, AND TREASURES, YET HE BARELY TOOK NOTICE.
HE STILL WEARS HIS OLD RAGS OVER THE SILK ROBES YOU GAVE HIM.
AMAZING.
THE MAN VALUES HIS HONOR MORE THAN ANYTHING ELSE IN THE WORLD!
MY LORD! URGENT NEWS!

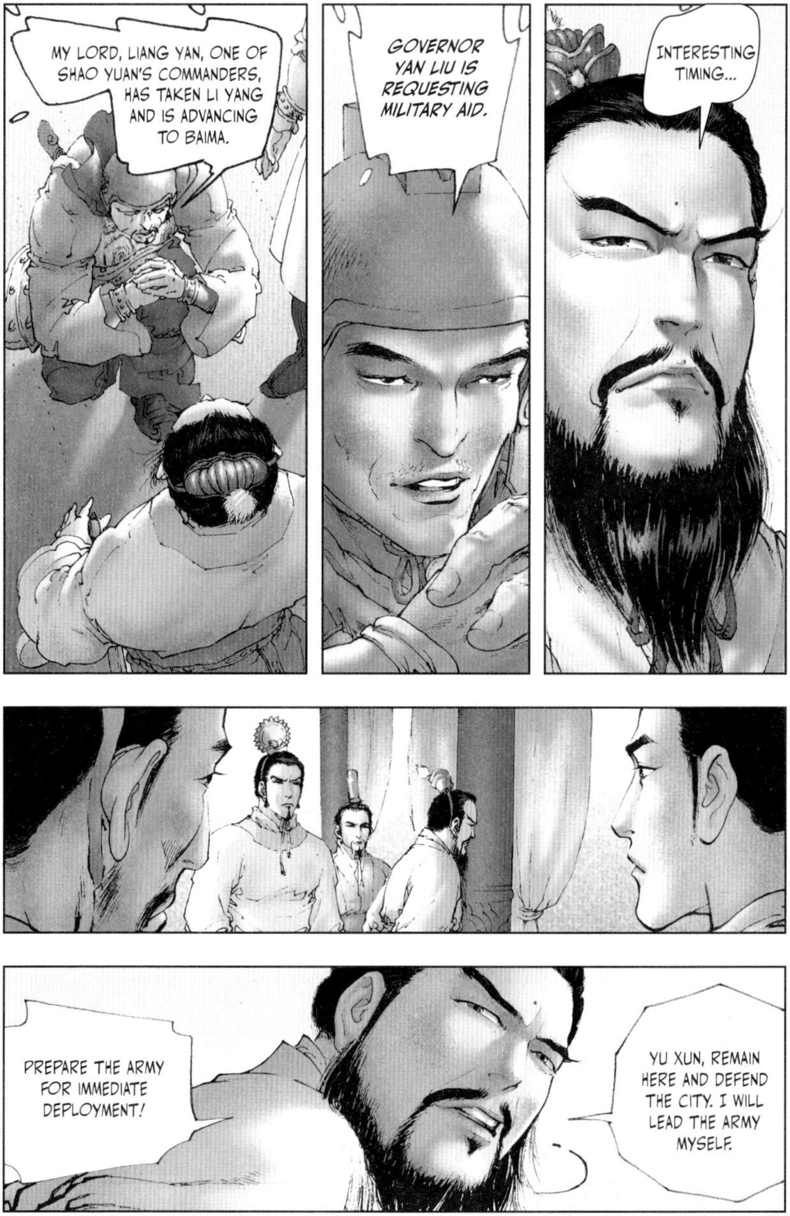
MY LORD, LIANG YAN, ONE OF SHAO YUAN'S COMMANDERS, HAS TAKEN LI YANG AND IS ADVANCING TO BAIMA.
GOVERNOR YAN LIU IS REQUESTING MILITARY AID.
INTERESTING TIMING...
PREPARE THE ARMY FOR IMMEDIATE DEPLOYMENT!
YU XUN, REMAIN HERE AND DEFEND THE CITY. I WILL LEAD THE ARMY MYSELF.

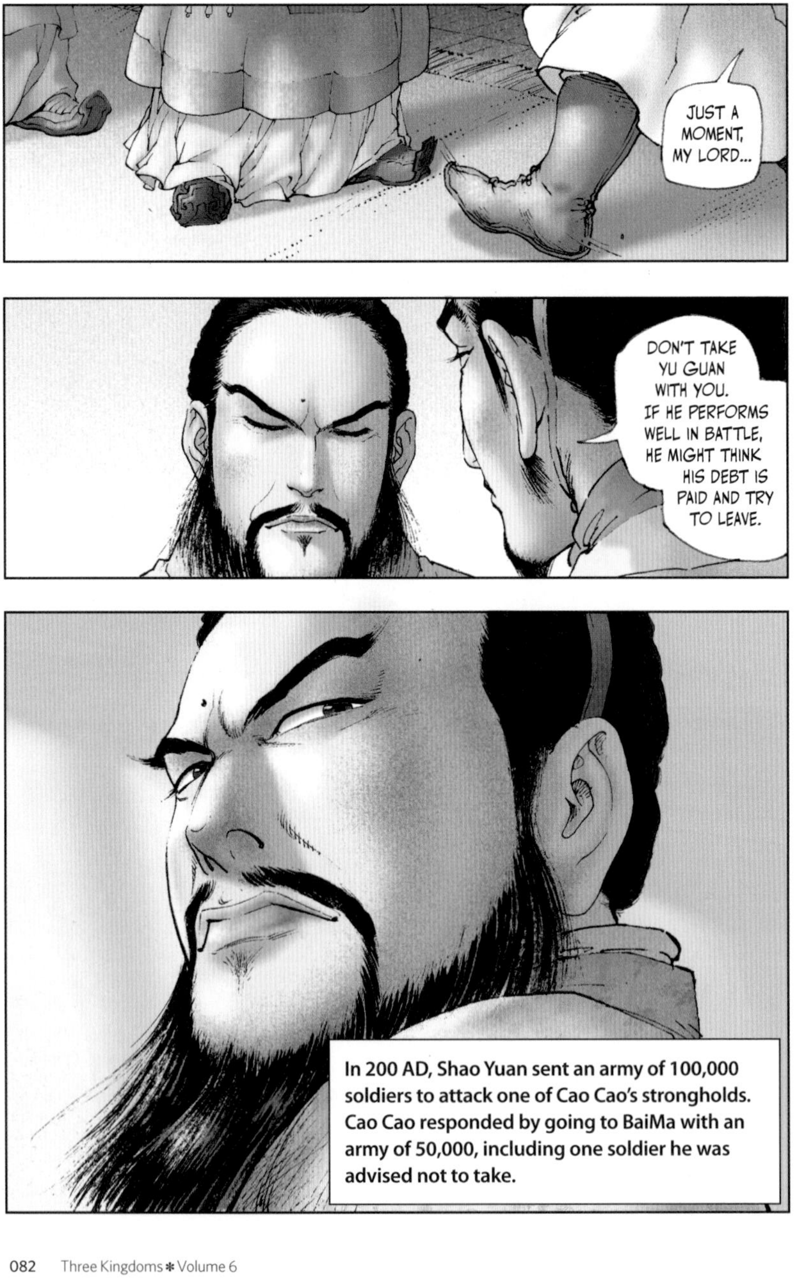
JUST A MOMENT, MY LORD...
DON'T TAKE YU GUAN WITH YOU. IF HE PERFORMS WELL IN BATTLE, HE MIGHT THINK HIS DEBT IS PAID AND TRY TO LEAVE.
In 200 AD, Shao Yuan sent an army of 100,000 soldiers to attack one of Cao Cao's strongholds. Cao Cao responded by going to BaiMa with an army of 50,000, including one soldier he was advised not to take.

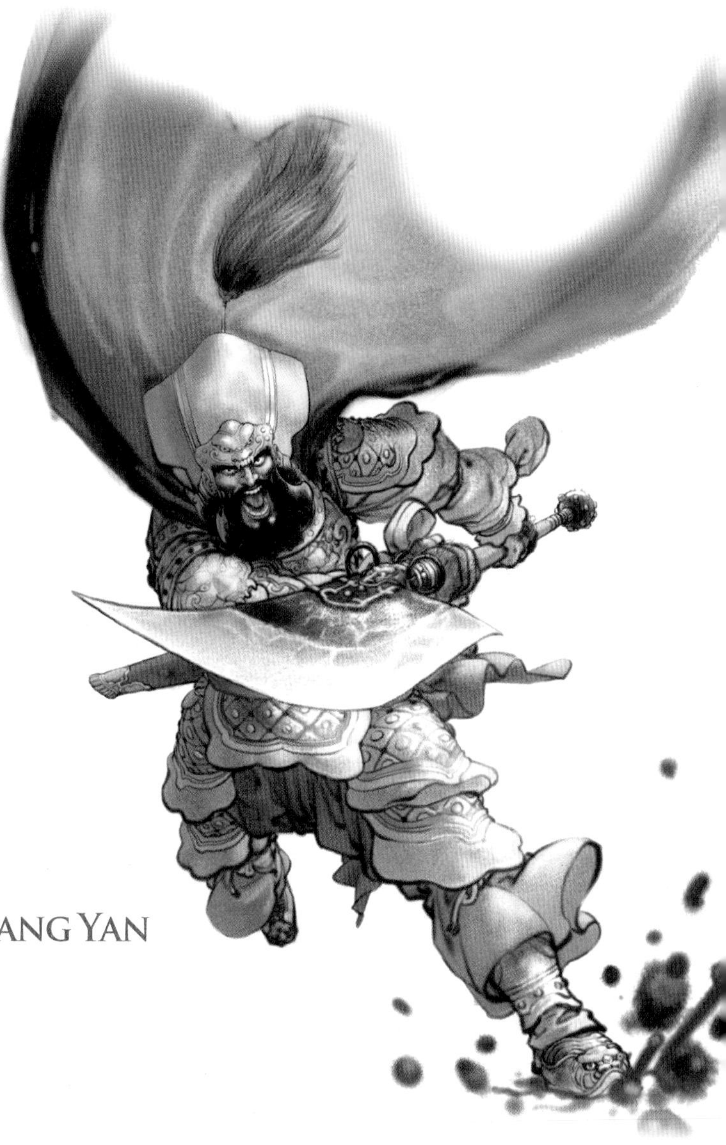

LIANG YAN

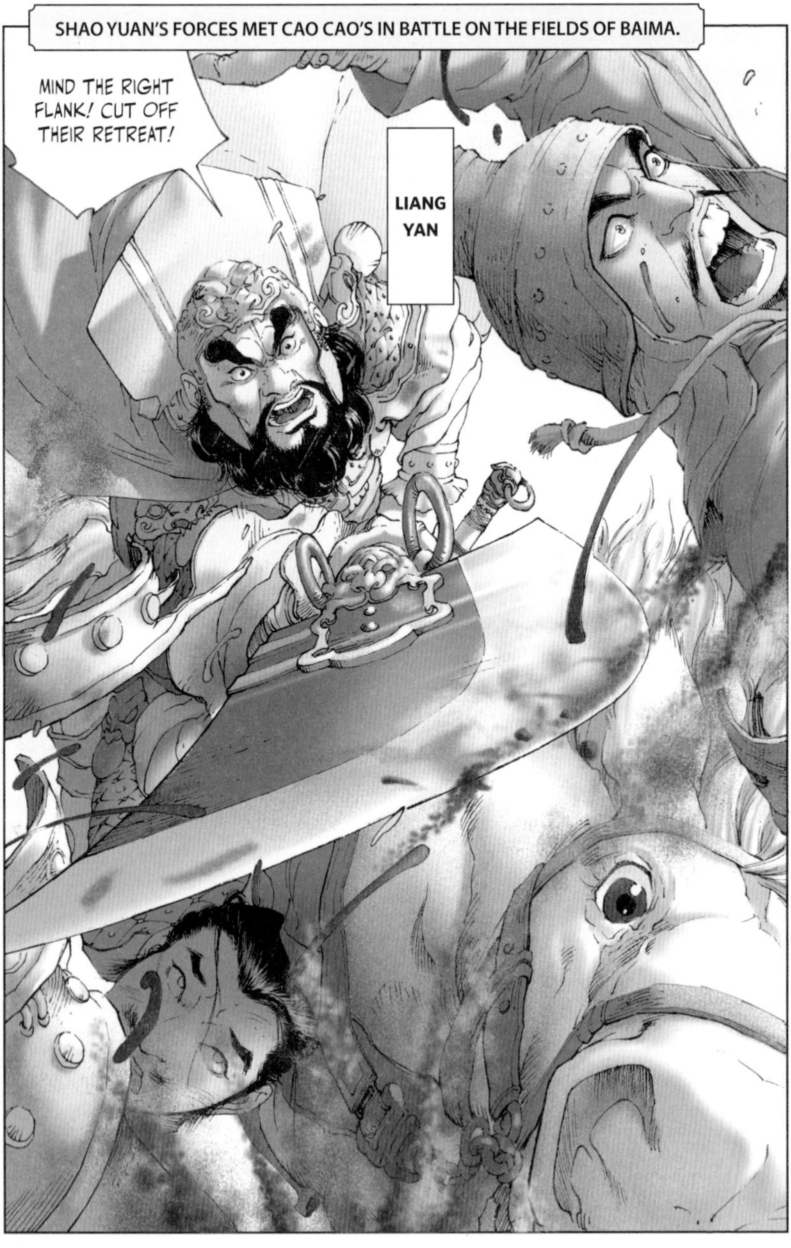
SHAO YUAN'S FORCES MET CAO CAO'S IN BATTLE ON THE FIELDS OF BAIMA.
MIND THE RIGHT FLANK! CUT OFF THEIR RETREAT!
LIANG YAN

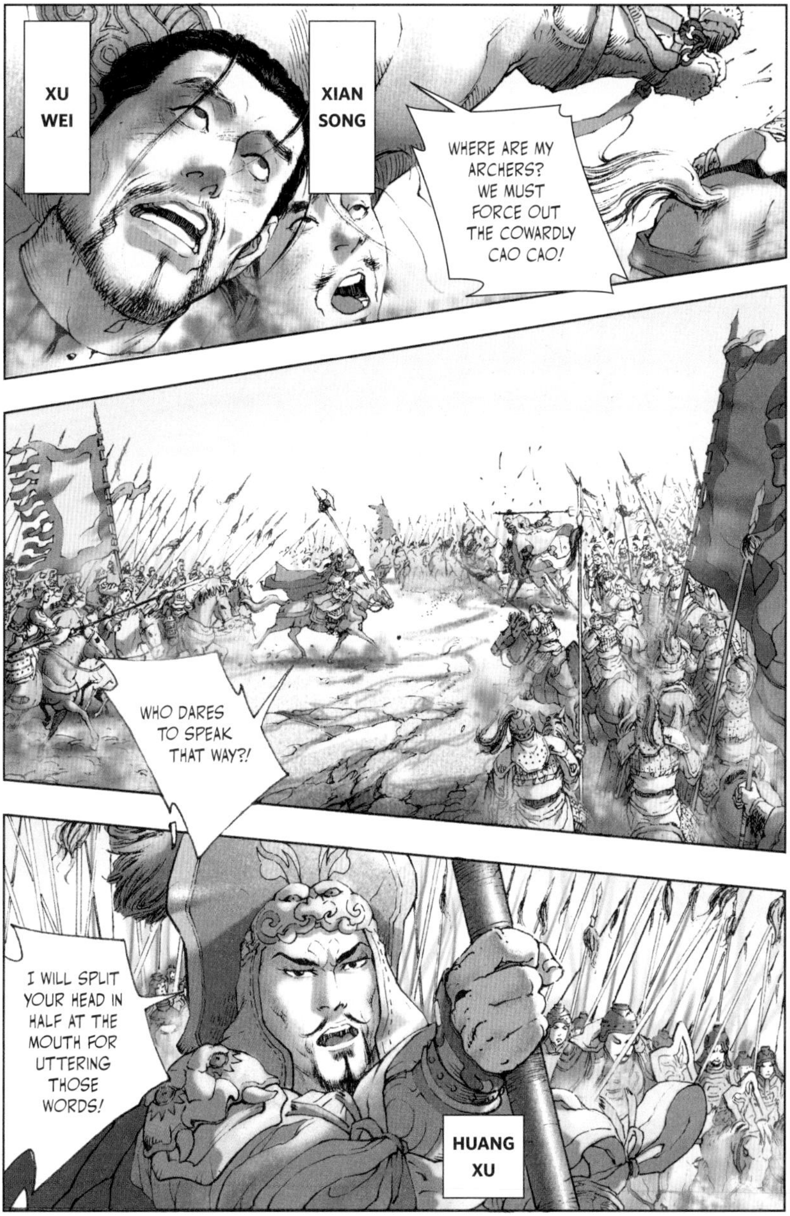
XU WEI
XIAN SONG
WHERE ARE MY ARCHERS? WE MUST FORCE OUT THE COWARDLY CAO CAO!
WHO DARES TO SPEAK THAT WAY?!
I WILL SPLIT YOUR HEAD IN HALF AT THE MOUTH FOR UTTERING THOSE WORDS!
HUANG XU

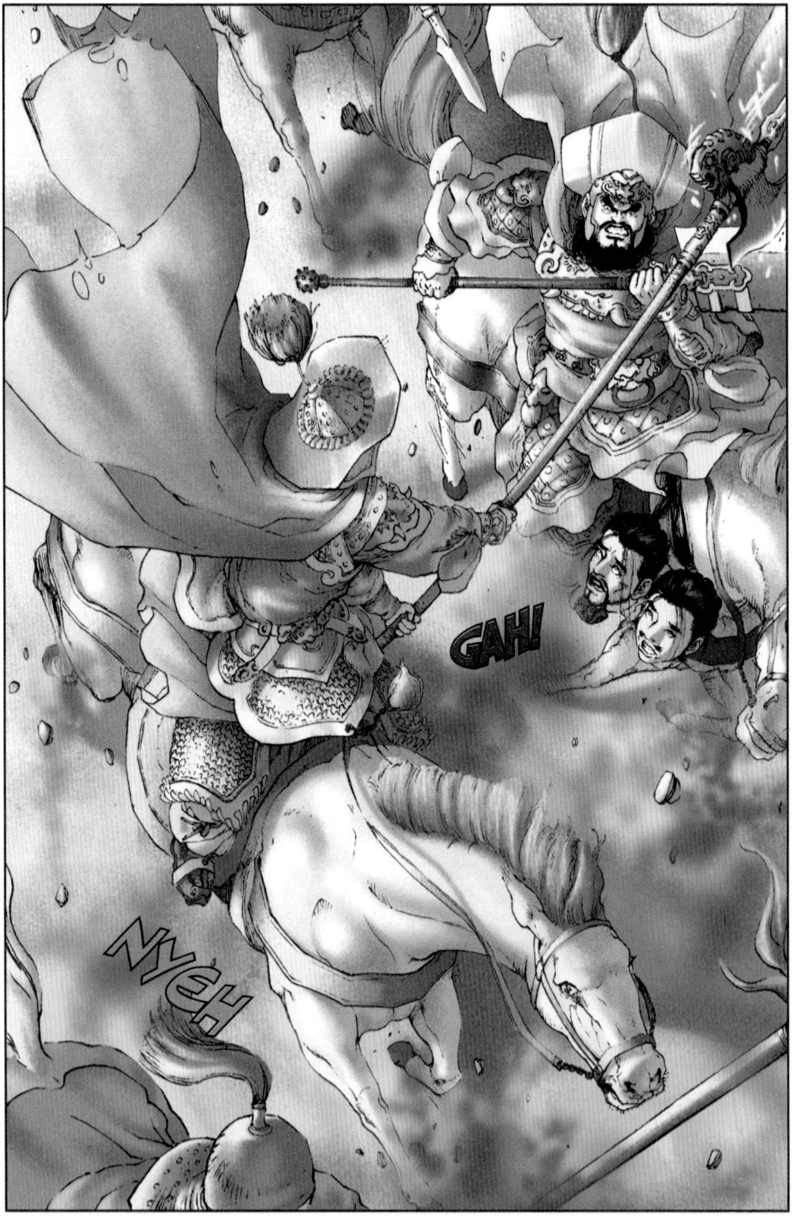
GAH!
NYEH

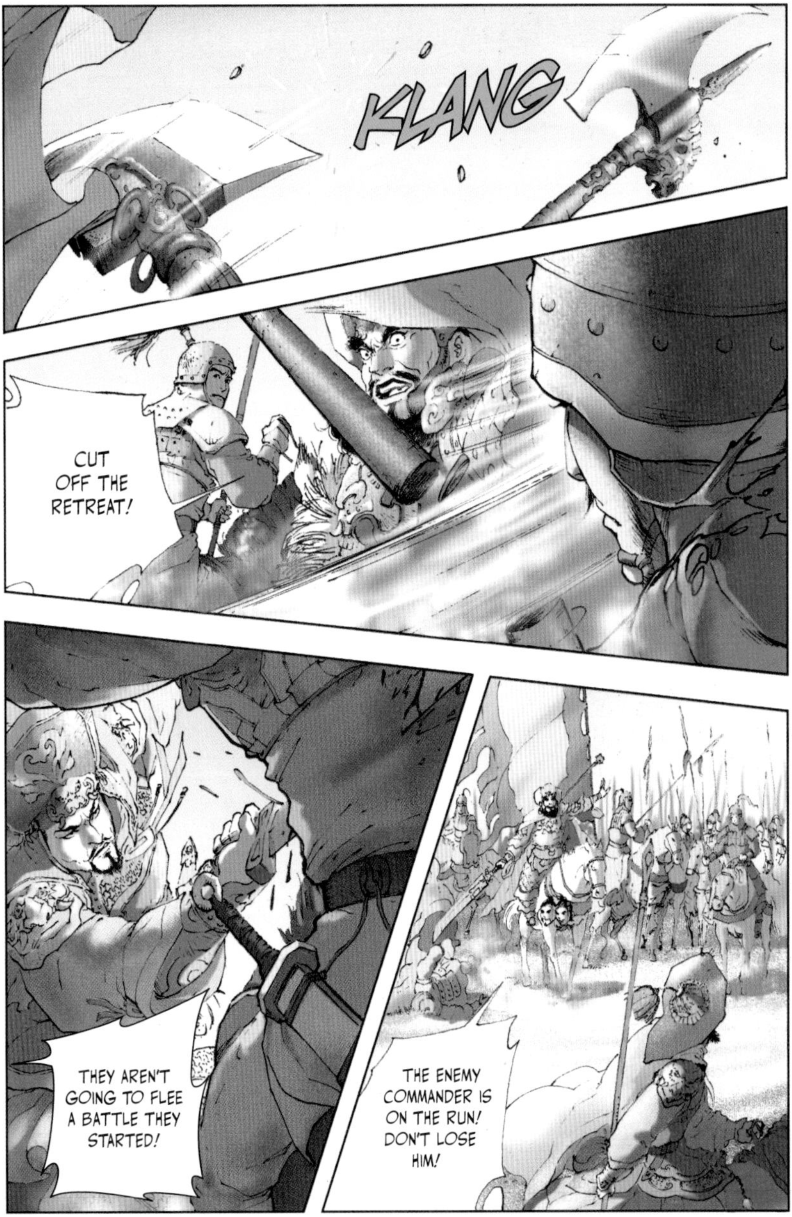
KLANG
CUT OFF THE RETREAT!
THEY AREN'T GOING TO FLEE A BATTLE THEY STARTED!
THE ENEMY COMMANDER IS ON THE RUN! DON'T LOSE HIM!

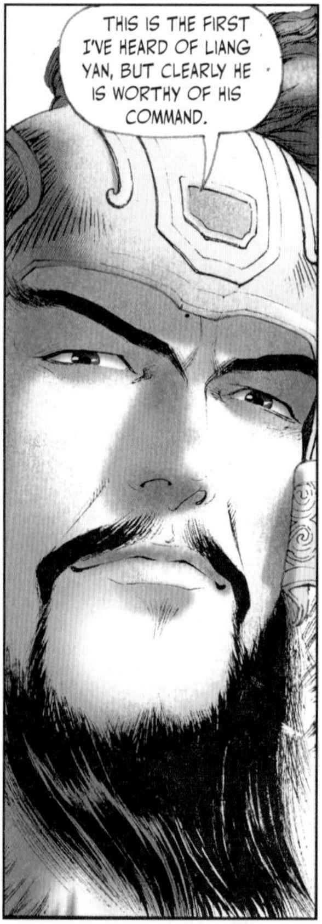
THIS IS THE FIRST I'VE HEARD OF LIANG YAN, BUT CLEARLY HE IS WORTHY OF HIS COMMAND.

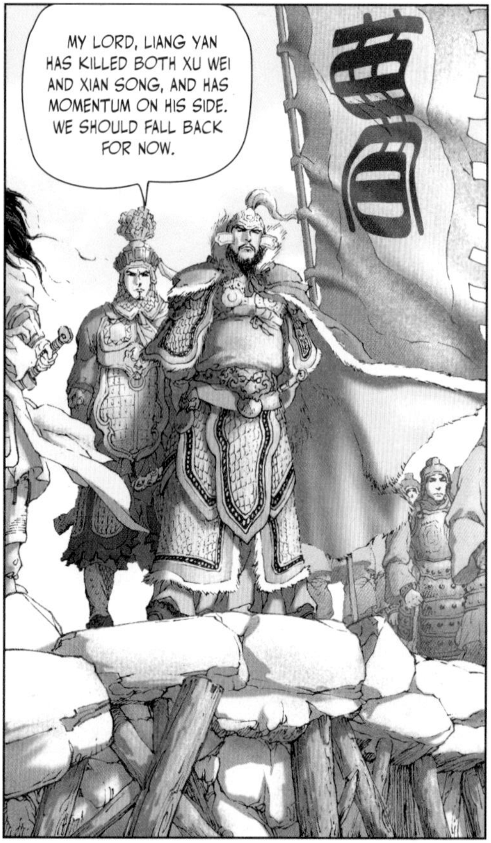
MY LORD, LIANG YAN HAS KILLED BOTH XU WEI AND XIAN SONG, AND HAS MOMENTUM ON HIS SIDE. WE SHOULD FALL BACK FOR NOW.

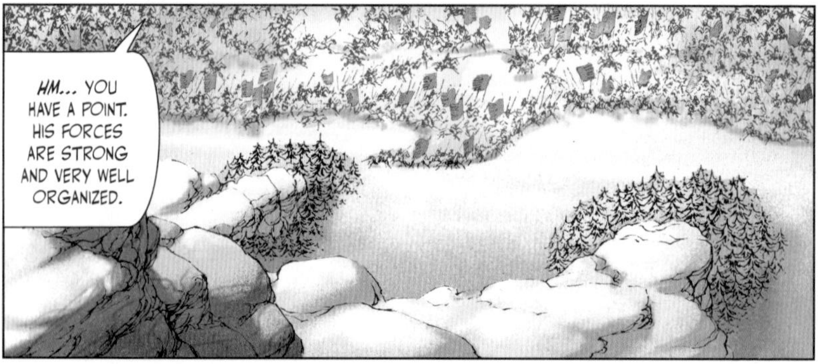
HM... YOU HAVE A POINT. HIS FORCES ARE STRONG AND VERY WELL ORGANIZED.

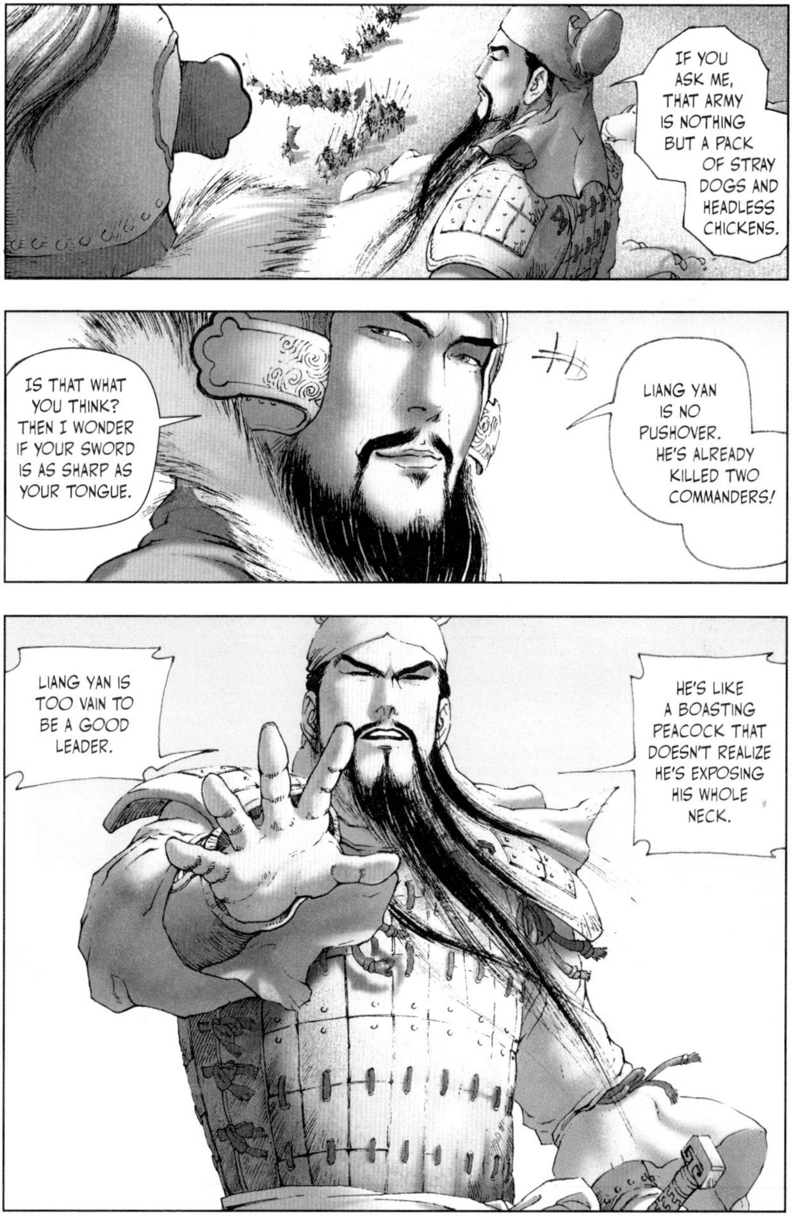
IF YOU ASK ME, THAT ARMY IS NOTHING BUT A PACK OF STRAY DOGS AND HEADLESS CHICKENS.
IS THAT WHAT YOU THINK? THEN I WONDER IF YOUR SWORD IS AS SHARP AS YOUR TONGUE.
LIANG YAN IS NO PUSHOVER. HE'S ALREADY KILLED TWO COMMANDERS!
LIANG YAN IS TOO VAIN TO BE A GOOD LEADER.
HE'S LIKE A BOASTING PEACOCK THAT DOESN'T REALIZE HE'S EXPOSING HIS WHOLE NECK.

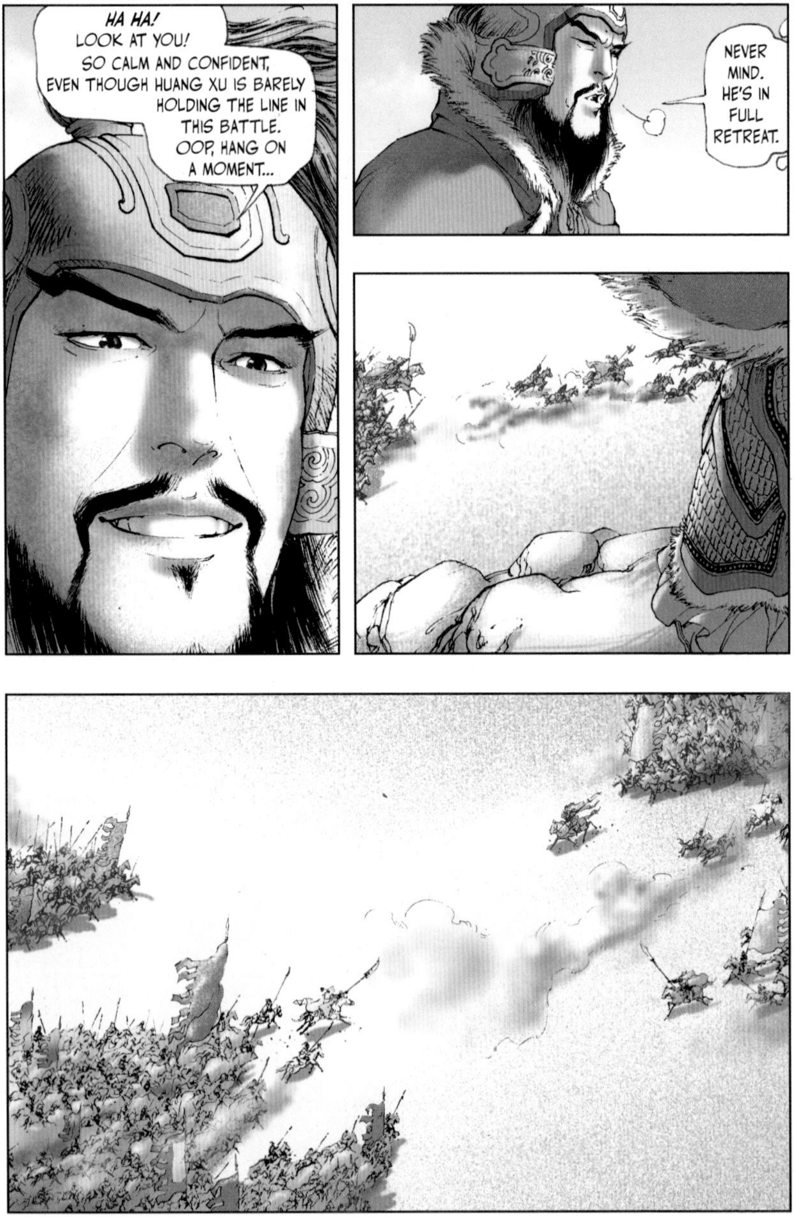
HA HA! LOOK AT YOU! SO CALM AND CONFIDENT, EVEN THOUGH HUANG XU IS BARELY HOLDING THE LINE IN THIS BATTLE. OOP, HANG ON A MOMENT...
NEVER MIND. HE'S IN FULL RETREAT.

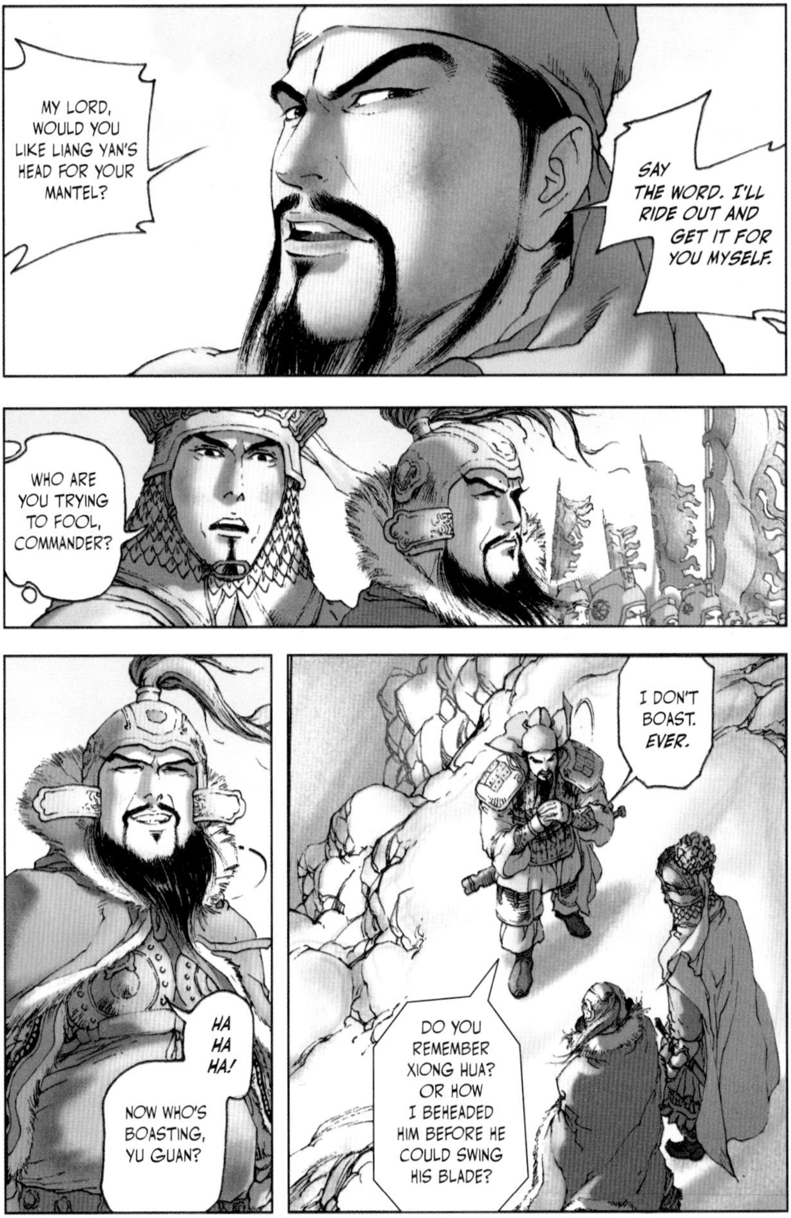
MY LORD, WOULD YOU LIKE LIANG YAN'S HEAD FOR YOUR MANTEL?
SAY THE WORD. I'LL RIDE OUT AND GET IT FOR YOU MYSELF.
WHO ARE YOU TRYING TO FOOL, COMMANDER?
HA HA HA!
NOW WHO'S BOASTING, YU GUAN?
I DON'T BOAST. EVER.
DO YOU REMEMBER XIONG HUA? OR HOW I BEHEADED HIM BEFORE HE COULD SWING HIS BLADE?

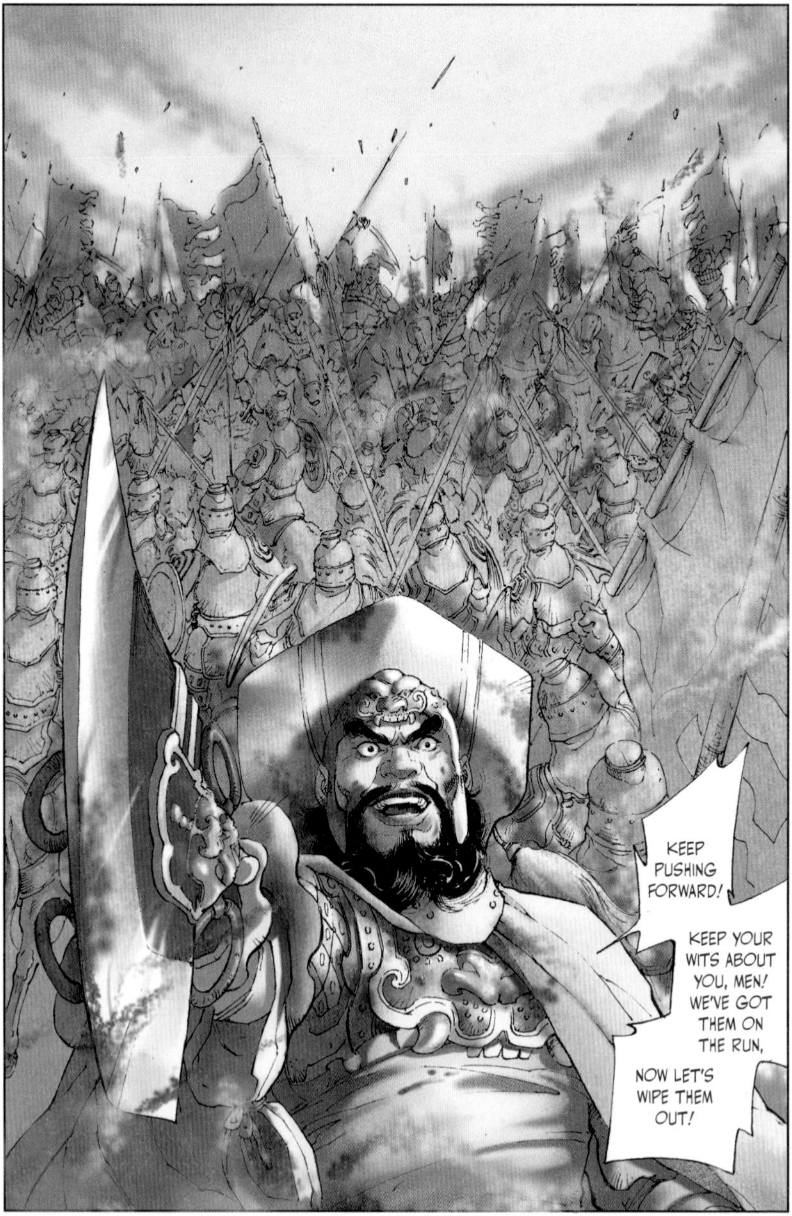
KEEP PUSHING FORWARD!
KEEP YOUR WITS ABOUT YOU, MEN! WE'VE GOT THEM ON THE RUN,
NOW LET'S WIPE THEM OUT!

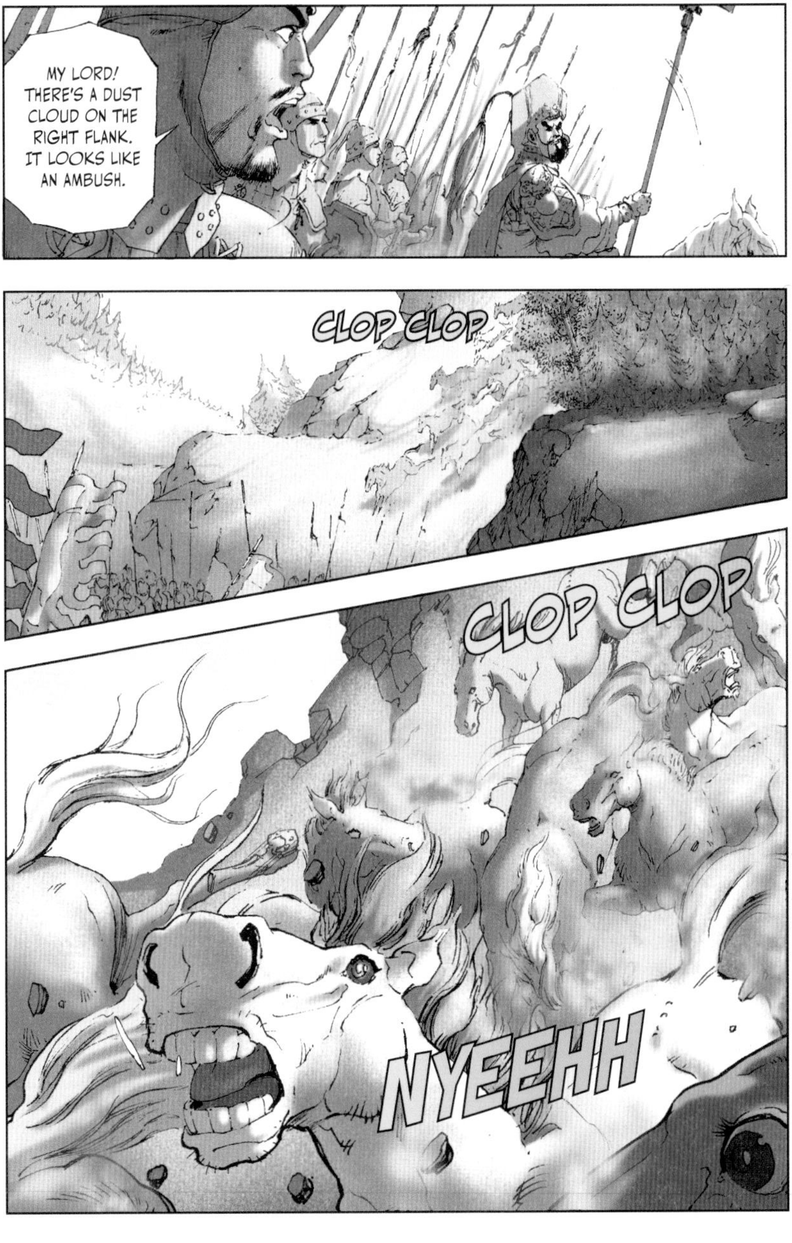
MY LORD! THERE'S A DUST CLOUD ON THE RIGHT FLANK. IT LOOKS LIKE AN AMBUSH.
CLOP CLOP
CLOP CLOP
NYEEHH

HMPH. WHAT A MISER-ABLE PLAN. CAO CAO IS SO DESPERATE TO BUY TIME HE SENDS A HERD OF HORSES TO BE SLAUGHTERED.

SHIELDS AND SPEARS UP, ALL OF YOU! RIDERS OR NO RIDERS, NOTHING GETS THROUGH!

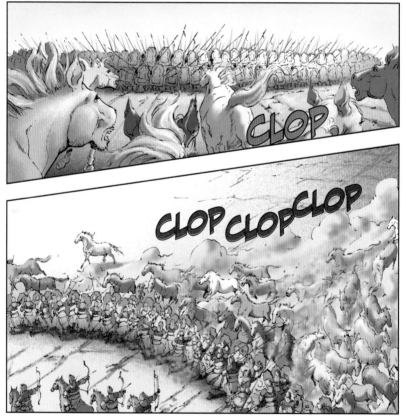

CLOP

CLOP CLOP CLOP

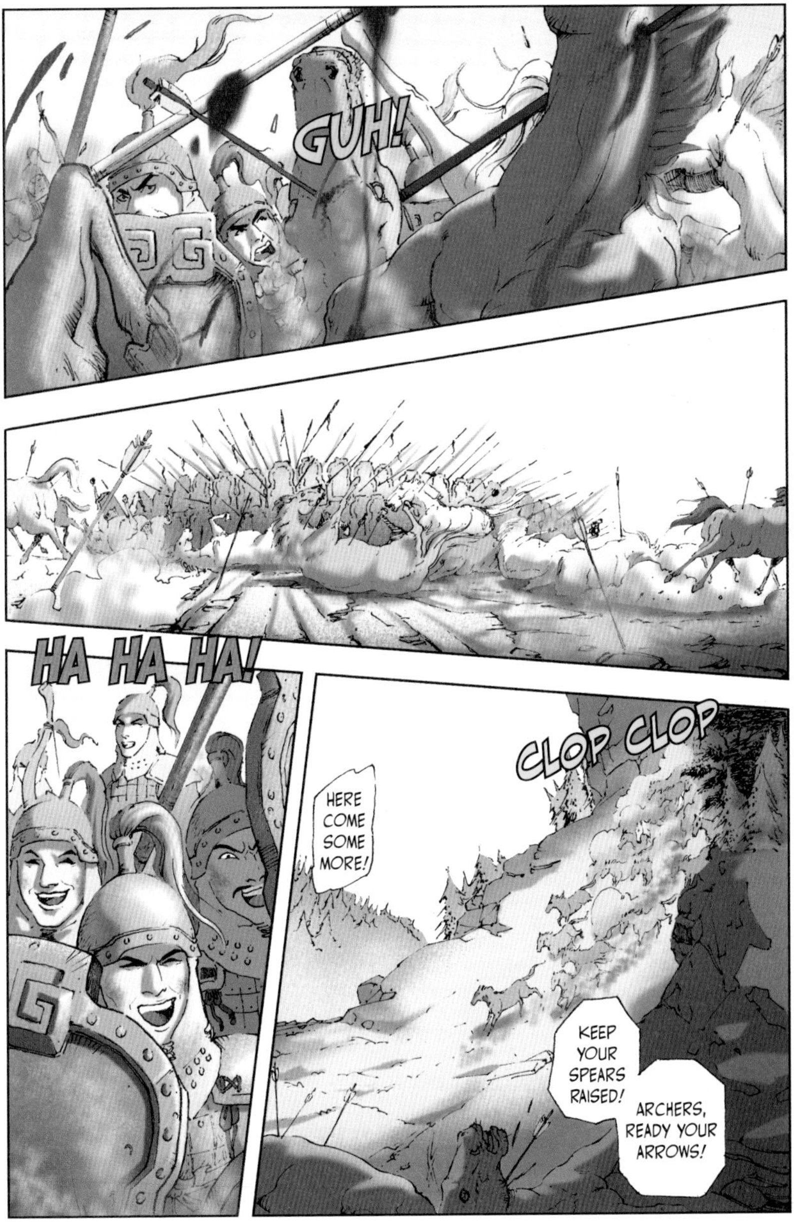
GUH!
HA HA HA!
CLOP CLOP
HERE COME SOME MORE!
KEEP YOUR SPEARS RAISED!
ARCHERS, READY YOUR ARROWS!

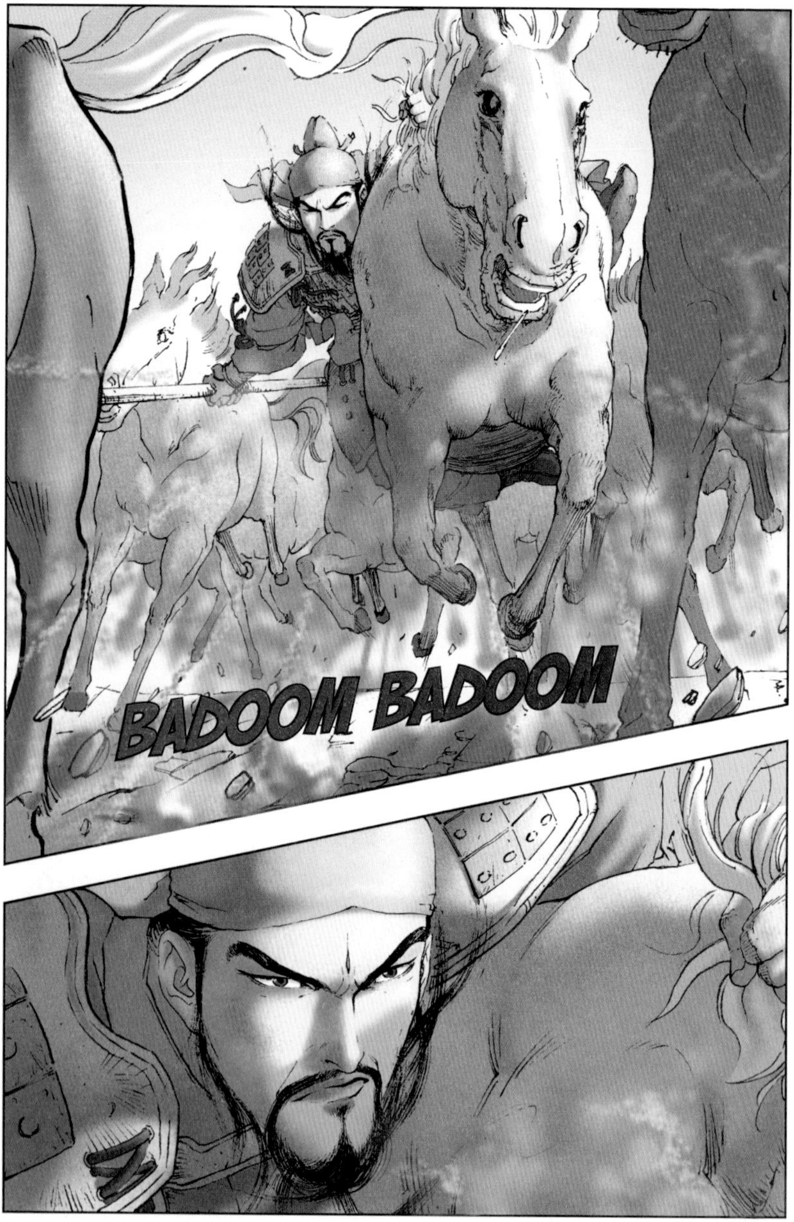
BADOOM BADOOM

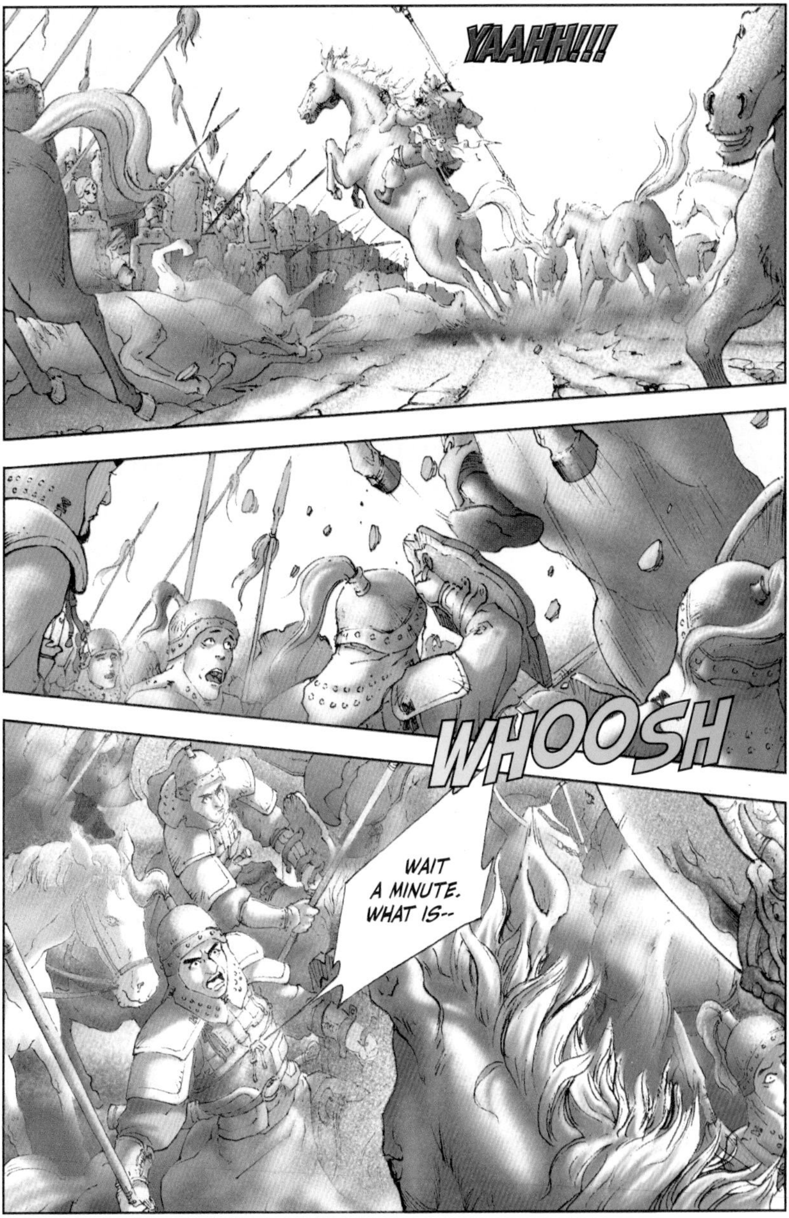
YAAHH!!!
WHOOSH
WAIT A MINUTE. WHAT IS--

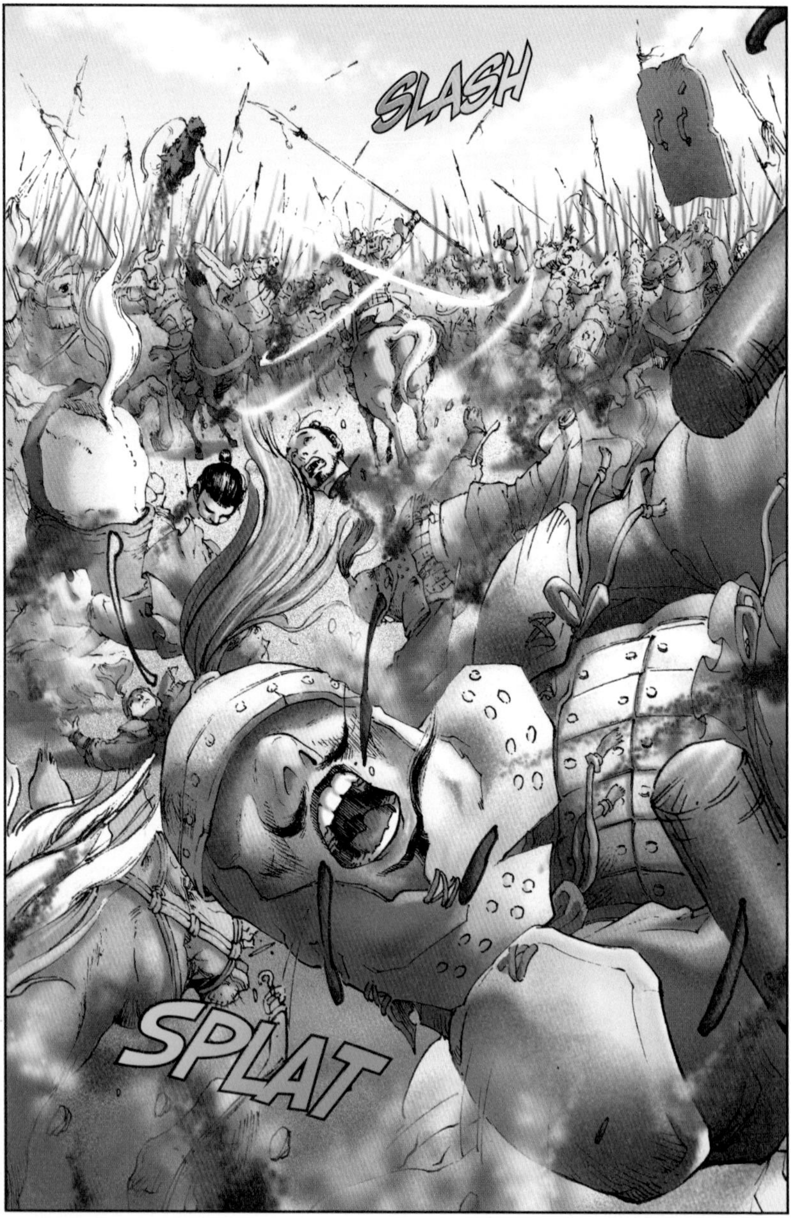
SLASH
SPLAT

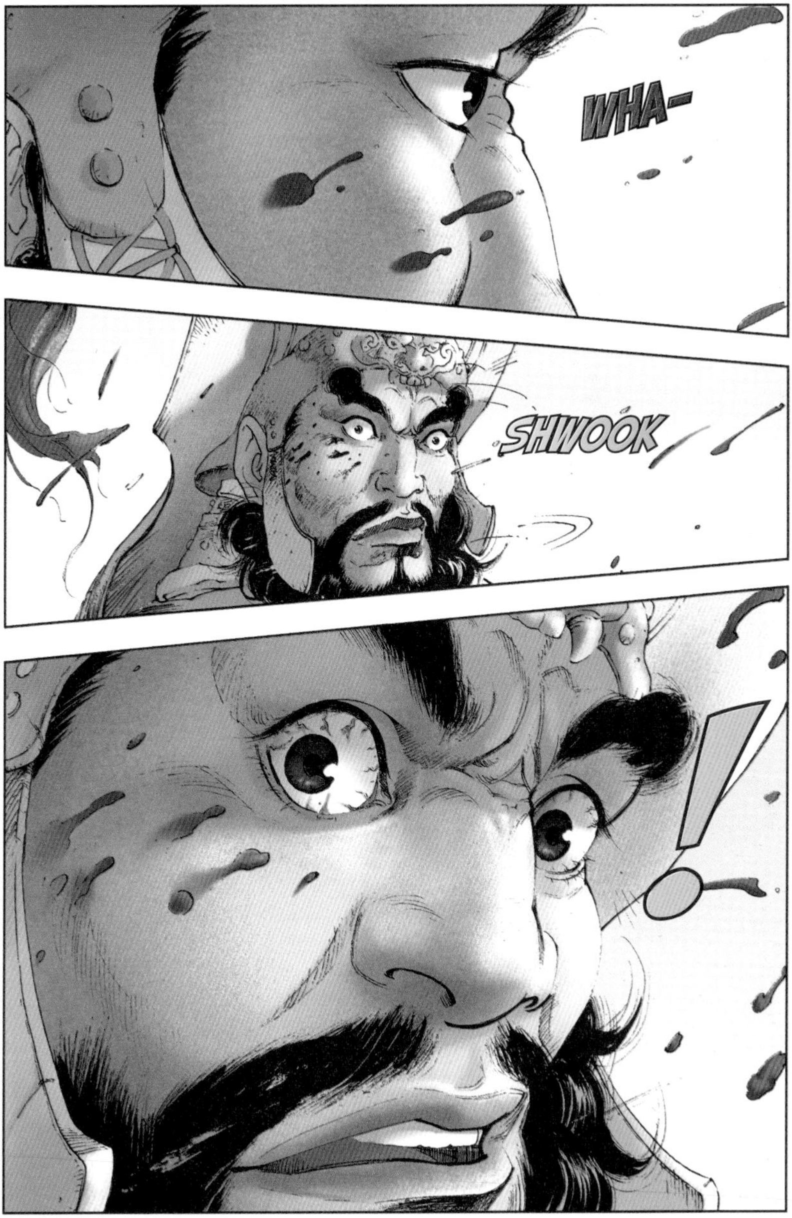
WHA-
SHWOOK
!

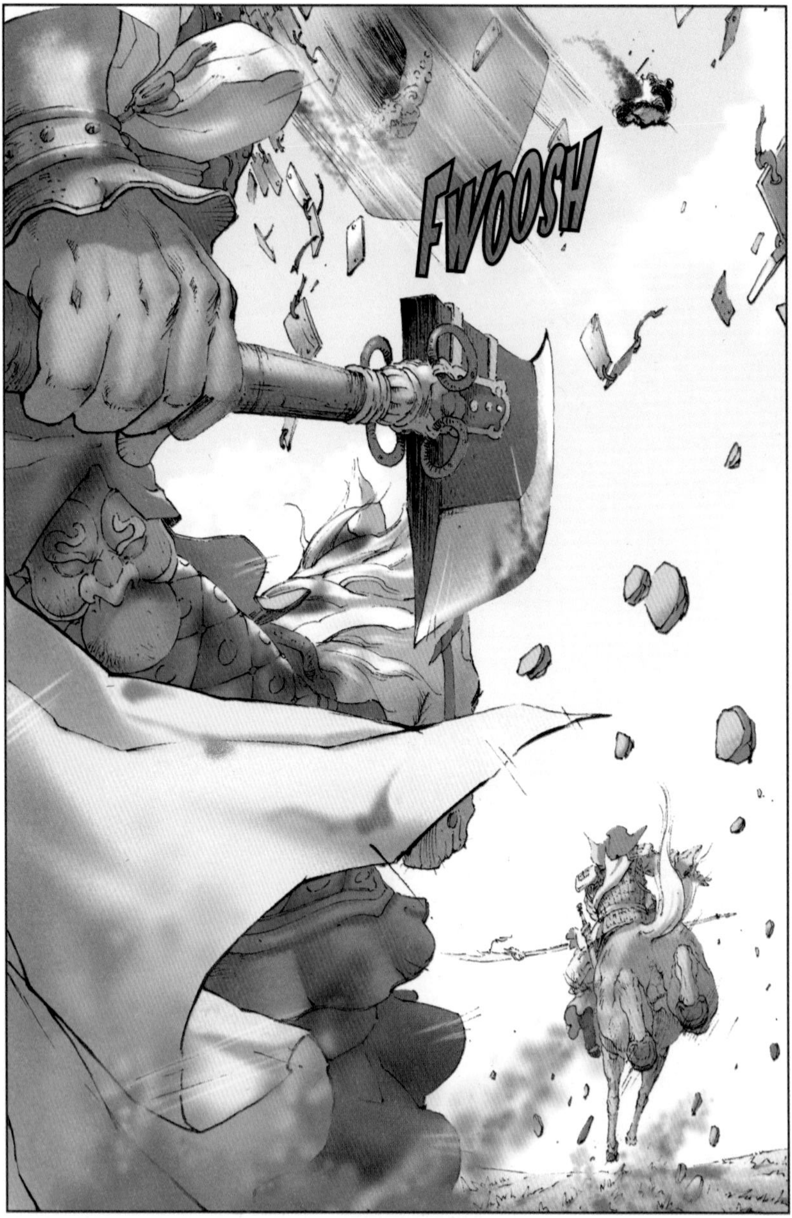
FWOOSH

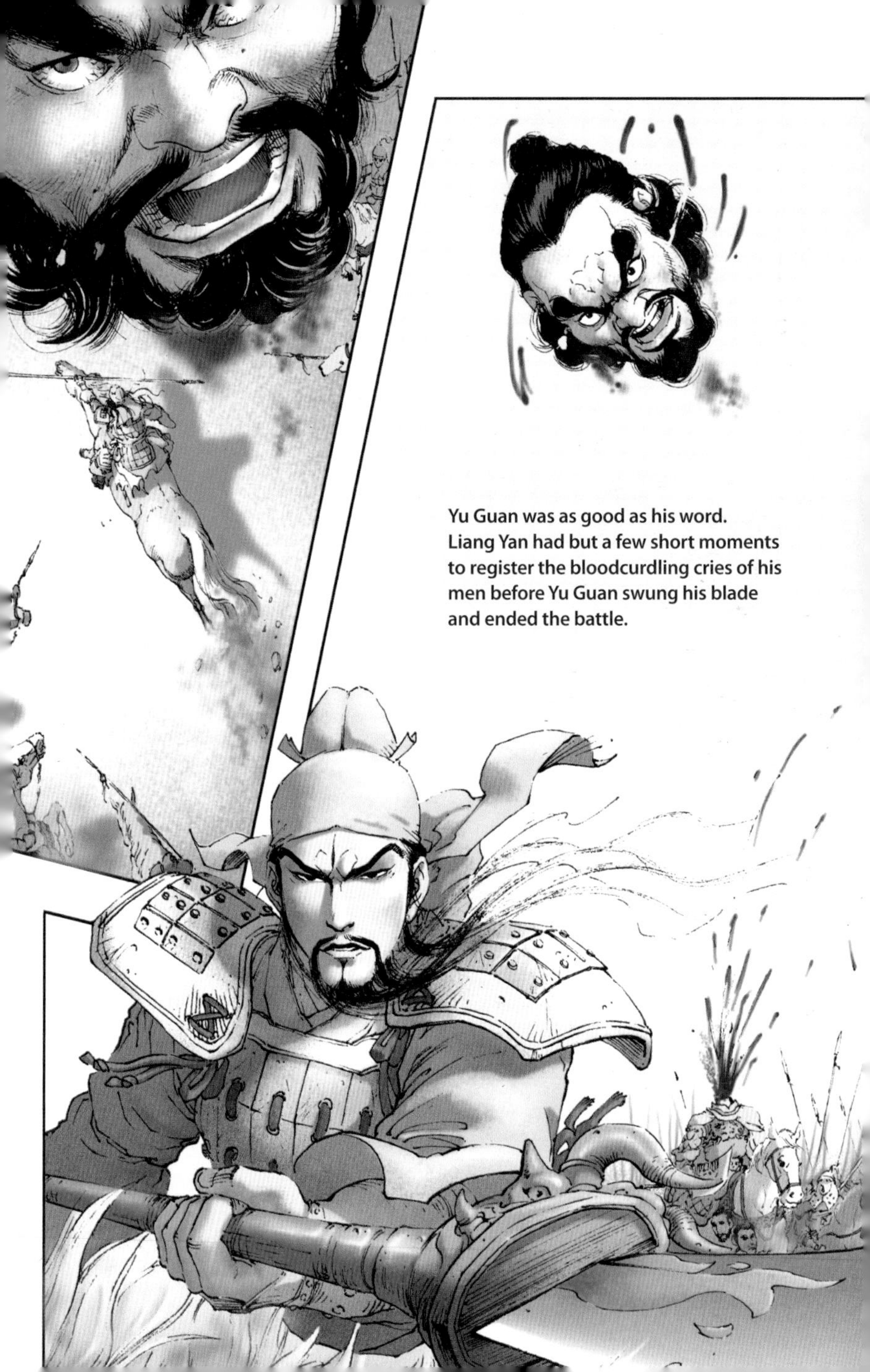
Yu Guan was as good as his word. Liang Yan had but a few short moments to register the bloodcurdling cries of his men before Yu Guan swung his blade and ended the battle.

Chapter 3

The Leverage of Brotherhood ^{200 AD}

Summary

Shao Yuan is furious upon hearing the news that Bei Liu's sworn brother is responsible for the death of his best field commander. He immediately suspects a conspiracy, but Bei Liu assures him there is no hidden agenda; if Bei Liu wanted Shao Yuan dead, he would have killed him already. Bei Liu understands that Yu Guan would only fight for Cao Cao if the lives of family had been threatened, but before he has a chance to devise a plan, Chou Wen, another of Shao Yuan's commanders, steps forward and offers to lead an army to avenge Liang Yan's death. Shao Yuan dispatches him with another 100,000 troops.

Chou Wen leads the army into battle with a different strategy: he uses thousands of archers to unleash wave after wave of arrows on the enemy, driving them back from the battlefront. The tide of the battle appears to be in Chou Wen's favor, but just as before the tide is abruptly turned when Yu Guan enters the battle. Despite being struck by numerous arrows, Yu Guan is relentless in his attack, and after intense fighting Chou Wen falls to Yu Guan, like many before him. Shao Yuan's forces are decimated, and both Shao Yuan and Bei Liu are dismayed to learn that Yu Guan is assuming an ever-more-active role in Cao Cao's army.

BATTLE OF BAIMA

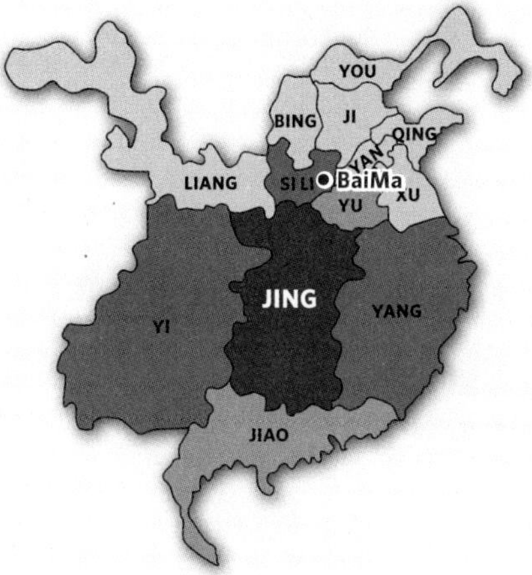
YOU
BING
JI
QING
YAN
LIANG
SI LI
BaiMa
YU
XU
JING
YI
YANG
JIAO

Origin

In 200 AD, Shao Yuan finally overcame his reservations and issued a war declaration on Cao Cao. His intention was to advance to XuChang, capture Emperor Xian, and defeat Cao Cao on his own terrain. Shao Yuan dispatched his army across the Yellow River, where they met Cao Cao's elite forces at BaiMa.

Strategies

Shao Yuan dispatched an army of 100,000 soldiers but was met in battle by an army of only 50,000 led by Cao Cao himself. Yuan Shao mounted an aggressive attack aimed at dividing and conquering the smaller force before his forces continued to push further south. However, Cao Cao accepted the counsel of You Xun, who advised that they send a portion of their army to the rear of Shao Yuan's forces. This maneuver maneuver would create a distraction, and Shao Yuan's army, being confident of their advantage, would divert attention and resources from the front line. As expected, Shao Yuan's forces took the bait, at which time Cao Cao sent Yu Guan to attack the front line. Yu Guan made short work of killing Liang Yan and driving back Shao Yuan's forces. Shao Yuan then dispatched Chen Wen and another armed force to confront Yu Guan. This attack ended much like the first one.

Outcome

Cao Cao defeated Shao Yuan and won the Battle of BaiMa in large part because of the superior fighting of Yu Guan. Since reluctantly agreeing to join Cao Cao's side, Yu Guan had been an invaluable soldier.

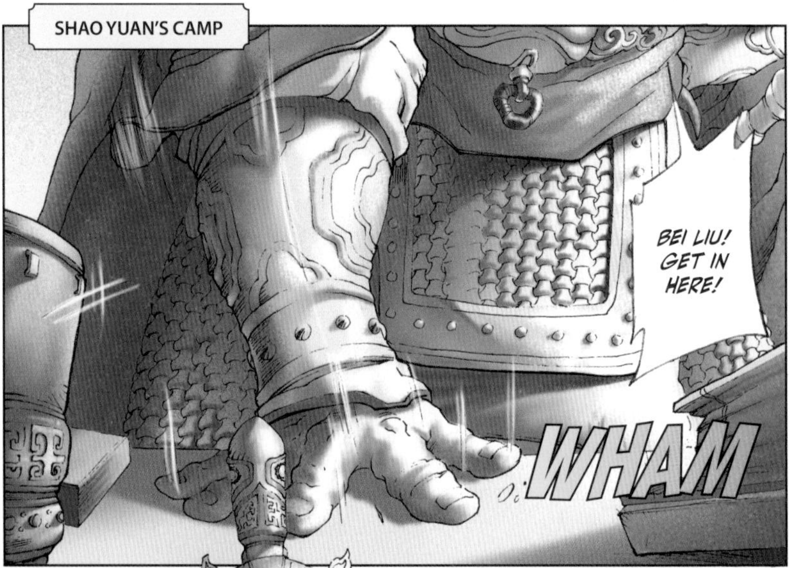
SHAO YUAN'S CAMP
BEI LIU! GET IN HERE!
WHAM

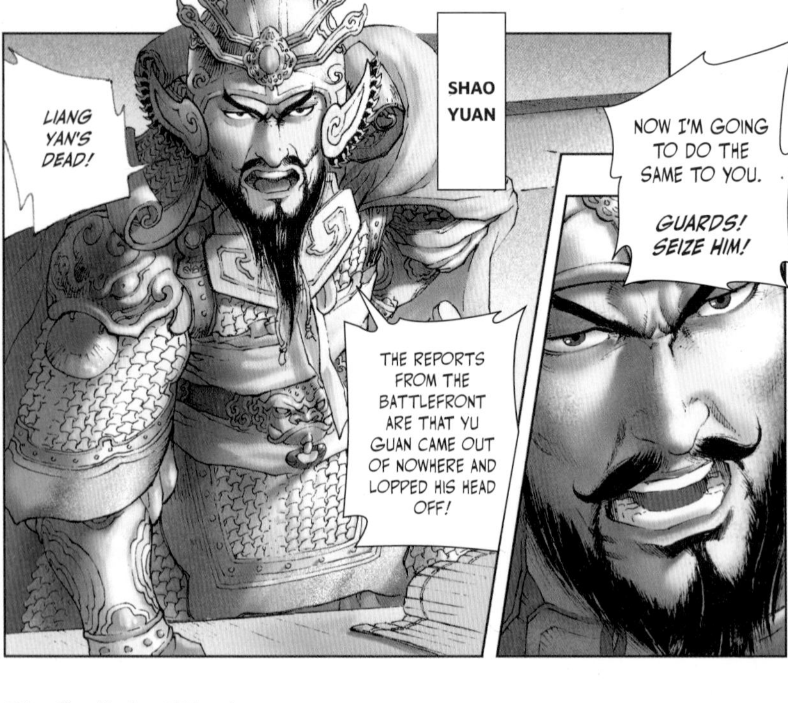
LIANG YAN'S DEAD!
SHAO YUAN
THE REPORTS FROM THE BATTLEFRONT ARE THAT YU GUAN CAME OUT OF NOWHERE AND LOPPED HIS HEAD OFF!
NOW I'M GOING TO DO THE SAME TO YOU.
GUARDS! SEIZE HIM!

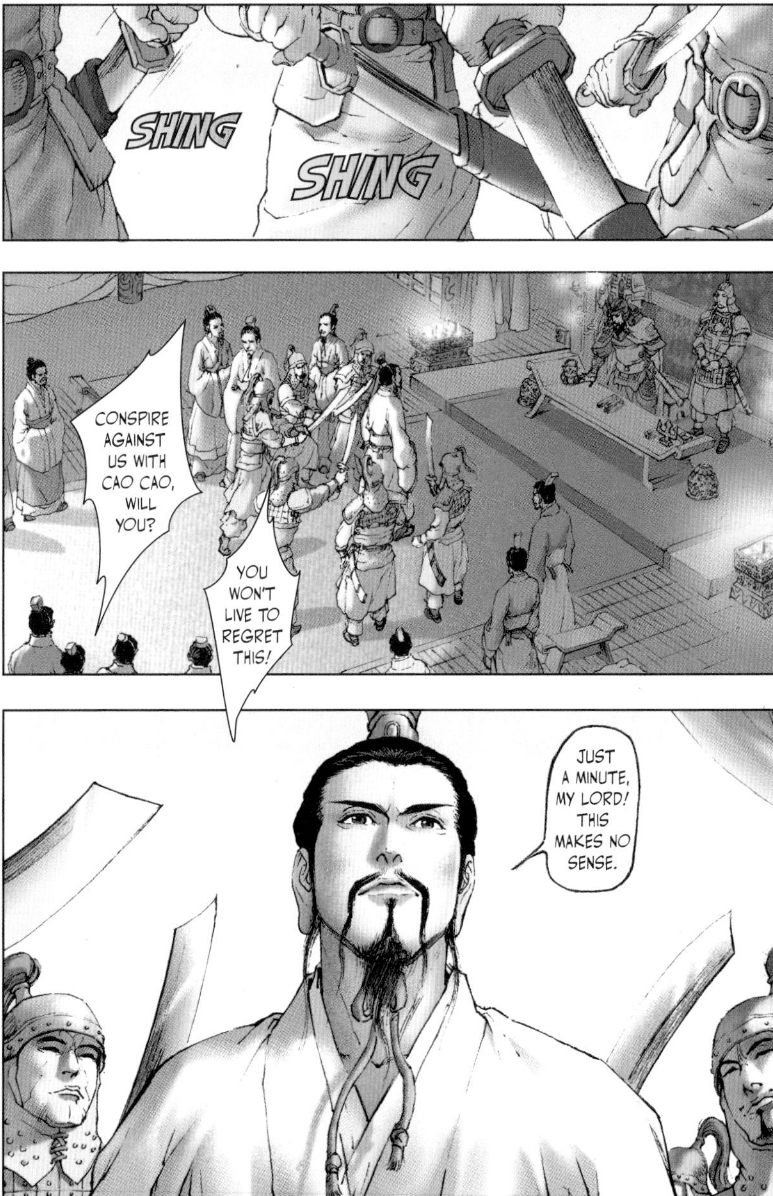
SHING
SHING
CONSPIRE AGAINST US WITH CAO CAO, WILL YOU?
YOU WON'T LIVE TO REGRET THIS!
JUST A MINUTE, MY LORD! THIS MAKES NO SENSE.

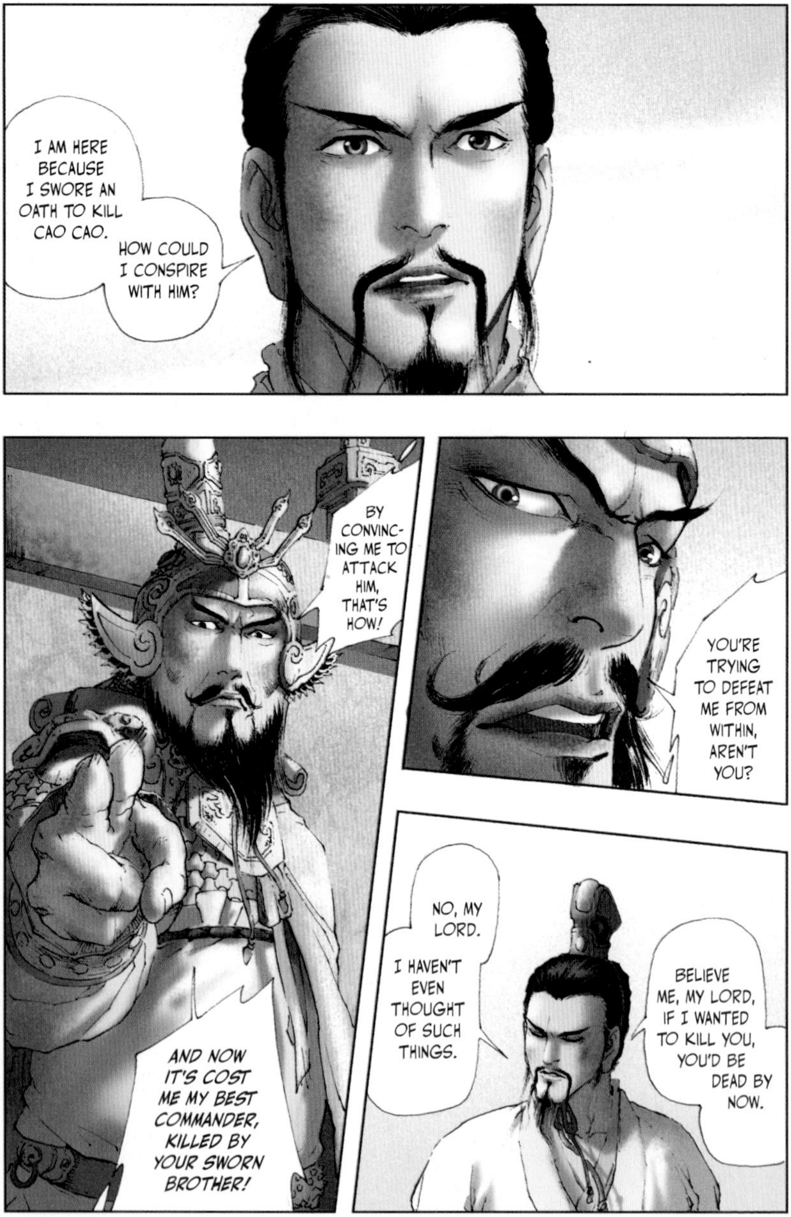
I AM HERE BECAUSE I SWORE AN OATH TO KILL CAO CAO.
HOW COULD I CONSPIRE WITH HIM?
BY CONVINC-ING ME TO ATTACK HIM, THAT'S HOW!
AND NOW IT'S COST ME MY BEST COMMANDER, KILLED BY YOUR SWORN BROTHER!
YOU'RE TRYING TO DEFEAT ME FROM WITHIN, AREN'T YOU?
NO, MY LORD.
I HAVEN'T EVEN THOUGHT OF SUCH THINGS.
BELIEVE ME, MY LORD, IF I WANTED TO KILL YOU, YOU'D BE DEAD BY NOW.

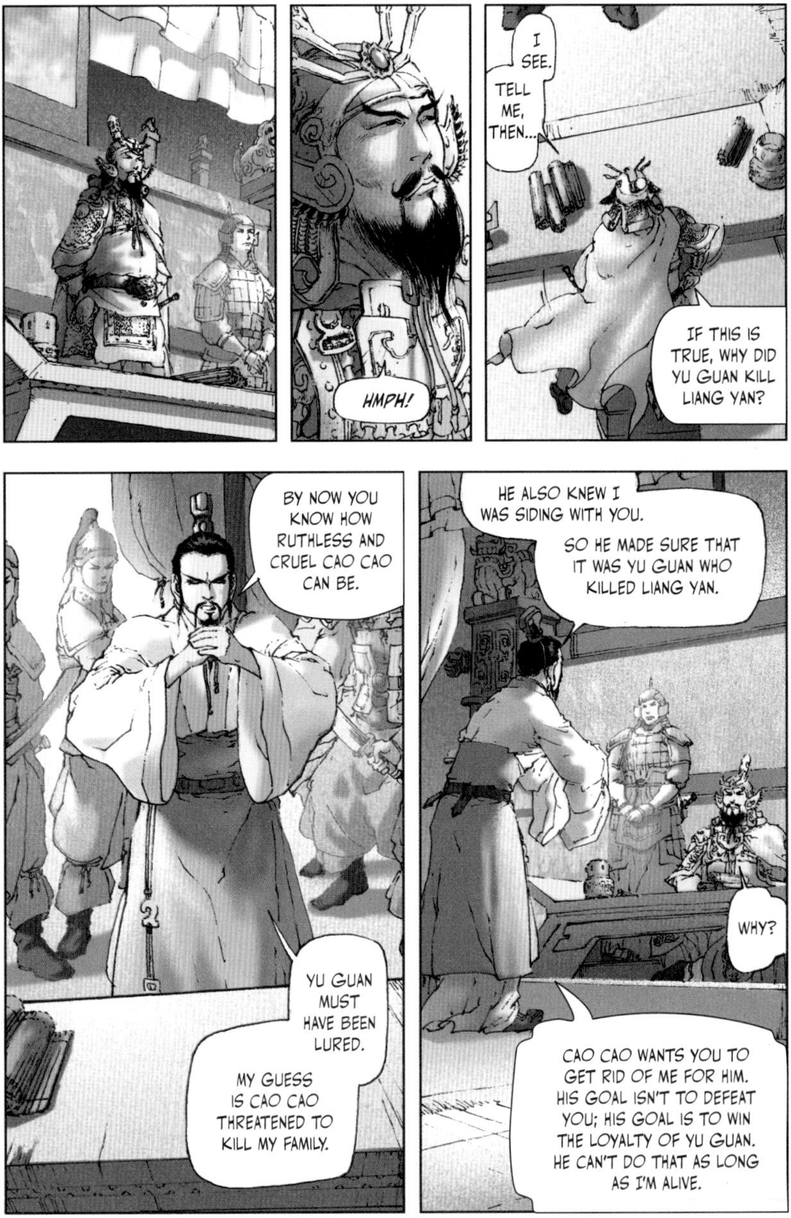
HMPH!
I SEE.
TELL ME, THEN...
IF THIS IS TRUE, WHY DID YU GUAN KILL LIANG YAN?
BY NOW YOU KNOW HOW RUTHLESS AND CRUEL CAO CAO CAN BE.
YU GUAN MUST HAVE BEEN LURED.
MY GUESS IS CAO CAO THREATENED TO KILL MY FAMILY.
HE ALSO KNEW I WAS SIDING WITH YOU.
SO HE MADE SURE THAT IT WAS YU GUAN WHO KILLED LIANG YAN.
WHY?
CAO CAO WANTS YOU TO GET RID OF ME FOR HIM. HIS GOAL ISN'T TO DEFEAT YOU; HIS GOAL IS TO WIN THE LOYALTY OF YU GUAN. HE CAN'T DO THAT AS LONG AS I'M ALIVE.

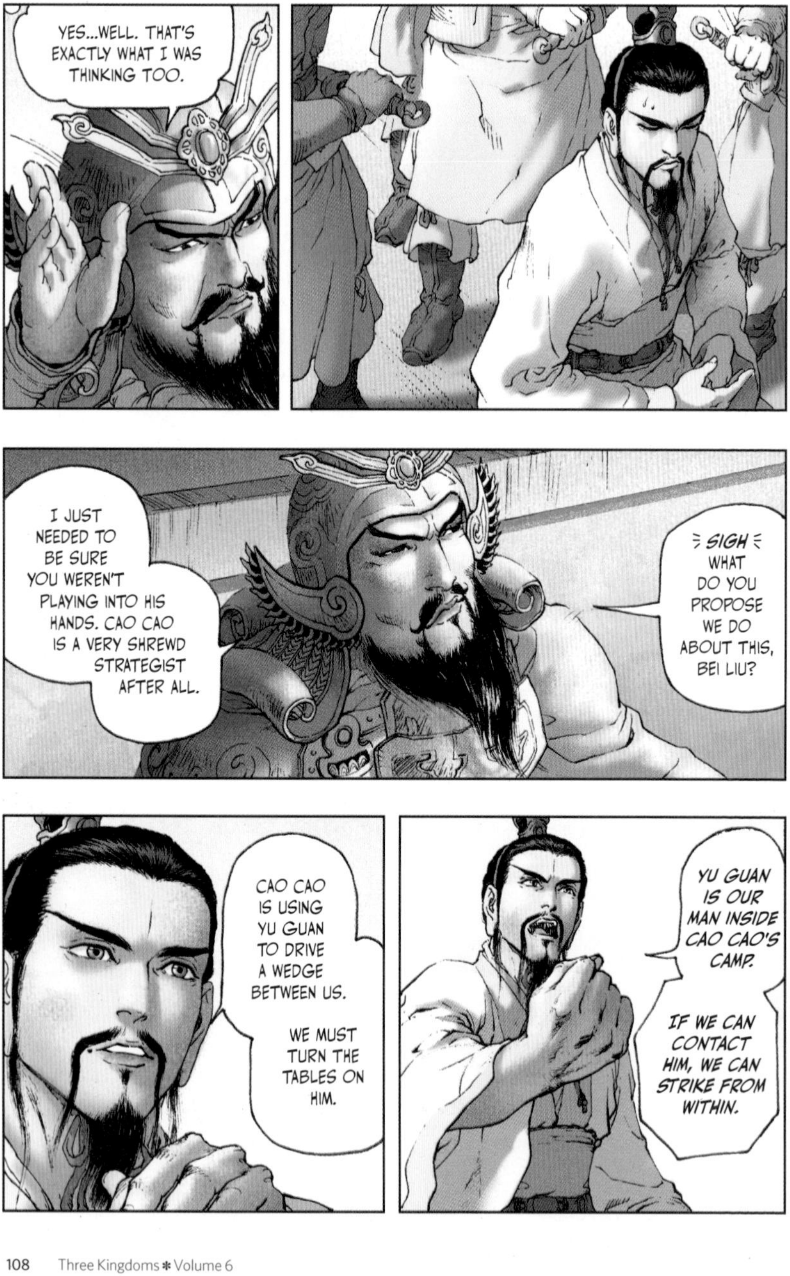
YES...WELL. THAT'S EXACTLY WHAT I WAS THINKING TOO.
I JUST NEEDED TO BE SURE YOU WEREN'T PLAYING INTO HIS HANDS. CAO CAO IS A VERY SHREWD STRATEGIST AFTER ALL.
SIGH WHAT DO YOU PROPOSE WE DO ABOUT THIS, BEI LIU?
CAO CAO IS USING YU GUAN TO DRIVE A WEDGE BETWEEN US.
WE MUST TURN THE TABLES ON HIM.
YU GUAN IS OUR MAN INSIDE CAO CAO'S CAMP.
IF WE CAN CONTACT HIM, WE CAN STRIKE FROM WITHIN.

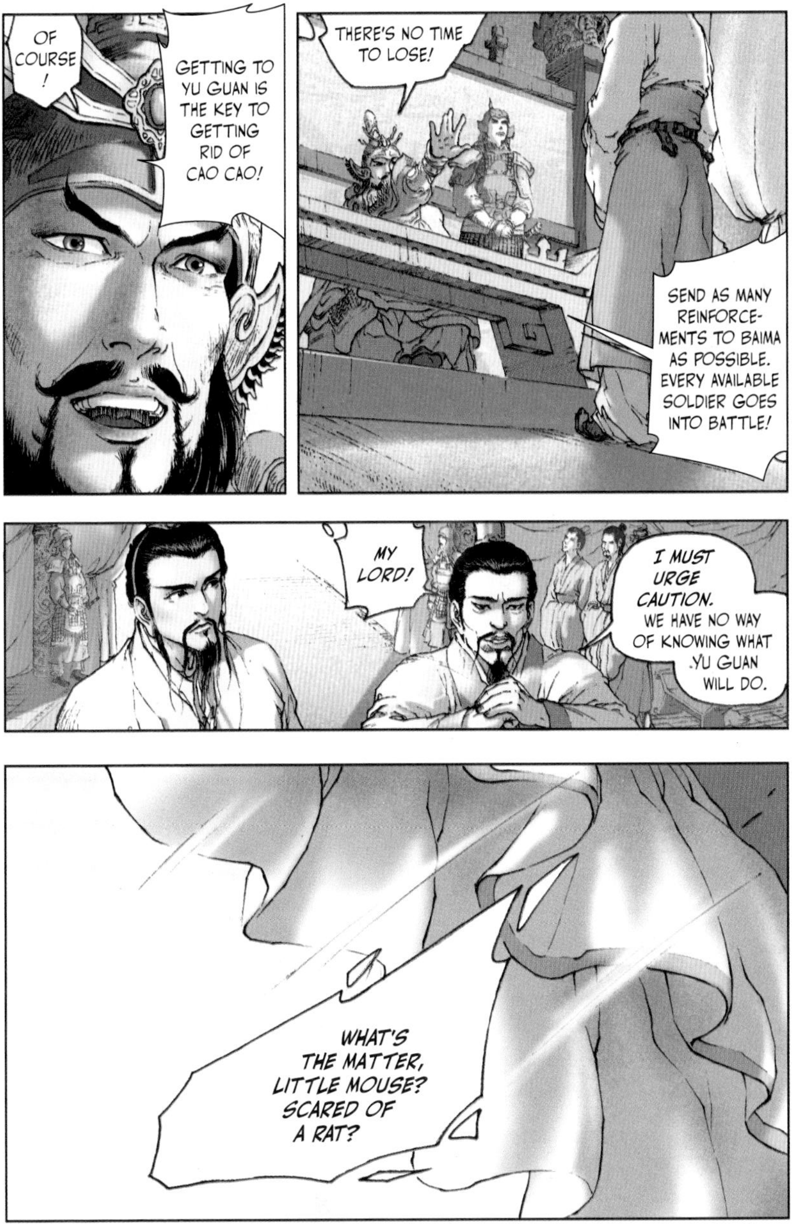
OF COURSE!
GETTING TO YU GUAN IS THE KEY TO GETTING RID OF CAO CAO!
THERE'S NO TIME TO LOSE!
SEND AS MANY REINFORCE-MENTS TO BAIMA AS POSSIBLE. EVERY AVAILABLE SOLDIER GOES INTO BATTLE!
MY LORD!
I MUST URGE CAUTION. WE HAVE NO WAY OF KNOWING WHAT YU GUAN WILL DO.
WHAT'S THE MATTER, LITTLE MOUSE? SCARED OF A RAT?

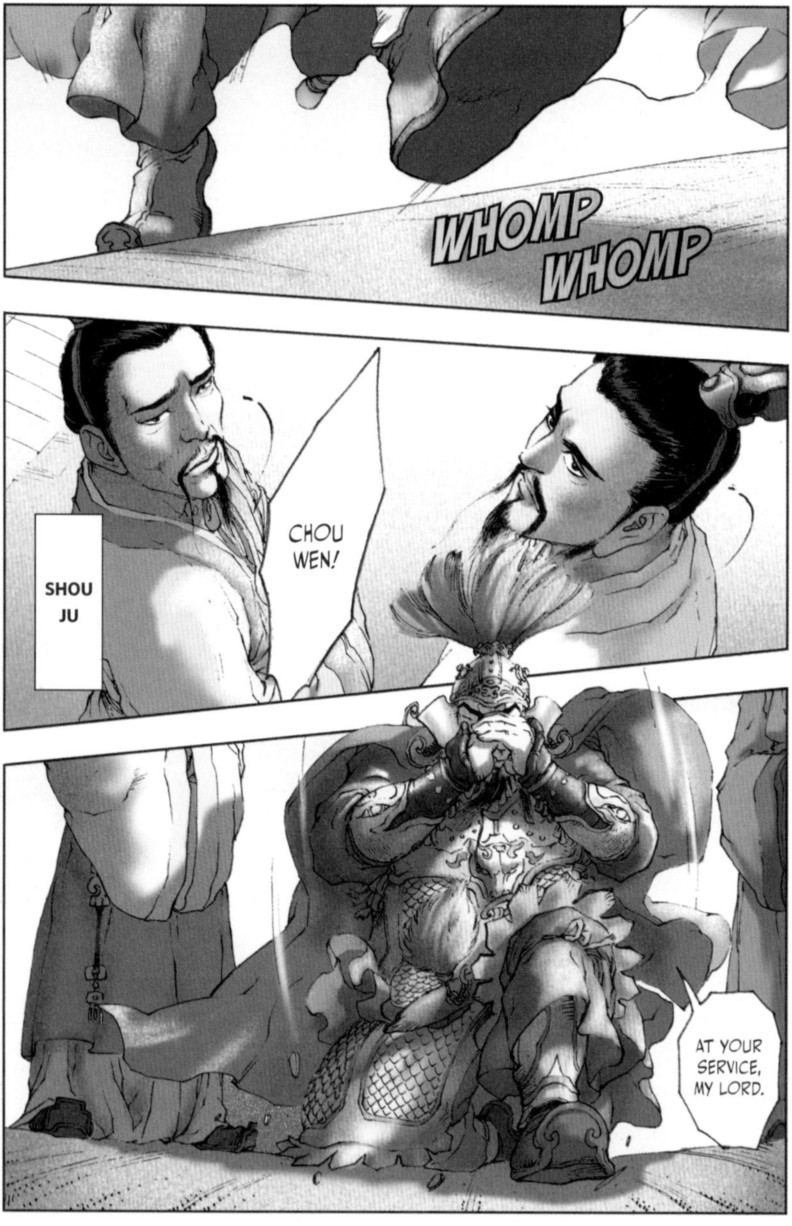
WHOMP
WHOMP
SHOU JU
CHOU WEN!
AT YOUR SERVICE, MY LORD.

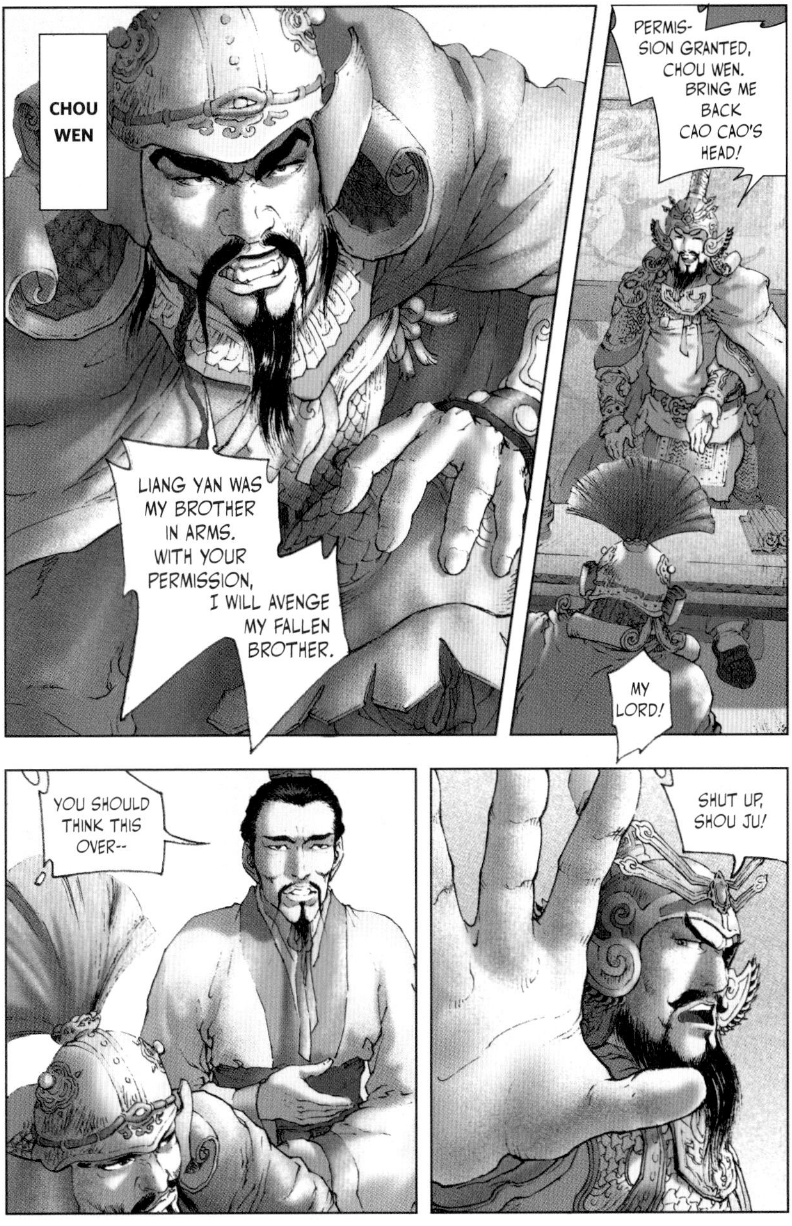
CHOU WEN
LIANG YAN WAS MY BROTHER IN ARMS. WITH YOUR PERMISSION, I WILL AVENGE MY FALLEN BROTHER.
PERMIS-SION GRANTED, CHOU WEN. BRING ME BACK CAO CAO'S HEAD!
MY LORD!
YOU SHOULD THINK THIS OVER--
SHUT UP, SHOU JU!

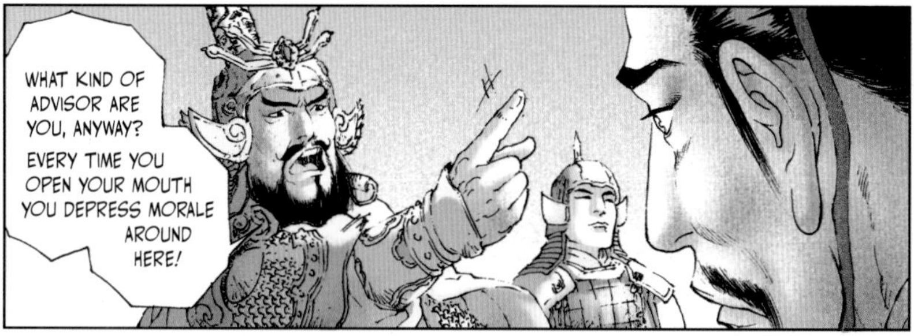
WHAT KIND OF ADVISOR ARE YOU, ANYWAY?
EVERY TIME YOU OPEN YOUR MOUTH YOU DEPRESS MORALE AROUND HERE!

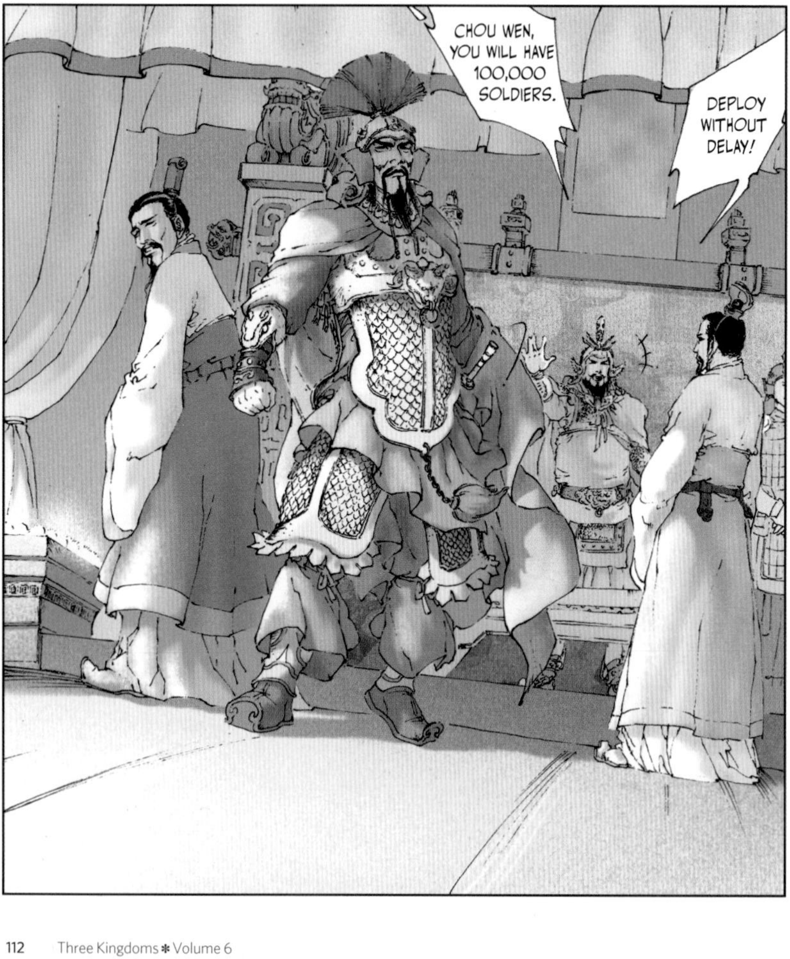
CHOU WEN, YOU WILL HAVE 100,000 SOLDIERS.
DEPLOY WITHOUT DELAY!

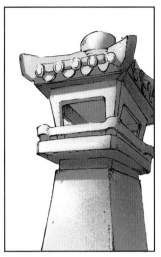

SHOU JU, WAIT A MOMENT!

PLEASE DON'T THINK US RECKLESS. WE JUST WANT TO BE RID OF CAO CAO.

WHAT I THINK NO LONGER MATTERS. THE DECISION HAS ALREADY BEEN MADE.

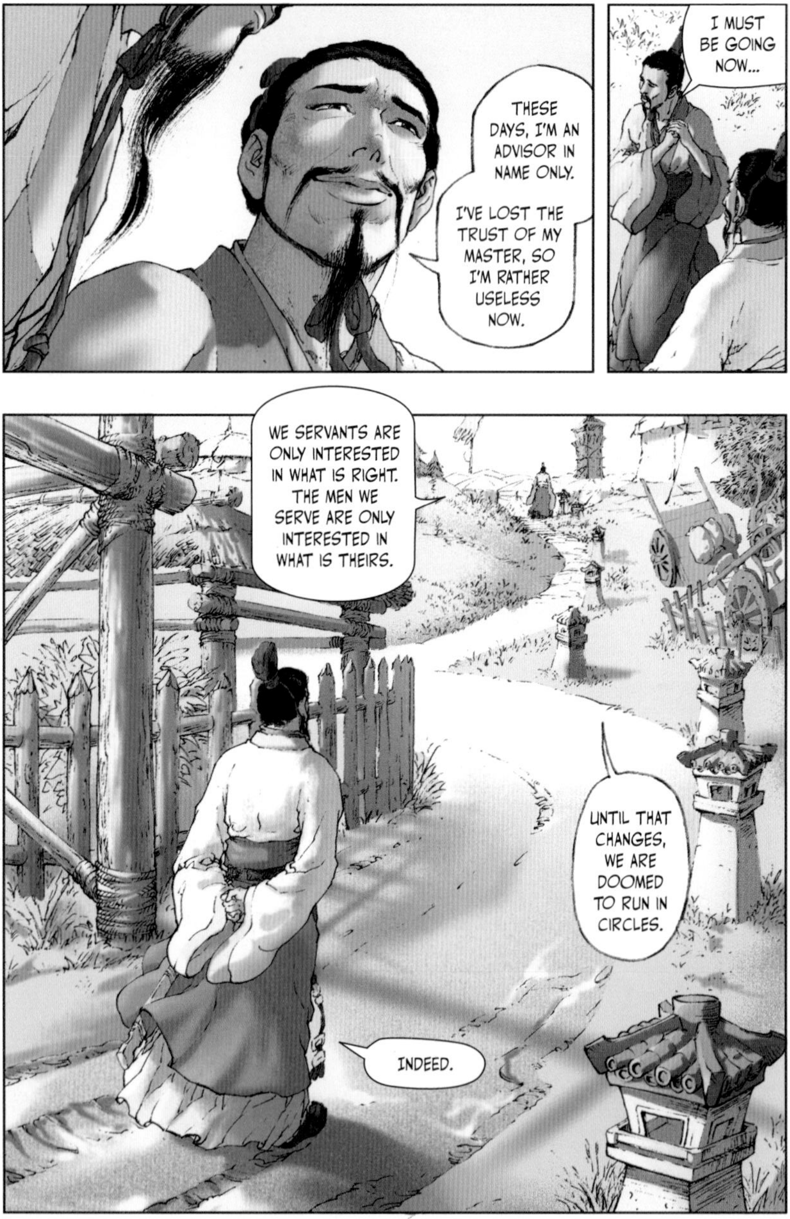
I MUST BE GOING NOW...
THESE DAYS, I'M AN ADVISOR IN NAME ONLY.
I'VE LOST THE TRUST OF MY MASTER, SO I'M RATHER USELESS NOW.
WE SERVANTS ARE ONLY INTERESTED IN WHAT IS RIGHT. THE MEN WE SERVE ARE ONLY INTERESTED IN WHAT IS THEIRS.
UNTIL THAT CHANGES, WE ARE DOOMED TO RUN IN CIRCLES.
INDEED.

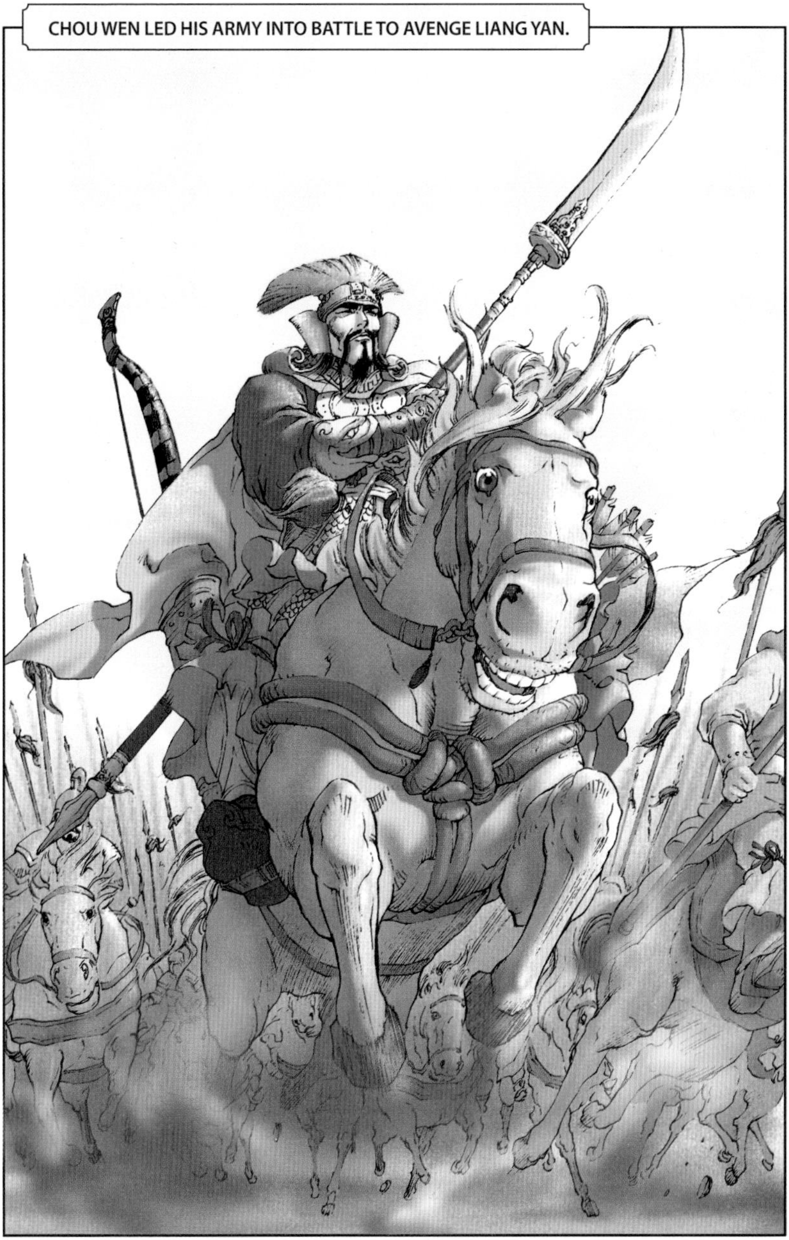
CHOU WEN LED HIS ARMY INTO BATTLE TO AVENGE LIANG YAN.

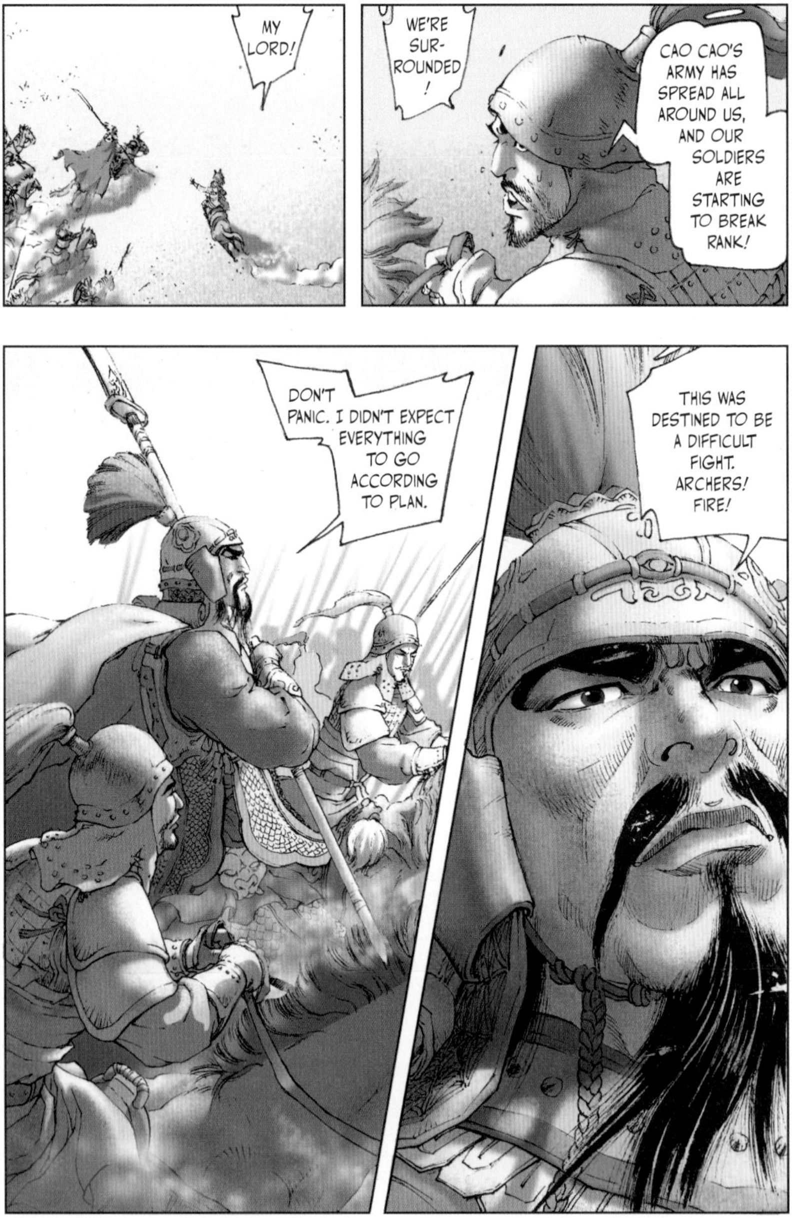
MY LORD!
WE'RE SUR-ROUNDED!
CAO CAO'S ARMY HAS SPREAD ALL AROUND US, AND OUR SOLDIERS ARE STARTING TO BREAK RANK!
DON'T PANIC. I DIDN'T EXPECT EVERYTHING TO GO ACCORDING TO PLAN.
THIS WAS DESTINED TO BE A DIFFICULT FIGHT. ARCHERS! FIRE!

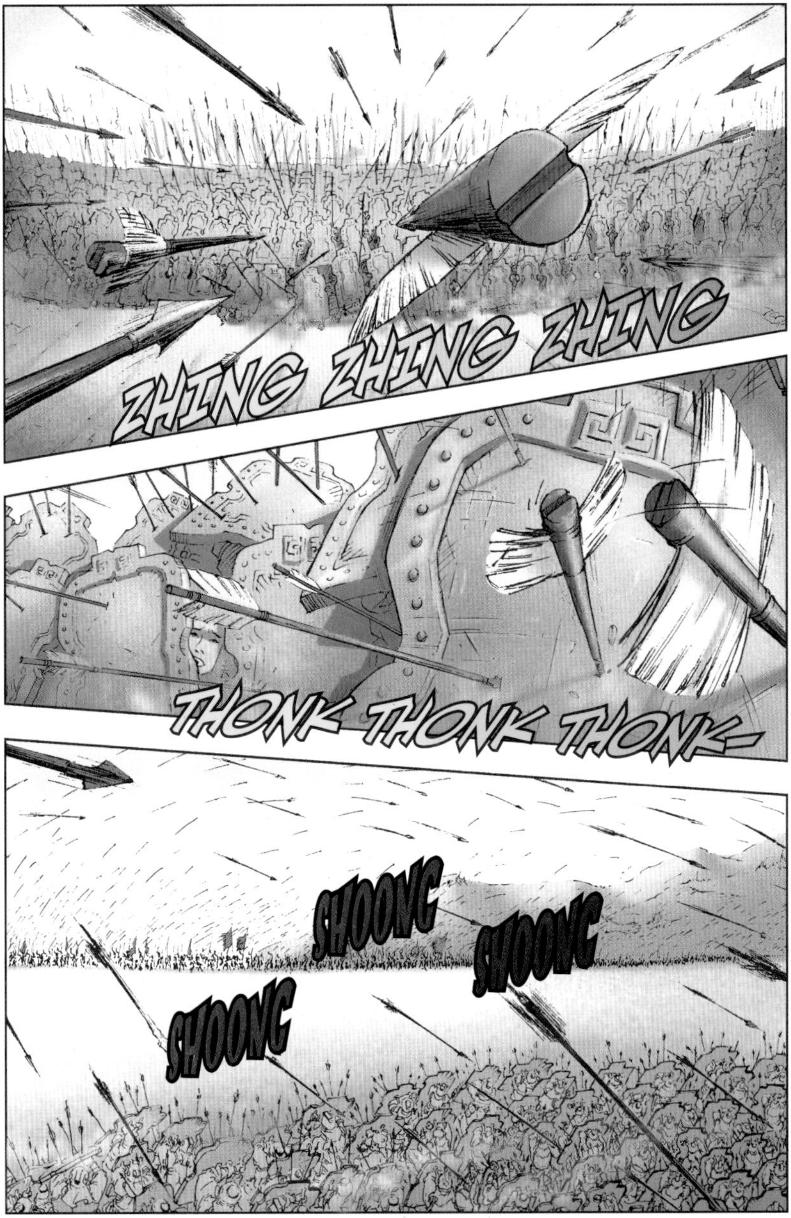
ZHING ZHING ZHING
THONK THONK THONK-
SHOONG
SHOONG
SHOONG

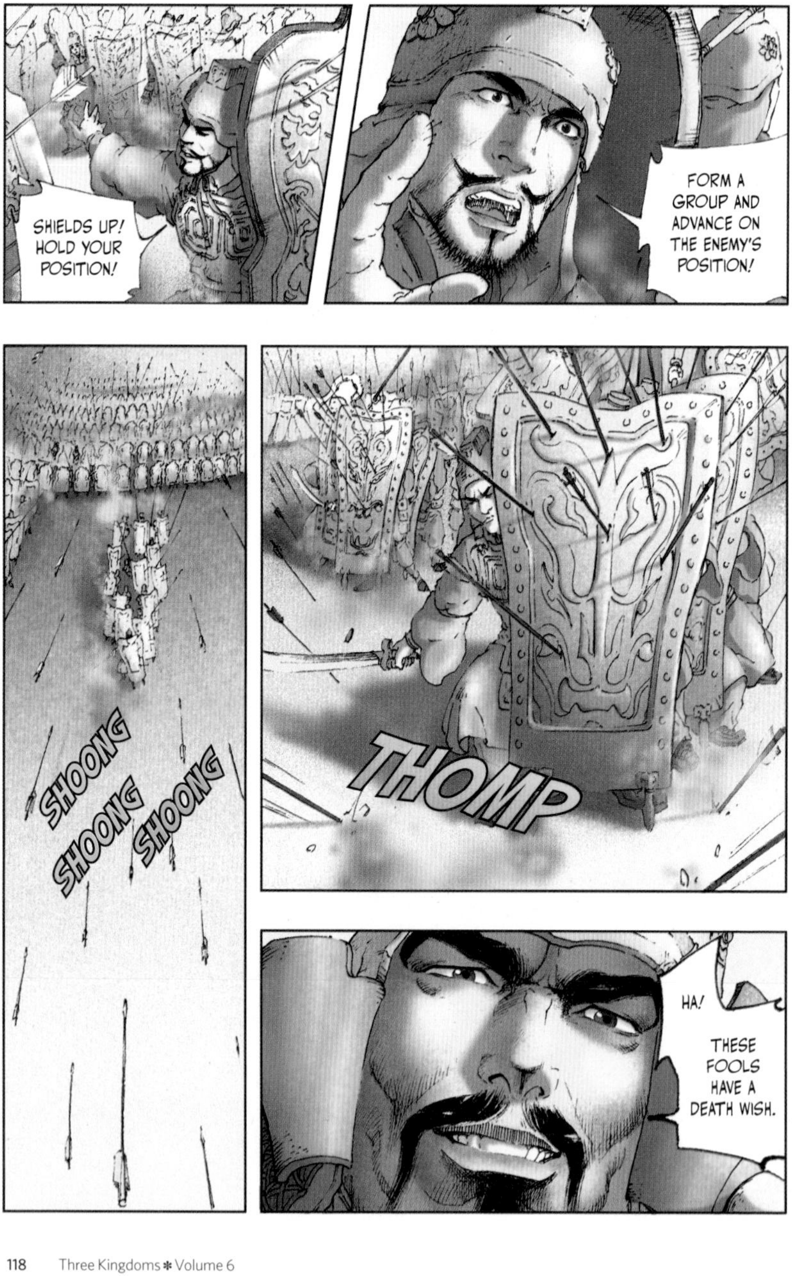
SHIELDS UP! HOLD YOUR POSITION!
FORM A GROUP AND ADVANCE ON THE ENEMY'S POSITION!
SHOONG
SHOONG
SHOONG
THOMP
HA!
THESE FOOLS HAVE A DEATH WISH.

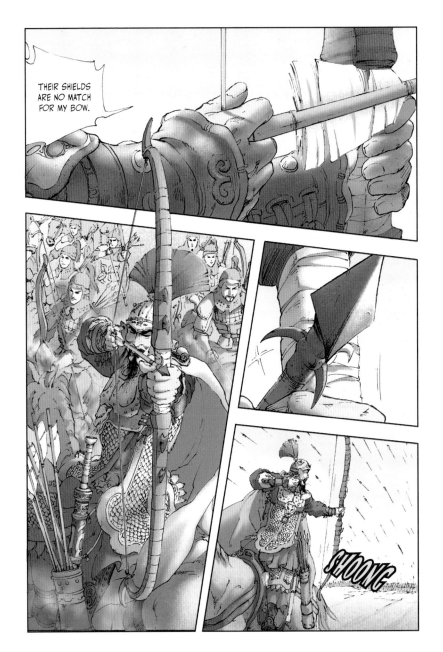

THEIR SHIELDS ARE NO MATCH FOR MY BOW.

SHOONG

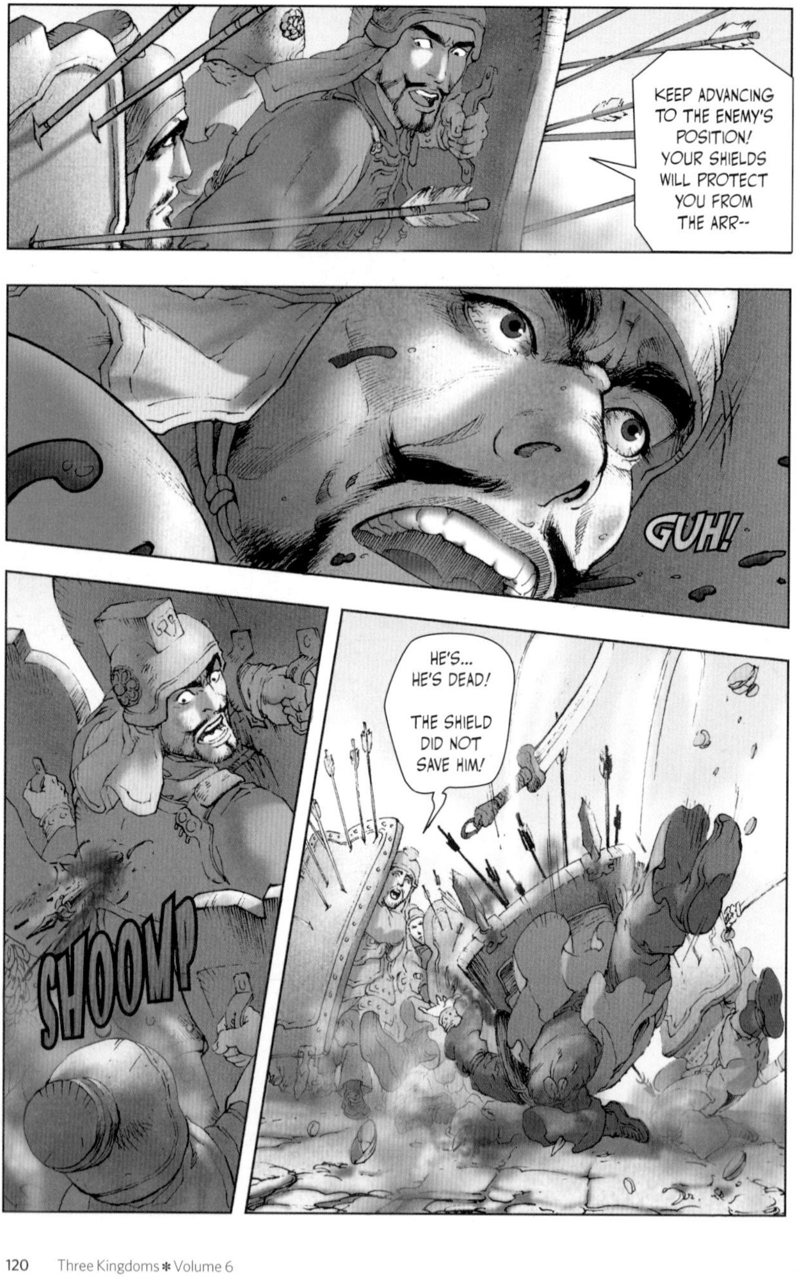
KEEP ADVANCING TO THE ENEMY'S POSITION! YOUR SHIELDS WILL PROTECT YOU FROM THE ARR--
GUH!
SHOOMP
HE'S... HE'S DEAD!
THE SHIELD DID NOT SAVE HIM!

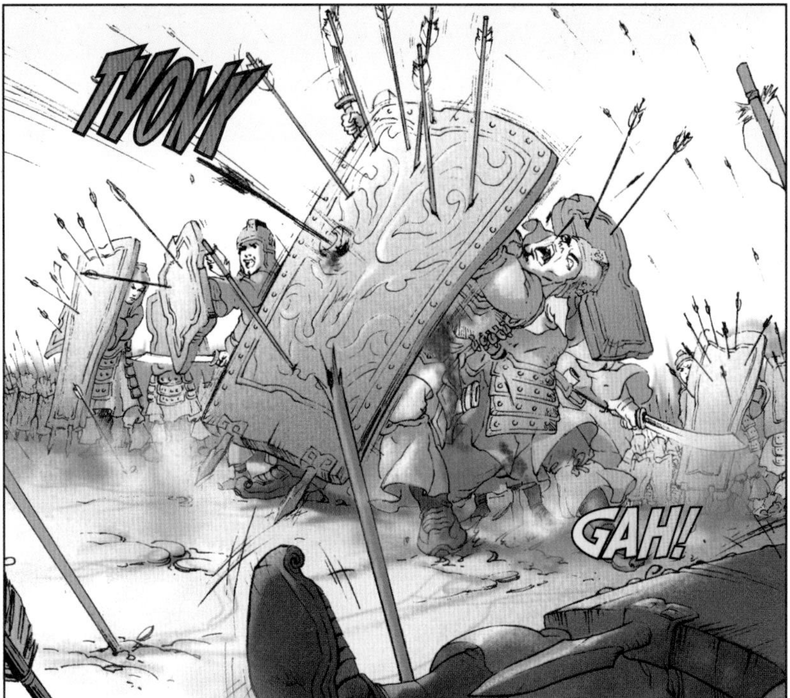
THONK
GAH!

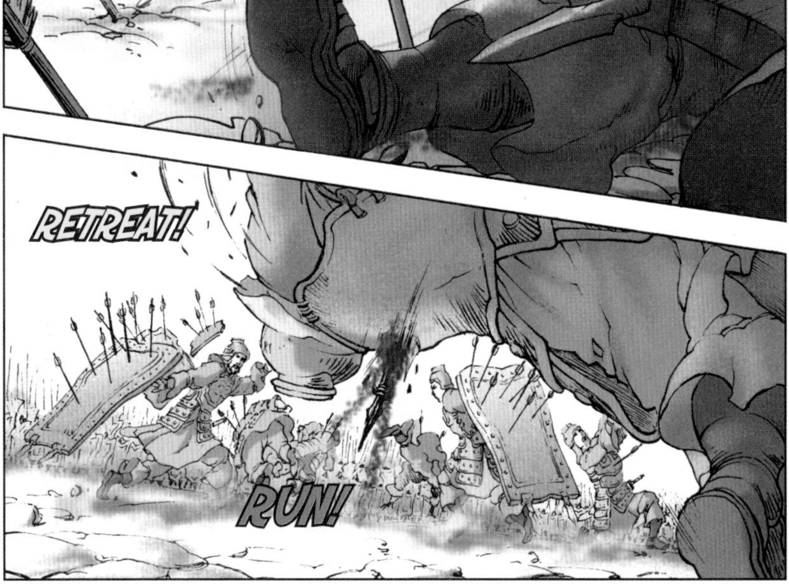
RETREAT!
RUN!

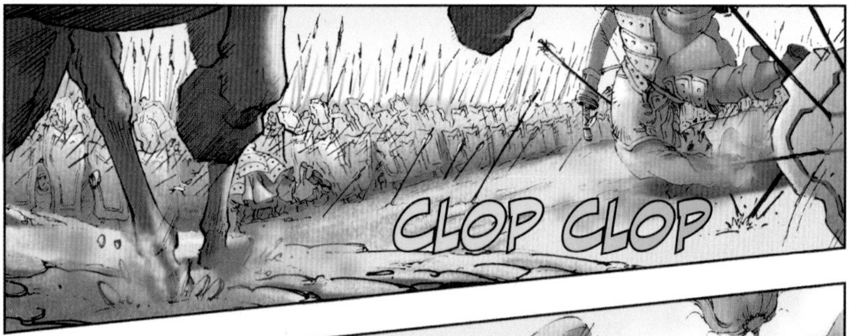
CLOP CLOP

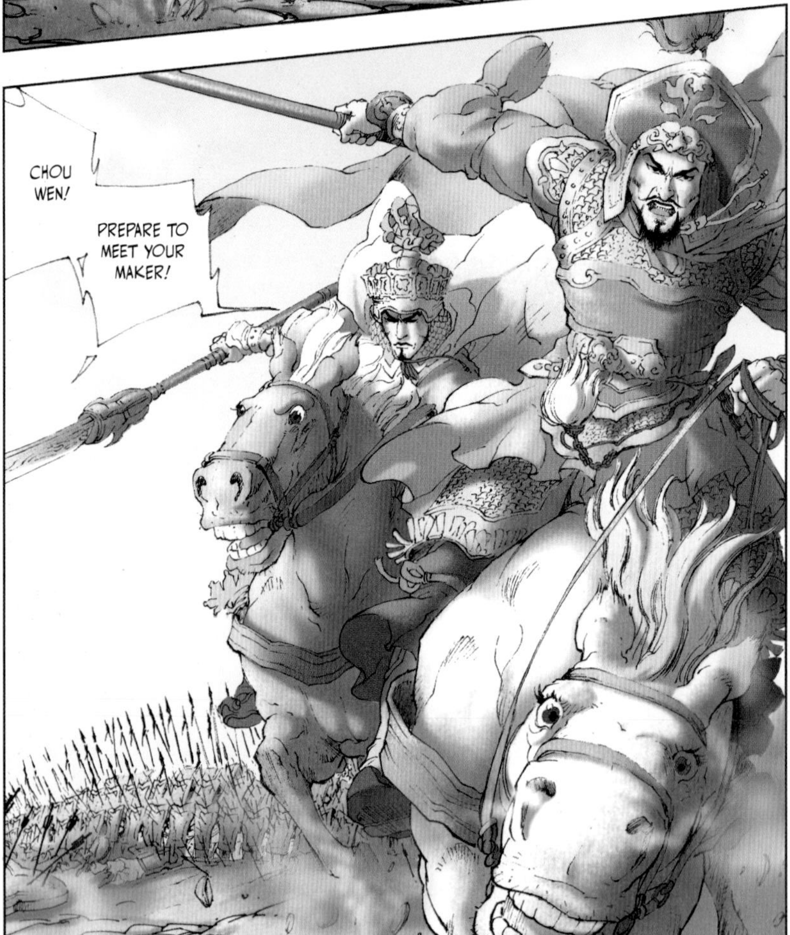
CHOU WEN!
PREPARE TO MEET YOUR MAKER!

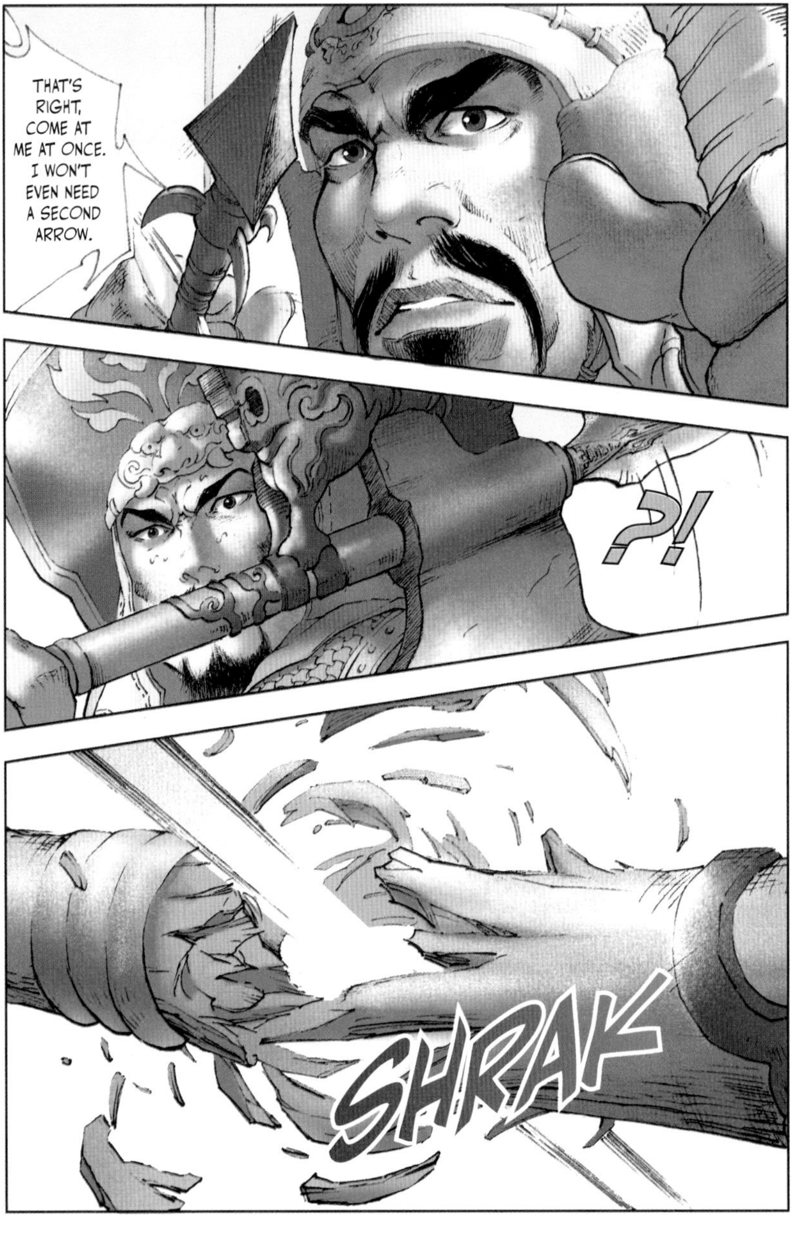
THAT'S RIGHT, COME AT ME AT ONCE. I WON'T EVEN NEED A SECOND ARROW.
?!
SHRAK

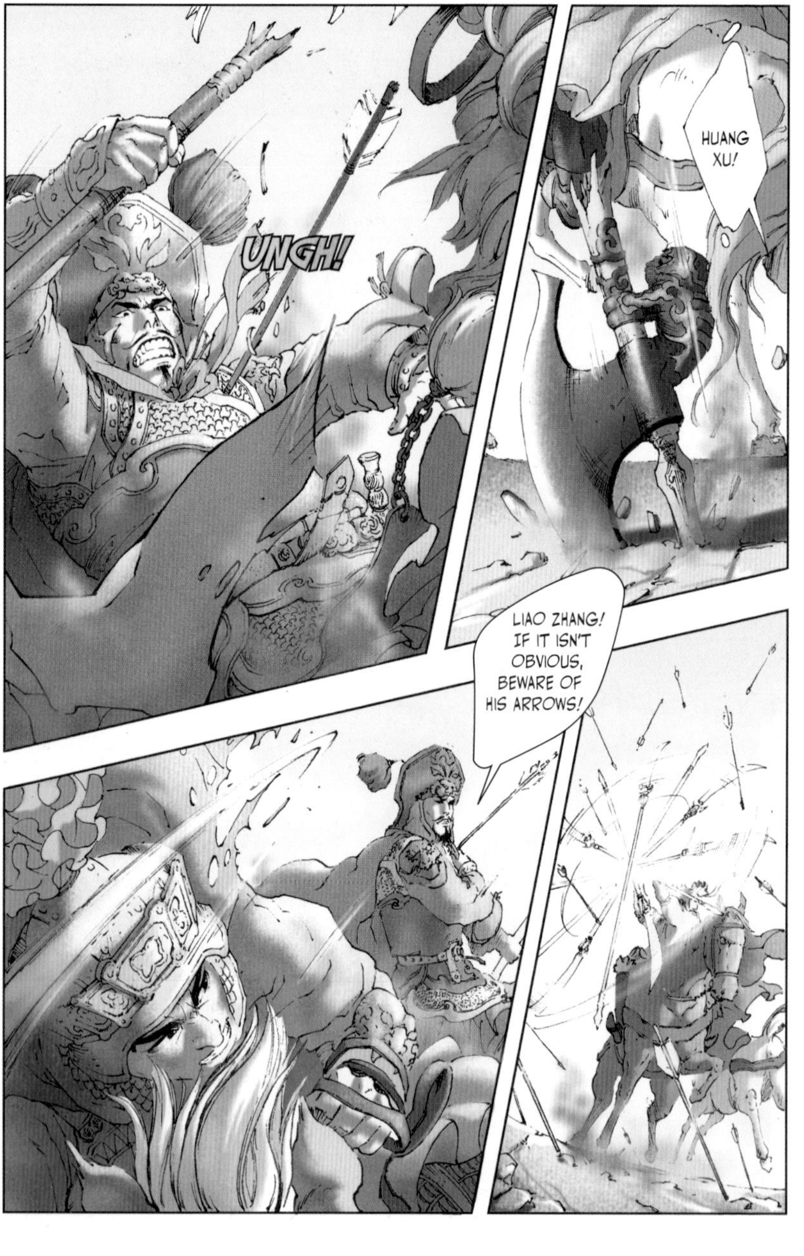
UNGH!
HUANG XU!
LIAO ZHANG! IF IT ISN'T OBVIOUS, BEWARE OF HIS ARROWS!

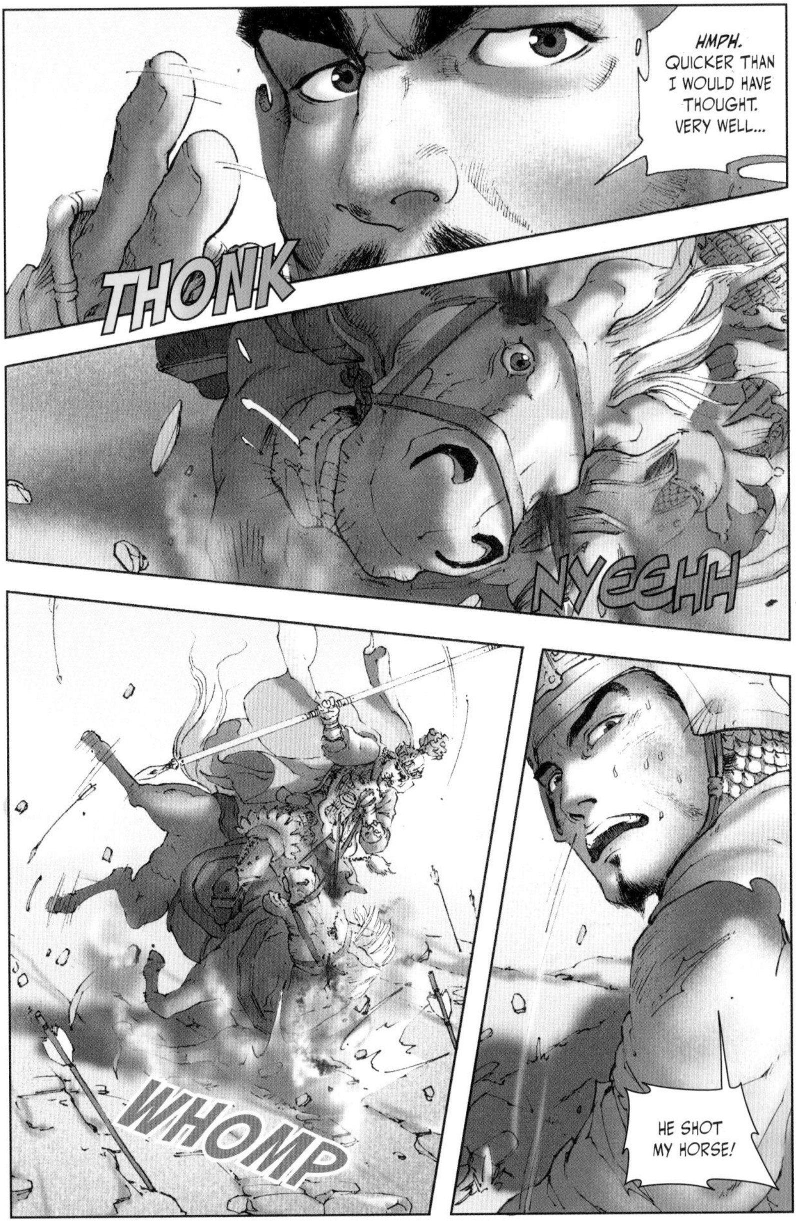
HMPH. QUICKER THAN I WOULD HAVE THOUGHT. VERY WELL...
THONK
NYEEHH
WHOMP
HE SHOT MY HORSE!

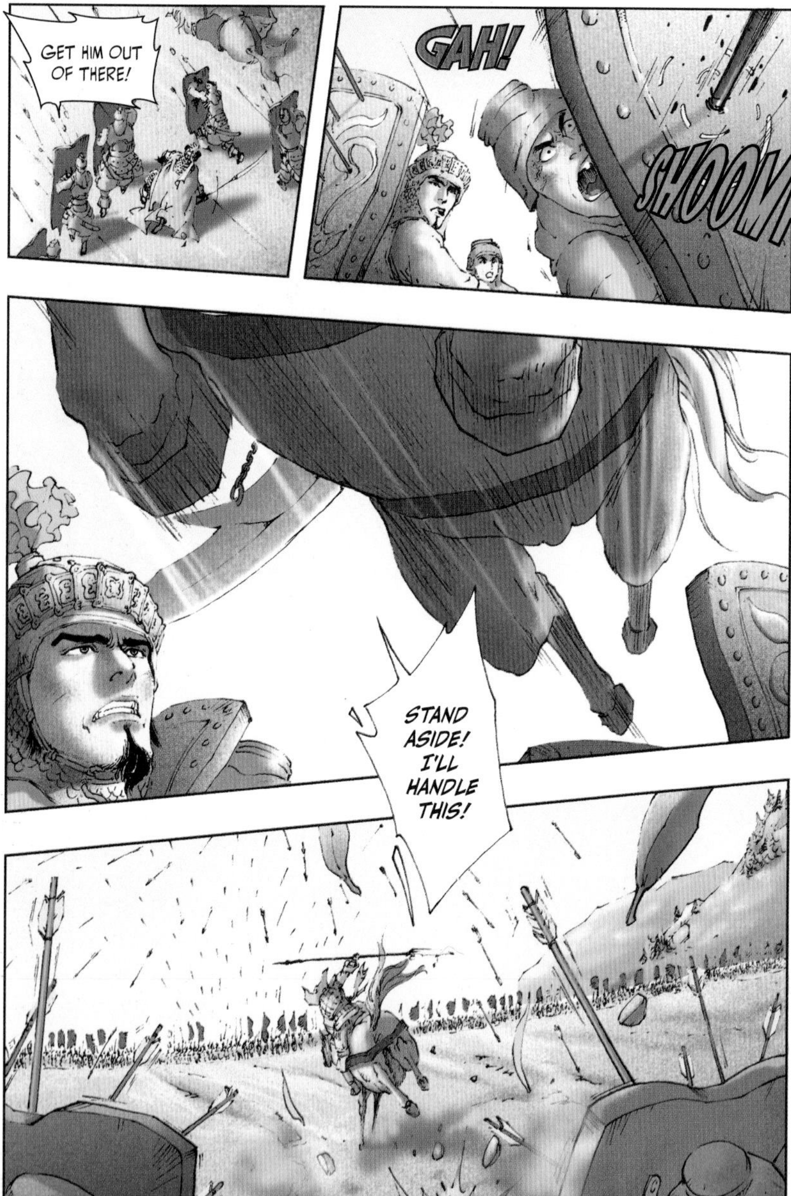
GET HIM OUT OF THERE!
GAH!
SHOOMP
STAND ASIDE! I'LL HANDLE THIS!

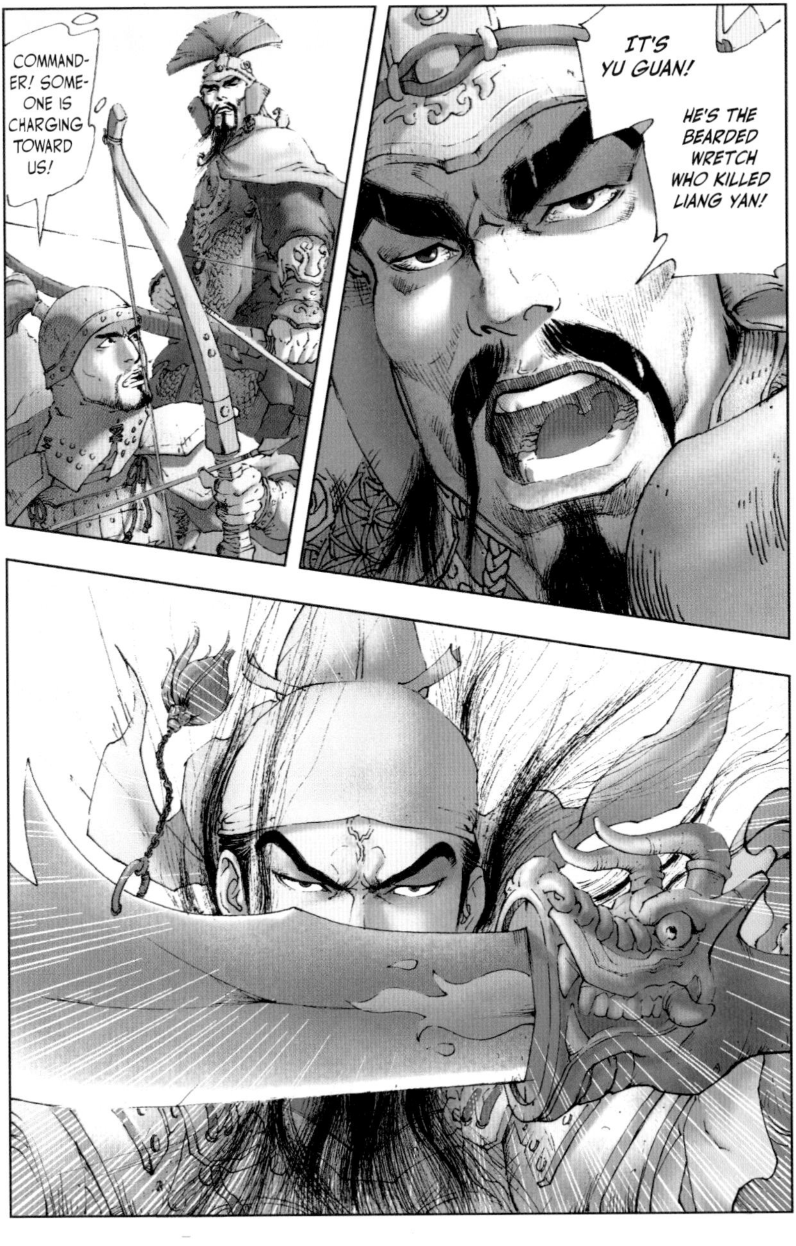
COMMANDER! SOMEONE IS CHARGING TOWARD US!
IT'S YU GUAN!
HE'S THE BEARDED WRETCH WHO KILLED LIANG YAN!

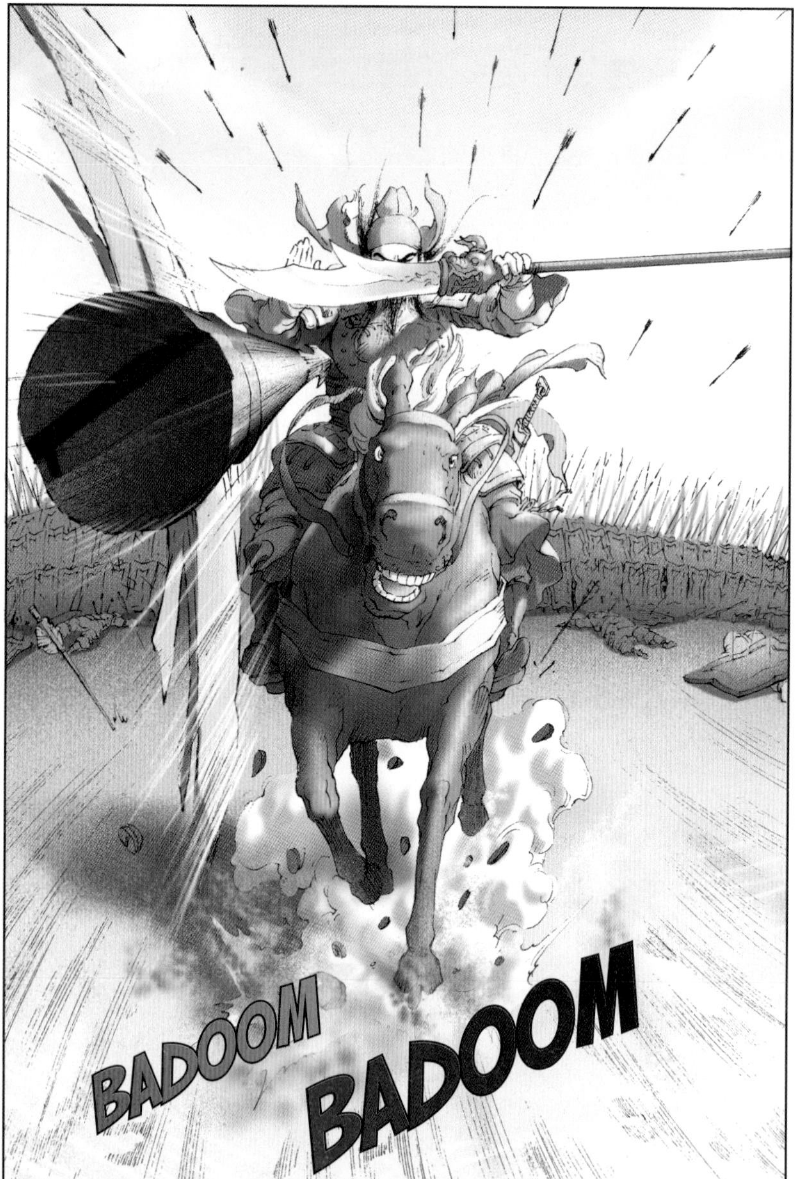
BADOOM
BADOOM

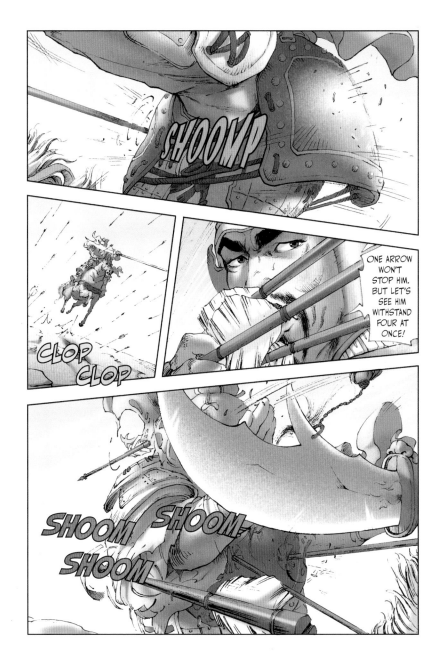

SHOOMP

CLOP
CLOP

ONE ARROW WON'T STOP HIM. BUT LET'S SEE HIM WITHSTAND FOUR AT ONCE!

SHOOM SHOOM
SHOOM

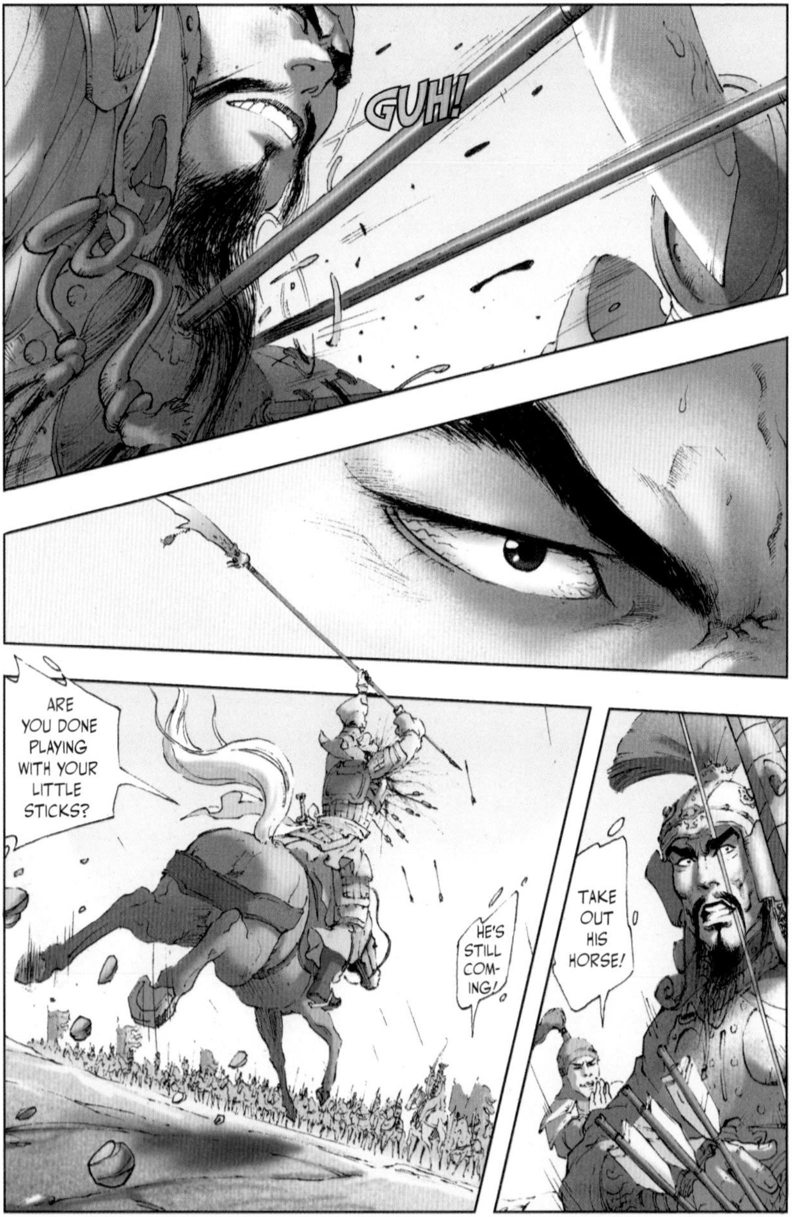
GUH!
ARE YOU DONE PLAYING WITH YOUR LITTLE STICKS?
HE'S STILL COM-ING!
TAKE OUT HIS HORSE!

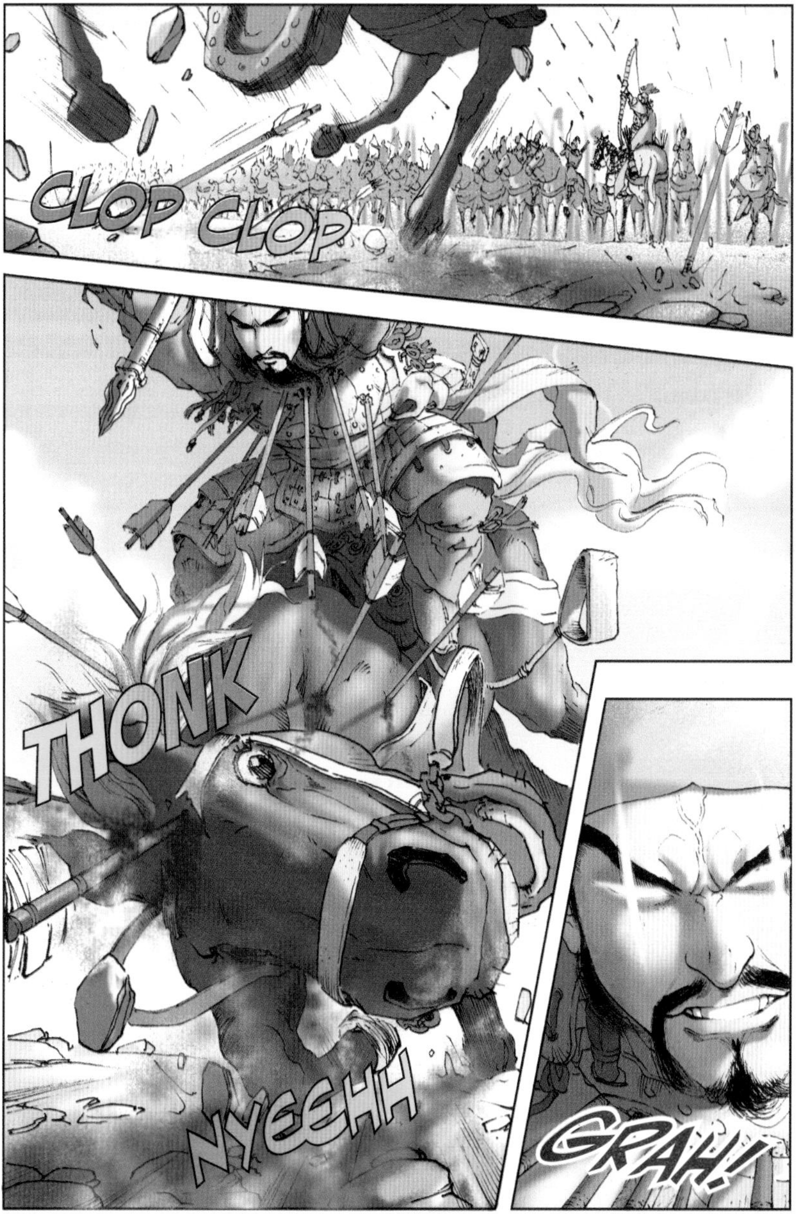
CLOP CLOP
THONK
NYEEHH
GRAH!

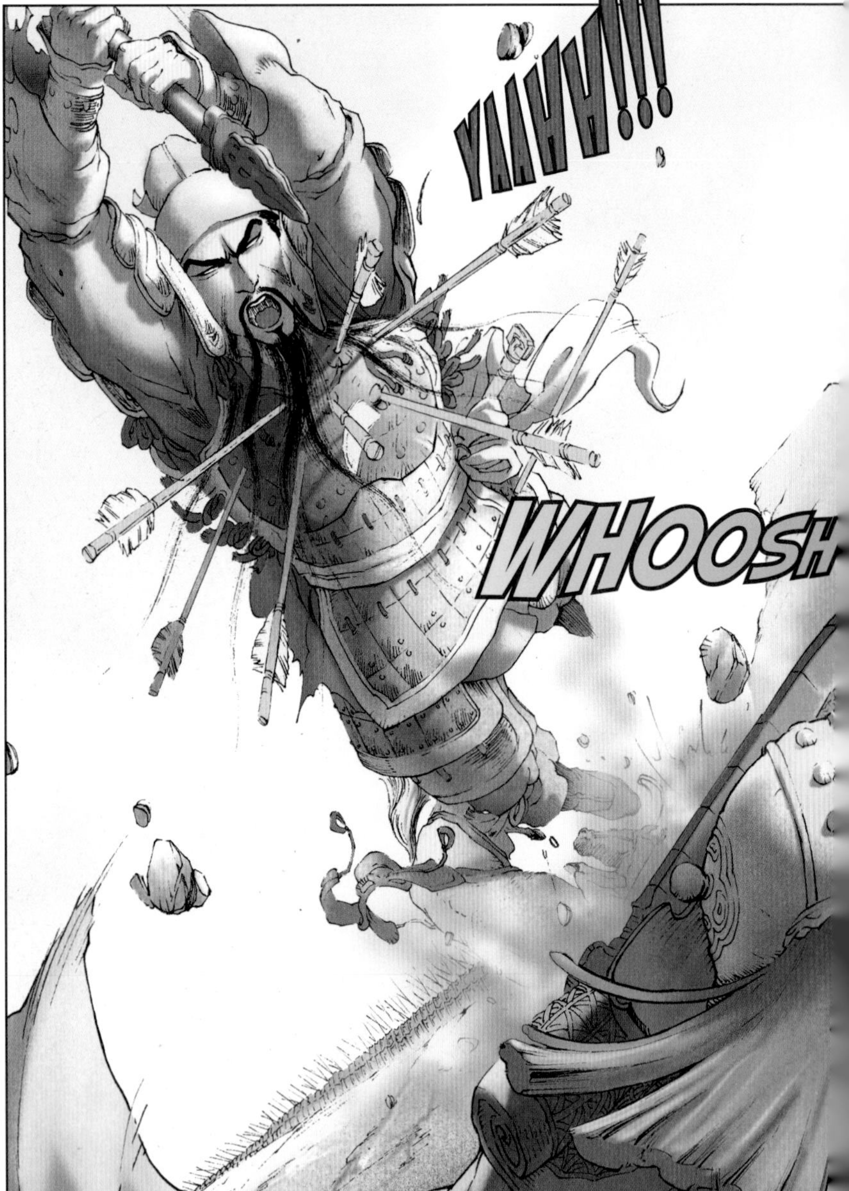
YAAAHH!!!
WHOOSH

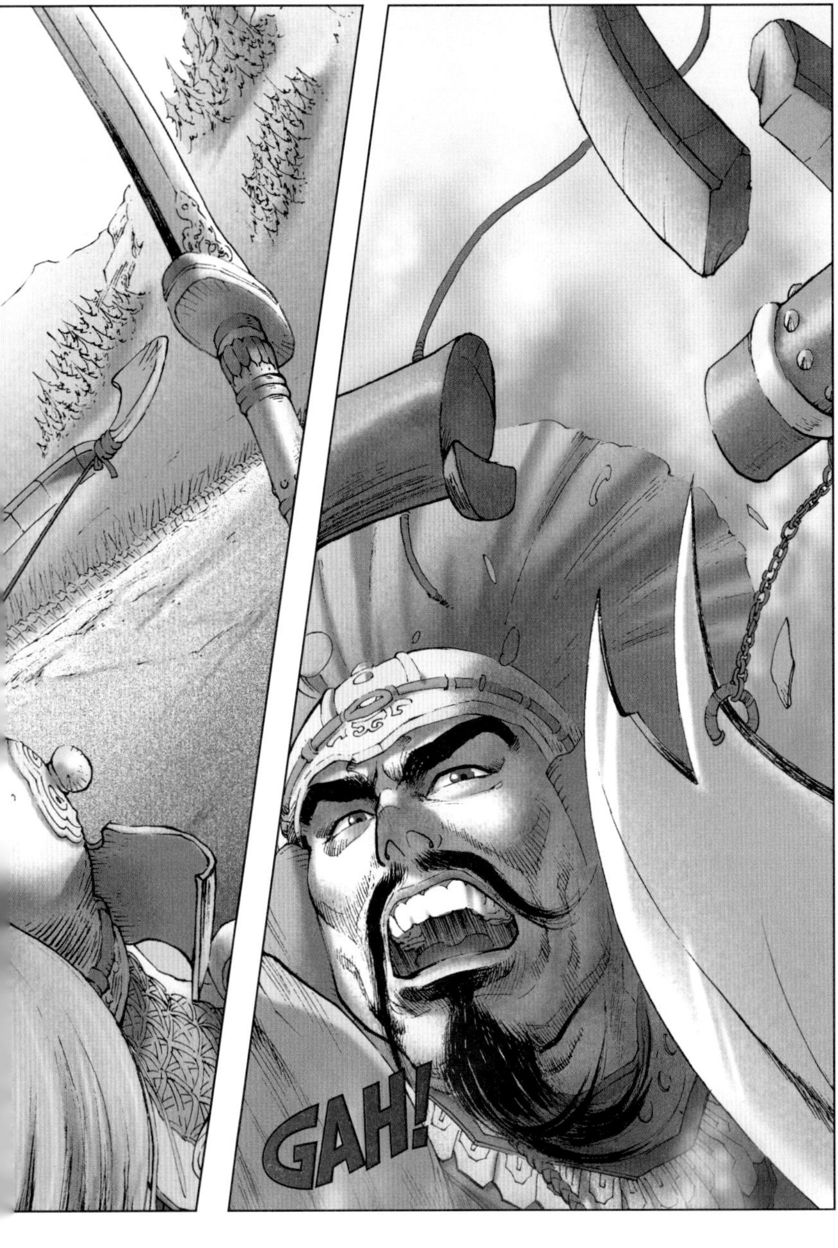
GAH!

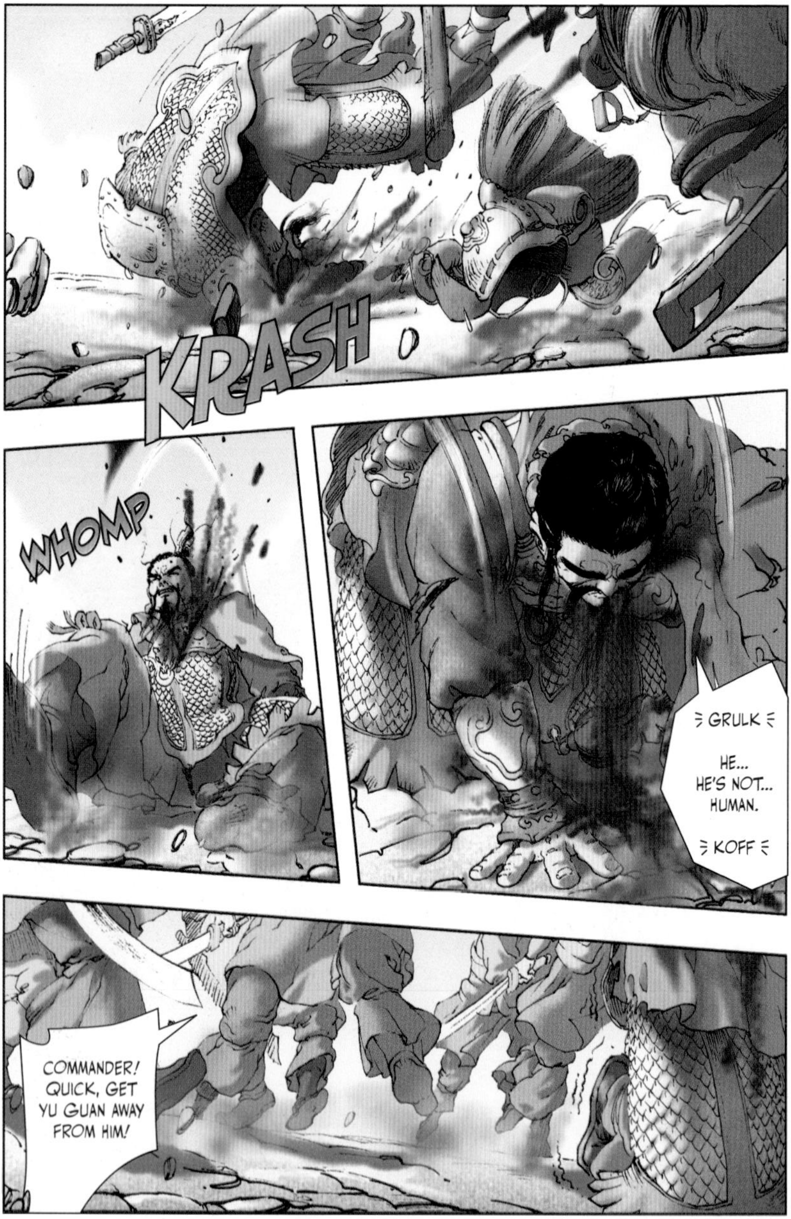
KRASH
WHOMP
≡ GRULK ≡
HE... HE'S NOT... HUMAN.
≡ KOFF ≡
COMMANDER! QUICK, GET YU GUAN AWAY FROM HIM!

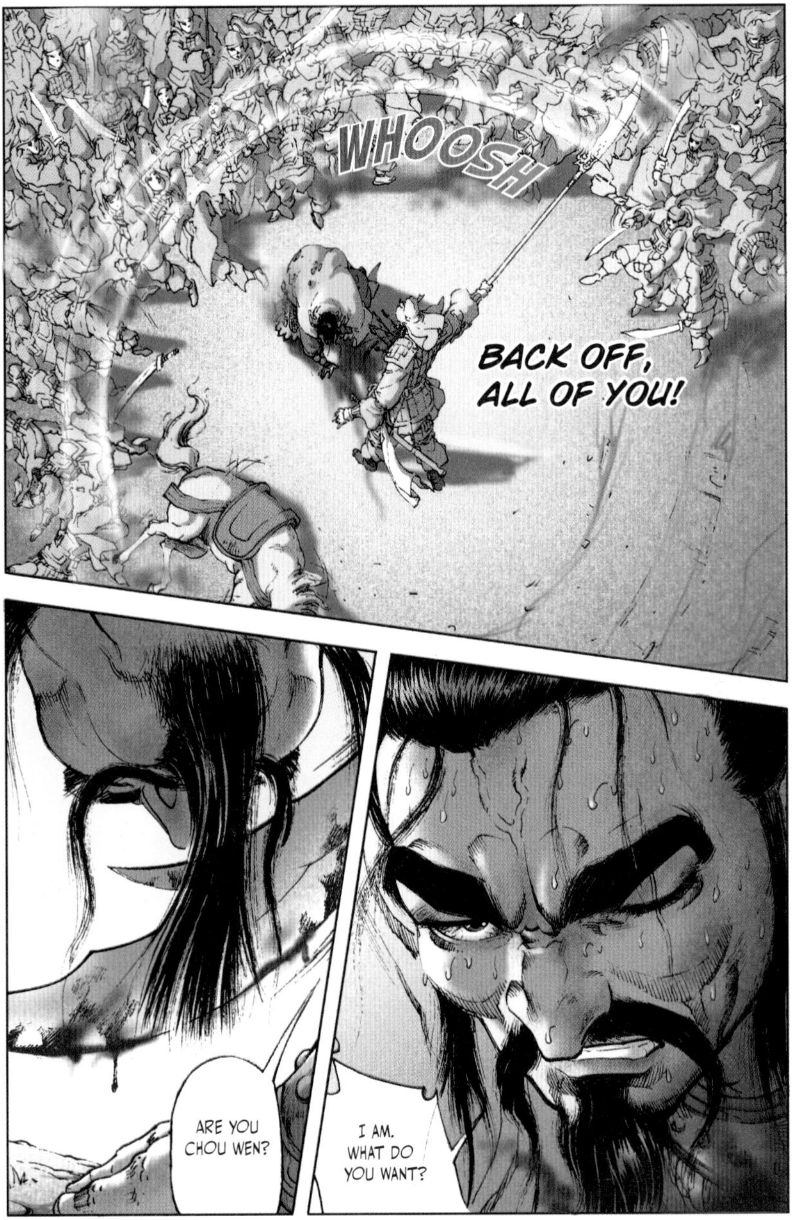
WHOOSH
BACK OFF, ALL OF YOU!
ARE YOU CHOU WEN?
I AM. WHAT DO YOU WANT?

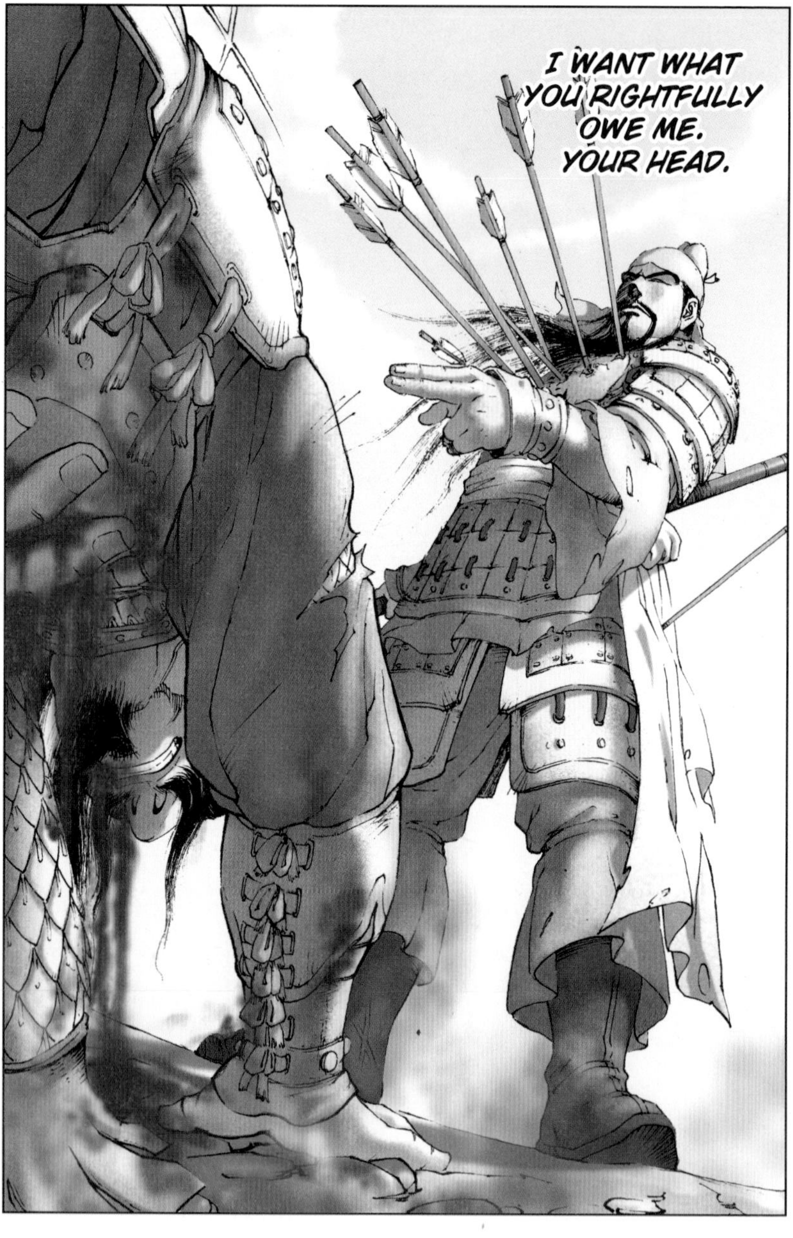
I WANT WHAT YOU RIGHTFULLY OWE ME. YOUR HEAD.

Chou Wen

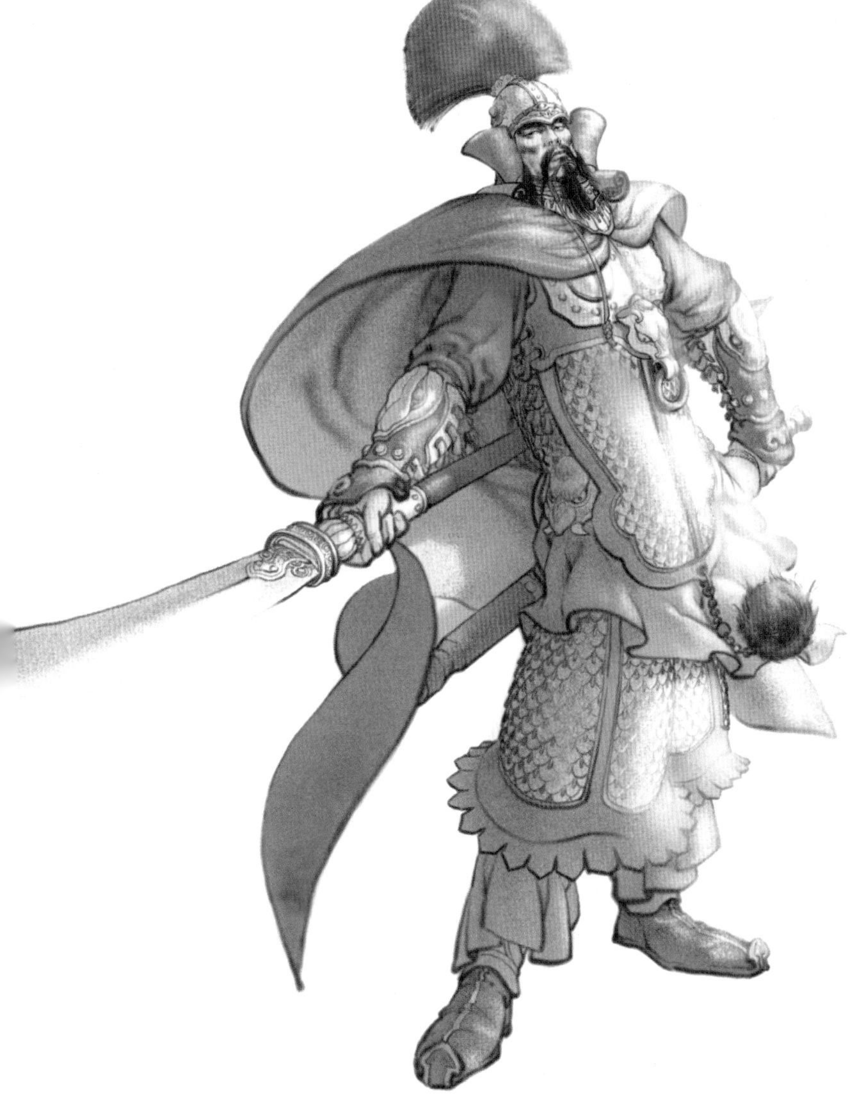

Chapter 4

Yu Guan's Long Journey Home [200 AD]

Summary

When Shao Yuan learns that Chou Wen has been killed, he confronts Bei Liu about his failure to win over Yu Guan. Bei Liu acknowledges the failure and is willing to accept Shao Yuan's punishment, but Shao Yuan declines to punish him. Time is running out, and they need to reach Yu Guan.

Gan Sun takes it upon himself to try to infiltrate Cao Cao's camp and is purposely caught as a spy. He is brought before Yu Guan, who recognizes Gan Sun and is elated to hear that Bei Liu is alive and well in Shao Yuan's camp. True to his word, Yu Guan writes to Cao Cao to explain his decision and departs to find Bei Liu. Cao Cao is not pleased with the development, but he finds much to admire in Yu Guan's steadfast adherence to his principles of loyalty, so he tells his counselors he will not prevent Yu Guan from leaving. Cao Cao does not, however, inform any of the several checkpoint guards Yu Guan will encounter of his decision, and leaves Yu Guan in the hands of fate.

As he makes his way back to his sworn brother, Yu Guan thinks back on the time they took their pledge, and vows to fulfill his oath to his brother. By the time he reaches the final river crossing that leads to Bei Liu, Yu Guan has met and beheaded five checkpoint guards. One final guard remains in Yu Guan's path, but many have stood between him and fulfilling his oath; none have lived to speak of it.

Yu Guan's Quest to Reunite with Bei Liu

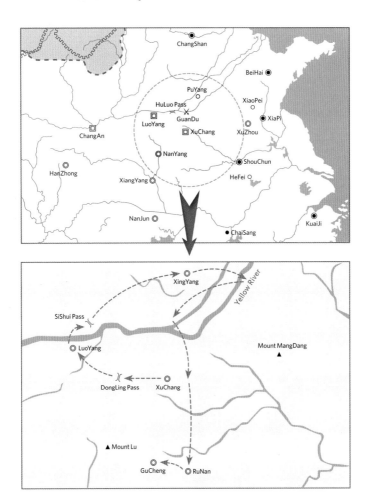

ChangShan
BeiHai
PuYang
XiaoPei
HuLuo Pass
GuanDu
XiaPi
LuoYang
XuChang
XuZhou
ChangAn
NanYang
ShouChun
HanZhong
XiangYang
HeFei
NanJun
KuaiJi
ChaiSang
XingYang
Yellow River
SiShui Pass
LuoYang
Mount MangDang
DongLing Pass
XuChang
Mount Lu
GuCheng
RuNan

● Yu Guan's quest to reunite with his brothers wasn't given Cao Cao's full blessing, as he did not alert his checkpoint guards to Yu Guan's passage. As a result, Yu Guan met and fought, Xu Kong in DongLing Pass, Tan Meng and Fu Han in LuoYang, Xi Bian in SiShui Pass, Zhi Wang in XingYang, and Ji Chen at the Yellow River.

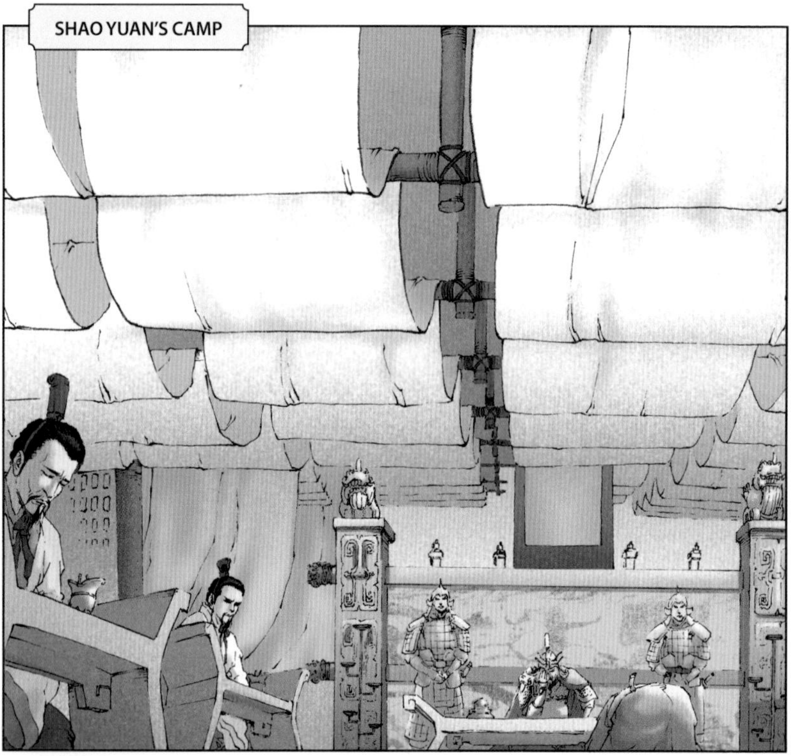
SHAO YUAN'S CAMP

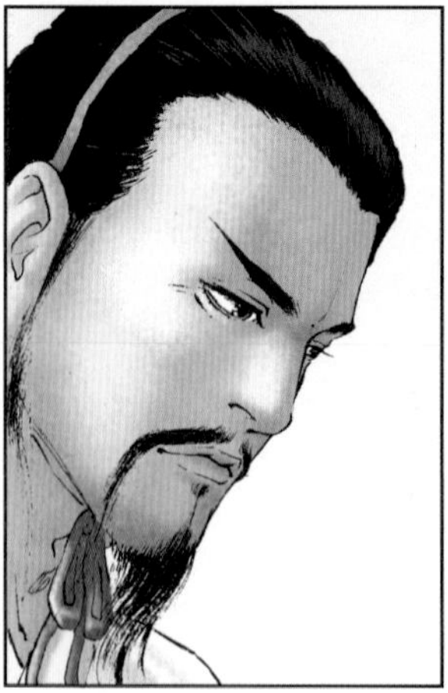

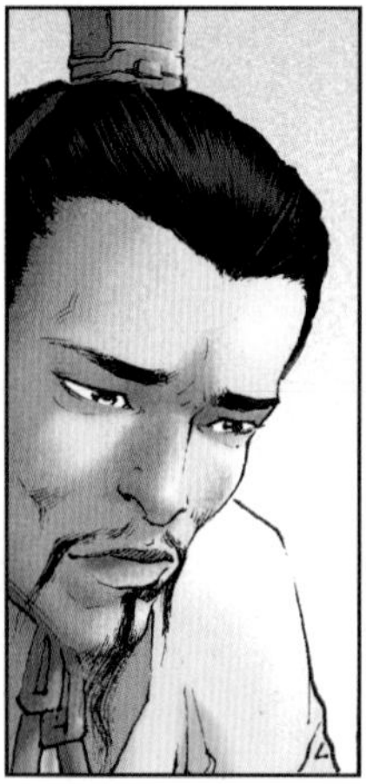

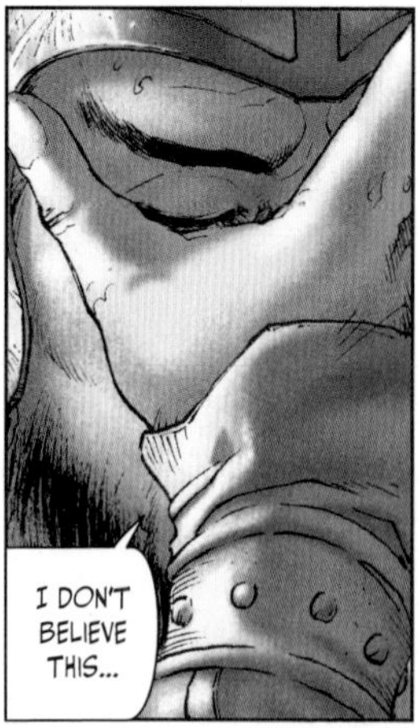
I DON'T BELIEVE THIS...

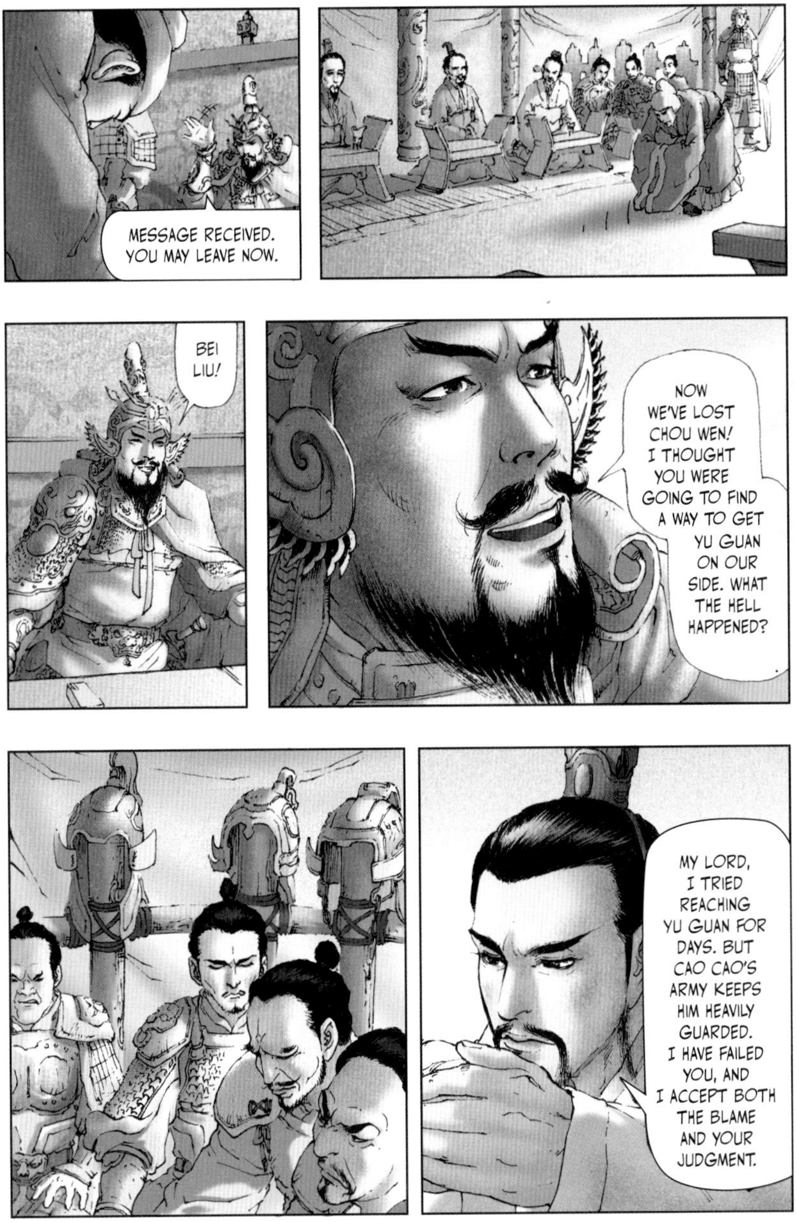
MESSAGE RECEIVED. YOU MAY LEAVE NOW.
BEI LIU!
NOW WE'VE LOST CHOU WEN! I THOUGHT YOU WERE GOING TO FIND A WAY TO GET YU GUAN ON OUR SIDE. WHAT THE HELL HAPPENED?
MY LORD, I TRIED REACHING YU GUAN FOR DAYS. BUT CAO CAO'S ARMY KEEPS HIM HEAVILY GUARDED. I HAVE FAILED YOU, AND I ACCEPT BOTH THE BLAME AND YOUR JUDGMENT.

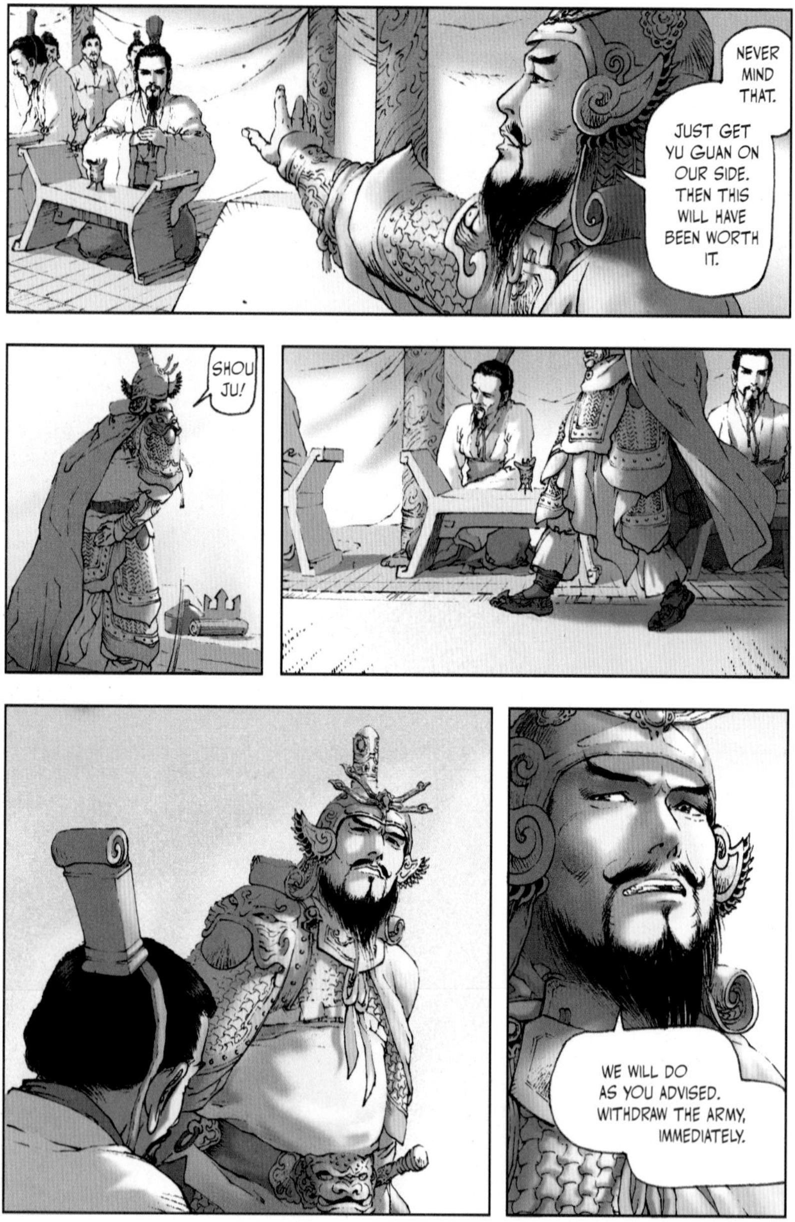
NEVER MIND THAT.
JUST GET YU GUAN ON OUR SIDE. THEN THIS WILL HAVE BEEN WORTH IT.
SHOU JU!
WE WILL DO AS YOU ADVISED. WITHDRAW THE ARMY, IMMEDIATELY.

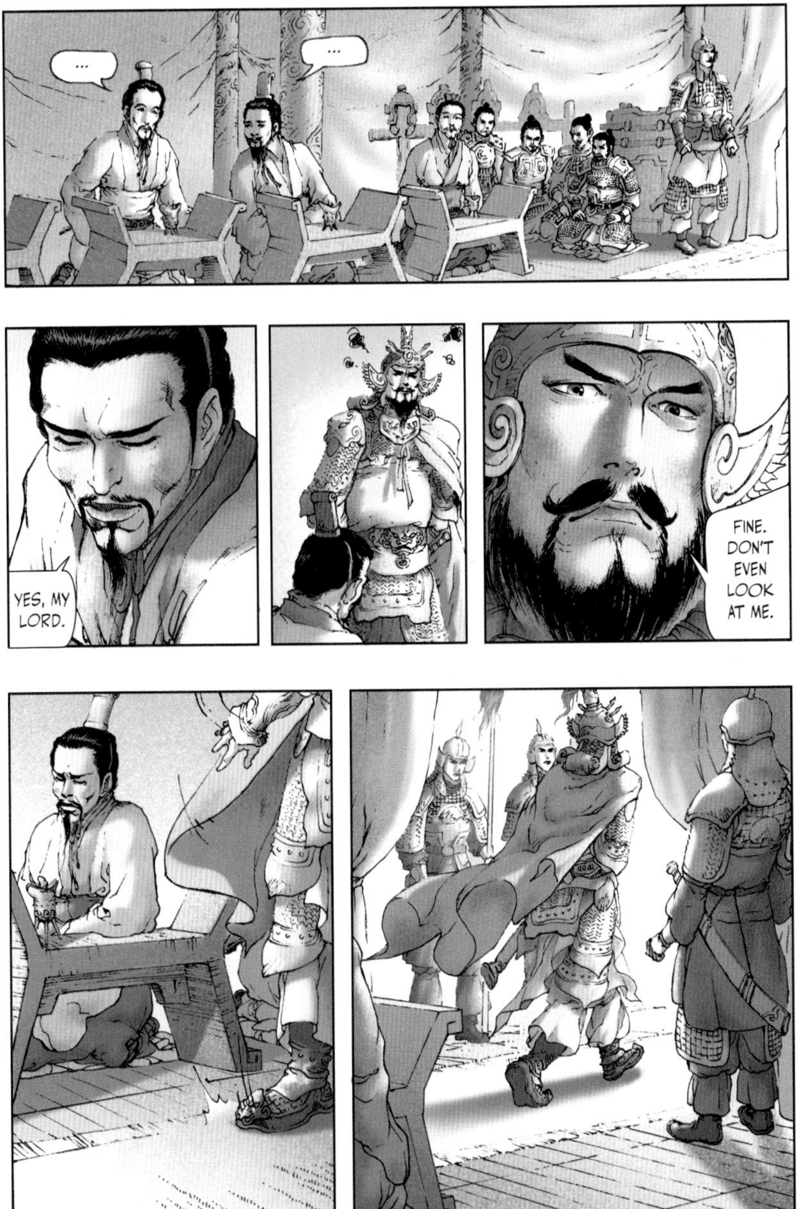
...
...
YES, MY LORD.
FINE. DON'T EVEN LOOK AT ME.

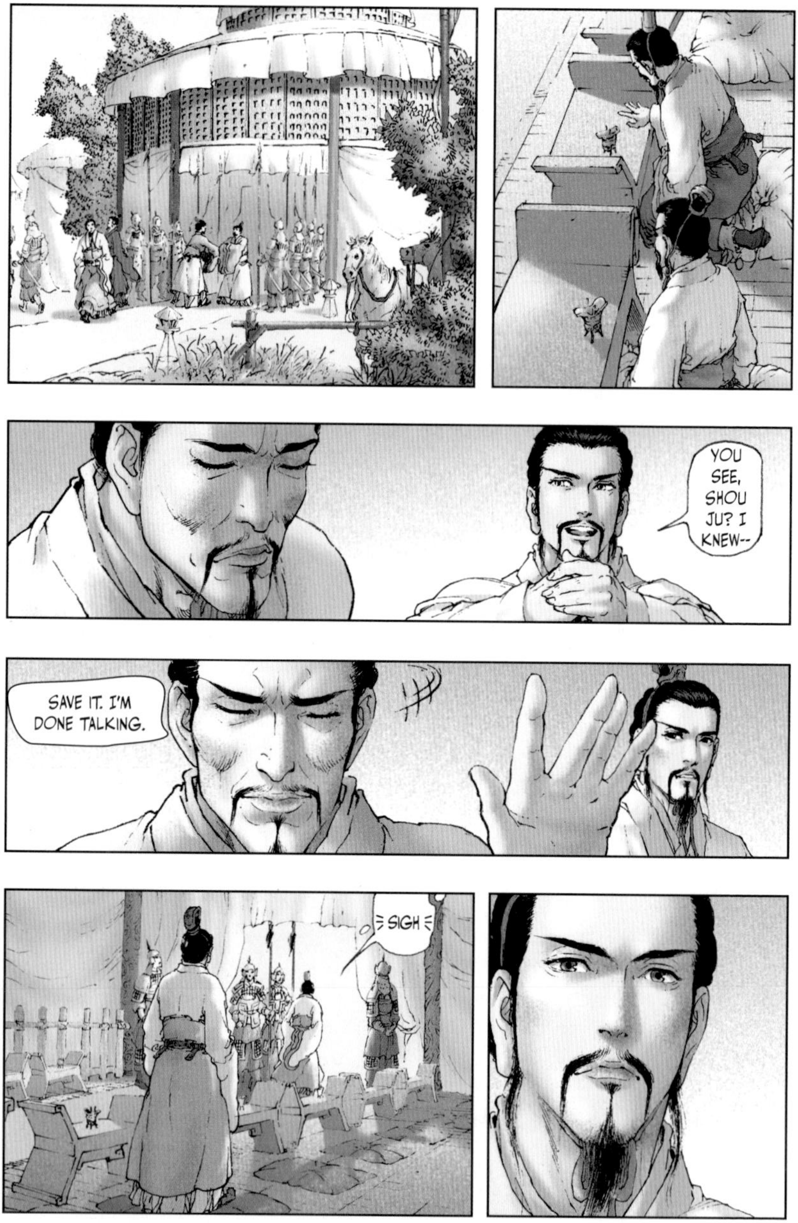
YOU SEE, SHOU JU? I KNEW--
SAVE IT. I'M DONE TALKING.
SIGH

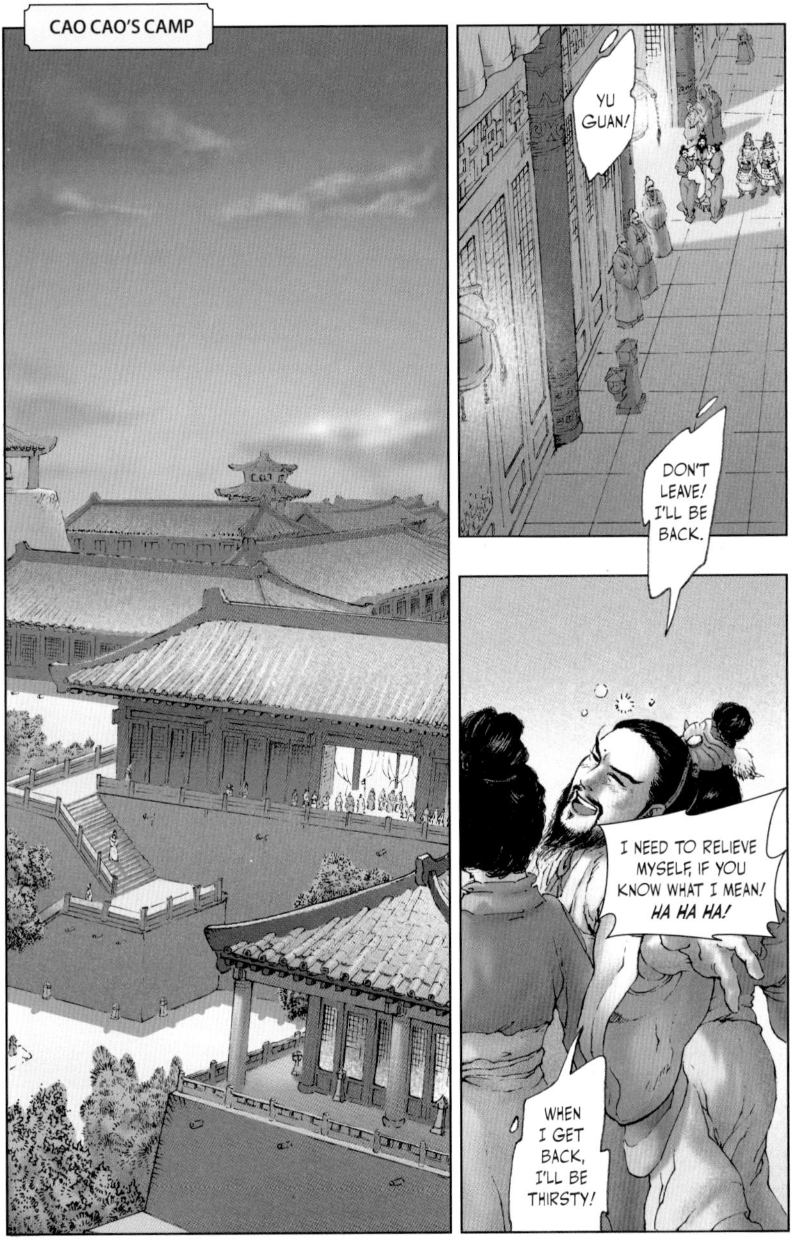
CAO CAO'S CAMP
YU GUAN!
DON'T LEAVE! I'LL BE BACK.
I NEED TO RELIEVE MYSELF, IF YOU KNOW WHAT I MEAN! HA HA HA!
WHEN I GET BACK, I'LL BE THIRSTY!

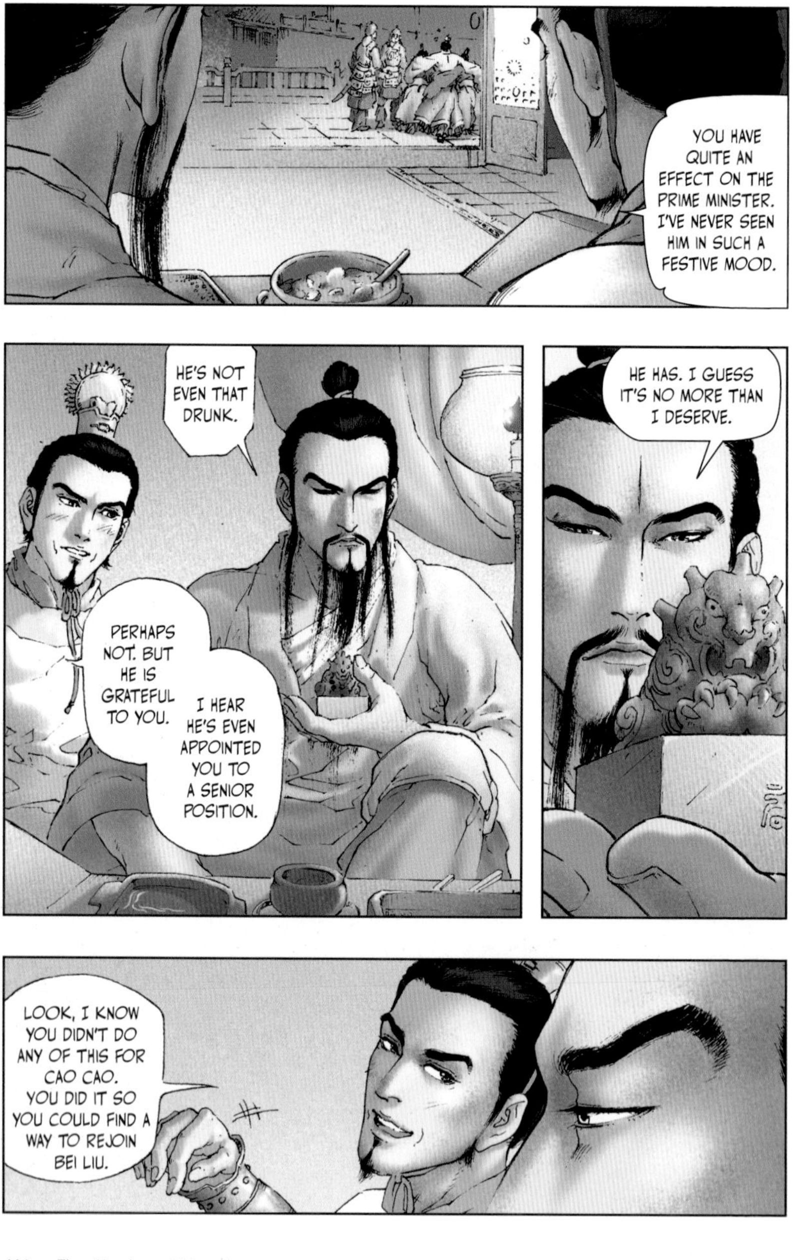
YOU HAVE QUITE AN EFFECT ON THE PRIME MINISTER. I'VE NEVER SEEN HIM IN SUCH A FESTIVE MOOD.
HE'S NOT EVEN THAT DRUNK.
PERHAPS NOT. BUT HE IS GRATEFUL TO YOU.
I HEAR HE'S EVEN APPOINTED YOU TO A SENIOR POSITION.
HE HAS. I GUESS IT'S NO MORE THAN I DESERVE.
LOOK, I KNOW YOU DIDN'T DO ANY OF THIS FOR CAO CAO. YOU DID IT SO YOU COULD FIND A WAY TO REJOIN BEI LIU.

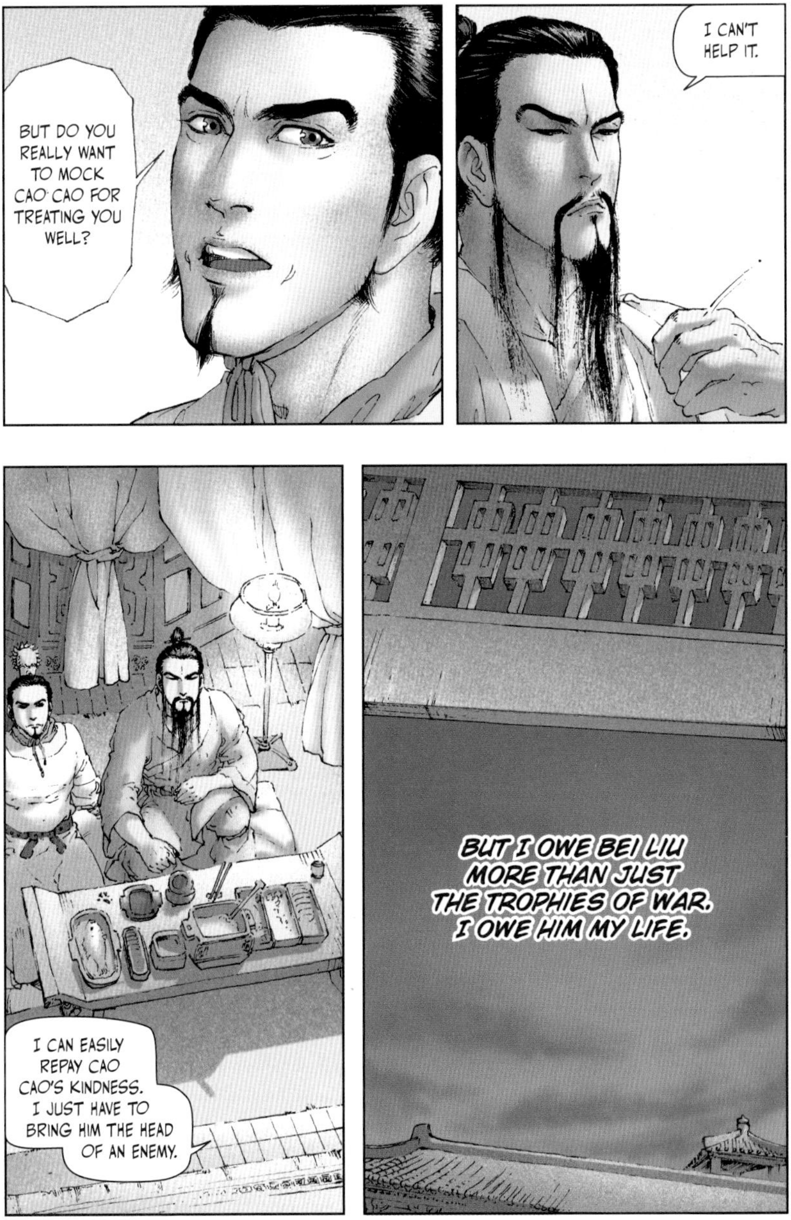
BUT DO YOU REALLY WANT TO MOCK CAO CAO FOR TREATING YOU WELL?
I CAN'T HELP IT.
I CAN EASILY REPAY CAO CAO'S KINDNESS. I JUST HAVE TO BRING HIM THE HEAD OF AN ENEMY.
BUT I OWE BEI LIU MORE THAN JUST THE TROPHIES OF WAR. I OWE HIM MY LIFE.

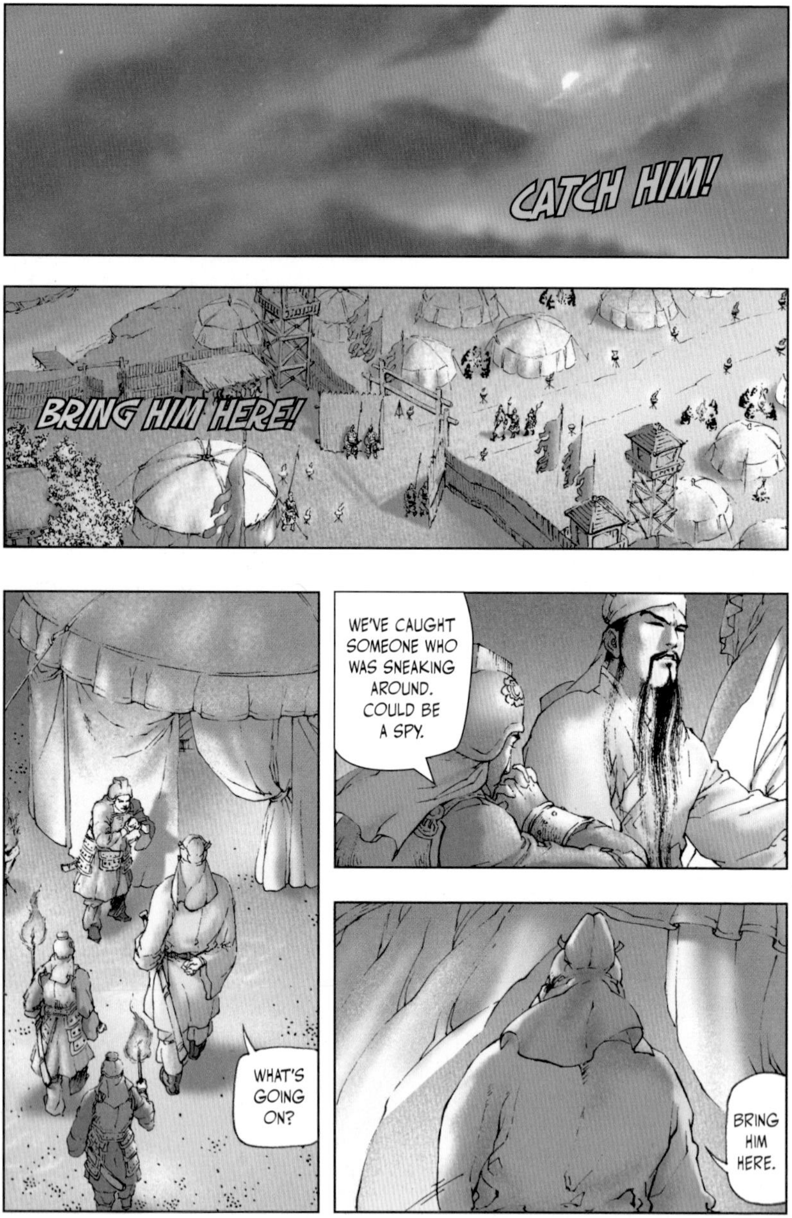
CATCH HIM!
BRING HIM HERE!
WE'VE CAUGHT SOMEONE WHO WAS SNEAKING AROUND. COULD BE A SPY.
WHAT'S GOING ON?
BRING HIM HERE.

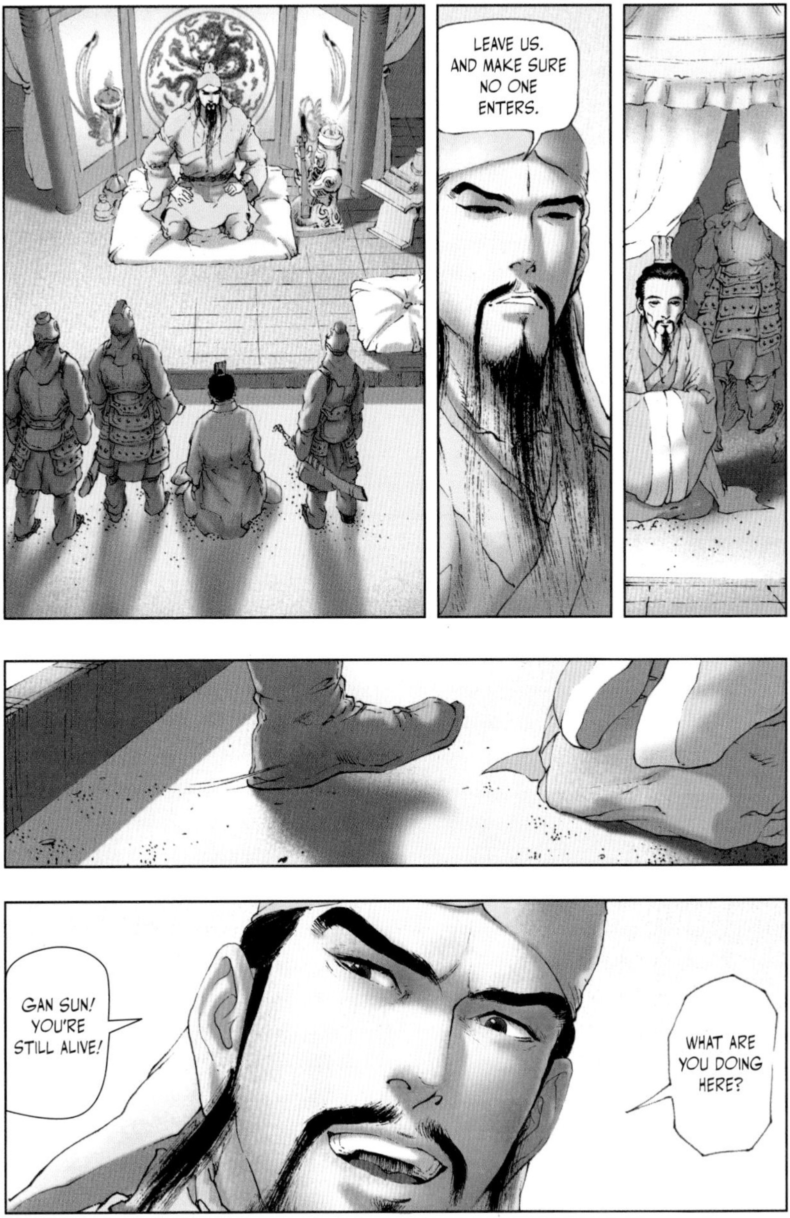
LEAVE US. AND MAKE SURE NO ONE ENTERS.
GAN SUN! YOU'RE STILL ALIVE!
WHAT ARE YOU DOING HERE?

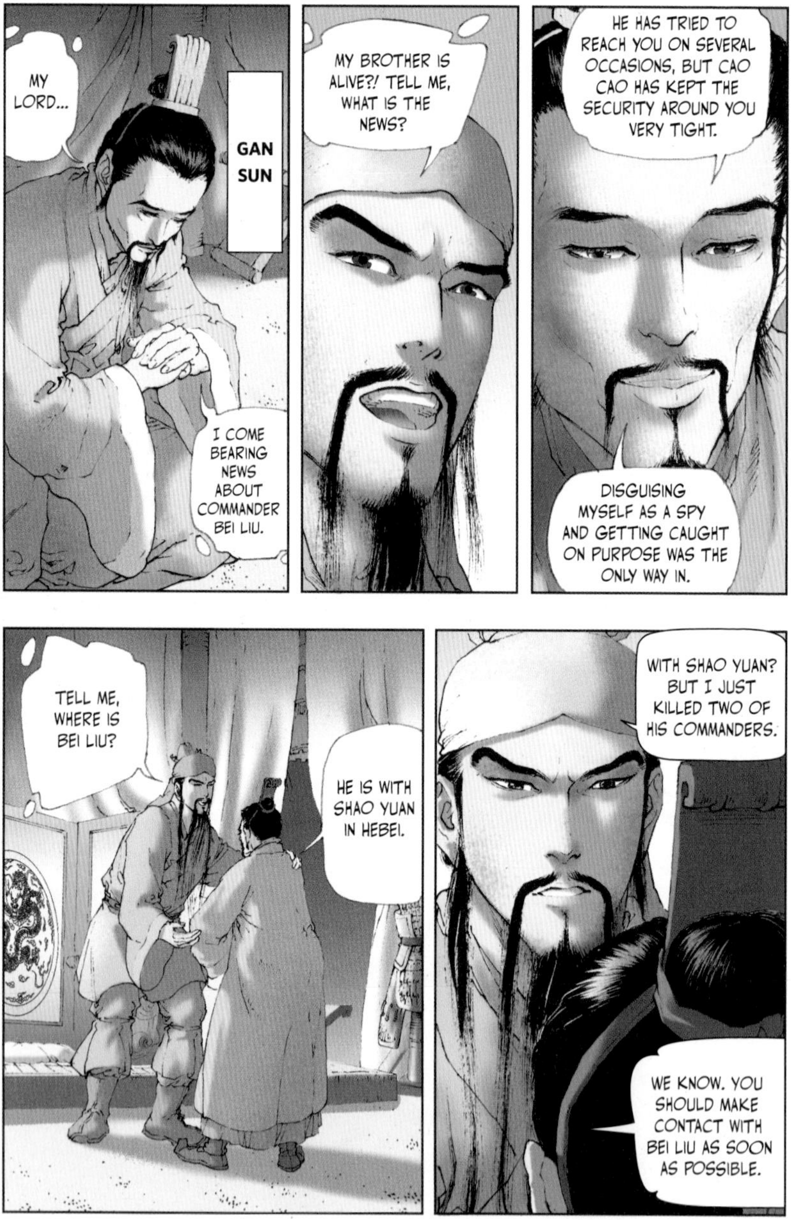
MY LORD...
GAN SUN
I COME BEARING NEWS ABOUT COMMANDER BEI LIU.
MY BROTHER IS ALIVE?! TELL ME, WHAT IS THE NEWS?
HE HAS TRIED TO REACH YOU ON SEVERAL OCCASIONS, BUT CAO CAO HAS KEPT THE SECURITY AROUND YOU VERY TIGHT.
DISGUISING MYSELF AS A SPY AND GETTING CAUGHT ON PURPOSE WAS THE ONLY WAY IN.
TELL ME, WHERE IS BEI LIU?
HE IS WITH SHAO YUAN IN HEBEI.
WITH SHAO YUAN? BUT I JUST KILLED TWO OF HIS COMMANDERS.
WE KNOW. YOU SHOULD MAKE CONTACT WITH BEI LIU AS SOON AS POSSIBLE.

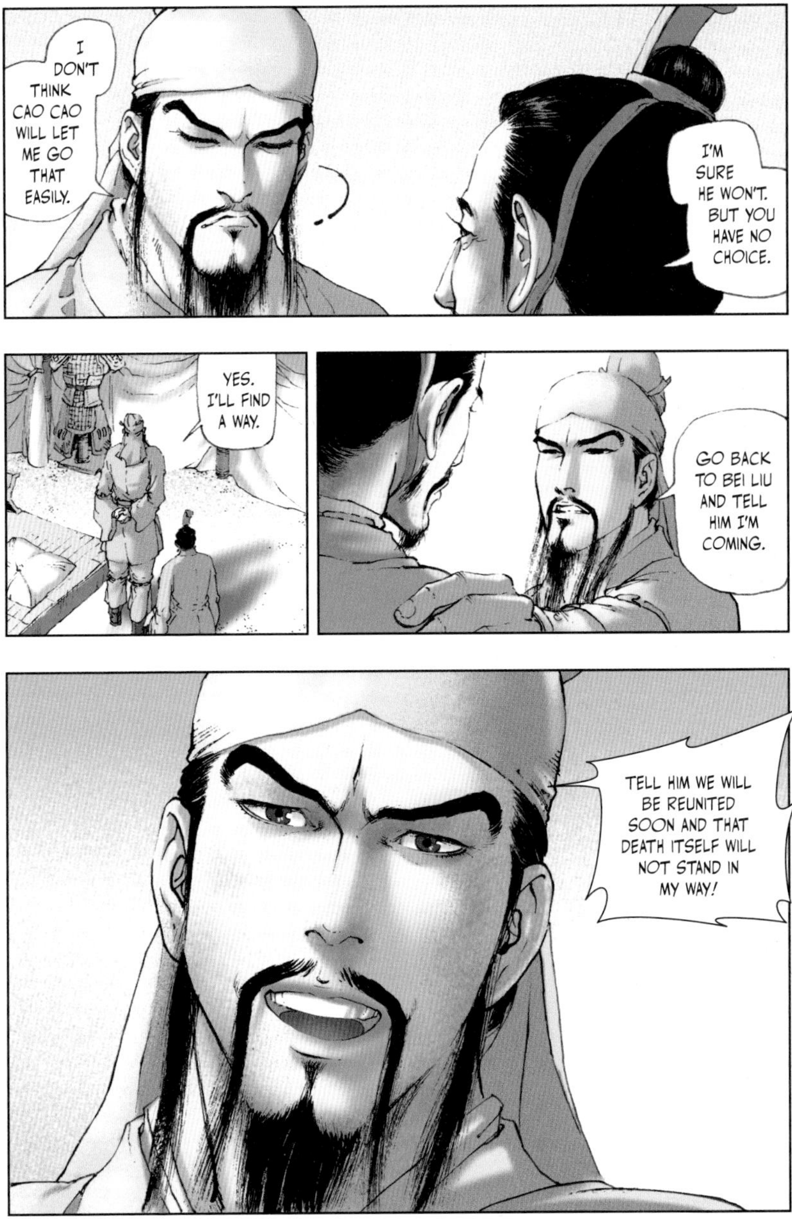
I DON'T THINK CAO CAO WILL LET ME GO THAT EASILY.
I'M SURE HE WON'T. BUT YOU HAVE NO CHOICE.
YES. I'LL FIND A WAY.
GO BACK TO BEI LIU AND TELL HIM I'M COMING.
TELL HIM WE WILL BE REUNITED SOON AND THAT DEATH ITSELF WILL NOT STAND IN MY WAY!

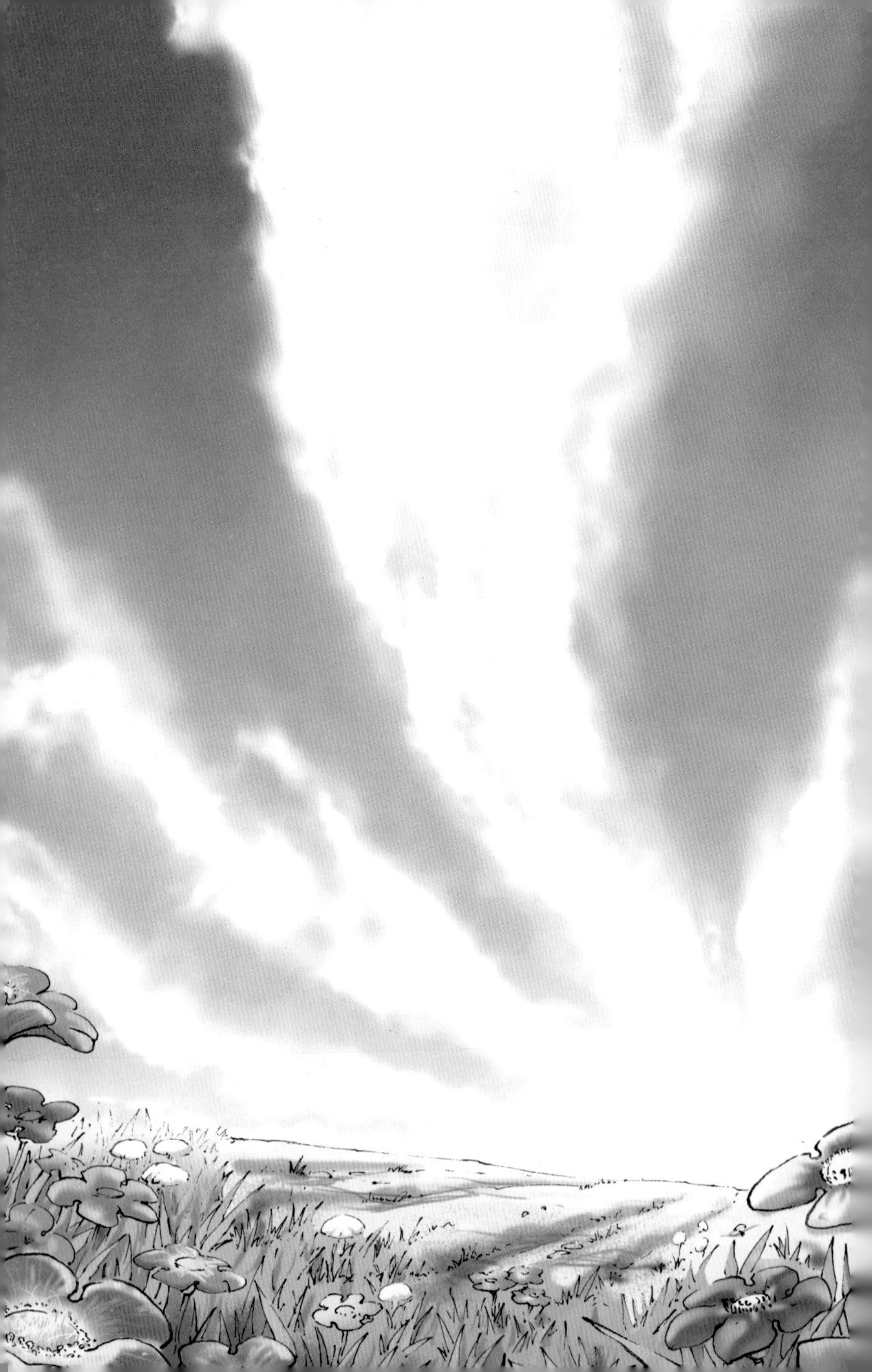

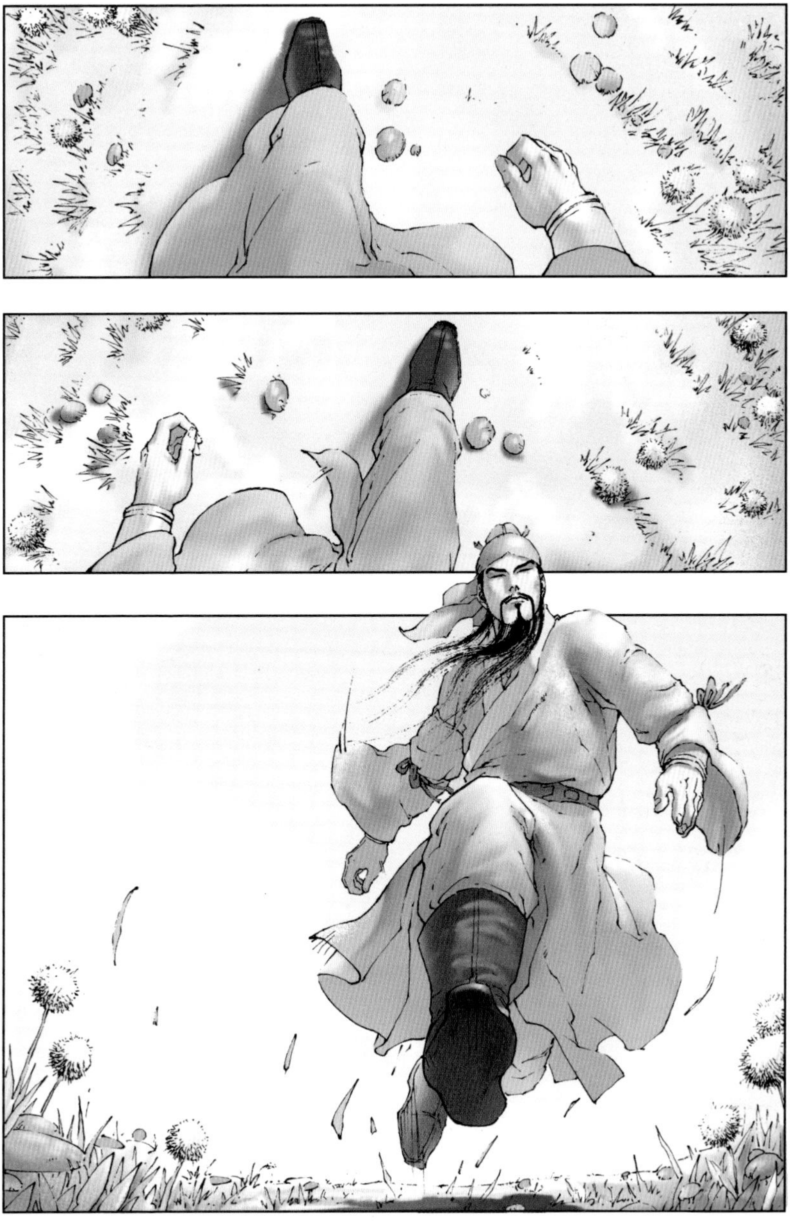

BEI LIU!
FEI ZHANG!
IT'S BEEN
SO LONG...

HA HA!

HURRY UP,
SLOW POKE!

YOU'LL
NEVER
MAKE IT!

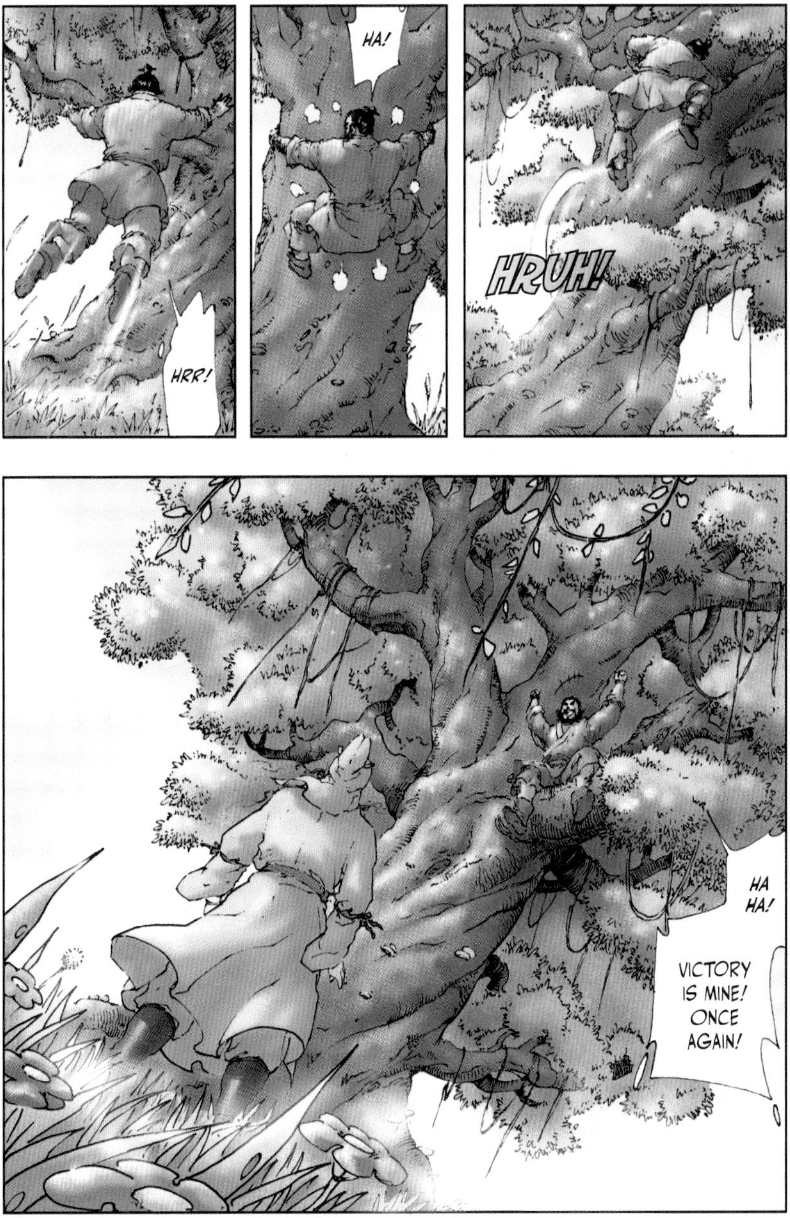
HRR!
HA!
HRUH!
HA HA!
VICTORY IS MINE! ONCE AGAIN!

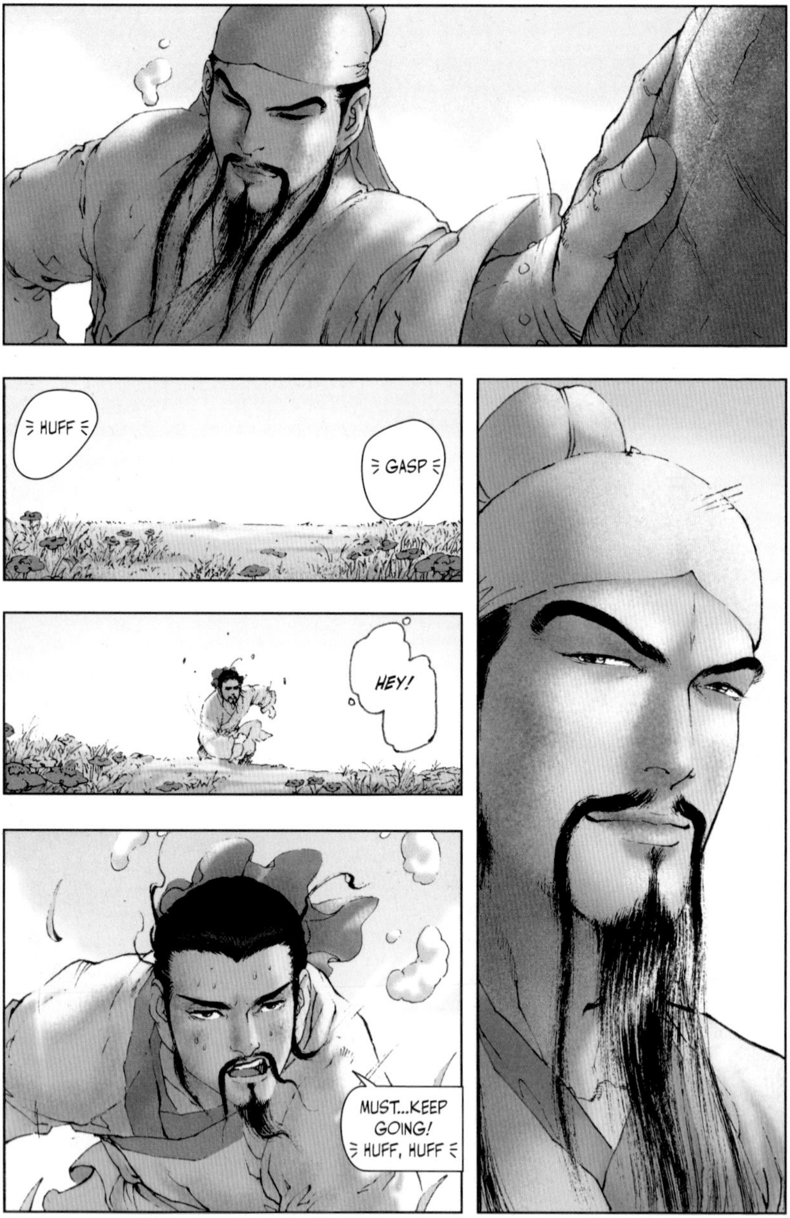
HUFF
GASP
HEY!
MUST...KEEP GOING!
HUFF, HUFF

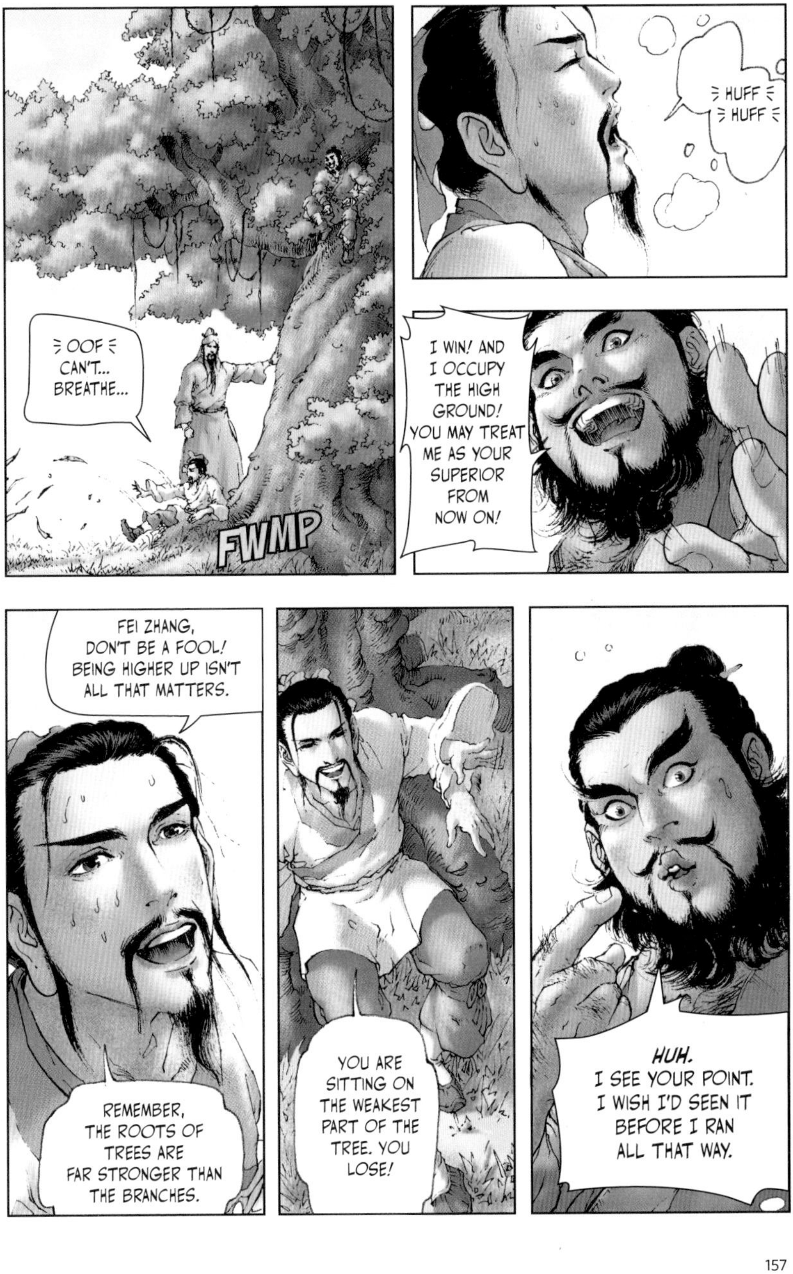
OOF
CAN'T... BREATHE...
FWMP
HUFF HUFF
I WIN! AND I OCCUPY THE HIGH GROUND! YOU MAY TREAT ME AS YOUR SUPERIOR FROM NOW ON!
FEI ZHANG, DON'T BE A FOOL! BEING HIGHER UP ISN'T ALL THAT MATTERS.
REMEMBER, THE ROOTS OF TREES ARE FAR STRONGER THAN THE BRANCHES.
YOU ARE SITTING ON THE WEAKEST PART OF THE TREE. YOU LOSE!
HUH.
I SEE YOUR POINT. I WISH I'D SEEN IT BEFORE I RAN ALL THAT WAY.

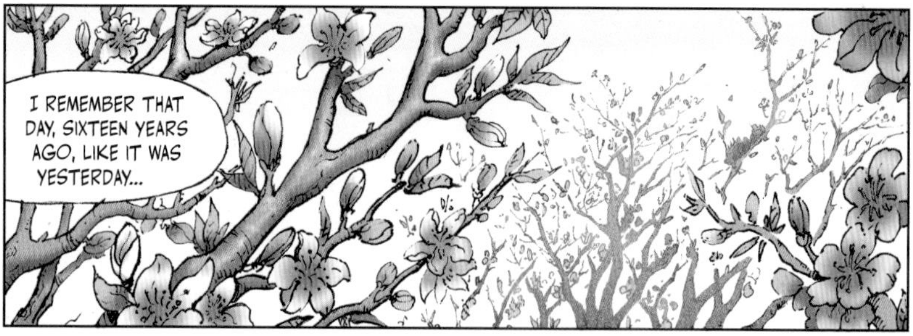
I REMEMBER THAT DAY, SIXTEEN YEARS AGO, LIKE IT WAS YESTERDAY...

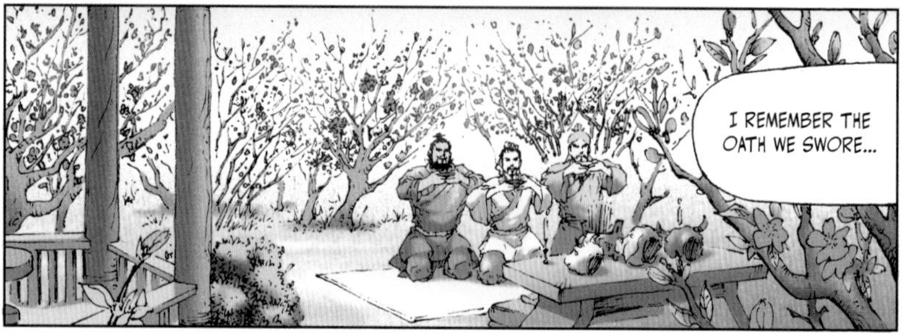
I REMEMBER THE OATH WE SWORE...

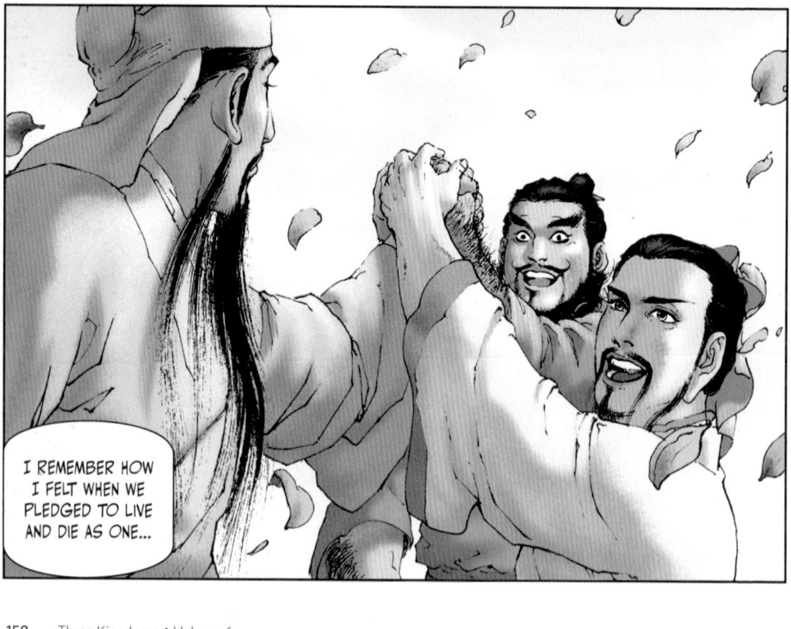
I REMEMBER HOW I FELT WHEN WE PLEDGED TO LIVE AND DIE AS ONE...

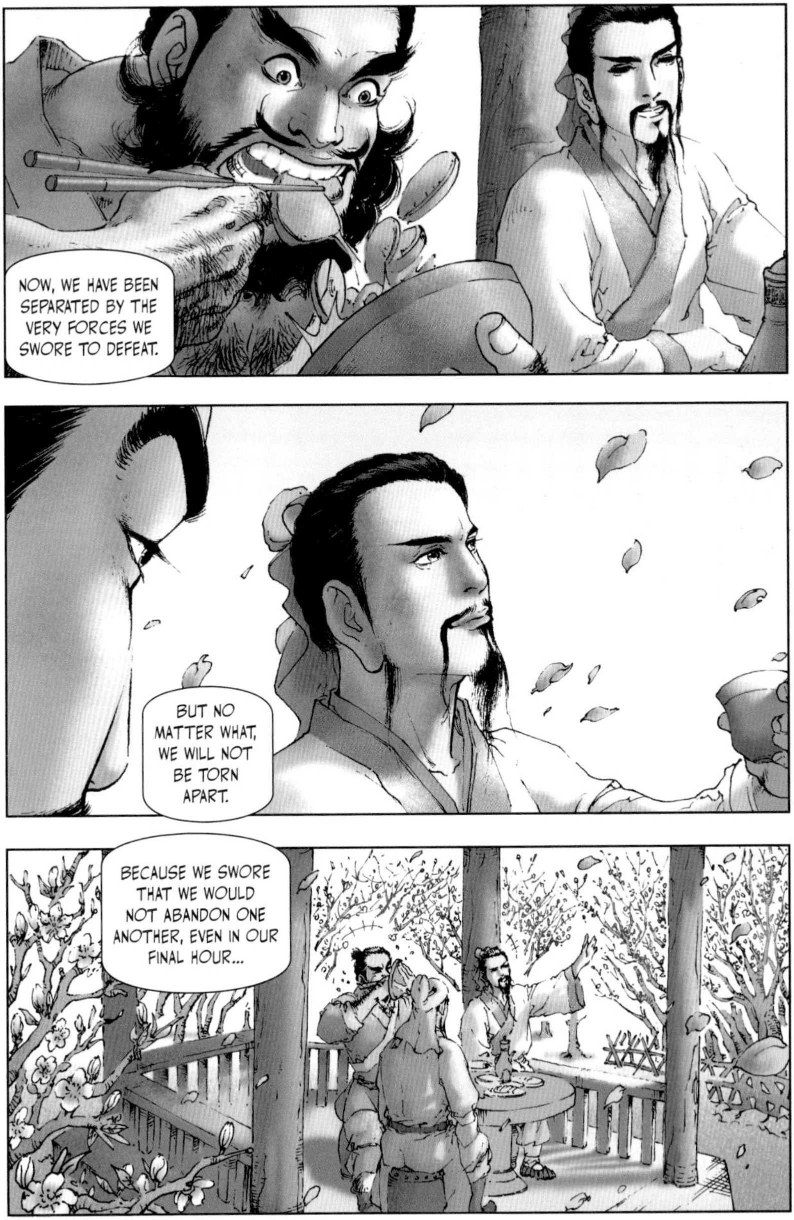
NOW, WE HAVE BEEN SEPARATED BY THE VERY FORCES WE SWORE TO DEFEAT.
BUT NO MATTER WHAT, WE WILL NOT BE TORN APART.
BECAUSE WE SWORE THAT WE WOULD NOT ABANDON ONE ANOTHER, EVEN IN OUR FINAL HOUR...

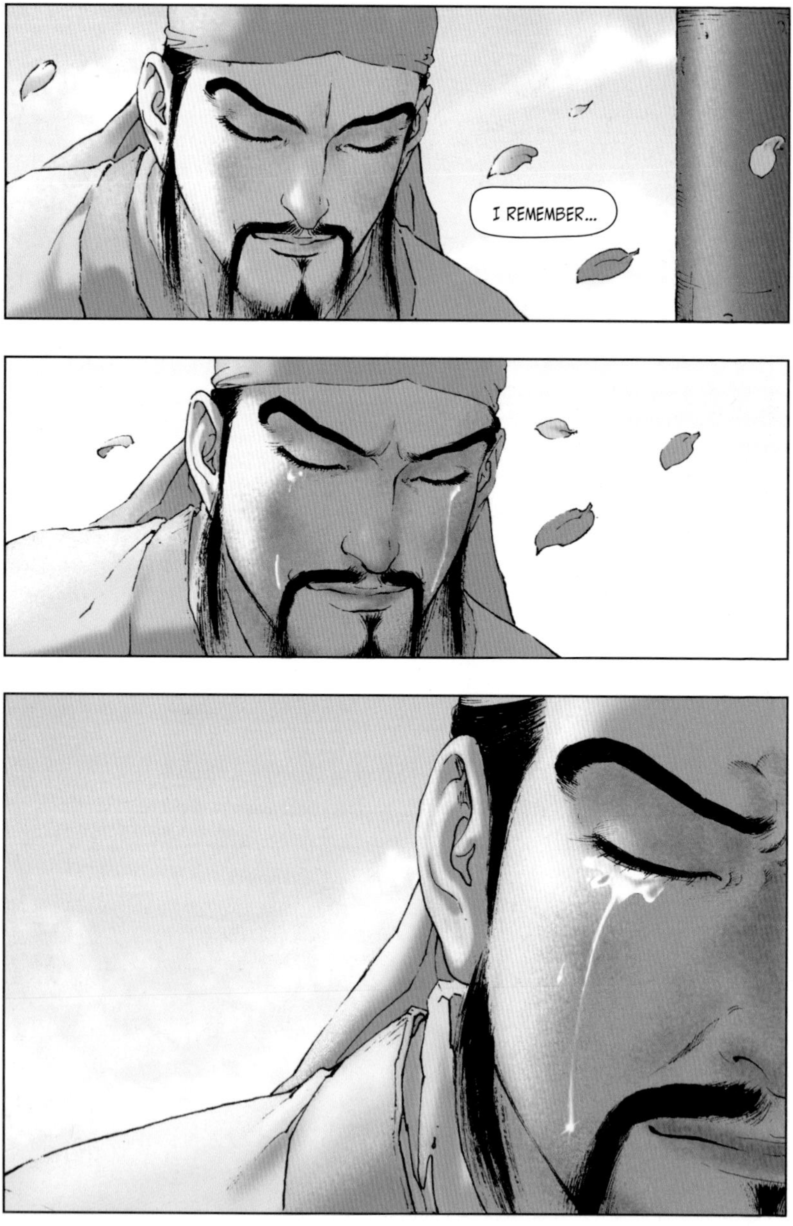
I REMEMBER...

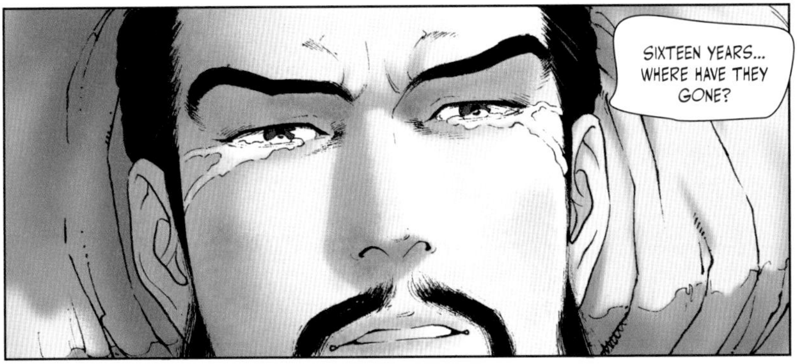
SIXTEEN YEARS... WHERE HAVE THEY GONE?

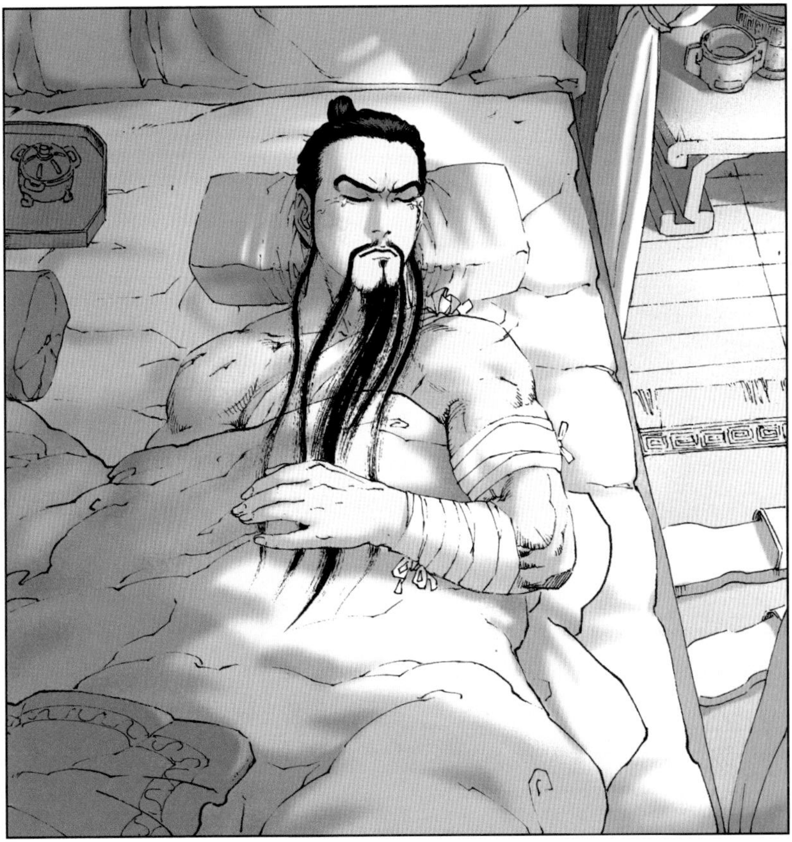

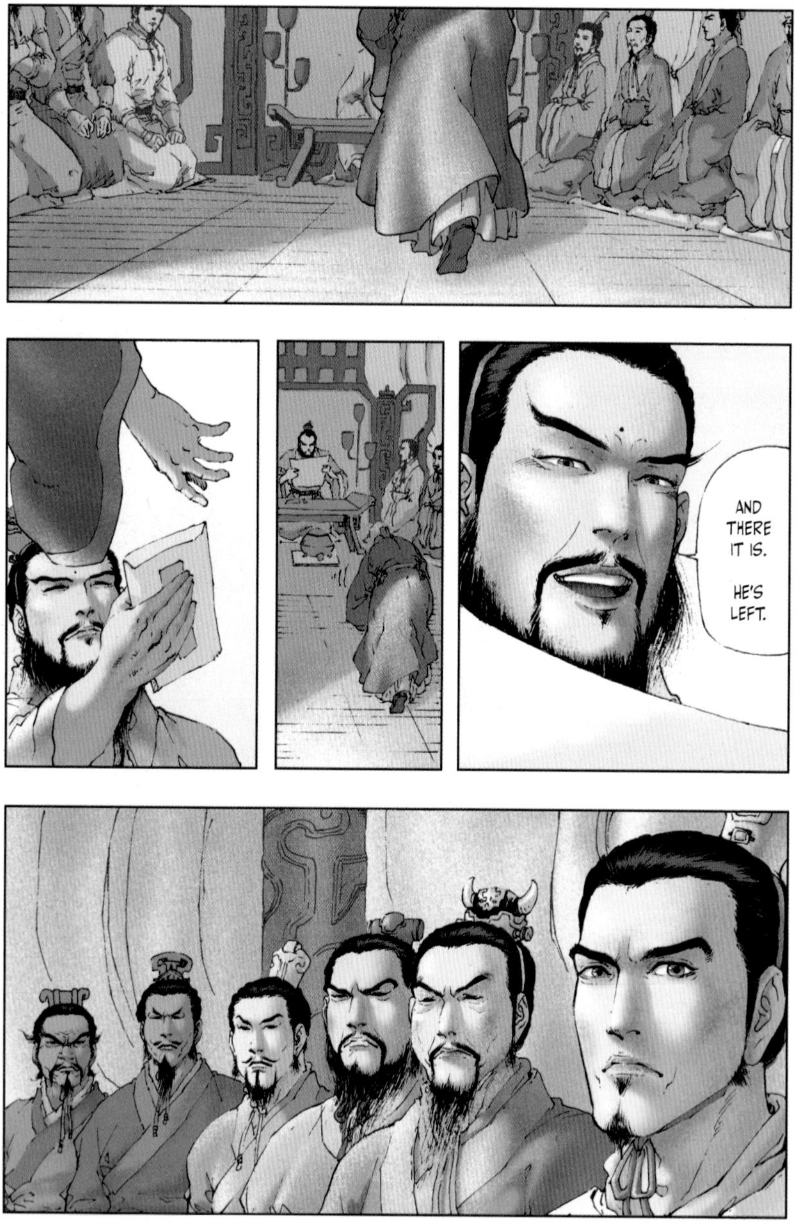
AND THERE IT IS.
HE'S LEFT.

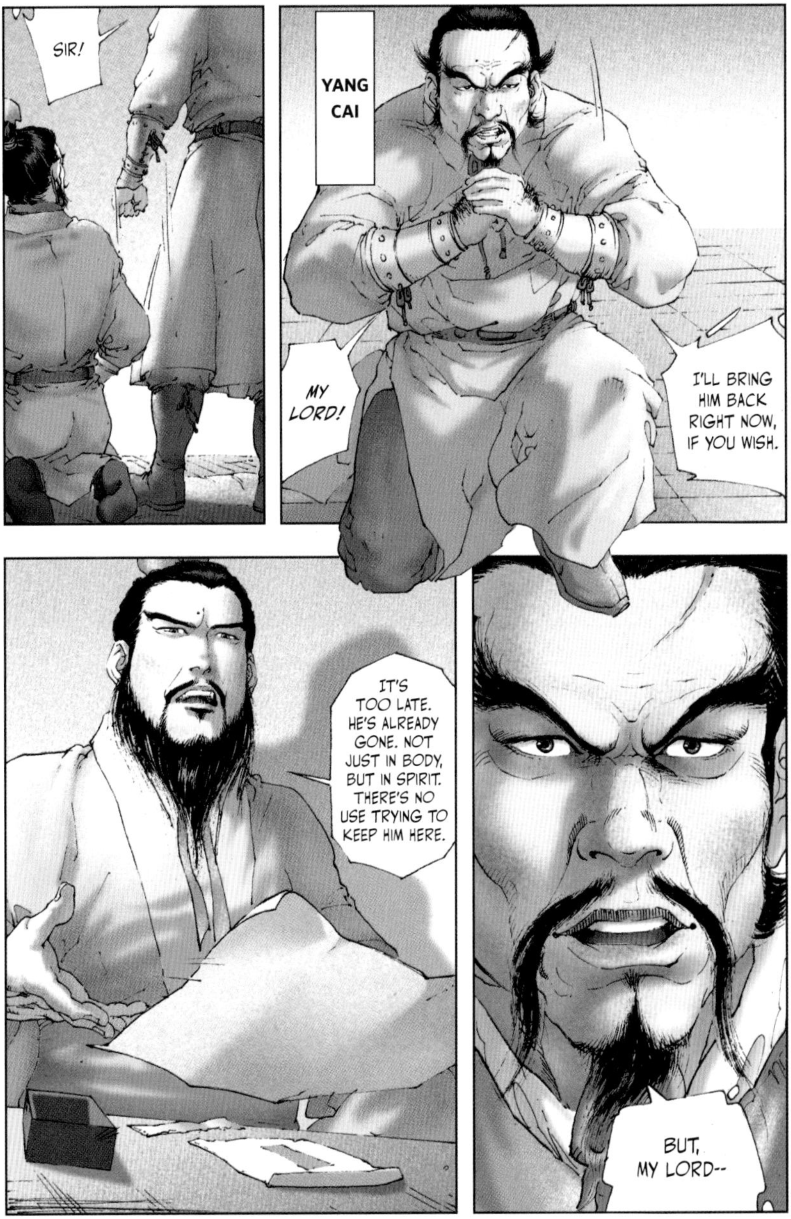
SIR!
YANG CAI
MY LORD!
I'LL BRING HIM BACK RIGHT NOW, IF YOU WISH.
IT'S TOO LATE. HE'S ALREADY GONE. NOT JUST IN BODY, BUT IN SPIRIT. THERE'S NO USE TRYING TO KEEP HIM HERE.
BUT, MY LORD--

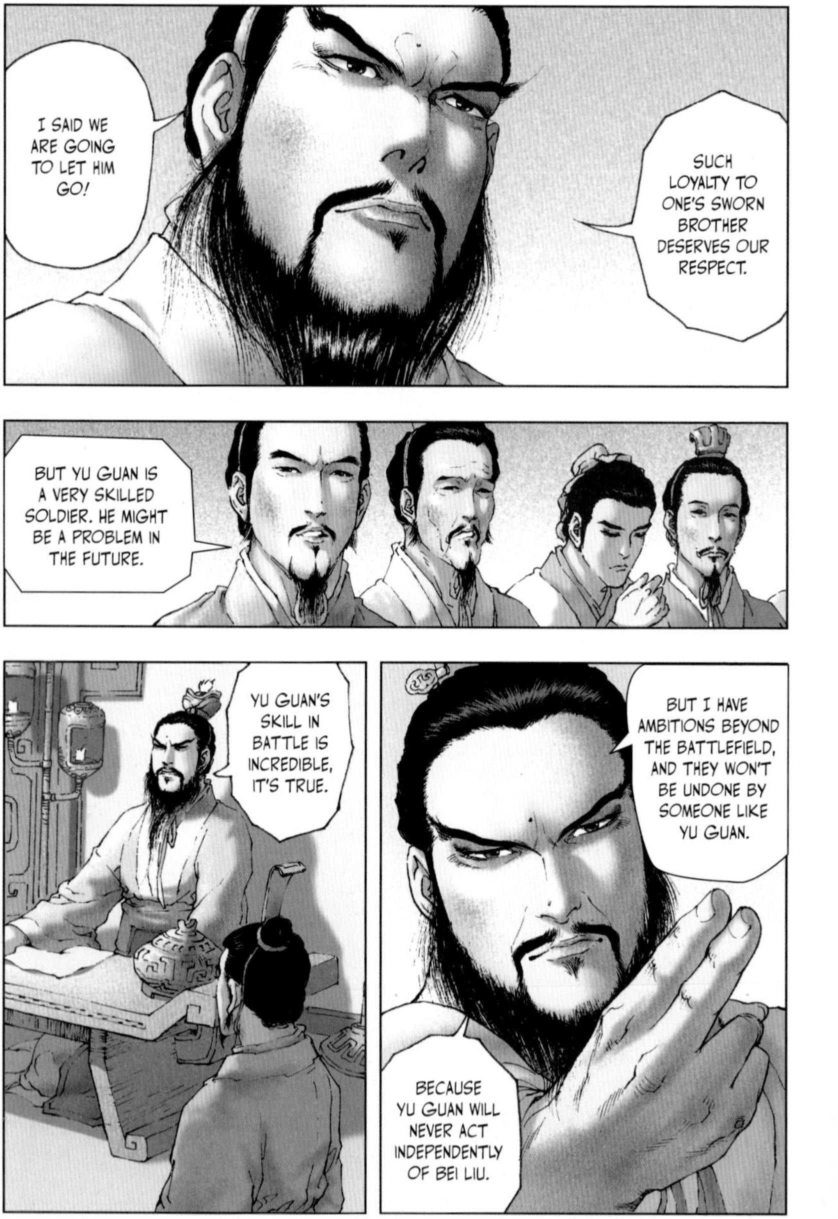
I SAID WE ARE GOING TO LET HIM GO!
SUCH LOYALTY TO ONE'S SWORN BROTHER DESERVES OUR RESPECT.
BUT YU GUAN IS A VERY SKILLED SOLDIER. HE MIGHT BE A PROBLEM IN THE FUTURE.
YU GUAN'S SKILL IN BATTLE IS INCREDIBLE, IT'S TRUE.
BUT I HAVE AMBITIONS BEYOND THE BATTLEFIELD, AND THEY WON'T BE UNDONE BY SOMEONE LIKE YU GUAN.
BECAUSE YU GUAN WILL NEVER ACT INDEPENDENTLY OF BEI LIU.

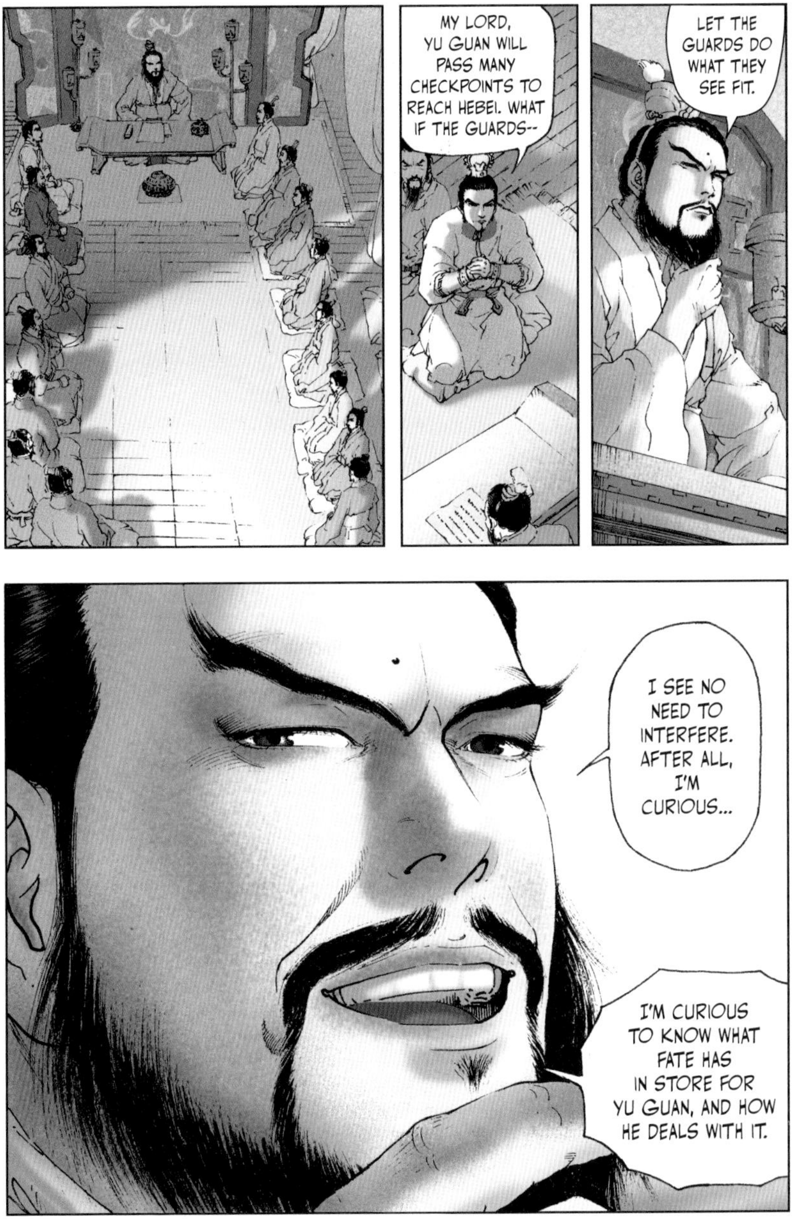
MY LORD, YU GUAN WILL PASS MANY CHECKPOINTS TO REACH HEBEI. WHAT IF THE GUARDS--
LET THE GUARDS DO WHAT THEY SEE FIT.
I SEE NO NEED TO INTERFERE.
AFTER ALL, I'M CURIOUS...
I'M CURIOUS TO KNOW WHAT FATE HAS IN STORE FOR YU GUAN, AND HOW HE DEALS WITH IT.

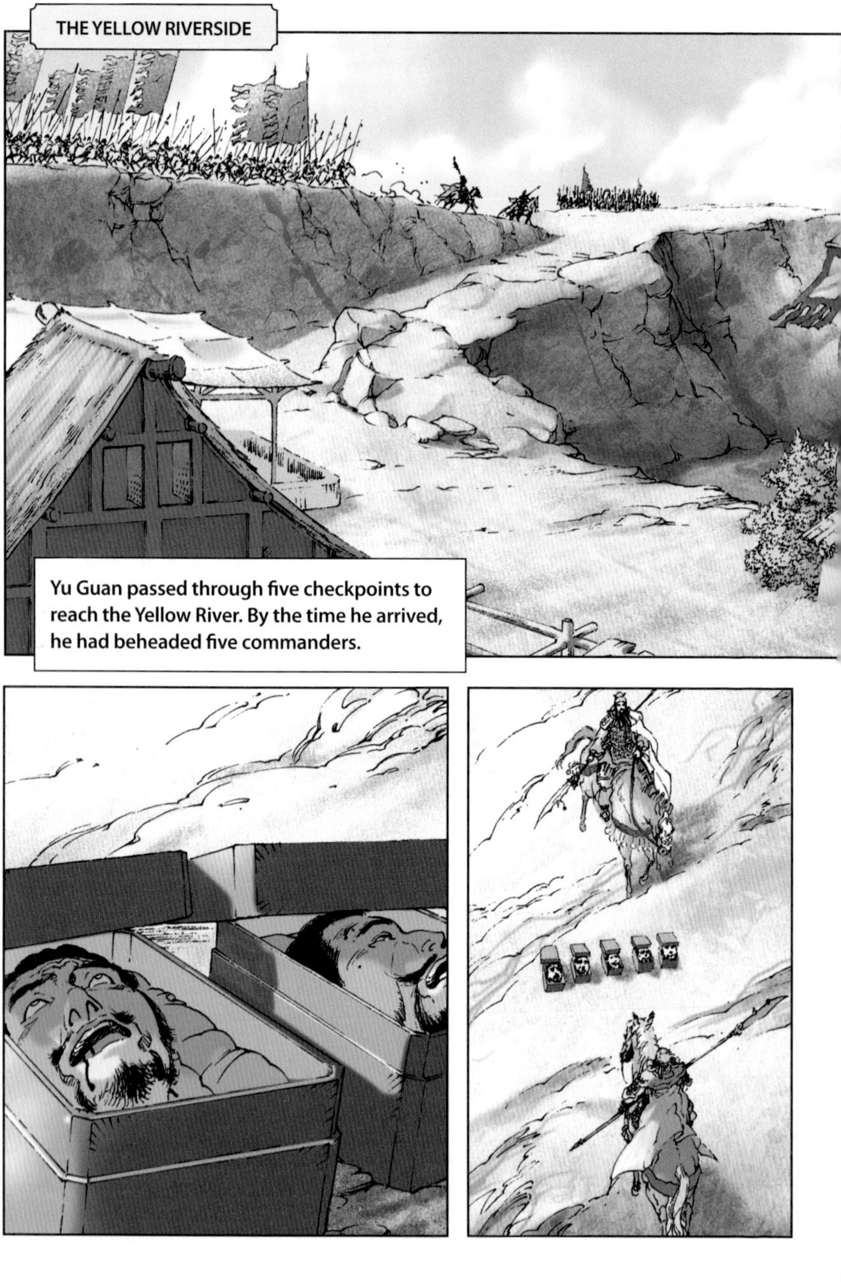
THE YELLOW RIVERSIDE
Yu Guan passed through five checkpoints to reach the Yellow River. By the time he arrived, he had beheaded five commanders.

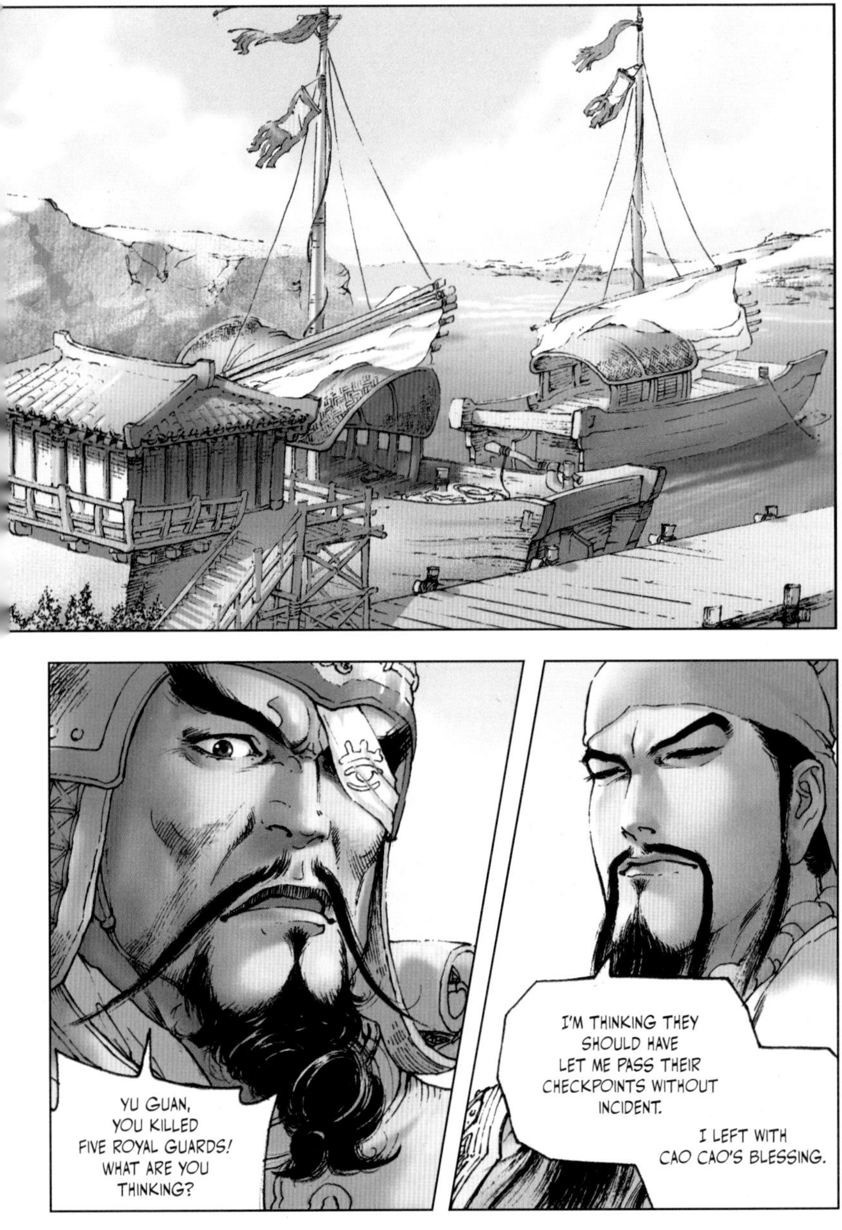
YU GUAN, YOU KILLED FIVE ROYAL GUARDS! WHAT ARE YOU THINKING?
I'M THINKING THEY SHOULD HAVE LET ME PASS THEIR CHECKPOINTS WITHOUT INCIDENT.
I LEFT WITH CAO CAO'S BLESSING.

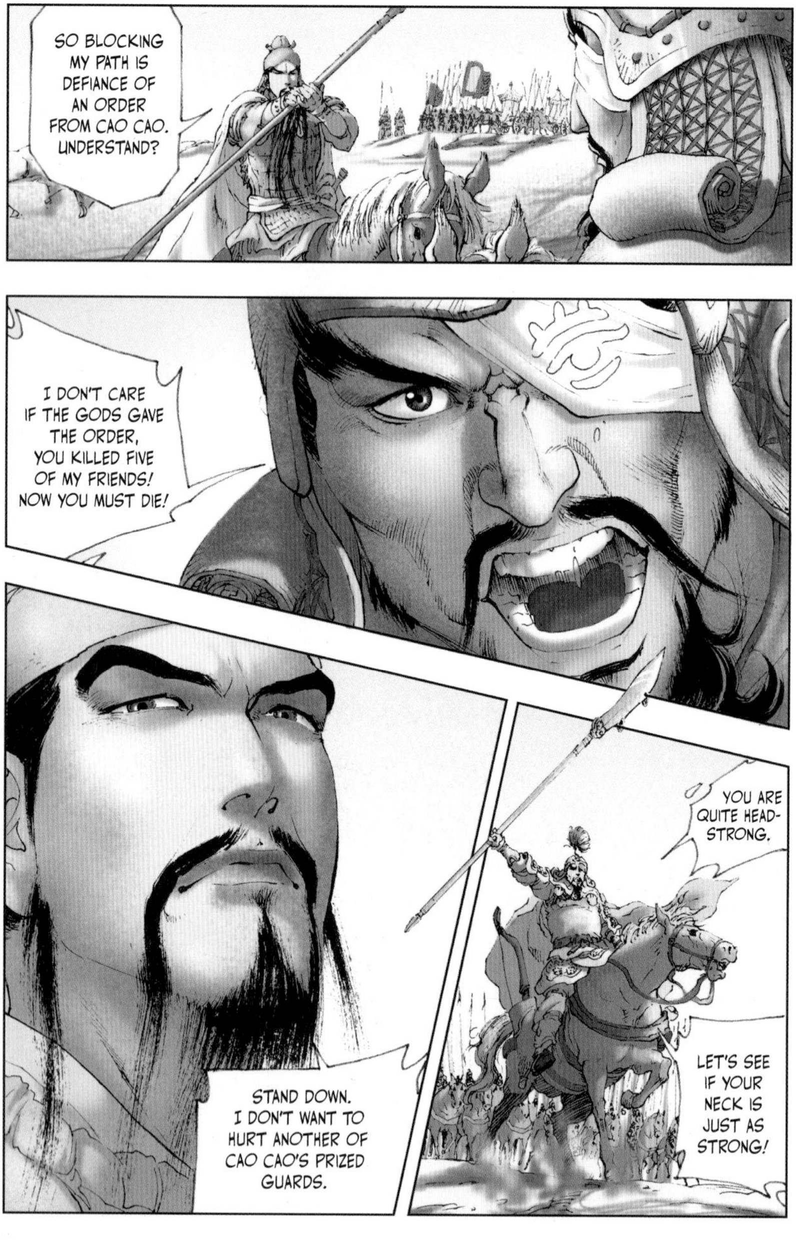
SO BLOCKING MY PATH IS DEFIANCE OF AN ORDER FROM CAO CAO. UNDERSTAND?
I DON'T CARE IF THE GODS GAVE THE ORDER, YOU KILLED FIVE OF MY FRIENDS! NOW YOU MUST DIE!
STAND DOWN. I DON'T WANT TO HURT ANOTHER OF CAO CAO'S PRIZED GUARDS.
YOU ARE QUITE HEAD-STRONG.
LET'S SEE IF YOUR NECK IS JUST AS STRONG!

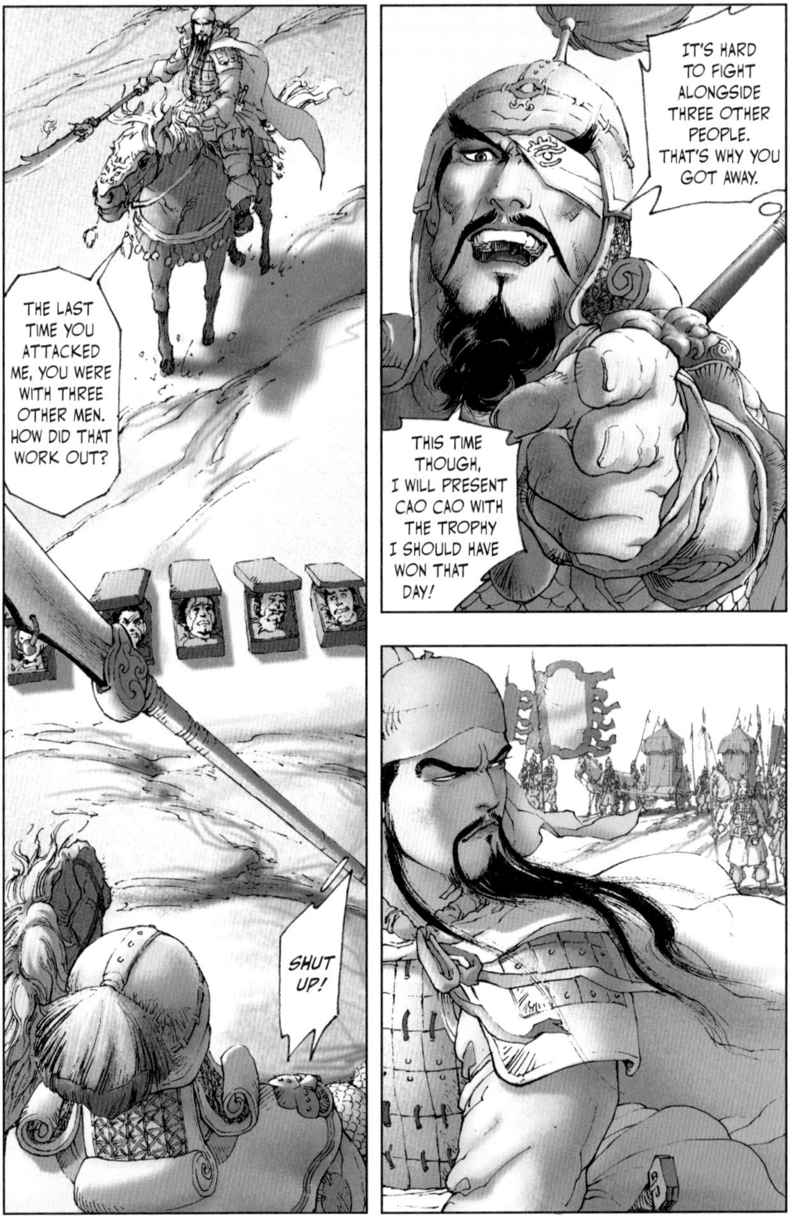
THE LAST TIME YOU ATTACKED ME, YOU WERE WITH THREE OTHER MEN. HOW DID THAT WORK OUT?
IT'S HARD TO FIGHT ALONGSIDE THREE OTHER PEOPLE. THAT'S WHY YOU GOT AWAY.
THIS TIME THOUGH, I WILL PRESENT CAO CAO WITH THE TROPHY I SHOULD HAVE WON THAT DAY!
SHUT UP!

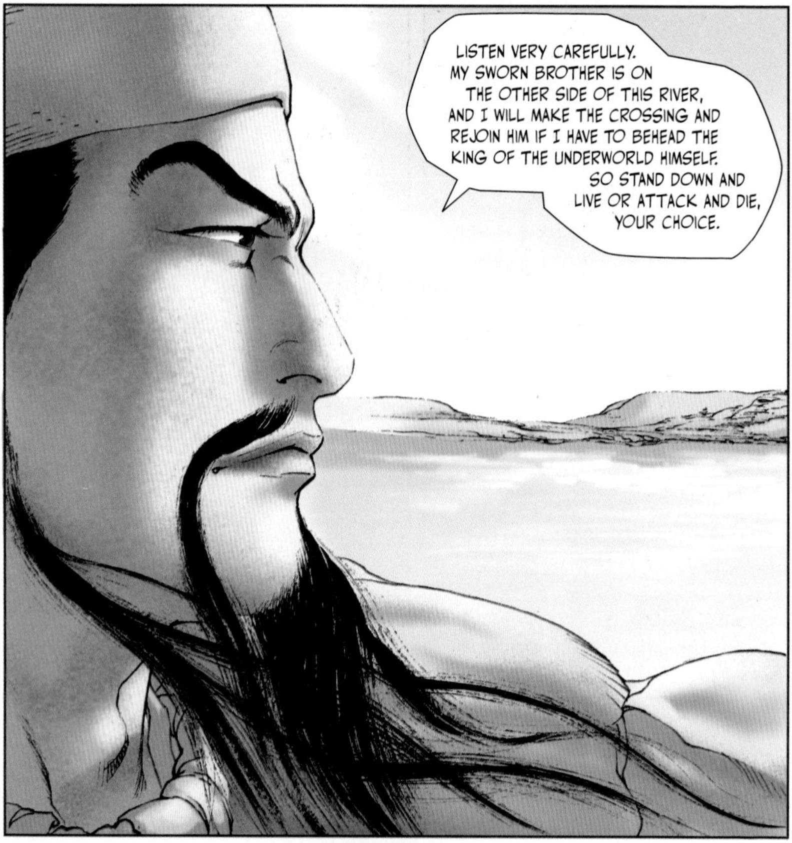
LISTEN VERY CAREFULLY. MY SWORN BROTHER IS ON THE OTHER SIDE OF THIS RIVER, AND I WILL MAKE THE CROSSING AND REJOIN HIM IF I HAVE TO BEHEAD THE KING OF THE UNDERWORLD HIMSELF. SO STAND DOWN AND LIVE OR ATTACK AND DIE, YOUR CHOICE.

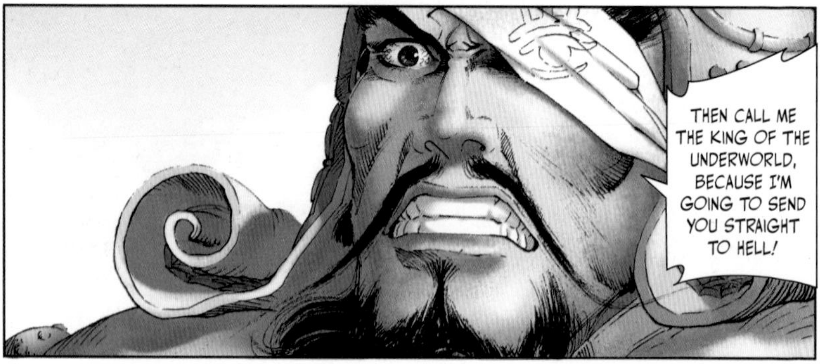
THEN CALL ME THE KING OF THE UNDERWORLD, BECAUSE I'M GOING TO SEND YOU STRAIGHT TO HELL!

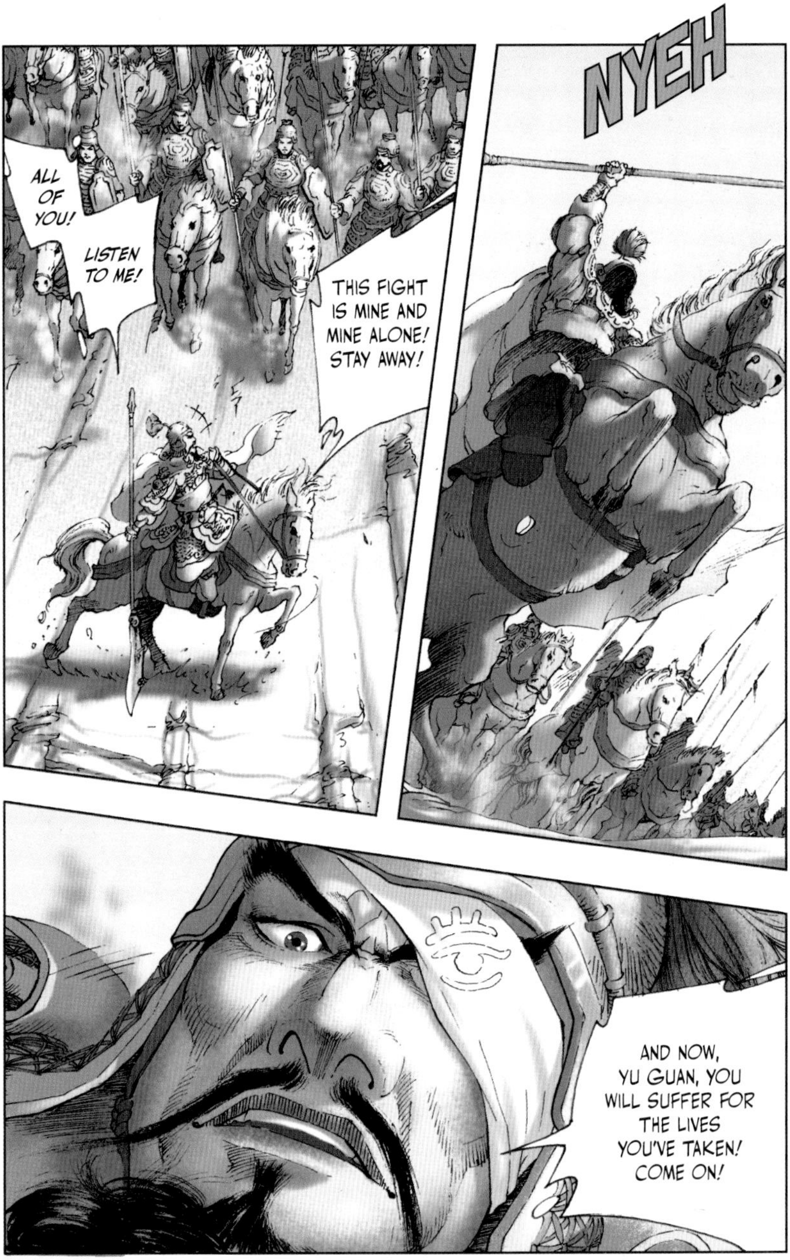
ALL OF YOU!
LISTEN TO ME!
THIS FIGHT IS MINE AND MINE ALONE! STAY AWAY!
NYEH
AND NOW, YU GUAN, YOU WILL SUFFER FOR THE LIVES YOU'VE TAKEN! COME ON!

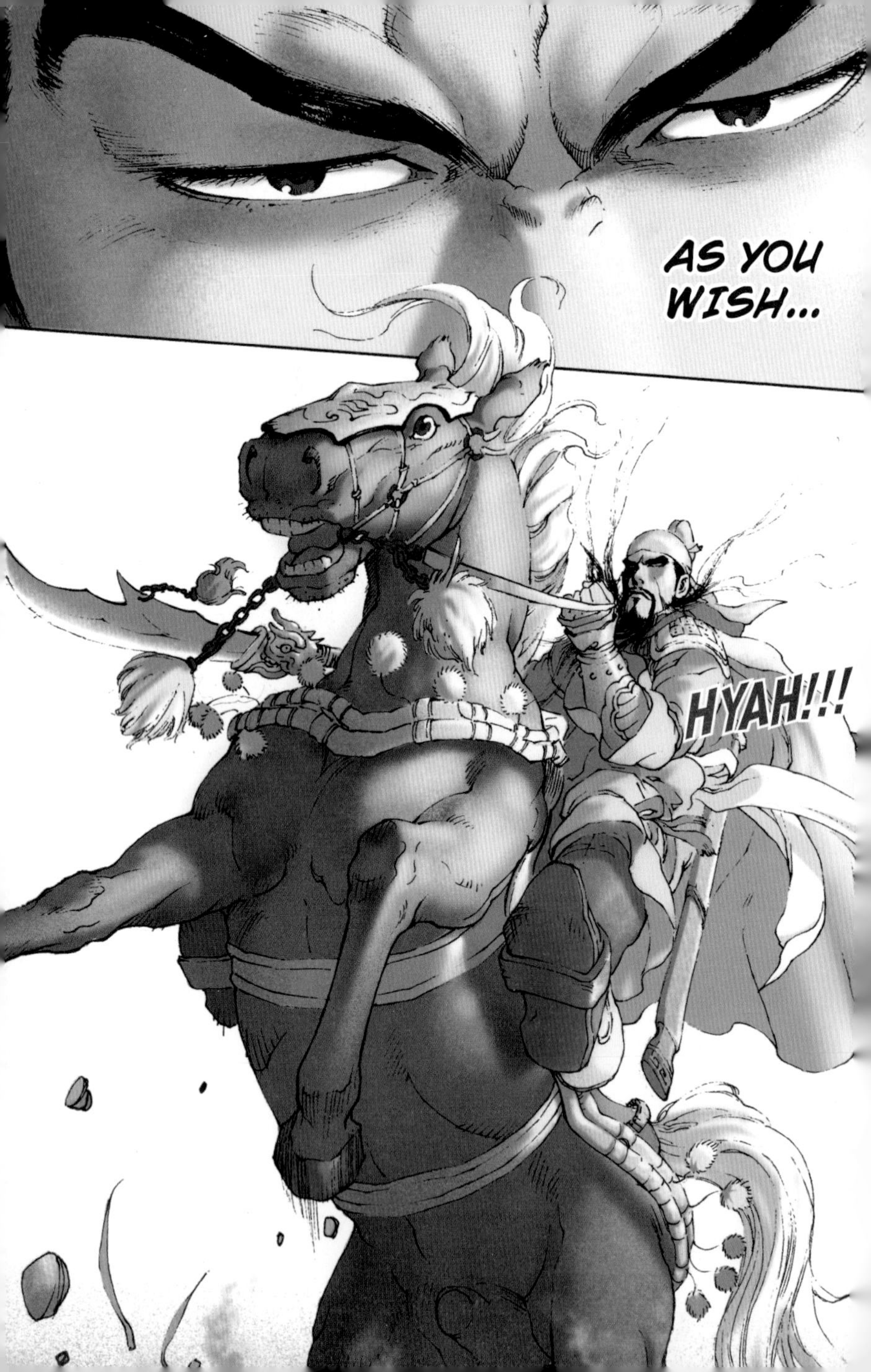
AS YOU WISH...
HYAH!!!